Also by

FRANCES PARKINSON KEYES

★

LARRY VINCENT

"A blessed companion is a book"—JERROLD

LARRY VINCENT

★

FRANCES PARKINSON
KEYES

THE COMPANION BOOK CLUB
LONDON

*Made and printed in Great Britain
for The Companion Book Club (Odhams Press Ltd.)
by Odhams (Watford) Limited,
Watford, Herts.
S.954.V*

CONTENTS

★

BOOK ONE

CREDIT EXTENDED

Winter, 1897—Spring, 1918

CHAPTER ONE

"Not so far off with those corn sacks, Le Maitre! How many times have I got to tell you we're unloading 'em at . . . Man alive, am I seein' straight? That couldn't be Clyde Batchelor of Cindy Lou coming toward the stageplank!"

The paunchy little officer, engaged in directing the disposition of cargo along the decks of a small stern wheeler, had interrupted himself abruptly, his bellow of reprimand softening to an exclamation of incredulous pleasure. Just as suddenly, the expression of his ruddy face, darkened by stubble along the cheek and jowl, changed from one of impatient irritation to one of genial welcome.

"Mis-ter Batchelor! Mis-ter Batchelor, sir!" he cried, raising his gold-braided blue cap and waving it in exuberant greeting. "I couldn't believe my eyes at first. This sure is a great surprise!"

The elder of the two men approaching the landing stage from Bienville Street smiled and stretched out his hand.

"I didn't know myself whether I could make it, so I couldn't send word I'd be coming aboard at New Orleans this trip. All the same, I hope to know I'm welcome."

"Welcome!" exclaimed the captain. "You know there isn't a man in Louisiana I'd ever be so glad to see. Just for himself, I mean, too. As for that no-'count Le Maitre up there and his chum Torrance, they'll start figuring straight off that they can win enough from you this evening to catch back on their last night's spending spree."

"It's a long worm that has no turning," Clyde Batchelor protested. "This is about due to be the time I send you all home for fresh money before we land at Cindy Lou. Meanwhile, Captain Bruner, shake hands with my friend, Valois Dupré."

"Major Dupré, the lawyer?" inquired the captain, obviously impressed. "Are we going to have the pleasure—yes, and the honour, if I may say so—of carrying you on this trip, too?"

"Wish I could, I do indeed," replied the younger man. "But I'm just down to see Mr. Batchelor off."

"In that case, go right aboard the *Parlour City*, gentlemen. Major Dupré can at least make himself at home until the 'All Ashore' bell sounds."

"Talk about seeing me off!" exclaimed Batchelor with assumed ruefulness. "Maybe you don't know it, Valois, but you're delivering me into the hands of the enemy. Right after dinner, I must tell you, these pirates and sharpers will inveigle me into a tall poker game—a two-bits' limit battle. And before we land at Cindy Lou tonight they'll have me skinned down to the buff—indeed, if there's time, they'll render what's left of me for my lard."

Bruner threw back his head to laugh the more heartily. "We do sort of rely on the two-three trips a year Mr. Batchelor makes on the *Parlour City* for money to buy presents for our wives, Major Dupré. If he'd only travel with us oftener . . ." The captain broke off to roar at the top of his voice, "I said not so far aft with those corn sacks, Le Maitre! How many times I got to tell you we're unloading them at New Sarpy?"

"Just once, Cap'n, just once!" Le Maitre shouted back. "You started to tell me and then you caught sight of Mr. Batchelor or someone you thought might be him an'——"

Bruner growled and then guffawed. "I don't put up with no back talk, generally speaking, Major Dupré," he said, gradually dropping his voice to its former conversational level. "But I got to admit it's like Le Maitre said, so I guess I better let that pass this one time. . . . What about your grips, Mr. Batchelor?"

Clyde gestured in the direction of a surrey, from which a top-hatted Negro was lifting a worn valise.

"I've only got one, this trip," he said. "Hoppy'll bring it aboard directly. Meanwhile, I'm taking Valois up for a farewell drink. Your bar's open, isn't it?"

"It will be as quick as I can send my mud clerk, Torrance,

to do the honours. The way things are, these days, there isn't enough business to warrant having a regular barkeep, so Torrance doubles in glass, so to speak."

Laughing at his own witticism, Captain Bruner stepped aside from the stageplank and hospitably bowed the two friends aboard. Both were spare and both tall, but there the resemblance ended. Clyde Batchelor, though still fresh skinned and erect, was unmistakably an elderly man; Valois Dupré, dark to the point of swarthiness, was in the prime of adult vigour. They differed as much in dress as they did in physical attributes: Clyde wore a wide-brimmed Stetson, of the type affected primarily by planters, a 'jim-swinger' frock coat and trousers of black broadcloth, a pleated shirt and a string tie; Valois a pepper-and-salt sack suit, a high stiff collar and a felt pork-pie hat. As they started across the stage-plank, Clyde paused to ask a question.

"Will you be leaving more or less on time, Captain Bruner?"

"On the dot, Mr. Batchelor. On the dot. Got most all the cargo stowed already and, so far as I know, just one couple more of passengers to come aboard. But there's time for you and Major Dupré to have that farewell drink together."

"Thanks. That's just what I wanted to know. By the way, is Captain Wellborn piloting you still?"

"Yes, but not this trip. He's staying ashore as his first grandchild is being christened and he said there weren't steamboats enough on all the Mississippi, or either the Red and the Ouachita, besides, to keep him from that. But he got Louie Sanchez to make the trip for him. Louie pilots the *General Gregson*, one of the government snagboats that's laid up for repairs, so he was right glad to make a couple of extra jitneys, and he's a real, old-time lightnin' pilot, too."

"Good enough. . . . Come along, Valois, let's get that drink while the getting's still good."

"Right."

They crossed the stageplank to the deck, which surged gently beneath their feet as the wave of a passing ferry washed along the *Parlour City's* mooring place. Then, after pausing a moment to steady themselves, they turned toward the grimed stairway and ascended to the boiler deck. Here, a freckled, sweater-clad man, his dingy cap askew on his shock

11

of red hair, stood at the forward guard, a sheaf of papers clutched in one hand.

"Howdy, Mr. Batchelor," he said over his shoulder. "Joe Torrance and I are all set for you tonight. Got to check the last of this cargo now, though."

"See you later then," Clyde replied, turning into the tunnel-like saloon where the oil lamps had already been lighted. However, they were few and far between and their chimneys were in sad need of polishing, so they seemed merely to punctuate the gloom, rather than to relieve it. Clyde glanced about him, as if prepared to comment on the dismal quality of this semi-obscurity, and then apparently changed his mind.

"I suppose the drinking whisky at the bar won't be too awful," he said, shrugging his shoulders. "Not if we make 'em bring out a bottle anyway. . . . I've got some prime bourbon in my portmanteau, but since I'll be home by midnight, I didn't engage a stateroom, so there's no convenient place to open it. Well, here we are."

The 'bar' was a mere shelf, backed by a smudged mirror. While they waited for Torrance, who was still occupied by his duties as mud clerk, Clyde waved his hand in a sweeping gesture that took in all their surroundings.

"I mind the time when nobody in this world would have believed steamboating would come down to this," he said. "Imagine having to wait for the barkeep!"

"Nothing about the waterfront's the way it used to be," Valois agreed. "Even I can remember when people would have laughed at the idea of having only four steamboats take off on a Thursday evening. To be sure, one of the four is the *St. James*—a real beauty, with all modern improvements. So why do you always take this ratty little tub?"

"It wouldn't surprise me a bit," Clyde chuckled, "if it wasn't to keep the old steamboating fever from taking hold again. It sure might, if I saw all that slick woodwork and white paint and electric lights on the *St. James*. I thought I might risk the *Betsy Ann*, for she does look like an old-timer outside, Steamboat Gothic railings and all, even if she does have new-fangled engines—'a deaf-and-dumb boat,' if there ever was one, and for once I was in the mood for a boat that doesn't chuff in her smokestack. But I wasn't going to take any chances. Nobody's going to fall back in love with steamboat life after a taste of the *Parlour City*. . . . Well, here comes our barkeep at last."

The man who now tardily approached them was so fat he seemed to roll along his course, and yet the sweater which enveloped the upper part of his person sagged at every possible point, at its wilted turtle neck, at the wrists and at the equator which really could not be regarded as a waistline. "Sorry to keep you waiting, Mr. Batchelor," he wheezed, badly winded. "But you know how they shove everything off on me."

"Quite all right, Joe. I bet that widow in Luling still thinks you're a bit of all right. This is Mr. Dupré. Joe Torrance, Valois. And now, break the news to us, Joe. Have you got anything that wouldn't be classed as Rampart Street rotgut?"

Torrance, still puffing heavily, was having a hard time unfastening a locker beneath the bar shelf.

"That I have, Mr. Batchelor," he grinned, turning his rotund body sideways so as to be able to look upward. "One bottle of the smoothest Old Crow that ever came out of Kaintuck! Must of knowed you was coming aboard when I put that bottle in stock."

He produced glasses, drew a pewter pitcher of water, and set these on the bar. "Put the bottle back and snap the lock for me when you gentlemen finish, please, sir," he added. "That will give me a chance to see some consignee doesn't steal us blind on claims." He rolled hastily away down the gloomy tunnel of the main saloon.

Clyde poured two fingers each into tumblers, and filled two others with water. "Happy days!" he said ceremoniously.

"And nights!" acknowledged Valois. "By George! This really is fine bourbon."

"Better get what you can of it while the getting's possible," Clyde observed. "I understand the people who make it are going to sell out to the trust, and once they do, it'll never be the same. How about another?"

"No, this'll do me nicely, thank you ever so much, sir. I expect I'd better be moving on toward home, if there's no further service I can render you."

"Especially with a lovely young wife waiting to greet you," Clyde said, smiling. "Under the circumstances, I'd be the last man in this world to detain you, Valois. Come along."

They passed out on to the deck, and Clyde grimaced as a puff of land breeze enveloped them. "When I talked about not getting a taste for steamboat life," he observed wryly, "I wasn't setting aside smells, either. Get a whiff of that perfume!"

He pointed in the direction of the lower deck, where a drove of Longhorn cattle, their huge horns clashing, stamped amid their bedding. "It'll be better to windward of those passengers," he said, walking forward and turning to watch the roustabouts, their heads and shoulders cowled with burlap bagging, who were still piling sacked sugar, rice and beans forward of the crates and bales which formed a solid tier on the opposite side of the deck. Then he glanced toward the old surrey in which he and Valois had driven to the Bienville Street landing. It was still where they had left it, the nag which had drawn it drooping so listlessly in the shafts that the grounded hemisphere of iron, to which it was attached by a heavy strap, seemed quite superfluous. But the Negro driver had come aboard in the wake of his patrons and now stood before them, lifting his top hat and wiping his bald pate with a huge bandanna.

"Whe' at mus' Ah put disyere grip, suh?" he inquired, pointing to the Gladstone which he had momentarily set down.

"Leave it with the mud clerk, Hoppy. He knows where to put it. And thanks."

The old Negro shuffled away. The roustabouts, who had finished piling the sacks, were pushing aboard a shiny buggy with red-spoked wheels. All the rest of the cargo had now been stowed. It was only a matter of minutes before the signal of 'All Ashore' would be sounded. Clyde stretched out his hand.

"I want to thank you again, before we say good-bye, for all your many kindnesses over and above the law part," he said. "It's made me feel right good to know that a Valois Dupré would go right on, helping me handle my business. All the same, I feel you ought to be paid standard prices, like I get for my perique. It was different with your pa. He was a

14

rich man. Well, you're no pauper, either, I know. But you're only getting started again at your practice after being gone a long while——"

"Please do hush, Mr. Clyde," Valois protested. "You know what store I set by carrying on just like Papa wanted. And one of the things he wanted most was that you and I should do business the same way you and he did. I wouldn't feel right to be making money out of our friendly dealings, especially after the terrible . . . there now, I shouldn't have mentioned it. I'm a dough-head for true."

"Now it's your turn to please hush. We've both suffered pretty much the same sort of loss, though I'm thankful your father lived long enough to see you come back from Cuba, medals and all. If you could have heard the loving pride with which he'd talk about you—why, when the *Times-Democrat* printed that story about your citation, he came all the way from New Orleans to Cindy Lou to tell me about it!"

"I'm not sure that medals always mean much, Mr. Clyde."

"You weren't thinking about my dear stepson, Bushrod Page, by any chance, when you said that, were you?" Clyde inquired with sudden sarcasm.

"No, sir, of course not," Valois answered quickly. He had spoken spontaneously and without conscious malice. But it was common knowledge that Bushrod Page, whose father had been a distinguished member of General Lee's staff, and whose mother, after a suitable period of widowhood, had become Clyde Batchelor's adored wife, had capitalized his heritage rather than glorified it. This was true not only of his military career; indeed, there was little about any part of his career which redounded to his credit. He had been suspended from college and forced to resign, both from the law firm in Richmond, where he had been accepted as a junior partner, and from the Westmoreland Club. Later, his marriage to a middle-aged heiress, Mabel Stoddard, the only daughter of a New York railroad magnate, had soon ended in separation; it had been saved from complete shipwreck first, because Bushrod's maternal grandmother had shrewdly divined that Mabel could be bribed with the promise of a plantation which would place her among Virginia's First Families; and

15

later, because Mabel enjoyed acting the role of a 'hero's' wife, in and out of season. Even while denying any intended reference to Bushrod, Valois realized it was quite natural that Clyde should suspect him of an *arrière pensée*.

"All right, I'll take your word for it," Clyde said, rather dryly. "But the fact remains that even Bushrod got a lot of medals—well, more than one anyway—and hustled home to show them to Mabel before he went off on a series of 'jubilees' and then on to the Philippines with good old General Wheeler. He's back at Cindy Lou now, though."

"So I heard. I'd like to show him some sort of a courtesy. After all, we both——"

"Yes, you both fought in the Spanish-American War. But that's where the likeness ends, Valois—at least, I'm happy to believe so."

"How long does he expect to stay?"

"Who knows? As long as the people around St. James Parish make over him as a hero, the way they're doing, I suppose. But no need for you to do it, too."

The old man's tone was bitter now. Well, that was not strange, either. It must be hard on him, having this stepson, whom he had always disliked, with him at Cindy Lou, now that the beautiful old place was bereft of Bushrod's mother, Lucy, whom Clyde had worshipped, and of her daughter, Cary, who had been hardly less dear to him. Lucy and Cary's husband, Savoie Vincent, had both perished in a terrible fire which had destroyed the young couple's home, and Cary had died only a few days later, as a result of the injuries she had sustained. Her baby boy, Larry, whom she had entrusted to her stepfather on her deathbed, alone had survived the holocaust.

"I suspect Mabel's just as well pleased to have Bushrod out from underfoot, too," Clyde went on, still more bitterly. "Her father, more than likely, would be paying him to keep away, if the old man were still alive."

"Well, perhaps we shouldn't be too hard on him," Valois said lamely. "He was a dashing officer and, after all, he was pretty badly wounded. Maybe while he was convalescing he had a chance to think things out and decided to turn over a new leaf. When he finds out you intend to give him a share of

16

the C. & L. Company's proceeds, perhaps he'll show that he's grateful to you, after all."

"No such luck! More likely he'll raise seven kinds of assorted hell because it's not bigger. . . . Well, there goes the 'All Ashore.' The old *Parlour City* will be pulling out directly."

"The best of everything to you, sir. You'll be home by midnight, won't you?"

"Yes, if all goes well."

Clyde watched the younger man out of sight and then walked across to the opposite side of the deck and continued to stand for a few moments beside the old-style wooden railing. In the gathering dusk he could just make out the light of the Algiers ferry house across the river, and he heard the two ferries exchange whistles in midstream as they passed behind the *Stranger*, an anchored yacht which he had not noticed before. This was the famous vessel upon which Rex, Monarch of Mardi Gras, would make his triumphal entry into New Orleans a few weeks hence. Hastily, Clyde shifted his gaze to a lumber-laden four-master which a noisy little steam tug was shepherding upstream. He wanted nothing to remind him of the Carnival gaieties in which Cary had revelled with such consummate delight. And yet, he could not help thinking about them. How beautiful she had been in her court costume of sapphire and silver, the year that her great friend, Armande Vincent, whose brother, Savoie, she had later married, had been Queen of Carnival. Cary had been one of the Maids and she had outshone all the others; she had even outshone the Queen. In fact, she had always outshone Armande. She had done it again, at a later Carnival, the year after she was married. She and Savoie were just back from their honeymoon, which they had spent in France, mostly with the de Chanets, who claimed kinship with Pierre Chanet, one of the first settlers in the region where the Vincents and the Batchelors lived. The Vincents also claimed kinship with this settler, and very proudly; for it was he, whose name the Indians had corrupted to Perique, who taught them to cultivate the tobacco which grew nowhere else in the world; and the yearly crop of this, now grown at the Vincents' plantation, Victoria, was the main source of their very substantial wealth. So it was natural that Savoie should take Cary to visit the French

17

branch of the family; but then they had stayed on and on, and had not come back until Savoie's father summoned them home. Afterward, he was sorry he had done so. For their homecoming coincided with that later Carnival, the one at which Armande was to have had her second great triumph, after years spent in mourning the death of the sweetheart who was stricken with yellow fever shortly before their intended marriage. And then Armande had not had her triumph after all, because Cary had stolen it from her. . . .

Still later, the score had been briefly evened, for Armande had married the current Marquis Pierre de Chanet, who, too late, Cary had discovered was the man she really loved. But even at Armande's wedding—a magnificent ceremony at the St. Louis Cathedral—Cary had eclipsed the bride. As he stood staring into space, Clyde ceased to see the ferries and the waterfront and visualized his beloved daughter as she came up the aisle, radiant in a gold-coloured dress, gold-coloured wings surmounting the lovely head she held so high and golden bracelets tinkling at her wrists. Afterward, to be sure, she had fainted dead away. But that was not until the convivial wedding reception, as well as the solemn marriage ceremony, was over—not until she was alone with her mother in their suite at the St. Charles. And the fainting fit had nothing to do, of course, with the fact that Armande Vincent had married Pierre de Chanet. It happened because Cary was pregnant already, because she was carrying the baby she later left to Clyde on her deathbed; and she should not have been at that wedding, overtaxing her strength and wearing clothes that were too tight for her, though these were so artfully cut that they concealed her condition, and it had been the proudest moment of Clyde's life when he saw her coming exultantly up the aisle of the cathedral in her gold-coloured dress. . . .

He turned abruptly and made his way to the small texas deck, which was gritty with drifting cinders; then he went up the four steps leading to the pilothouse. "Mind if I come up for a bit, Captain Sanchez?" he asked of the dimly visible figure staring past the wheel spokes. "I'm Clyde Batchelor of Cindy Lou."

"Come right in and make yourself at home, sir. You'd be

18

more than welcome in any pilothouse I had the running of."

So this was Clyde Batchelor, the pilot added to himself; the man who had become a legend along the river, but whom, through some curious chance, Sanchez had never seen in the flesh before—a tall, spare man, the slight awkwardness of whose movements might be due in part to advancing age, but whose height probably also had something to do with his difficulty in settling himself comfortably on the rather hard seat which was all the pilothouse afforded. In the semi-obscurity, Sanchez could not have told whether his visitor's hair was blond or white, though it probably was the latter, for Batchelor must be past sixty by now. His features were not really discernible, either. Nevertheless, the pilot had a general impression of essential alertness, which neither age nor fatigue could destroy, of eyes that had not lost their keen watchfulness and hands that moved more swiftly than an unenlightened observer might expect. But Sanchez was not unenlightened. All up and down the river it was known that Batchelor had been a waif whose success at crapshooting had taken him from the dives of St. Louis to the shantyboats, and then to the gaming tables of those floating palaces whose flamboyant *décor* had given rise to the term, Steamboat Gothic. Sanchez knew that when gunboats invaded the river, at the beginning of the War Between the States, Batchelor, already wealthy, left the Mississippi to become richer and richer as a purveyor to sutlers and a speculator in tobacco and cotton. Sanchez also knew that, although this adventurer's first Southern associates had been hoarders and profiteers who betrayed their own people, a great change had come about when Clyde Batchelor married Lucy Page, the widow and daughter of distinguished Confederate officers. For her he had bought the great planta-tion which its first owners, Marchand and Dorothée Labouisse, had called St. Cloud—a name which the Negroes had corrupted to Cindy Lou. To justify himself in Lucy's eyes—and his own—Clyde had turned from evil ways and become a substantial citizen, a landed proprietor and a great boat builder. With her as his partner, he had organized and operated the fleet of steamboats which carried the C. & L. flag on the Mississippi from St. Louis to the Gulf and on many a lesser river besides. And then he had lost almost

19

everything—the fortune, the prestige, the woman for whom he had won the world as he knew it. All that was left to him was the land—much of it reputedly worthless—some desultory shipping, and a house which had once been the glory of a convivial countryside and was now desolate with the emptiness of lost life and lost love. . . .

Sanchez did not put it all to himself in just that way; nevertheless, the substance of it made up the burden of his thoughts and he felt the deep pity of one riverman for another as he glanced, now and again, toward the silent figure beside him. Yes, the man was essentially a gambler. To be sure, he no longer gambled with cards, at least by the standards generally classified as gambling—his casual two-bit games with Captain Bruner and others of that ilk did not count. But for a long while he had gambled with everything he touched and finally, his fabulous luck had failed him; he was now an impoverished, defeated, lonely old man. . . .

The pilot would have liked to put his sympathetic understanding into words; but he had not the vaguest idea how to do it. Moreover, he realized that you did not talk to strangers about matters which were amiss; you only congratulated them on their shining successes. But he was beginning to feel a strain in the silence which usually seemed so soothing to him, and he was thankful when his visitor finally broke it.

"Wouldn't that be Nine Mile Point, Captain?" Clyde asked, indicating a cluster of shuttling lights on the west bank.

"Avondale, just above the Point," replied the pilot. He puckered the lips beneath his majestic oxhorn moustache and scored a fastidious bull's-eye into the tall brass spittoon. "The damn railroad ferry. Many's the time I've wanted to ram that scow they use to carry trains across the river. But hang it all, I'd be destroying government property at the same time, seeing's as how my regular job is on the River Commission boat——"

"Any time you decide to go into action, call on me," interrupted Clyde. "I wouldn't miss the chance to be there and take a hand, not for a whole ranch in Texas."

"Sure you wouldn't," agreed the pilot, moving from one side of the wheel to the other as he spun the spokes. "No real riverman would. Pity there's so few of us left. Can't remember back to when I had the pleasure of seeing a genu-wyne active steamboat man in my pilothouse."

"Well, as to that," began Clyde, pausing to clear a sudden huskiness from his throat, "I might as well break the news first as last that I'm not an active steamboat man any longer."

"How come?"

"I've closed down the C. & L. Navigation Company for keeps."

"Get out! . . . Since how long?"

"Since about three-four hours ago. That was young Valois Dupré, my lawyer, who came aboard with me. He'd just finished handling the business and kindly offered to carry me down to the levee."

"Ain't that one hell of a note?" mourned the pilot, scoring another bull's-eye into the spittoon. "I hate to hear it, Mr. Batchelor. Even if this is the first time I've actually come to meet you, man to man, I sure do hate to hear the C. & L.'s a gone thing."

"Well, when you come right down to it, the company's been a gone thing for a long time. What happened today was just the burial."

The two men fell silent again, the pilot because he still could neither find nor utter the words he wanted to say, Clyde because he was returning from New Orleans in a state of almost overwhelming fatigue and depression. The fatigue was understandable enough. His general health was good and his strength sufficed for the activities which came within the sphere of his regular routine; but under any additional exertion, he tired very quickly. Admittedly, he had reached an age where this was inevitable and perhaps the depression was inevitable, too. Of course, the C. & L. Navigation Company had long since ceased to be anything more than a skeletal organization. He and Lucy had acted quickly upon a decision, taken some years earlier, to sell all their barges and towboats and to confine their projects on the river to chartering steamers at cotton-shipping time. Seasonal revivals of this sort had defrayed the cost of a so-called office in the rear room of a St. Peter Street building, where an elderly, stoop-shouldered book-keeper also acted as manager, accountant and janitor. Even when the railroads threatened to gobble up the little freight business there was left, a shipping contract with some planters at Hard Times Landing had produced enough revenue to provide both Lucy and Clyde with some special treat on the occasion of their wedding anniversary—the only one, at the only time, to which she would consent, once they had agreed on a policy of retrenchment. After Lucy's death, Clyde had put a similar sum aside for Larry's education, on the same day, every year. But the profits of the C. & L. had now almost reached the vanishing point; and though the plantation was doing sufficiently well so that there was nothing to prevent him from carrying on the custom, he could no longer pretend that the money came from the moribund steamboat company. In a sense, he felt that its house flag was a memorial to Lucy, even though it flew for only a brief period each autumn; and he had a further sentimental attachment to the property, since it was the only one which he and Lucy had owned jointly, under Louisiana law. But increasingly, he found himself able to look hopefully toward the future rather than sorrowfully to the past. There was peace after war and the world was beginning not only a new year, but a new century. What better time could there be to close forever the door of that rear room, holding fast to the belief that somehow and somewhere another would open?

Over and over again, as he sat silent in the pilothouse, Clyde told himself that there was only one answer to this question: there could have been no better time. He had done the wise thing, the right thing, the thing Lucy herself would have been the first to advise. Even the stoop-shouldered book-keeper could not be a logical object of sympathy; he had a small pension as the veteran of a former war, and a widowed daughter was eager to have him make his home with her. Clyde who, as usual, had erred on the side of generosity when he severed his connection with his forlorn employee, had no reasons for self-reproach because the man was losing his means of livelihood. But the mood of depression continued.

It was no whit lightened by the call to supper; for Clyde, who was something of a gourmet, was inevitably offended by the steamboat hash and watery grits which characterized the greasy cuisine aboard the *Parlour City*. He tried to make an adequate show of relishing these and the contents of the various side dishes containing canned peas, mustard greens, lumpy mashed potatoes and other vegetables; and later, he made a similar effort in order to give the impression of sharing the impatience with which others waited for the table to be cleared, so that the nightly game of ten-cent-ante-two-bits' limit poker could begin. But the cards were so worn that they felt almost like blotting paper to his sensitive fingers; and, try as he would, he could not focus his attention on the play, or derive either distraction or amusement from the game. It was temporarily suspended for the protracted stop at Edgard, where the shiny, red-spoked buggy was pushed ashore, along with other freight; so he took advantage of the break and returned to the pilothouse, thankful for the darkness and the silence in which he could continue to commune with his thoughts.

Gradually, his mood lightened. After all, he reflected, the picture was not wholly dark. To offset the depressing effect of the C. & L.s liquidation, there was the letter he had received the morning before from Mrs. Vincent, the mother of his late son-in-law, Savoie. The Vincents had gone to France to visit their daughter, Armande, after her marriage to Pierre de Chanet, and had stayed on for the christening of her baby, Pierrot, who was only a few months younger than Larry. The news of Savoie's terrible death had reached them at Monteregard, the De Chanet's château in Charente and, inevitably, had been a great shock—so great a shock, indeed, that Mr. Vincent had suffered a stroke as a result of it. The first letter bringing this sad news had come from Armande, who told Clyde that her father was very low; indeed, the attendant physician had emerged from the sickroom looking extremely grave, and had said it would be well to summon a priest and that, until other instructions were issued, the patient was to be given nothing except champagne. Though Clyde had never come in close contact with the Sacrament of Extreme Unction, he was acquainted with its grave significance; the reference to champagne, however, puzzled him, until his old friend and neighbour, Mrs. Surget, to whom he showed the letter, clarified it for him.

"I haven't heard of its usage, in such a connection, for a long while. But I do remember, vaguely, having heard that it was customary, in certain parts of France, for a physician to make such a recommendation, instead of saying outright that the end was near. The family was supposed to understand, and still feelings were spared, scenes averted and all amenities observed. You must admit, Clyde, that the French make a fine art of *savoir faire*!"

"All right, I'll admit it," he had said. But he spoke rather grudgingly, and Amy Surget had no trouble in gathering that the admission carried with it no admiration and that probably his lack of enthusiasm had other causes than the one under discussion. "Well, evidently poor Lamartine is in a bad way," he had gone on, looking at the letter again. "But I don't believe he's dead, after all. This was written over two weeks ago and I haven't had a cable since. I think I would have, if the worst had happened."

Clyde's surmise had proved correct. About ten days later, he had received a second letter, this time from Mrs. Vincent, which told him that, though Extreme Unction and champagne had both been administered, as directed, her dear husband had rallied after all and was even beginning to regain some of his powers of speech, though his physical helplessness was as great as ever. "In fact," she had continued, "I am writing you now in accordance with Lamartine's expressed wish. It is evident that our sojourn in France must be greatly prolonged, and that when—or if—he is able to return to Victoria, he will still be unable to take an active part in its supervision. Under these circumstances, it would mean a great deal to him—and, I may add, to Armande and me, also—if you would assume the management of the plantation on a business basis. Of course, you have had a hand in its management for a long time already. Both dear Lamartine and poor Savoie relied on your advice and your help, and I know that since we suffered our great loss, you have taken a more active part in the direction of the plantation. Grateful as we are for your good offices, however, we cannot permit you to continue them, as a favour, indefinitely. (Naturally, in a sense, everything you did would be considered a favour, but I think you will grasp my meaning.) We should, therefore, be most

24

appreciative if, without false pride, you would set forth the terms on which you feel such an arrangement would be not only fair, but profitable, from your point of view."

So it had come—the chance for which he had so greatly hoped. He had not lifted a finger, he had not voiced a wish, and still it had come. Late that same night, after Larry had been put to bed and Clyde had spent several hours in figuring, he wrote to Mrs. Vincent, telling her that he would be glad to assume the management of Victoria on a business basis and suggesting a salary of five thousand a year. He had reckoned that, with careful management, he could gradually pay off the mortgage at Cindy Lou and still have enough for Larry and himself to live on, from the proceeds of his own crops. Everything that came from Victoria could be salted away for its eventual purchase. If that were done, in ten years' time he would have fifty thousand dollars. Even if he could not live to see Larry grow up, he could live for ten years. He would. He must. . . .

The third letter from France had arrived the morning prior to his departure for New Orleans. In it, Mrs. Vincent had accepted his terms and thanked him for his co-operation. . . .

For some time already, he had been taking Larry through the gardens and orchards and to the stable and dairy, carrying the baby over his shoulder when he himself made his daily rounds. More recently, he had set Larry in front of him on the saddle when he went to the drying sheds and the sugar-house. Now at last he had gone farther afield with his precious charge—as far as the Big House and wide arpents of Victoria. Holding the baby firmly enclosed in the hollow of one arm, Clyde had raised the other and waved his hand back and forth in an encompassing gesture.

"That's going to be yours, some day, Larry," he had said. "*All* of it."

Larry had gurgled and pounded on the pommel. Clyde had understood this to mean that the baby wanted to be off again and the ride had been resumed at a lively pace. . . .

"Hell almighty, Mr. Batchelor!" Louie Sanchez's voice was breaking the silence, abruptly ending the reverie. "Often as I've made this run in my time, I could find Cindy Lou in a fog at midnight, during the black of the moon. Wish you'd

25

kindly say as much, with my compliments, to whoever built that big blaze!"

Flames were indeed leaping high from a fire of dried cane reeds—similar to those kindled at Christmastime—on the batture of Cindy Lou. Clyde hastened to explain.

"That's meant for a welcome to me, not a beacon to you, Captain," he said. "Zack always does something of the sort when I'm expected back. But he knows as well as you or I do that, even if there were no other landmark, the anchor light on the *Lucy Batchelor* yonder would be more than enough navigation aid for any pilot."

He pointed into the blackness along the shoals near the west bank, where the first of the floating palaces he had built rode at the permanent mooring to which she had been retired. From her jack staff gleamed the anchor light which Zack tended as faithfully and with as much devotion as he gave to his deaconship in the True Word Baptist Church. Before Lucy's death, she and Clyde had often rowed out to the moored boat for a picnic supper, made doubly pleasant by the evening coolness which pervaded the river at sundown, even in the hottest months. They had both known—though neither would have dreamed of putting the knowledge into words—that the proud vessel would never again make her stately way along the river. Lately it had required more and more work to keep the weakening old hull pumped out and afloat. But Clyde was not ready to admit this, even to himself, and the glimpse of her from the pilothouse intensified this reluctance. Looming up through the darkness, she became again a vision of loveliness and an abode of romance. . . .

The jangling of bells and the churning of engines brought him abruptly back to the present. He rose and stretched himself.

"Good night, Captain Sanchez," he said. "And thanks for your courtesy to an old man."

"'Night," replied the pilot noncommittally. But his gaze followed his departing visitor, and he shook his head sympathetically.

"Poor old Cholly-off-the-spot!" he muttered to himself. "Once they get to goin' down hill, it's fare-thee-well, my love, for true."

Clyde made his way to the foredeck, where deckhands were running out the landing stage under Captain Bruner's shouted directions, and waited until the far end of this rested firmly against the batture. Then he turned to say good-bye to Le Maitre and Torrance. The captain insisted on going ashore with him, though his faithful servants, Old Zack and Zack's brawny son, Nappy, were waiting to greet him, their wide grins of welcome flashing white in the firelight.

"Been a pleasure to have you with us, Mr. Batchelor," Captain Bruner said heartily, wringing Clyde's hand. Nappy had already hastened on to the stageplank and taken Clyde's valise from the deckhand who was apparently bent on carrying it ashore. Motioning the intruder back, as though to indicate that he would tolerate no trespassing on his own domain, Nappy swung the heavy satchel to his shoulder with effortless ease and tramped triumphantly off with it.

"Don't make it so long a spell between trips!" the captain urged, once more wringing Clyde's hand. Then, shouting directions again, this time for departure, he hastened aboard the *Parlour City*. The bells jangled anew and the pitmans plunged along their appointed paths as the stern wheel took up its task. The boat backed away from the batture, the smoky and fitful light of its lanterns reflected in zigzags of radiance trailing downward into the black water. Sparks glowed scarlet as otherwise invisible smoke chuffed upward from the stacks, and mellow Negro voices took up the strains of a jump-along-Josie chant, the melody and the chuffing both becoming fainter and fainter as the distance between the steamboat and the landing widened.

Clyde turned to Zack, placing an arm affectionately about the old servant's shoulders.

"Everything's all right at the house, I'm sure, Zack, or you'd have told me different," he said. "But tell me anyway."

"Everythin' couldn't sca'sely be no better, suh," Zack replied. "Titine done fix you a bait of vittles on a tray in de gamin'-room and I got a good fiah goin', too. All both of us knowed you wouldn't get no fitten food on that trashy boat nohow."

"That'll be fine, and I'm looking forward to a snack, for a fact. And Larry's all right?"

27

"He's mo'n jus' all right, suh. He growing' right out his britches. I ain' never done see a young 'un grow like disyere one, not in all my days, I ain't."

"I'm glad you didn't wake him to bring him down to the landing."

"Huh! Dat Tudie, she snatch me ball-haided was I to try it," Zack chuckled infectiously.

Clyde laughed, too, and, side by side, they started slowly toward the lighted house through the terraced gardens. As they came abreast the lowermost of the fountains that adorned these, one of the peacocks which also contributed to the general show of splendour, screeched raucously somewhere off in the night. Zack shivered and muttered under his breath, drawing closer to Clyde; but Nappy, who had never shared his father's superstitious fear of the gorgeous birds, swung gaily past, whistling the air of 'Just One Girl.' He had already stowed the grip away in Clyde's bedchamber, and was waiting at the door of the gaming-room when his master reached it.

Once inside, the tired traveller warmed his hands gratefully before the embers which glowed in the fireplace, then seated himself beside the tabouret spread with cheese, ham and spicy sausages. These were soon supplemented by steaming coffee and hot cornbread, which Zack brought in from the kitchen. Clyde nodded his thanks, told the men he would look after himself now, and began to eat, savouring his supper slowly.

He would have liked to go to the nursery when he had finished, to wake the baby and tell him that future proprietorship in a moribund steamboat company had been bartered for the solid assurance of a vast productive enterprise, in which Victoria and Cindy Lou would be merged into a single great empire. But of course that would never do; however manfully Larry might seek to knuckle sleep from his eyes, he was not old enough to grasp the portent of this turn in his prospects. But it would not hurt merely to peep into the nursery, to make sure all was well. Clyde banked the fire, went quietly upstairs and opened the door of Larry's room.

In the dim light shed by a vigil lamp, he could see the child sleeping peacefully beneath the quilted covers of his small bed. Less quietly, but quite as soundly, his nurse, Tudie, was sleeping in a nearby cot. Reassured and heartened, Clyde closed the door again, making certain that it was fast, so that there would be no chance of later disturbance. Bushrod had not yet come in, and sometimes he did so rather noisily. As was his habit, he had gone to one of the neighbouring plantations, where a Negro orchestra, alternating with a large music box, would provide tunes for dancing and where he would be the lion of the evening. But he had left the door of his room open and evidently he had left a window open also, for cold air was pouring out into the hall. Picking up a lamp, Clyde entered the empty chamber, prompted only by the idea that he would find the source of the draught and put an end to it.

Once inside, however, he paused and looked around him. The room was in a state of complete disarray and, after closing the rear window and setting down the lamp, Clyde began, almost automatically, to pick up the stray garments which were strewn about. He was orderly by nature, and years of association with Lucy, who had been the personification of daintiness, had increased his instinctive aversion to slovenly habits. Moreover, he realized that in Lucy's lifetime no room in their house could possibly have looked like this in the evening; however negligent its occupant, some servant would have put it in proper condition during the course of the morning and returned to it, later in the day, to rectify anything that might since have gone awry. He would have a word with Delphie, the housemaid, who was still supposed to give meticulous care to the upper story; but there was no use in trying to do so tonight, as by this time she would have returned to the quarters. In any case, he was too tired, at the moment, to deal with a servant who had grown slatternly in her ways, now that she had no mistress to supervise her. It would be less bother to straighten things out himself.

In order to see better, he pulled down the lamp which was suspended on metal chains from the centre of the ceiling and lighted it. As he swung it back into place, his attention was caught by a rectangular packet, wrapped in brown paper, tied with white cord and tagged with a blue express label, which lay on the littered centre table. Frowning with impatience at himself, he turned aside; then, conscious of some strange compulsion, he looked back again; there was something vaguely familiar about the appearance of the parcel, though he did not instantly realize what this was. Still acting almost involuntarily, he picked it up and scrutinized the label.

'Ever-True Novelty Company, St. Louis,' he read with growing dismay and mounting rage. Then, his fingers shaking, he untied the knotted cord and laid back the wrapping. The brown paper unfolded to disclose two dozen decks of cards—the same kind which, over and over again during the old days, he had seen slipped, by sleight of hand, into a friendly game which was taking place in the gentlemen's cabin of a floating palace.

CHAPTER TWO

His FIRST impulse was to throw the cards into the fire, leaving the empty, telltale wrappings to confront his stepson when Bushrod returned from his night of revelry. Indeed, Clyde had already picked up the decks and stridden toward the hearth, when sober second thought brought the realization that this was no way to deal with such a serious situation. What the best way might be could not instantly be determined; but at least it was not through the destruction of material which might prove valuable evidence in an emergency. He carefully rewrapped the cards, restored the package to its original position and, making no further effort to create order out of the prevailing chaos, left the chamber and went slowly down the two flights of stairs which took him to the gaming-room. Then he poured himself a stiff drink and sat, sipping it slowly, until he heard the sound of wheels outside, followed by footsteps along the gravel path. A moment later, Bushrod opened the door and walked in.

Undeniably, he made an impressive showing. His unimpaired figure set off his uniform to immense advantage; pallor gave a Byronic touch to his fine features; and the dark circles under his eyes, far from suggesting dissipation, only added to this air of romanticism; in every way he embodied the popular conception of a patriot who had suffered in a noble cause, and who was still suffering from the results of its hardships and its dangers, but who was making a valiant effort to conceal his pain under a cloak of buoyancy. And this was the dissembler who was accepting hero worship from a generous and cordial people at the same time that he was preparing to abuse their hospitality, so prodigally offered, with practices as adroit as they were dishonourable!

"Anything wrong?" Bushrod inquired, casually acknowledging his stepfather's greeting and turning toward the open cellaret.

"Not that I know of. Why should there be?"

"No special reason. Except that it's rather late. I don't usually find you up at this hour. When I saw the light there, I thought something might be amiss with you. That's why I came on to the gaming-room, instead of going straight upstairs."

"I appreciate your concern for my welfare. I seem to remember other occasions when something rather different brought you to this room. You can't blame me if I still associate your presence here with very unpleasant interviews. Not that there's any real connection, of course. Though, as a matter of fact, I've got some money for you this time, too."

"Money?"

"Yes, I meant to give it to you in the morning, but if I do it now instead, we'll be square that much sooner. I don't know whether I mentioned that I intended going to New Orleans today. But that's where I've been. The C. & L. Navigation Company was liquidated this afternoon—at least, what remained of it. The Cooley folks bought out the name and good will, leaving me what I'd banked from last year's shipping and paying a tidy enough sum for the contracts already signed—enough to cover the coming crop."

Bushrod, who had been fingering the glass he held and looking down at the drink he had poured himself, as if he enjoyed its mellow light, glanced up with a sudden show of interest.

"And part of that tidy sum would be mine?" he inquired. "Is that what you waited up to tell me? I haven't wanted to hurry you, of course, but I've been wondering when . . . Don't keep me in suspense. What does my share come to?"

"Six hundred and eighty-four dollars and some odd coppers."

"Oh!" Bushrod looked down again and began to drum on the table, first with a slow, rhythmic movement and then with

31

jerky irregularity. Clyde glanced at him contemptuously and, for the first time, some of his contempt crept into his voice.

"When you say 'Oh!' like that, it's evident you really mean, 'Is that all?' Yes, that's all—and whatever it is, it's just that much more than what, under the law, you can rightfully claim. Is that plain?"

"No, it isn't. If you think I mean to sit idly by and let you pass me a sugar-tit, you're mightily mistaken."

"Very well. I'll try to explain. The steamboat company was formed after your mother and I were married, and so became community property, jointly owned, half and half, by her and myself. It was the only piece of community property we owned. I bought the plantation before our marriage. Hence that was mine alone, because it was separate and paraphernal, under the law."

"I know. Under the Napoleonic Code which so amply assures protection for married women!"

The sneer in Bushrod's tone was now as unmistakable as the contempt had been in his stepfather's. But Clyde answered quietly.

"That is correct. It is also correct that the fifty thousand dollars I gave your mother at the time of our marriage was hers. I could not touch it or compel her to give me any part of it."

"Fifty thousand dollars!"

"Actually, more than that, by quite a good deal. Your mother had invested most of it very shrewdly, thanks to advice given her by Lamartine Vincent and others. She had done this without consulting me; indeed, without my knowledge. I did not learn about the existence of that sum until you bled me of what was just about my last penny in ready cash . . . the last time we were together in this room."

"Then what's all this palaver about six hundred dollars when I have coming to me a share—at least a quarter share—of more than fifty thousand?"

"You have coming to you exactly nothing, as a matter of law."

"We'll see about that!"

"Indeed we shall. But it will be worth your while to hear me out, so that you understand what your position is. I had mortgaged everything I owned at the time of Cary's wedding to build her a house and provide the sort of marriage she had counted on. Those loans were necessary because of an unlucky flier in the cotton market and the drain of our steamboat operations on the plantation earnings. So when you black-mailed me out of twenty thousand dollars I was ruined. That was the one thing I might have used to make a fresh start. And you robbed me of it."

"It wasn't a fraction of what you should have given me, and you know it. Cary and I were to share alike as far as you were concerned, and . . ."

"We'll discuss that some other time, if we must. Let me get on with this explanation of what utter and complete ruin I faced the day Cary and Savoie left on their honeymoon. I don't know to what shifts I might have been put—but for your mother. She had guessed something of how things stood with me, and offered to help. I told her the situation was beyond help, because I had exhausted my credit, was head over heels in debt, had mortgaged even the coming crops—and it was then that she gave me not only the money I had settled on her years before, but all the gains her wise investments and the income from these had added to the original sum."

"And you mean that was all swallowed up in your mis-management?"

"From then on she and I managed together. Thanks to her, we paid the interest on my debts and made other pressing and immediate payments on principal. We bought some bitterly needed equipment—and before the year's end we were taking in more than we were paying out. Had she lived, not only this plantation, which she helped to redeem, but the money, which it would have repaid, would have been community property. But she—she did not live."

"How does that affect the money that was due her?"

"It means that at the time of her death she and I were technically insolvent. It means our liabilities—our debts—were greater than our assets. It means that the community, such as it was, consisted of nothing but unpaid and unpayable debts."

"But they have been paid."

"Last year's operation finally cleared away the last of the

loans we made to meet our mortgages. For the first time, Cindy Lou was free and clear once more. But none of that, under the law, affects your mother's share of the community."

"We'll see about that, if there's any law in the land."

"That we will. As a matter of fact, I had your mother's succession opened before Judge Chretien. He appointed an appraiser, whose report on the insolvency of your mother's estate had been filed. But because you were abroad, I asked that the proceedings be held up. So that if you want to contest them, you can do so, at any time. Meanwhile, the solvency of the plantation made it possible for me to liquidate the navigation company at last, and while no court could compel me to give you a share of that, I was and am ready to do so."

"While you pocket the rest?"

"For Larry. As his tutor. Under the agreement made with your grandmother at the time of—of the funeral—he will be my heir to all of Cindy Lou."

"Tutor?"

"Guardian then, if that term suits you better. But the legal guardian of a minor is called a tutor in Louisiana. I hardly thought a barrister would need to be told that."

"And since when, if it isn't asking too much, have you been made my nephew's legal guardian?"

"I haven't been. That is, not officially. But I have spoken to Judge Chretien of the district court and written to Mrs. Vincent about the matter. Since the appointment won't be contested. . . ."

"What makes you so certain of that?"

"Mrs. Vincent has answered my letter, assuring me that her husband is satisfied. As you know, he's completely crippled. But, fortunately, his mind has remained clear."

"Is he the only one who might object?"

"I feel sure he is, since your grandmother had already assured me that she didn't. Don't you think I'm right?"

For a moment, their eyes met. Then Bushrod shrugged his shoulders, as if the matter were of no further interest to him.

"About my share in the proceeds from today's transaction," he said. "I suppose there's some sort of an accounting I could see, merely as a matter of form, naturally. But so as to verify the calculations."

"Certainly. In fact, Valois Dupré prepared a notarized attest at my request. I felt reasonably sure you'd make such a demand and you're entitled to an accounting."

"Of course I am. And while we're on the point, I might add that I'd like a similar statement from you, acknowledging my ownership in a part of this plantation."

"You don't own any part of this plantation. You never will. You agreed, in writing, that if your maternal grandmother's Virginia plantations, Amalfi and Sorrento, were left to you outright, you would forgo any claim you might have to a share in Cindy Lou."

"As you said a few minutes ago, 'that is correct.' Otherwise, you've made a mistake, and a mighty big one. I own the entire back part of this plantation—that strip of land along Bayou Boisblanc, where Cary was always setting out to find treasure —and never did!" From somewhere out in the garden came an unearthly shriek. Bushrod leaped up. "For God's sake, why don't you get rid of those damned peacocks!" he cried. "That noise would drive a preacher to drink!"

Clyde reached into a bowl which stood beside his empty toddy glass, took out two pecans, pressed them side by side into his hand and knotted his fingers over them until the shells burst noisily. Then, opening his fist, he looked at the fragments for a moment before picking out a few kernels and putting them into his mouth.

"Well, now, you amaze me," he said slowly. "Not by asking me why I don't get rid of the peacocks. I know you don't like them, but Larry does. So I think I'll hang on to them. What you say about the land does come as a surprise though. I know for a fact that old Dupré didn't sell you the property and no one else had a right to. Or the title, either. I take it you're not lying— this time. So somebody must have sucked you in. Instead of selling you a gold brick, or a diamond mine in Brazil, or a key to the river, someone sold you a worthless deed to Cindy Lou. Well! . . ."

"The state of Louisiana sold it to me! I bought it for the taxes. And if you think you can make a joke out of that, you're welcome to!"

"I won't try to make a joke out of it. But I'd like to hear a little more about it."

35

Clyde reached for more pecans, cracked them as he had the others and sat thoughtfully chewing the kernels. Bushrod's sneering tone gradually rose to something very near a shout.

"I'd be very glad to explain. Dupré found a better gravel bed than yours on the Tangipahoa River—close to New Orleans, too, with a sand bar hard by. It's easy to follow how he figured things out. Here was this parcel on Bayou Boisblanc that wasn't worth a jitney to anybody, *except* as a gravel bed, and he didn't want to waste any more money on it. Naturally, he wasn't going to offer to sell it back to you and no one else wanted it. So he decided to let the state take it over for taxes. My father-in-law—not to mention my dear wife—keep me pretty short; but I manage, one way and another, to have some ready cash most of the time. So I had enough to buy in the Bayou Boisblanc property for the first verse and chorus of a short song. So it's mine. Do you understand? *Part of Cindy Lou is mine!* And I dare you to put up a fourth interest in the rest of the plantation against that part in a poker game and see who picks up the marbles!"

"And supposing I won't? After all, you just said that what you claim you own is worthless, except as a gravel bed. And it seems nobody wants a gravel bed there."

"I did say so and it's true—generally speaking. But it happens to have two other values as far as you're concerned. One is you want it so badly you can taste it. That was where you and Cary used to spend a lot of time, and anything connected with Cary, in your mind . . . She had a few faults, too, but we won't go into those."

"No. We won't go into those."

Clyde's voice was still as even as before. Nevertheless, something in it caused his stepson to decide, rather hurriedly, that the last statement was conclusive.

"Well, there may be treasure there, too, for all I know," he said. "I mean the kind you and Cary were hunting for. But you'll admit it's pretty doubtful. However, there's no doubt at all that tract of land could be a gold mine for me—not a gold *brick* or a *diamond* mine in Brazil, but a *gold mine* right here in Louisiana. I could start a gambling house on it—a saloon, a dance hall, maybe some cribs upstairs. A neighbour to Cindy

36

Lou, on what used to be Cindy Lou land. What would you say to that?"

Bushrod had expected that this suggestion would bring forth another cold statement made with menacing finality or even, this time, a violent outburst. Instead, Clyde merely shook his head and, for a few moments, seemed absorbed in thought.

"I don't know," he answered eventually. "I suppose if I were a 'hero,' I'd say such a venture would be unbecoming an officer and a gentleman. As I'm just an old river gambler, I look at it differently. I can't see why you bother to risk a 'gold mine,' like what you've described, against a share in the plantation. The gambling den, booze parlour and whore house would be a lot more profitable. The odds aren't good enough."

"Name your own odds, then."

"Very well. I'll play you draw poker for your claim to the Boisblanc gravel land *and* a written statement from you acknowledging the insolvency of your mother's community estate at the time of her death, against an assignment to share all of Cindy Lou's profits with you henceforth."

"An assignment to how much of a share?"

"A third of whatever's turned over to Larry, or to me as his tutor, each year. Even you are bound to realize I wouldn't cheat him."

"But what's the idea of acknowledging mother's insolvency?"

"At the time your mother's succession was appraised as insolvent, Judge Chretien wanted to have you present so that you could, if you wished, assume your share of the insolvent estate's debts. I asked that the whole matter be held up until you returned. If you will sign an acknowledgement of that insolvency, and recognition of the fact that there was no community, Judge Chretien can enter a judgement recording the fact that there is no other claimant to the estate, such as it was at the time of your mother's death. . . . That agreement against a third of all profits Cindy Lou will ever earn. What do you say?"

Bushrod made no attempt to conceal the sudden surge of elation that swept him to his feet. "Why, I say, done with you!" he cried. "What'll it be? Winner-take-all on the first hand?"

"Winner-take-all on one hand's no test of anything but

luck. We'll play for chips till one of us picks a hand by his own choosing to tap out the other player for everything."

"That's all right with me. First hand, last hand, four-in-hand, any old hand. Trot 'em all out—foot, horse and heavy artillery—and let the firing commence!"

"That can't all be done in a minute, as you ought to know after your recent glorious military career. Besides, there are documents to prepare and it's rather late, as you said yourself when you came in. I've been to New Orleans today and you've been—well, I don't know exactly where, but anyhow this is 'After the Ball is Over.' I wouldn't say either one of us was in the best shape to play—even for peanuts. And this isn't going to be that kind of a game. What about tomorrow night?"

"I'm taken for tomorrow. The Naquins and their cousins are making up a party to see the ball game at Donaldsonville and spend the night there."

"Day after tomorrow then. Any time you like, except tonight."

"Very well. Day after tomorrow. Though I warn you I'll be on the lookout for any rigs you may try to run in the mean-time."

"Run any rigs? As if I'd need to. But you'd be well advised not to run any on me. I knew all the tricks long before you started your brief career at the Westmoreland Club. Well, that's neither here nor there. I'll be looking for you around eight Wednesday night."

Clyde twitched the reins so that they flickered along Spice's back, but the motion was quite without conscious direction. His relaxed posture in the cabriolet was as easy as the mare's gait, and she jogged along the familiar road, early Wednesday afternoon, just fast enough to outdistance the dust cloud raised by her hoofs from the powdery surface of the highway. Along one side of it ran the low, endless molehill of the levee. On the other lay the fields, separated here and there by arching, moss-hung live oaks, by the ornamental shrubbery of a plantation garden or by clustered cabins weathered to the same silvery grey as the cypress palings of the fences surrounding them. At one such cabin, Clyde drew Spice to an abrupt halt and banged the butt of his whip against the side of the cabriolet in a sharp tattoo.

"Ma'y Lou!" he called. "Ma'y Lou! Rustle your bones!" There was no immediate response, and he was on the point of raising a fresh halloo when an enormous Negress turned the corner of the cabin, billowing into sight. Her splayed feet were bare and a single shapeless garment of faded calico clung to the more voluminous bulges of her body. But a bright print cloth was tied about her head in an elaborately knotted tignon, and large loops of yellow metal dangled from the lobes of her ears.

"Bless Jesus, Mr. Clyde, you'se too welcome, suh," she beamed, "even iffen mah house is that upset I could faint. I could so. Do leave me unhook dis gate. . . ."

"No need, Ma'y Lou. I'm only passing by. But I'll be back directly, and when I come I want you to have a sugar-tit for me."

The big Negress cupped one fat elbow with her palm, whipping the other hand over her mouth as she cackled shrilly.

"No sugar-tit couldn' be for you, suh, no," she giggled, spluttering. "You just a'funnin' with old Ma'y Lou, dat you is."

"Don't act like you never had good knowledge," he said with an answering grin. "I want a sugar-tit and what I need it for doesn't concern you the first particle."

"Does you mean just a plain, everyday sugar-tit lak us gives our babies, Mr. Clyde?"

"Exactly. And I'll be back for it in less than no time, so stir your stumps."

"Yessuh, I sho'ly will. As soon as ever you gets back, suh, I has a sugar-tit tied for you."

Clyde nodded a goodbye, twitched the reins and clicked a command to Spice. Then, as the mare resumed her peaceful jogging, he continued along the river road to the Grand Hotel Pierre Chanet. This hostelry had prospered greatly as river traffic fell off for canvassers and drummers—Knights of the Grip, as they like to call themselves—now went about the countryside in their own buggies, because steamboats were so few and far between and so unreliable of schedule. The Pierre Chanet housed a good poker game in one of the back rooms, and the travelling salesmen found it pleasant to while away the Saturday-to-Monday tedium there. This meant excellent business for the bar, as well, and here Clyde, having secured Spice to the worn cypress arc of the hotel's hitch rack, purchased a deck of cards.

"Just one, thanks, Celestin. Steamboats, either pink or blue. It makes no difference which."

He found Ma'y Lou waiting for him at the weathered fence, a clean, neatly tied bit of white cloth that looked like a miniature rag doll held proudly in her great black hand. Tucking it into the pocket of his grey moleskin vest, he gave her a silver dollar, nodding acknowledgement of her shrill thanks and a broad jest to the effect that the older the stallion, the prouder he be's to claim ary wood's colt as his own get. Then, chuckling as he thought of Ma'y Lou's parting comment, he sat back in the cabriolet, relaxed, while Spice drew it homeward through the deepening dusk.

CHAPTER THREE

Now THAT he was alone, Clyde had discontinued Lucy's pleasant practice of serving afternoon tea. Instead, he had a hearty supper, early enough for Larry to be at the table with him; and while Delphie, the housemaid, had grown slack in her ways, Belle, the cook, aged and slow as she was, had not lost the skill that went with having 'a free hand and no conscience' when it came to cooking. She had never yet sent in a meal that was not a credit to her and tonight it was actually something of a feast. Dumaine, the overseer, had sent a couple of fine green trout to the Big House and these had been baked in a *sauce piquante*; fluffy white rice and Whippoorwill peas accompanied these. So did a mixture of late-gathered winter greens, which had been simmered with a hunk of fatback in an iron pot, after leaves of sweet basil, finely minced with bird's-eye peppers, and a couple of garlic pods, stuck with cloves, had been added for seasoning. Crackling bread made with buttermilk and home-ground meal went with this *pièce de résistance* and crisp waffles with pecan cuite followed it. When he had finished, Clyde pushed back his chair from the table with a gusty sigh.

"A man my age hasn't any business eating that much rich food," he said. "Remember that, Larry, when you get to be as old as I am. From the way you scoop everything up now, it looks as if you might need a word of warning."

Larry's hearty laugh showed that he understood his grandfather was 'funning' even though he did not know what all the words meant; and after the two had hugged each other hard, he ran noisily off to Tudie. Clyde looked after him dotingly and turned to Zack. "Bring my coffee down to the gaming-room," he said, "and light a fire in both the heating stove and the fireplace. It was hot enough through the day, but it's turned off chilly. . . . I don't expect Mr. Bushrod for an hour or so yet, but when he comes in, tell him I'm waiting for him."

"Ah done light the fires already, suh. Ah figured as how you might be wantin' 'em."

The gaming-room's warmth was benign; the crackle of wood in the grate mingled cheerfully with the purr from the draught of the heating stove. The large central lamp of the girandole had been lighted and its height so adjusted that only the top of the card table came within its cone of radiance; the rest of the room remained intimately wrapped in semi-darkness. With an increasing sense of well-being, Clyde let himself down into an armchair facing the fireplace. On the serving stand at his elbow, Zack placed a tray bearing a small silver coffeepot, a bowl of cracked loaf sugar, a decanter of brandy and one eggshell cup, which Clyde promptly filled with the fragrant black brew. Then, into the bowl of a coffee spoon, he dropped a small chunk of sugar, which he saturated with brandy. Zack touched the end of a *roseau* sliver to the coals and quickly applied the tiny flame to the sugar. A blue light clothed its crest for an instant, before sliding down to envelop the sides and dance lightly over the bowl of the spoon. Clyde held the small flambeau steady until the sugar lump collapsed with a syrupy bubbling, then quenched it all in the coffee, stirring the aromatic mixture and sipping it with lively relish.

"Only one, tonight," he said to Zack. "But wait in the kitchen, even after Mr. Bushrod gets here. I might be wanting you later on."

His sensation of well-being continued to increase. It would

not matter how soon Bushrod came; on the contrary, the stage had been set for hours now and he was eager for the play to begin. He had realized, from the beginning, that whatever methods his stepson had in mind, the latter must have taken the precaution of working these out before he issued his challenge. Otherwise, he would not have talked so brashly. Yet a close scrutiny of the cards and chips, kept on an inlaid rack in the gaming-room, had revealed nothing out of the ordinary. The cards were the same Steamboat and Congress decks Clyde always kept there and most of them were new, their revenue stamps still intact. So much for that.

An equally detailed examination of Bushrod's room had likewise brought nothing of a suspicious nature to light. The package from the Ever-True Novelty Company, which Clyde had accidentally found on his return from New Orleans, was gone; but that was to be expected. Bushrod had, no doubt, taken its contents with him when he went to Donaldsonville for a 'ball' game and to spend the night and the following day with the Naquins and their cousins at an adjacent plantation. This interval would certainly be largely given over to poker. But it was here at Cindy Lou that Bushrod was preparing for the supreme gamble of his career. . . .

The answer to the puzzle was so simple that Clyde was astonished he had not found it at once; but it was not until he had passed a sleepless night, restless and irritated at his failure to solve the mystery, that he suddenly did so: the package of his discovery could not have been the first which had come to the house. There must have been at least one other—perhaps several others—and from one of these had come the decks which Bushrod intended to use now. He was far too shrewd to suppose that his stepfather would accept any he might bring into the gaming-room at the last moment. The marked cards must be there already, and so placed that Clyde himself would unwittingly introduce them into the game. But he had examined the contents of the inlaid rack and everything had appeared to be in order. Hold the deal a moment. . . . Appeared to be. . . . Appeared to be. . . . Why that must be it!

Clyde had dressed hurriedly, returned to the gaming-room and, from the inlaid rack, had again taken an unopened deck and peered with frowning intensity at the intact revenue stamp which sealed it. Finally he had sawed through this with his thumbnail, pulled out the contents and carefully lifted the flaps of their waxy wrapping with the blade of a penknife. No more than a glance was needed to reveal that the apparently normal latticework pattern on the backs of the cards was marked with the familiar Ever-True design, so that anyone who knew the key could read the value of each card as clearly from the back as from the front. But the unbroken government seal? . . . Of course! Bushrod would have in his possession forged—or even stolen—revenue stamps, to be applied over what was left of the torn seals after marked decks had been substituted for the original contents of the genuine Steamboat or Congress boxes. An old, old dodge. But it had come within a hairsbreadth of taking him in.

Well, forewarned was forearmed. A skilled player, knowing that marked cards which he could also read were being used against him, enjoyed a tremendous advantage over a cheat who was not aware of his intended victim's knowledge. Clyde wondered what sort of a deal Bushrod planned to use in the crucial hand. The marked cards had been rearranged; the cold deck was already stacked. And Bushrod would deal that hand. He must have arranged the packs for himself to handle with a false shuffle, being prepared to reverse Clyde's cut when he packed the cards. Clyde took two poker hands off the top of the substituted deck, turning the cards of one up. Sure enough, there it was. The hand that would be dealt him showed a pat full house—three queens and a pair of fours. Bushrod's hand held two kings, two tens and the five of diamonds. Obviously, he had assumed Clyde would stand pat. Bushrod would discard one on the draw—the five of diamonds, naturally—and would receive . . . Clyde flipped over the next card—a third king. Thus Bushrod's three kings and two tens would top Clyde's three queens and a pair of fours. Old as the hills, but suckers were still taken in by it.

Clyde riffled through the deck to draw out the fourth queen from far beneath the carefully stacked hands that topped it. Taking this card to his office, he slipped a fine-pointed new steel nib into his penholder and diluted a few drops of red ink with water from the cedar drinking keg. Turning the pink lattice of the card's back uppermost, he set to work with knife point and pen. Progress was slow; it was achieved by no more than a touch of blade or pen point at a time. But when he had finished, the markings on the back of this queen of clubs showed it to be a four; and though his eyes were tired, they twinkled as he returned to the gaming-room and substituted this queen for one of the two fours that were to have been dealt him.

Otherwise, he left the deck arranged exactly as he had found it, rewrapping it in the original glassine cover which he closed fast with a drop of mucilage from the bottle on his desk. He had no way of replacing or repairing the broken revenue stamp, after he had slipped the rewrapped cards back into their flat box. But this was no great matter since it was virtually certain Bushrod would call for a new deck and ask him to take it from the rack; otherwise there would have been no reason to substitute 'cold' marked decks for all the genuine ones in the rack. Moreover, Clyde could always make an adequate pretence of breaking an already broken seal. Certain of his ground, Bushrod would not be watching closely at that stage, in any case. . . . Replacing the deck in its rack, Clyde went through a rear passage to the kitchen garden where a bell swung from the top of a slender pole. He gave its cord a sharp pull, and as the bell pealed, a stableboy came running quickly toward him.

"Hitch Sugar or Spice to the cabriolet," he directed. "It doesn't matter which, but be quick about it."

What a pity it was, he reflected, as he waited for the cabriolet, that this rare jest could not be shared. So Bushrod did not mean to have anyone fob off a sugar-tit on him, eh? The joke was really too good for a man to keep to himself. Clyde went into the garden and plucked a wine-coloured, belated bloom for the buttonhole of his jimswinger; then, returning to the house for his Stetson, he cocked this at a rakish angle. It certainly made a man feel young again to whet his wits.

He took the reins from the small darky, gave the cabriolet's spidery wheels an approving glance and set off in the direction of Ma'y Lou's cabin and the Grand Hotel Pierre Chanet.

This had been several hours ago and now he was seated in the big armchair, gazing quietly at the embers and sipping his coffee with that increasing sense of contentment. He was still sitting there when Bushrod came in.

"People, people, it's cold on the river!" he exclaimed, spreading his hands to the welcome warmth of the grate fire. "In that open launch of Naquin's, the wind cut through me straight to the marrow."

"I expected you rather earlier."

"God almighty! You ought to know how these Creoles are. They've got kinfolk back of every tree and tucked away in every fence corner. Before we could think of leaving Donaldsonville, we had to pay courtesy calls on Cousin Constantine and Cousin Clovis and Parrain This and Marraine That, because any relative who was overlooked would be mortally hurt. But here I am, better late than never, I reckon, and ready to receive the warm and affectionate welcome of a stepsire who loves me as though I were Bronze John's own twin."

"Coffee?"

"No, thank you just as much. But a hooker of blue ruin would be gratefully received as a sovereign preventer of *la grippe*."

Clyde waved his hand toward the rosewood cellaret. "You'll find whatever you need there, I think," he said. "And if you're not feeling up to snuff, I wouldn't object to postponing the game until——"

"Hell no!" Bushrod tossed off a small glass of bourbon, neat, and smacked his lips. "You said you expected me earlier. I won't hold you up any longer. Bring on the cards and counters."

Clyde rose, placed the rack on the table, raised the cover and began to count out chips.

"I should think a couple of hundred dollars would be aplenty," he suggested, with just enough of a rising inflection to leave the decision to Bushrod. "I mean for the warm-up. One of us will probably make it winner-take-all before it's used up."

Clyde produced a worn pigskin wallet from the inner pocket of his coat and extracted a folded sheet of paper from it. "Here's the statement, all in good shape," he said. " 'Whatever money is paid to Lawrence Vincent's account from Cindy Lou Plantation, through sale, rent or crops, whether

45

paid to him direct or to his tutor during his minority, a sum equal to one-third of every such payment is to be remitted within seven days to Bushrod Page or to his lawful agent.' "

Clyde tossed the sheet across the lighted table to Bushrod, who scanned the document briefly and shrugged.

"I expect it'll hold water," he observed. He scraped a chair across the floor to the table and sat down. "All right. Shall we start the sociable?"

"When I have your written agreement," Clyde answered, still standing. "This will be table stakes. Until the paper is with the chips in front of you, we don't turn the first card."

"What the hell's eating you? How could I chiprack you on a proposition like that?"

"I'll never know, because you won't have a chance to show me. Stop playing the gentleman, will you? I'm all the audience there is this time. Bring what you need in the way of paper, pen and ink from the office, and then write me a signed statement of your promise to leave and another stating your disclaimer to any part of this property. Put those statements with your chips, and afterwards we'll play. Not before. And we won't play with any cards of yours. I've taken the time and trouble to go to the Chanet and buy a new deck. You needn't bother asking if I don't trust you. The answer is I sure as hell don't. I wouldn't trust you as far as I could carry the river in my vest pocket."

Bushrod rose, without answering, and, going into the office, brought back a pad of ruled foolscap paper, a pen and a small bottle of purplish ink. Then he sat down and wrote scratchily, signed the two documents with a flourish and read them aloud. Clyde nodded and Bushrod ripped the paper from its pad, passed the sheets quickly back and forth over the lamp chimney several times to dry the ink, then laid them beside his varicoloured chips.

"Satisfied?" he asked.

"Well, not exactly. But we can start playing any time. Here's the deck. Shuffle it yourself. Then we'll cut. High deals."

Without a word, Bushrod opened the new deck, stripped the glassine wrapping from the cards, pushed it and the two jokers to one side and shuffled dexterously, riffling the cards

46

with practised skill. At length, he spread them in an arc across the baize centrepiece.

Clyde turned a jack to Bushrod's six of hearts. As he shuffled the cards anew, his expression was as blank as a newly whitewashed wall; but behind that imperturbable mask he was wondering by what means Bushrod would substitute one of the marked decks for this unmarked one. He was not left long in doubt. On the first deal, Bushrod tossed two ten-dollar chips into the pot, along with two cards.

"I'll take a couple off the top, if you feel like seeing how the luck's running tonight," he said. Then, as an earsplitting screech again slashed through the quiet night, he exclaimed, "God damn those peacocks! Every last one of them would be in the market for a new neck if I had my say-so."

"But you haven't. As for this hand, I wouldn't care for any part of it," Clyde observed placidly. "I wouldn't choose to draw against you this time."

"You mean all I win is my own double sawbuck?" Bushrod asked testily. "And with three natural aces to draw to?" He made as if to display the cards, but, as though goaded beyond endurance, he tore them across and threw the pieces on the floor. Then he did the same with the two he had discarded, snatching them back from the table's centre. "That calls for a new deck. And, by the way, I'm not afraid to play with your cards, even if you are scared of mine. Pick any deck you please out of your own box, for all of me."

Not so well done, reflected Clyde behind the blank front of his poker face. To be sure, tearing up an ill-favoured hand and demanding a new deck was a traditional gesture. But a cleverer sharp would then have offered to bring in cards of his own. When Clyde demurred, as he was reasonably certain to do, Bushrod could have waved aside the objection with a casual, "Hell, if you're all that worried, I'm agreeable to playing with your cards. Anything for a quiet life." But he was too impatient for his grand coup to let the suggestion come from his opponent.

Clyde lifted the cover of the container and, apparently without looking, withdrew from it one of the decks. Running his thumbnail swiftly along the upper edge of this, as if he were slitting the revenue stamp, he took out the cards and shoved them, still in their glassine wrapper, across the table to Bushrod, who removed the wrapper and the two jokers and tossed them into the grate.

Bushrod riffled the cards, crisply, apparently shuffling them with his swiftly moving fingers, before offering the deck for a cut, in a way that suggested he half expected the tender would be waived. But Clyde reached across and divided the pack. He appeared wholly intent on stacking his chips in more meticulous alignment; nevertheless, he caught every detail of Bushrod's reversal of the cut: the tip of the left little finger inserted between the two portions of the deck, the swift left-hand flip under cover of the right hand, which was brought forward as though merely to take the first card in making the deal. He picked up the hand Bushrod dealt him, squeezed the edges cautiously to inspect it, closed it into a book and laid this face down upon the table before him. There lay the four queens and the single four he had arranged in this deck earlier in the day.

"I'll tap you on this first hand," he said quietly. "Do you want me to do it now or after the draw?"

Bushrod examined his cards, shifted in his chair and otherwise made a show of indecision and doubt. "That means your hand's pat," he said musingly. "What a hell of a note! A pat hand on the first deal, with me over a barrel, because I can't lay down my hand, however sorry it might be. And I don't mind saying it's a sorry two pair—the hardest hand in the deck to improve. So it makes no difference when you tap me."

"What makes you so all-fired sure my hand's pat?" Clyde challenged.

Beyond the cone of illumination, the room still lay in shadow. Then a sudden jet of yellow flame hissed from a dying ember and subsided into a dusky glow. Clyde again picked up his cards and studied them, as though seeking reassurance. Apparently still preoccupied with his thoughts, he arranged his cards face down before him, one beside the other, so that each back was plainly visible.

"I might have four and a kicker, you know," he argued pensively, "or I might have nothing but a rinctum tiddy— a cooler—a strong case of measles, having overlooked my hand, maybe. *You'd* never believe a body'd be gambler enough to shoot the moon on a chance. That'd tempt me to run a windy on you just for the hell of it. But whether the hand's pat flush, or four of a kind or just a wild dream makes no difference. So put up your poke right now if you aim to draw cards."

Bushrod had darted a surreptitious glance at the face-down row in front of Clyde. There could have been no error. Nevertheless, he felt the cold clutch of doubt. If by some wild mischance anything had gone wrong. . . . But no, the marks showed that his stepfather had a full house: three queens and a pair of fours. Yet he swallowed several times before tossing his statements on the green centrepiece in front of Clyde.

"Domino!" he said, not very steadily. "Now—how many cards?" He picked up the deck and held it towards Clyde, waiting with his right hand poised as if to deal on demand.

"I'm pat. You were right. I'll play what I've got."

"I reckoned as much," Bushrod answered rather smugly. "Neither do I think you're running a windy. That's why I'm going to draw one card to my two pair. If what you've got is a straight, a flush or a small full house, I can improve enough to take the pot. If you've got four of a kind, or a straight flush though, I can't. Here's what I'm drawing to—kings and tens." He faced up his hand and flipped the fifth card, the five of diamonds, to one side and lifted the top card slowly from its resting place on the deck until he could read it. Then he turned it over and brought it down on the table with a resounding bang of knuckles against the wood. "And a king it is!" he said exultantly. "Twenty sweet miles of railroad track and three kings to walk them!" He cast a triumphant glance at the backs of the cards still aligned in a row before Clyde. "Well, speak up. Which of us sleeps on the levee tonight? Show me that pat hand of yours!"

Clyde faced up his cards one at a time: the queen of hearts, the queen of diamonds, the queen of spades, the four of hearts. . . . He waited, looking up to watch Bushrod's face as the last card was turned: the one whose marked back proclaimed it a four, but whose face revealed the stylized mirror images of the queen of clubs, four-petalled blossom in hand.

"Why, Bushrod!" he said mildly. "What in time's the matter with you? You're the colour of a toad-frog's belly."

"B-b-but . . ." Bushrod caught himself just in time; he had

been on the point of reaching across the table for the queen. "I mean. . . ."

"I know exactly what you mean." For the first time since the game began, Clyde smiled. He turned the queen and skimmed it across the table so that it came to rest, back up, in front of Bushrod. "You mean the mark on the hindside showed it to be a four-spot? Those Ever-True people must be getting downright careless."

"You—you've had that card right from the start!"

"I expect I must have. While you were visiting the Naquins, I did a little prospecting—and bless me, if I didn't trip right over a cold deck, all stacked for the whiskery old caper that went out of style about the time McClellan was beaten for president. So I took the notion of playing fox to your possum. Well, you know as much about the rest as I do." He pushed the cards aside and, taking the document of assignment, tore it into small pieces. "I've had a very pleasant evening," he continued. "It's been worth a little trouble to show you that you'd better not step out of your class—when it comes to gambling or anything else. While we're at it, let's get one fact mighty clear: whether you believe it or not—and on that point I don't give the first God damn—I've never cheated you out of anything that belonged to you and I wouldn't have done so this time. I made a promise to myself, as well as one to your mother—well, never mind about that—you wouldn't understand anyway. But you didn't have anything for a stake tonight. Your renunciation of a share in the property is no more than you had already agreed to when your grandmother made you sole heir to both Amalfi and Sorrento. And your claim to the Boisblanc acreage is only lettuce and wind. You've got no more title to it than a field mouse."

CHAPTER FOUR

STILLNESS suddenly closed in upon the room, and in the semi-darkness beyond the sharply edged cone of radiance, this silence became something almost palpable. At his stepfather's final words, Bushrod had glanced swiftly down toward the folded sheet of foolscap that had just been returned to him, conscious that his eyes might betray his thoughts. Now he tapped it lightly against the polished edge of the table.

"What you said doesn't make sense, but you evidently believe it does," he remarked evenly. "I mean about my claim to the Boisblanc acreage being nothing more than lettuce and wind."

"Quite so," Clyde agreed.

"And you gave this back to me"—Bushrod lifted the folded sheet and let it drop again—"of your own accord. I didn't so much as ask you for it."

"No, you didn't."

"Which means that even if you beat me at my own game— and you did, I'm bound to admit—you wouldn't take this quit claim on any such terms," Bushrod went on, almost as though musing aloud. "So you gave it back to me. Is that right?"

"That's about what it amounts to."

"In other words, whatever title I may have to the Boisblanc tract, good, bad, indifferent, worthless or whatever, that title is still mine. Do you agree to that?"

"Yes indeed. You couldn't be more welcome to whatever claim you think you have, not if I handed it to you on a silver platter with *sauce piquante*. Because what you call your 'title' is still nothing but lettuce and wind and I tell you so plainly."

"And I tell *you* plainly it's as good as gold. After all, I know something about land titles—you seem to have forgotten that I'm a lawyer. And titles don't come any sounder than tax titles. I bought that Boisblanc acreage from the state of Louisiana."

"You had every reason to think so. I'll go that far with you. But fortunately or unfortunately—whichever way you choose to look at it—the title the state of Louisiana gave you wasn't worth the match you'd use to set fire to the paper it's written on—at least, if you took a notion to burn it up."

"That's impossible. The state is a sovereign and . . ."

"If you've a mind to listen, I can explain to you. If not, that suits me, too."

"I'll lose nothing by listening, I expect. Besides, I'm interested to know just what sort of yarn you've cooked up in

51

an effort to prove that a title direct from the state itself isn't worth the price of a matchstick."

Bushrod's chair made a scraping sound on the furbished brick flooring as he pushed away from the table and crossed one leg over the other. He still held the folded paper in his hand and he now began tapping it against his knee.

"It's really quite simple," Clyde began. "Just one sorry little mistake, made by a clerk, set everything topsy-turvy. You know how it is with a file of dominoes: maybe you knock only one, but that knocks down the next one and so on until they're all flat. This is something like that."

"Dominoes hasn't ever been my game. And so far, I haven't heard a word to prove that a tax title isn't as sound as a nut."

Bushrod was smiling now, and his smile was condescending rather than mocking. He continued to tap his knee with his folded paper, but there was still nothing in the gesture that suggested impatience.

"I'll have to go back quite a ways in order to explain, so I'm glad that you don't seem to be in a hurry," Clyde remarked equably. "The mix-up began right after your sister got back from Europe, early in '96. I'd been hard hit, in a money way, at the time of her marriage—well, you ought to know something about that. I still wasn't out of the woods a year later, though your mother'd helped me every way she could, and by scrimping and saving we'd got to the place where we could see daylight ahead. In fact, we knew that if we could just get hold of a little more ready cash, to make some improvements . . ."

"Weren't we supposed to be talking about tax titles? I mean about my purchase of the Boisblanc part of Cindy Lou at a tax sale two years ago?"

"Is that when you think you bought it?"

"Think hell! I *did* buy it!"

"All right. We'll come to that presently. About that Boisblanc tract now. Old Valois Dupré had been pestering me for a long while to sell it to him. I never would listen, because I had the idea Cary set great store by that particular tract. But when she came back from Europe she acted and talked as though she weren't even interested in it. So, as your mother and I needed the ready cash to make those improvements, I sent word to Valois Dupré that I was ready to sell him the gravel land."

"Well, I know about that already. I know he bought it from you and I know he let the taxes lapse."

"So he did," Clyde interrupted quietly. "But still they didn't lapse. That's what I'm trying to explain."

"He did . . . they didn't . . . what sort of talk is that? What's it all leading up to?"

The tapping had become a little more insistent and one slender leg was now swinging back and forth over the other. The smile was gone. Bushrod's face, as well as his gestures, reflected increasing annoyance.

"You'll see, if ever you'll hear me out," Clyde answered, still imperturbably. "Dupré bought the land from me in April of '96, and it was agreed that he'd assume that year's taxes—due in '97. Everything was shipshape and the transfer of title to Dupré was recorded at the courthouse. The cash we got out of the sale put Cindy Lou over the hump. We knew then—your mother and I—that, barring the worst kind of luck, we could pull through. And that summer we didn't have to squeeze the pennies quite so hard before we'd let one go."

"I still say all this is beyond the point. The point is that you did sell that Boisblanc tract to a man named Dupré, who let the taxes lapse."

"I'm coming to that now. During the late spring of '96, we were all more or less upset by Cary's illness and the preparation for Armande's wedding and the De Chanets' visit. Then in the midst of this general confusion, Dupré came to tell me about the other gravel bed he had found—the one a lot closer to New Orleans than our Boisblanc piece. He offered to sell my land back to me, then and there. And I had to tell him I was too hard up to buy it."

"Why, you just said you'd reached the point where you didn't need to pinch pennies any longer!"

"I said we'd got to the point where we didn't have to pinch them *quite so hard*—to the point where we thought we could pull through. But we still had to keep on pulling. So I refused Dupré's offer, even though he went as far as to say he'd sell the land back to me for a dollar and lend me the dollar to buy it with! He kept insisting that the extra profit he'd make out of the new gravel bed would more than make up for the cost of mine and that he really *wanted* me to have that."

"And still you refused?"

"I expect you wouldn't understand. But yes, that's just what I did. I had all I could do to keep the rest of Cindy Lou going and lay by enough for taxes on that. Valois understood how I felt, even if you don't. But he said that since I didn't want the property the state could have it, for all he cared. He was going to abandon it. It wasn't a bit of use to him, and he didn't propose to worry with book-keeping on it. He hadn't paid the first year's taxes yet and he wasn't going to pay them—those or any others."

"So we're coming to it at last. He *didn't* pay the taxes, did he?"

"Indeed he didn't. And if one lone clerk in the office of Fernand Lemieux, the old assessor, hadn't made a mistake, your title to that Boisblanc property might have been worth gambling for in dead earnest. But see if you can follow me now: I told you the sale of that Boisblanc land to Valois Dupré was recorded at the courthouse and that the purchaser assumed the '96 taxes."

"Yes and that he didn't pay them. That he never paid them or any other taxes on the property."

"That is correct. But the tax bills were sent to him. The clerk in Lemieux's office saw that a proper entry was made on the books, so that the sheriff sent the notices to Valois Dupré at New Orleans—I assume you know that the sheriff collects taxes in Louisiana—the assessor merely computes them."

"And if those notices were duly sent, what was the mistake?"

"The clerk made the mistake. He neglected to make a second entry to the effect that my tax bill be cut by the amount of Dupré's. So, in April of '97, when they sent Dupré his bill, they also sent me mine at the old figure—the figure based on my ownership of *the entire Cindy Lou Plantation, Boisblanc and all*."

"And you paid it? You didn't high-tail it up to the courthouse at Convent and raise holy hell until somebody corrected the mistake? What sort of a Simple Simon do you take me for? You ought to know I wouldn't swallow a yarn like that!"

Bushrod's voice rang with the contemptuous anger which he was no longer making the slightest effort to control or conceal. He leaped to his feet and leaned across the table, gripping its polished edge and looking down at his stepfather with an expression of sneering hatred. Clyde neither moved nor answered and, just at that moment, Zack entered the gaming-room with an armful of firewood. The Negro plied an iron bar among the embers and laid fresh bolts of wood against the smouldering backlog. Then he glanced at Clyde, as if in silent inquiry. But the latter shook his head without speaking and Zack withdrew. It was not until the sound of his footsteps had died away in the distance that Clyde answered his stepson's outburst.

"I said I would explain to you. Also, that I didn't give a damn whether or not you believed me. Yes, I paid the full amount. That was right after your mother, your sister and Savoie Vincent had died horrible deaths. It wasn't until after your grandmother left Cindy Lou that I so much as looked at my books. Up to then, I was just going through some motions. When I got back to realities and went over my accounts, I saw right away that there must have been some mistake. But as long as the money had been paid, I decided to let matters stand as they were for the time being. I still wasn't in any mood or in any shape to take on extra problems."

"Though only the summer before, you wouldn't put out so much as one lousy dollar to buy back the land!"

Clyde looked up quickly. "I didn't propose to be the object of Valois Dupré's charity, then or at any time," he rapped out. "I'm neither a panhandler nor a blackmailer. When I set out to buy something . . . oh, what the hell! I've already said there are things you wouldn't understand. But maybe you can understand when I say that we did a lot better in '96 than we had ciphered we might. I mean your mother and I. Before the harvest, we couldn't say more than that we saw daylight ahead. But we had a bumper yield of cane that year and got top prices for our sugar, even allowing the Vincents their toll for grinding and granulating. Our tobacco crop did better still. Everything was coming our way at last. By the spring of '97 we not only saw daylight ahead, we were out of the woods. It really looked as if life would be wonderful again . . . until the fire. . . ."

Suddenly, his voice broke. But almost immediately it was under control again.

"That's got nothing to do with you," he continued harshly,

glowering at Bushrod. "But it does concern you that as long as I was paying taxes on all of Cindy Lou, those on the Boisblanc tract were never in arrears."

"That's only your view of it."

"No, it's been generally admitted. When old Fernand Lemieux finally found out about the mistake in his records, he almost had a spasm. He said he would do anything I wanted him to, in order to get everything straightened out. He fired the clerk who was responsible for it. He offered to have the sheriff send Valois Dupré a receipt for all past-due taxes. All in all, he took on so bad that I told him to wait until he got quieted down before we tried to get things fixed up. And the next day he dropped dead of a heart attack."

"So the matter was not straightened out. That's exactly what I've been saying. The land was advertised for sale by the state and I bought it."

"As I told you before, you had reason to think so. But I wouldn't advise you to count on it. You see, the next time I was in New Orleans I called on Valois and explained to him what had happened. I also said I was ready to buy back the Boisblanc tract for what he had paid me in the first place. And he said no, he had made me a price on it, which was one dollar, no more and no less, and he would stick by that price. If I cared to take it for that it would be a deal. He had got mighty rich by that time, dealing in building materials, and his schooners were bringing in shell and sand and gravel from over the lake to his yards on the New Basin Canal. I knew he meant what he said, just as I had, so I finally bought back the Boisblanc tract."

"For a dollar?"

"That's right."

"And would it be too much to ask what became of your high and mighty notions of not taking handouts, or whatever you called them?"

"By the time I bought back the land I had the money to pay for it, and that made all the difference. This was in the early spring of '98, another good crop year; it was no longer a case of having to take the land for a dollar because that was all I had. If you can't see what a difference that'd make, there's no use talking about that end of it."

"Suit yourself. But what you've said still doesn't alter the fact that a year later the high sheriff advertised the land to be sold for delinquent taxes and that I bought it—and own it."

"That's the last domino that fell. Lemieux, the old assessor, was dead. His clerk, the one who made the mistake, was fired. Young Sigur Hymel, who was elected to succeed Lemieux, and his staff didn't know anything about all this. All they knew about was what stood in the office records. And, according to those records, a certain number of properties—the Boisblanc tract among them—were in arrears. So Hymel handed the sheriff a complete list of what should be advertised in the *Regisseur du St. Jacques* to be sold for taxes. Naturally, if any of those properties had been in my name I'd have seen the notice, or someone would have told me about it. But it wasn't. The name of Valois Dupré didn't mean the first thing to any of the folks around here and I didn't look at the list myself, for the simple reason that all my taxes were paid. I wasn't hunting around to grab more land off the people who couldn't keep up their taxes. Apparently, you were."

"You're quite welcome to think anything you like about my motives. That won't alter the fact that I did buy the land."

"My prior purchase of it and the record, showing that no taxes on it were ever delinquent, alters the fact, though."

"Where is the record of that sale? The first one was recorded at the courthouse. What about the second one—if there was a second one?"

"Before Valois got around to recording it, or having his attorney do it for him, the war broke out. Young Dupré was on Colonel Billy Dufour's staff in a regiment of immunes and they were among the first to be sent to Cuba. The boy's father wasn't thinking about getting an unimportant scrap of paper recorded—unimportant to him anyway. And the attorney who would ordinarily have handled such matters for him was his son—the son who was in Cuba. So the matter was neglected. Then, by the time the war was over both he and I had forgotten about recording the transfer, although young Valois had drawn up a regular act of sale, when the deal was consummated, with all the whereases and the business about one dollar and other good and valuable considerations, so the mistaken entry on the assessor's books never did get corrected. What's more, as long as the tax notices were now going to you, it probably never would have been corrected, till either old Valois or I died. But it doesn't really signify."

"Well, something'd better signify, or I'll . . ."

Without haste, Clyde rose. "Or you'll what?" he inquired casually. Then he stood, waiting for a reply, with the thumb and forefinger of each hand hooked into the pockets of his grey moleskin vest. "Go ahead, Bushrod. Finish what you were saying. You'll do what?"

"A man has his rights," Bushrod insisted sullenly. "And don't stand there like an old fool. You never saw the day you could scare me, not even when I was a child. And now . . ."

"Now you're a bold hero and I'm just a decrepit old man?" Clyde chuckled in such genuine amusement that Bushrod looked up in equally genuine surprise. "Certainly I'm no bull of the woods. I never was. But Zack, who is old, too, and his son Nappy, who isn't, and who can take some of the bend out of a horseshoe with his bare hands, are still up. They wouldn't like it if anybody got to worrying their white folks too much. Sounds like storybook stuff, doesn't it? But it's real. So is what I told you about your deed to any part of Cindy Lou not being worth the match you'd strike to set fire to the paper it's written on. As for me, decrepit or not, I propose to keep my health and strength till Larry's old enough to fend for himself . . . no!"— he interrupted himself as Bushrod seemed about to speak— "you abide where you are and let me do the talking for now.

"You renounced all claim, right or interest to Cindy Lou when I told your grandmother Larry wanted and needed no part of the Virginia properties. But you tried to buy your way in through the back door and then cheat your way into more yet. If your title to the Boisblanc tract had been valid, you'd have lost it to me at poker tonight, by trying to run in some nursery tricks that wouldn't have fooled a bunch of school-teachers playing 'Authors.' In other words, you forfeited any right to any share or part of Cindy Lou I don't know how many times over."

"Your sermons don't interest me any more than your real estate dealings," Bushrod said, rising. "If you must talk, talk to the walls. I'm going to bed. As to who has title to the

Boisblanc land, I'll look into the records before I tell you what I'll do in the matter."

"You'll find it would pay you better to listen to me," Clyde went on. Bushrod, who had already started toward the door, half-turned and waited. But his bearing showed plainly that he was merely pausing, momentarily, between one step and the next.

"As I said before, you've forfeited any right or claim to consideration," Clyde continued evenly, "but I've always been willing to pay for what I want. And what I want is that Larry should be left alone by the likes of you. So I'll do this: as long as you stay away from Cindy Lou, I'll pay you an allowance that will keep you from any need to panhandle or engage in any of the other ways you've used in making ends meet. It won't be enough to fit you out with a private apartment at the Gibson House or the Waldorf . . . but perhaps you can sweet-talk or blackguard Mabel into giving you a remittance to stay away from Amalfi, except when she wants you to make an appearance there. With two remittances, you'll be secure against everything but your own folly . . . and before you go, by way of lagniappe, here's something that's about your speed. Matter of fact, you suggested it."

Withdrawing right thumb and forefinger from the pocket of his vest, he tossed a clean, white sugar-tit on to the brightly lit table. Outside in the night-cloaked garden, one of the peacocks again burst into a raucous screech. Furiously, Bushrod flung the sugar-tit into the fire and stormed from the room.

Much later, Clyde was aroused once more from the light slumber of old age by the peacocks' clamorous discord. He realized that some sort of commotion was afoot on the grounds; but his energy had been deeply drained by the events of the day and he did not rise to investigate. Not until he came downstairs the following morning, after noting that Bushrod's room, deserted, had been left in chaotic disorder, did he learn from Zack that all the peacocks had been found dead in the garden, where someone had wrung their jewel-sheathed necks during the night.

It was only after he had superintended their burial, and

the rage which surged through him mingled with the consciousness that another link with the happy past was gone, that he remembered to speak to Zack about the anchor lights. He had had many other things on his mind and, subconsciously, he might have used this as an excuse for the delay: he had not been willing to believe that anything was amiss aboard the *Lucy Batchelor*, which was a still more important link with the past, and Zack had not noticed the change in her. But when they went out to her together, they both realized that there must be a slow leak somewhere, that she was gradually settling. Before expert help could locate the cause of the trouble, she had sunk without a trace.

CHAPTER FIVE

IT DID not surprise Clyde to find Larry playing with his blocks; this was one of the little boys' favourite pastimes. Neither did it surprise the old man to find that Larry had brought the blocks to the office, instead of playing with them in the nursery or in the library, as he had done heretofore. Clyde had always encouraged Larry to stay with him and there was no reason why the child should have thought he would not be fully as welcome to bring his playthings with him as to come himself. To be sure, the box in which the blocks were kept was rather heavy; it was about a foot square and it was made of wood, ornamented with etched Oriental figures framed in bands of dark green. Originally, it had contained tea. Clyde could remember when Lucy bought their tea in large wooden boxes like that, shipped direct from China. They had used a great deal of tea in those days—a long, long time ago. . . .

That was not the point, of course. The point was that Larry, though he was large and strong for his age, could not possibly have carried that big box from the nursery—or even from the library—down the steep stairs to the office. He must have asked Tudie or Nappy to do this for him, and he must have had some special reason for it. Without impatience, but with considerable interest, Clyde waited to find out what this was.

The blocks had belonged to Cary and, as she also had been a very sturdy child, they had suffered considerable hard usage before they came to Larry. In the beginning they had been bright blue and bright red, in equal quantities, and the letters on them had all been bright black. Now the blue and red surfaces were streaked and faded and the bold lettering was faint at best, even where it had not been almost obliterated. The sharp corners of the blocks had either been unevenly chipped off or rubbed to roundness, and many of them were faded or cracked. But Larry had always played with them quite contentedly, ever since he had been old enough to play with blocks at all, and it had never occurred to Clyde before that perhaps he ought to get new ones—stone blocks, for instance, with which Larry could build houses and churches, instead of just making piles and rows. However, it occurred to him now.

"I reckon that maybe we ought to be thinking about getting you some new blocks, one of these days," he remarked. "Eh, Larry?"

Without answering aloud, Larry shook his head. He was very busy putting some of the blocks in two short rows near his grandfather's desk. He turned them this way and that and arranged them with great care. When he finally looked up, Clyde saw that his cheeks were flushed and his eyes shining.

"These are *alphabet* blocks!" he said. "You didn't tell me so, but Aunt Amy did." His tone was not reproving. His adored grandfather could do no wrong in his eyes, and consequently could commit no sins of either commission or omission. Nevertheless, Clyde instantly accused himself of negligence and started to say he was sorry Aunt Amy had got ahead of him, that he should have realized Larry was old enough now to know about alphabets and not to think of blocks merely as playthings. But Larry went on so fast that Clyde had no chance to get very far. "She was surprised because you hadn't taught me my letters," Larry was saying excitely. "So *she* taught them to me! I can say them all! A—B—C—D—E—F . . ." Without a mistake he chanted through the alphabet to the end. "She taught me something else, too," he concluded in triumph. "So that I could surprise *you*. Look at those blocks I fixed!"

Clyde glanced down. His eyesight was not keen any more and besides, his vision seemed to be somewhat blurred at the moment. But as he focused his gaze on the blocks in front of him, he saw that they had been so arranged that the letters in one row would spell LARRY and that those in the other row would spell DADDY. Larry had always called him Daddy and not Grandfather or any abbreviation of this. And now he knew how to spell that and his name. . . .

"Well!" Clyde said, clearing his throat. "Well, you certainly have surprised me, Larry! You've given me a very fine surprise. . . . Do you know how to spell anything else?"

"Yes, lots of things. I'll show you."

Swiftly he demolished the two rows of blocks which were standing and began to arrange others. "M-A-N. B-O-Y. D-O-G. C-A-T. H-E-N. P-I-G. C-O-W." Clyde read in swift succession. Then Larry began to fumble a little. He was trying for HOUSE and HORSE and he became slightly confused. Clyde rose from his chair and knelt down on the floor beside him.

"Maybe I could help——" he suggested a little hesitantly.

"Oh, Daddy, will you? Aunt Amy said she thought you would. She said she'd ask you to get me a primer, too."

"Of course I'll help. Of course I'll get you a primer, too. It's just that I didn't realize . . ."

This time he succeeded in saying what he had started to say before. Then, until suppertime, he and Larry sat on the floor together, arranging and rearranging blocks. And after supper, while he was reading aloud to Larry from Grimm's *Fairy Tales*, he stopped every now and then and asked the little boy to point out words that he knew. It was great fun for them both. The trouble was that Larry became so excited over it all he could not go to sleep. He did not sleep in the nursery any more, with Tudie watching over him. He slept in the youth bed which had been his mother's and which was now drawn up closely beside his grandfather's four-poster. Only this time, he kept sitting up in bed to make one important announcement after another.

"Larry, it's getting late. You won't feel like riding Tophile tomorrow morning, if you don't quiet down now."

"Yes I will, too. I always feel like riding Tophile. You

know that, Daddy. But I've thought of another word. I could show you if I had my blocks here."

"Well, but you left your blocks down in the office. You can show me tomorrow."

"But I can *tell* you now, can't I, Daddy? It's a nice word. It has four letters in it."

"All right, tell me now. But after you've told me, I want you to turn right over and——"

"B-O-A-T."

Clyde did not answer. It did not matter, in the darkness, that his vision was blurred. But something seemed to have happened to his voice, too.

"Don't you think that's a nice word, Daddy? Aren't you pleased?"

"Yes," Clyde said at last. "Yes, I think it's a very nice word. Yes, I'm very much pleased."

Larry finally went to sleep, but Clyde still lay awake beside him, thinking hard. He had not paid much attention when Larry teased Zack, who was handy with a jack-knife, to whittle little boats. He had thought the boy's request accidental—it might have been for animals or wagons or something else, just as logically. Afterward, to be sure, he had noticed that Larry's favourite pastime, next to riding his pony, seemed to consist in steering the little boats about in an old sugar kettle, now used only to hold rain water. But he had not regarded that as significant, either. Perhaps he should have. And of course he should have realized that a child, who could ride and swim as well as Larry could already, was old enough for book learning, too; and yet he had not given it a thought. He was grateful to Amy, of course; but he was chagrined that she should have had to point the way; he was also slightly jealous because it was she who had taught Larry his letters. Probably he himself would not make much of a teacher; but he could at least have done that much and perhaps a little more. He would look, the first thing in the morning, to see if there were not an old primer in the library. Cary must have had a primer. Yes, he remembered now, Lucy had taught her to read out of one called by the astonishing name of *Warner's Holiday Album*; and then there had been *McGuffey's First Reader*, and *Second*

Reader, and *Third Reader*. They were certainly around some-where. But perhaps now there was something newer, something more modern. He must make inquiries. And not only of Amy. She meant well, she had done her best, better than he had done himself. But certainly someone else could do better still. . . .

Larry would need other things besides a primer. A slate. Slate pencils. A blackboard. Chalk. If he could learn to spell he could learn to cipher. Well now, he had said nothing about numbers. Perhaps Amy had not stolen a march on Clyde when it came to numbers. He did not believe she had, either. Most women did not seem to realize that numbers were just as important as letters. And Larry would be quick at figuring, too. Clyde felt sure of it. He and Larry would have a good time together, over sums. Even the multiplication table . . . there must be some way of teaching a child the multiplication table so that it would not mean bewilderment and misery. He would find out. . . .

People talked about the three R's—Readin'—'Ritin'—'Rithmetic. And 'Ritin', not 'Rithmetic, came next after Readin'. Maybe. But he was not going to let any old method stand in the way of his teaching Larry to cipher—straight off, too. Besides, if he remembered correctly, Lucy had taught Cary to print before teaching her to write. Well, he could do that also—he could do both. He would get some of those ruled copybooks that had a page of letters in the front—capital letters and small letters, too, formed with an almost incredible degree of perfection and enclosed in a decorative scrollwork. Then he would practise secretly at copying these before he tried to teach Larry to do so. His penmanship had never been bad—in fact, it had once been a source of considerable pride to him. Lucy had complimented him on it more than once. But he would try to improve it. . . .

Perhaps Larry should be taught to read and write French at the same time he was taught to read and write English. That was the way Savoie had been taught, Clyde knew; if Savoie had lived he would have wanted his son taught in the same way. And Cary had not been much older than Larry when she had begun to study French. Lucy had not taught her that, because Lucy had insisted that the Madames of the Sacred

64

Heart at Convent would do it so much better. But the nuns themselves complimented Lucy on her knowledge of French. Though she did not speak it as fluently as Cary quickly learned to do, she read it with ease and wrote it with grace. Even Mrs. Vincent admitted that. . . .

Perhaps he should write to Mrs. Vincent for suggestions. She was entitled to express an opinion about the education of her only son's only child and to expect that this opinion would be respected. Clyde resolved that he would write to her the next day—well, perhaps not the next day, because he and Larry had planned to ride out on the levee and watch Nappy catch a mess of shad sardines in the yellow flood that writhed seaward below the plantation at high water. But certainly very soon. However, it might be necessary to start on some sort of a programme before he heard from Mrs. Vincent, for he had no assurance that she would reply promptly. With each succeeding season her letters had been farther and farther apart. Poor Lamartine still lingered on, a helpless cripple; and two years after the birth of the heir Pierre Lamartine, whom they called Pierrot, Armande had had another child, a little girl this time, who had been named Janine. Mrs. Vincent's outlook seemed to be bound by solicitude for her invalid husband, her pride in her daughter and her doting fondness for her two French grandchildren. She hardly ever mentioned her son-in-law and occasionally Clyde wondered whether there were any special reason for this; but he avoided giving the matter much thought. Sometimes Mrs. Vincent did refer with a certain arrogance to the reconciliation between the two branches of the De Chanet family, which Armande had effected, and spoke of the visits which Pierre's half-sister, the Princess D'Ambly, and her daughters—Josephine, now the Baronne de Courville, and Isabelle, who had recently married Gilles de Lorne—periodically made at Monteregard. The old marquis had died and Pierre was now at the head of the family; his son Pierrot was still the only male descendant—a fact on which Mrs. Vincent commented, with little apparent regard for the disappointment this must have caused, but rather with great personal satisfaction. However, it appeared that Josephine had a darling little daughter—Louise—who was a little younger than

Pierrot and a little older than Janine, and that the three children had wonderful times together. Obviously, Mrs. Vincent was interested in Louise only because she was such a perfect playmate for the others; and though it pleased her to speak of her important connections with such families as the D'Amblys, the De Courvilles and the De Lornes, Clyde was sure that her enjoyment was based on a sensation of vicarious prestige rather than on any feeling of genuine affection. Nevertheless, the effect of such a milieu had been to alienate her from the one in which she had formerly lived and which she had never regarded as quite worthy of her. Larry, the little American grandson whom she had not seen since he was a baby; Cary, his mother, who had not—in her estimation—been the social equal of her son Savoie; and his grandparents, Lucy and Clyde Batchelor, who by no stretch of the imagination could ever have 'belonged' to the Creole aristocracy, were all part of that milieu. She was only dimly aware of Larry now and she had no desire that the vague image should become more real to her. Clyde would write to her, that was the proper thing to do; however, he thought he could tell beforehand what she would say in her tardy reply: she was sorry to have left his nice letter so long unanswered, but poor Lamartine required more and more attention; and the children had had the mumps—light cases, fortunately, but one could never be too careful of adverse symptoms which might develop suddenly. Since their recovery the chateau had been full of company. Dorothée, as usual, had been in Paris, so it had been necessary that she herself help Armande oversee the household and entertain all these people who were coming and going. (Here would follow a formidable list of names culled from the *Almanach de Gotha*.) She was happy to say that Josephine's husband Jehan had been able to accompany her on her latest visit, though Gilles had been prevented from bringing Isabelle because of pressing duties on his own estate, which was one of the finest in France. Louise was not nearly as pretty as Janine, but she was a very cheerful child, and Janine, who was rather grave, needed exactly that sort of companionship. Oh yes—about Larry! Well, of course Savoie had always had a tutor. Probably that would be the best solution for Larry, too—at least, if Clyde could find a suitable young man of exemplary habits who was also an accomplished classical scholar. But Mrs. Vincent had an idea that tutors, like servants, were not what they used to be. . . .

Lying thoughtfully awake in the darkness, Clyde dismissed the idea of a tutor then and there. When the time came, he would write to Mrs. Vincent and tell her that her surmise had been correct, that, unfortunately, he had not been able to find a suitable young man of exemplary habits, who was also an accomplished classical scholar; it would not hurt his conscience to omit mention of the fact that he had not searched for any such paragon. However, the next evening, after he and Larry had returned from their swim in the old barrow pit on the *batture*, and Larry had tumbled contentedly into bed—not excited and wakeful this time, but drowsy from fresh air and exercise—Clyde rode up the river road to confer quietly with Mrs. Surget.

She had been hoping he would come, she told him; she had not liked to hurry him, to seem in any way to interfere, but it was really high time . . . Well, what specifically would she recommend? . . . Would he consider Jefferson College? she wanted to know. Generally boys were not received there until the age of ten or twelve, but occasionally exceptions were made for special cases. It was out of the question, Clyde answered, with more heat than he intended. He could not take Larry back and forth from Convent every day, or spare one of the hands to do so. That would mean four trips; besides, it was a long ride, too long for a little boy. As far as that went, Mrs. Surget replied quietly, Larry would not go back and forth every day; he would have to be a boarding pupil from the start. . . . All right, he might have known in advance what his answer would be to that, Clyde responded, still more heatedly; he had not the slightest idea of permitting Larry to be separated from him. He would teach the child himself, as well as he could. Of course French would have to wait. . . .

Mrs. Surget forbore to say she had known that was what he wanted to do, all along, that his call had been simply a gesture of courtesy. Nevertheless, she smiled to herself when he had gone. Now that he had been driven to it, Clyde would probably make a very good teacher. However, she had done the driving—quietly, secretly even, but none the less skilfully. That was the way women often had to work. Results proved that it was not a bad way.

The lessons were a success from the beginning. Clyde emptied a ground floor chamber of its furniture and fitted it up as a schoolroom. It was one of the bedrooms which had formerly been in frequent use by his business associates, and had always been kept in readiness for their reception. Now that he no longer had such visitors or, indeed, visitors of any kind, except at very rare intervals, it had outlasted its original purpose and it should have another. The lessons provided this. Larry was delighted with his primer, his slate, his copybook, his well-filled pencil box, his varicoloured chalk; he was even more pleased with the little desk, placed beside his grandfather's large one. Its opening was on the top, and there was room inside for all his new treasures, except the blackboard; moreover, there was a row of little drawers down one side, in which future treasures could be stored. This desk had been bought on purpose for him; it had not belonged to someone else first, like all the rest of the furniture in the house. It was his very own.

They did not have lessons at regular hours, but fitted them, more or less haphazardly, into the periods which the management of the plantations left free. Larry nearly always accompanied his grandfather in riding the crops and Clyde marvelled at the boy's natural aptitude for the saddle. Apparently, it never occurred to him to remain on the headlands and trot sedately over bridges; if something along one of the drainage banks caught his eye, he kneed Tophile, his small plantation pony, out into the field and sent him briskly over the ditches in beautifully timed jumps. He had outgrown the fat little Shetland on which he had learned to ride, and Clyde had purchased Tophile for him in Tennessee. From the beginning, there had been an extraordinary degree of understanding and attraction between horse and rider. Almost instinctively, Tophile seemed to divine what Larry required of him; and he fulfilled these requirements with the same zest that Larry himself showed in revealing them. No day was long enough to provide all the hours which the boy wanted to spend in riding, and it did not occur to him that lessons should interfere with a pursuit which was already habitual, nor did Clyde see any reason why he should make an issue of the matter.

But though the lessons were so irregular, there were just as many of them—if not more—than there would have been if Larry had been going to school. Saturday was not automatically a holiday merely because it was a Saturday; in fact, if there were rain, Clyde and Larry sometimes spent the entire day in the schoolroom and more than made up for their absence on a Friday, which might have been such a pretty day that they had taken a picnic basket and gone in a buggy with Nappy to the ditches back of the Boisblanc area for a big mess of scarlet swamp crayfish—'mud bugs,' Nappy called them. On such occasions, Larry was fascinated by the great square nets, and watched with gleeful interest as Nappy tied a piece of raw meat in the centre of each and then set them all upright in the shallow water, stirring the mud beneath until it spread upwards in great dark clouds. The bait was allowed to rest until these mud clouds settled. Then Nappy took a long myrtle pole and snatched out the nets, one by one. A dozen or more startled crayfish were often still gorging themselves on the bait which had lured them to their undoing, and Nappy tilted them from the net into a bucket, which Larry proudly held out toward him, and from the bucket the mud bugs were transferred to an oat sack, which was well filled by mid-afternoon.

There were all sorts of excursions like this; and sometimes Clyde and Larry went to the old gravel bed, where the buried treasure still lay undisturbed—if, as the Negroes continued to insist, it were really there—and Clyde watched Larry dig for it, just as he had watched Cary dig, more than a quarter of a century earlier. Larry did not tire as easily as Cary had or become so restless; he did not throw down his shovel and come to fling himself in Clyde's arms, demanding distraction. In fact, very often Clyde had to insist that Larry must stop digging, because it was getting dark and it was high time they went home. Larry always put down his shovel with reluctance; if he could only get just a little farther down, he insisted, he might find the treasure; nothing ever shook his belief in its existence.

Despite all such interruptions, however, the 'book learning' progressed faster than Clyde had expected. In summer when it was very hot outdoors at midday, the schoolroom was always cool and that was a fine time for lessons; and in winter, when first evening came so early and it was cold in the fields and on the river road, it was warm and cosy in the school-room. So the lamps and the fires were lighted and Clyde and Larry stayed at their desks until Larry began to rub his eyes, or said, "Gee, Daddy, I'm hungry." Then they went upstairs together to their waiting supper and, very often, Clyde went to bed immediately afterward, just as Larry did. But because they both went to bed so early, they were both ready to get up early, too; and since it was still dark and cold outdoors, it seemed natural to go back to the schoolroom and stay there, with the lamps and the fires burning, until the kindly sun had brought light and warmth to the day.

So, all in all, Larry galloped through the primer at top speed and plunged almost as fast from the *First* to the *Second Reader*; and meanwhile he had learned to print every word he could read and to write a good many of them. He could also count and add and take away; and Clyde realized that in little or no time the experiments in making the multiplication table pleasant could begin. Every now and then, Mrs. Surget was invited to visit the schoolroom and remain through lessons, and she always complimented Clyde on his prowess as a teacher and Larry on his progress as a pupil and went away smiling to herself.

Eventually, they had another visitor in the schoolroom. This was Father Le Grand, the pastor of St. Michael's Church in Convent. Larry recognized him because the priest had come and spoken to them, several times, when they went to the cemetery to put flowers on the tomb where Larry's father and mother were buried. He did not understand about that very well yet. He had seen dead animals, and knew they had to be put in the ground after they had died; but he had never seen a dead person, and his grandfather had not explained to him yet what happened to persons who died, or why they were buried differently from animals; and, for some reason, he had felt shy about asking, though he asked Daddy almost everything else that came into his head. He associated the priest with the cemetery, and the thought crossed his mind that perhaps Father Le Grand was the person to ask about death, though he was not an old friend, like Aunt Amy, and Larry did not think he had been invited to the schoolroom, the way she so frequently was. However, his grandfather received Father Le Grand respectfully and invited him to be seated.

"We're almost through for the day, Father," he said. "If you don't mind, Larry and I'll finish this lesson before we go upstairs. Then I hope you'll accept some refreshment."

"Thank you," Father Le Grand answered pleasantly. "I'd enjoy that very much—hearing the end of the lesson and taking a little refreshment afterward, too."

"Go on reading, Larry," his grandfather directed.

Larry was delighted to finish the story. He had been a little afraid, when the visitor arrived, that his grandfather would say, well, that would be all, until tomorrow. It was a very interesting story about a horse named Black Beauty. He read it aloud carefully, but with eager interest, and when he had finished he looked from his grandfather to the visitor, not because he wanted them to praise the way he had read it, but because he hoped to discover that they had shared his enjoyment. He was not disappointed.

"That was a very fine story," Father Le Grand said enthusiastically. "I never happened to hear it before, either. You've given me a real treat, Larry. I'll have to see if I can't find a story you haven't heard before and read it to you some day— or send you a book that it's in, so that you and your grandfather can read it together. Do you know the story about David and Goliath?"

"No, sir," Larry answered.

"Or the story about Daniel and the lions' den?"

"No, sir," Larry said again.

"Well, I have a book with both those stories in it. I'll bring it to you the next time I come this far down the river road."

"Thank you very much, sir," Larry said promptly. He was quite sure he had spoken politely, yet evidently something was wrong, for his grandfather started to say something and then stopped, because the priest shook his head. However, appar-

71

ently nothing was *very* wrong since both men were smiling. Larry put away all his treasures and closed the lid of his desk and slid out of his chair. Then he waited expectantly. The word 'refreshment' was not one he had heard often, but he knew in a general way what it meant and he had reason to hope that cookies might be involved.

"I mentioned going upstairs, *Father*," his grandfather was saying. He stressed the last word and then Larry understood: you did not call a priest 'Sir,' you called him 'Father.' He was very grateful because he had been permitted to learn that in such a pleasant way, instead of being reproved for making a mistake, which would have embarrassed him very much. But then, his grandfather hardly ever reproved him; that was one of the many wonderful things about Daddy. "However," Clyde Batchelor went on, "perhaps instead you'd just come into the gaming-room. That's where Larry and I usually have refreshments, at least between meals. We have so few visitors nowadays that I'm afraid the drawing-room's closed. But of course if you'd prefer——"

"Thank you, Mr. Batchelor. I'd consider it a compliment if you'd let me come to the gaming-room."

Larry's grandfather opened the door and the priest stepped into the passageway that connected the schoolroom with the gaming-room. He had never seen the ground floor of Cindy Lou before, he said; he had heard about the series of arches which gave it such distinction, besides acting as supports for the superstructure; but he had not realized that this series was so extensive or so impressive. He was using big words, but Larry knew what most of them meant; he knew that this visitor appreciated Cindy Lou, and that made him very happy. Zack, or one of the other servants, must have guessed that he and his grandfather would be going to the gaming-room, even if they did have a visitor, for a glass of milk and a plate of cookies were already standing on the centre table, besides the silver coffee service and a silver basket heaped with fruit-cake. But his grandfather paid no mind to the coffee; he opened the door of the cellaret and asked the priest what he would like.

"If you still have some of Carteret Paine's bourbon——" Father Le Grand suggested.

"I have, indeed. And you couldn't make a better choice."

The bourbon made a rich gurgling sound as it was poured out. The two men lifted their glasses and sat down in easy chairs on either side of the fireplace. Larry stood beside the gaming-table, eating his cookies and drinking his milk. He understood that it would be all right for him to do so now, though nothing had been said to that effect. In fact, nothing had been said to him on any subject. His grandfather and the visitor were talking to each other and for the moment they were not including him in the conversation.

"You said you'd never been on the ground floor of Cindy Lou before, Father. It's a long time since you've been anywhere in the house."

"Yes. Not since——"

"Not since Cary died. You were kind enough to come and see her during her last illness, even though she wasn't a member of your church."

"I wanted to come. I was fond of Cary and I thought of her as at least partly belonging to us. After all, I married her to Savoie Vincent, I baptized their son." He glanced toward Larry, smiling again, and Larry found he wanted to smile back. "But later . . . I didn't like to intrude."

"It wouldn't have been an intrusion. It would have been a very kindly act, like the other. But of course I should have realized that I ought to invite you. I'm afraid I've been very negligent about a great many things."

"Not negligent. Forgetful, perhaps. But I understood."

There was a short silence. The priest lifted his glass and took a slow sip. Larry reached for another cookie.

"Nevertheless, I decided that the time had come to jog your memory a little."

"Yes?"

"Yes. You see, having baptized Larry, I know how old he is. And as his godparents apparently haven't done it, I thought perhaps you wouldn't take it amiss if I suggested that he ought to be coming to church now and learning his catechism pretty soon. . . ."

There was another silence, a longer one this time. Neither man took a drink in the course of it, so Larry did not think he ought to reach for a cookie again, either. At last his grandfather spoke.

"You're right, of course, Father. His godparents—well, I'm not sure, but I think they both live in New Orleans. They were school friends of Cary and Savoie, I remember that much. But they haven't kept in touch with us since . . . I'm afraid they've been even more forgetful than I have."

"I can give you their names, of course. They signed the registry at the time of the baptism."

"Yes . . . well, I suppose I ought to write to them to remind them. But I'll bring Larry to St. Michael's myself next Sunday, Father. Next Sunday and every Sunday from now on, unless there's some good reason why I can't."

"I was sure you would, Mr. Batchelor, when I reminded you."

"About the catechism, though. I'm afraid there are some other things Larry ought to learn first. I'm afraid he'd be very much puzzled."

"You won't let him be puzzled. We'll see that he learns the other things first, if he doesn't know them already. But perhaps he does. . . . Come here, Larry."

Larry went around the table and stood between the priest and his grandfather. The priest put his arm around Larry's shoulders and spoke to him very kindly.

"You have a Christmas tree every year, don't you, Larry?"

"Yes, si—yes, Father."

"And you hang up your stocking and get lots of presents?"

"Yes, Father."

"You know there's some special reason why you have all those nice things at Christmas, don't you?"

"Yes, Tudie told me. Tudie took care of me until I was big enough to take care of myself. She told me lots of things."

"Such as——"

"She told me Christmas was a sort of birthday party."

"I see. Well, Tudie was right. Did she tell you whose birth-day it was?"

"Yes. She said a boy named Jesus was born at Christmas. A long time ago. She said his own people were very poor and he was born in a stable, with lots of animals around—cows and sheep and donkeys. But his mother was very pleased with the baby and lots of other people, besides her, were pleased. Some shepherds. They were poor, too. And some kings. They weren't

74

poor, they were very rich. They brought the baby nice presents. And there were some other people—that is, sort of people, called angels. And there was a star."

"I see that Tudie has done her very best to teach you about Christmas. I'll give you a story about it, too, in the same book with the story about David. . . . Now, tell me something else, Larry. Did Tudie teach you to say your prayers?"

"Yes, Father."

Larry thought he heard his grandfather say something very quickly, as if he were surprised, the way he had been about the alphabet. But when Larry turned at the sound, his grandfather was not saying anything at all, and his face had a strange blank look, without any smile on it.

"What did she teach you to say?" Father Le Grand went on.

"Well, first she taught me to say,

'Now I lay me down to sleep,
I pray the Lord my soul to keep. . . .'

"And did you understand what that meant?"

"No. But I said it every night because Tudie asked me to. Tudie's always been awfully good to me so I was glad to do something to please her. Then, last year, before I moved into Daddy's room to sleep, she taught me two more prayers. One begins, 'Our Father,' and the other begins, 'Hail, Mary.' Do you want me to say them to you?"

"No, not just now, Larry. But you do say them, don't you— every night before you go to sleep and every morning when you wake up?"

"Yes, Father."

Again Larry thought he heard a strange sound, but again, when he turned, his grandfather was silent and motionless.

"Do you kneel down when you say them?"

"No. I used to, when I slept in the nursery, because Tudie knelt down with me. But when I moved into Daddy's room he didn't say anything about kneeling down. So I just say them in bed."

"Well, it's all right to say them in bed. The place doesn't matter so much. The thing that matters most is just to pray. Sometimes it's easier to do it kneeling down, that's all. Sometimes if we wait until we get in bed, we're so sleepy that we don't pray very well."

"I thought of that. But still——"

Larry looked inquiringly from the priest to his grandfather. Suddenly he felt very tired, not a nice kind of tired, as if he had been outdoors all day, but a different kind of tired, as if he were going to cry. He hadn't cried in a long while, not since he could remember, and he hoped very much he wasn't going to now. He thought perhaps if they could talk about something besides prayers, he wouldn't. Or maybe they wouldn't have to talk about anything else—anything, at least, that he didn't understand very well. Maybe Father Le Grand would go away now and leave him and Daddy alone. . . .

Evidently, Father Le Grand realized that this would be a good idea, for he rose, still with his arm around Larry's shoulders, and said he'd enjoyed his visit very much and, now that he had found his way back to Cindy Lou, he was promising himself the pleasure of coming there fairly often. Meanwhile, he looked forward to seeing Mr. Batchelor and Larry at St. Michael's—and he wouldn't forget about the storybook.

After he had gone, Daddy did not say anything for such a long while that Larry thought perhaps he had gone to sleep. He tried to keep very still so that if Daddy was tired, too, he would not be disturbed. But at last he stirred in his chair, and Larry went over to it quickly and climbed up in his grandfather's lap. He knew he was welcome to do so, though when Daddy was funning he said that Larry was such a big boy now it was hard to hold him.

"I'm afraid there are a great many things I should have taught you that I haven't," his grandfather said in a sad voice. "I realize more and more all the time——"

"Why, Daddy, you've taught me lots of things! Everything I know, except the alphabet and the prayers."

"Yes, but I ought to have taught you those, too. I shouldn't have waited until after an old lady and an ignorant coloured girl——"

"I think Aunt Amy and Tudie were pleased to be able to teach me *something* when you'd taught me everything else, don't you?"

"I suppose they were. But I'm not pleased."

76

"I don't see why not. I should think you'd be very pleased. We're having all those nice lessons together just because I learned the alphabet. And now that you know about the prayers we could say those together, too, couldn't we? Every night before we go to bed. Out loud. Kneeling down. Then we'd be sure we wouldn't be too sleepy."

Lucy had always knelt to pray and she had taught Cary to do the same. But even she had not suggested that Clyde should kneel with her or her child. She had never discussed prayer with him at all. She had known that he was without religious faith, and she had not wanted to do or say anything that would seem to put the slightest unwelcome pressure upon him—about that or anything else. But Larry did not know that his grandfather was without religious faith; Larry was unconscious of any unwelcome pressure. He only knew that he and his grandfather did things together.

That night, for the first time since he had run away from the orphanage, when he was only a little older than Larry, Clyde Batchelor knelt beside his bed and repeated the Lord's Prayer. Larry repeated it with him. Afterward, still speaking in unison, though Clyde missed a word now and then, they said the Hail, Mary.

CHAPTER SIX

WHEN LARRY was twelve years old he made his First Holy Communion at St. Michael's. The next autumn he entered Jefferson College as a boarder.

Their first parting was a terrible wrench for both him and Clyde. But though it had taken him time to do it, his grandfather learned to face the fact that Larry needed better and other teachers and also companions of his own age. He had been very shy, at first, in the catechism class, but gradually he had made a few friends. Those friendships should now be ripe for development.

The school year was a long one, beginning in September and ending in June, with no vacation at Easter and only a short one at Christmas. On the first Sunday of every month Larry was allowed to go home, and on the other Sundays and on Thursdays Clyde was allowed to see him at the college. These brief visits were tantalizing rather than satisfying. They both counted the days from September to Christmas and from Christmas to June; then they made the most of every moment they could spend together. It did not occur to either of them, for a long while, that Larry might wish to visit some of his schoolmates, or invite them to Cindy Lou. They were so happy in each other's company, after their long parting, that neither was conscious of any need for other society. In time, however, after Larry had declined several invitations quite automatically, he mentioned one of them casually to his grandfather. Clyde answered quickly.

"If you'd like to go home with Blaise Bergeron, Larry, I hope you will. I hope you don't feel you have to come to Cindy Lou."

"I don't feel I have to come to Cindy Lou. I want to come to Cindy Lou."

"Well, of course I'm glad, in a way. But you haven't seen many other places yet. Perhaps you ought to."

"I don't believe any of them are as nice as Cindy Lou."

"You can't tell until you go and see them."

Larry made no reply. Taken by and large, he had always been an exceedingly tractable boy; still, deep within him, there was a stubborn streak.

"If you don't want to go home with Blaise, why not ask him to come home with you?" Clyde persisted.

"Because I don't want Blaise or anyone else around, except you, when I come home. I see all I want to of Blaise and the other boys at school."

If he had not been good at games, this insistent periodic withdrawal from his schoolmates might well have resulted in lack of harmony with them. But he was a born athlete, and his mode of life at Cindy Lou had tended to develop his natural talents. He made both the basketball team and the baseball team in the first try-outs, and his fancy dives were a source of secret envy and constant emulation at the swimming pool. He was always close to the head of his class, when he did not actually lead it, and this might have been another menace to widespread popularity; so might his flat refusal to join the debating society, though this refusal was not due to any lack of interest in controversial matters. When topics were subject to argument, he preferred to think them over by himself, or to discuss them quietly with his grandfather. Indeed, he could appear to be completely lost in a book, unaware of the tumult raging around him, and would look up with an expression as blank as Clyde's could be at will when angry questions were hurled at him by his classmates. At home, after a talk with his grandfather, he would sometimes sit silent for hours, mulling over everything that had been said, or saddle his horse and ride off alone toward the solitary swampland, or take his pirogue and paddle away through the drainage canals and the sluggish bayous.

In like measure, he declined, courteously but with unmistakable finality, to join either of the sodalities at the college. He had a great reverence for religion, but his shyness still persisted when it came to his devotions. He was not self-conscious when the college attended chapel in a body; but it was hard for him to approach the Communion rail unless so many others were doing it at the same time that he would not be noticed in the crowd. The prayers which meant the most to him were those which he and Clyde said by themselves in the chamber which they still shared when he was at home.

It was not until Larry was halfway through his third year at Jefferson College that his grandfather Vincent finally died, and his grandmother and his aunt Armande returned to Victoria, bringing the body with them for burial in the family vault at Convent. Probably they would not even have done this if the unhappy man had not extracted from them a promise that he should not lie in foreign soil. It was Clyde's impression that Lamartine had never become as fully expatriated as his wife and daughter, that his years of helplessness had been all the more bitter for him because they had been passed amidst the alien corn, and that his unimpaired mind had been active until the end; and this impression was quickly confirmed by the demeanour of his widow and daughter. Clyde met them at the station when they arrived, accompanied by a French maid and wearing the longest and heaviest veils that he had ever seen, even in a community addicted to *crêpe*. He escorted them to Victoria and assisted in the arrangements for the interment which, in accordance with their wishes, was the most elaborate that had ever taken place in Convent. But nothing which could be called a real conversation took place on these occasions; and for a few days after the obsequies the two ladies remained secluded, allegedly in a state of complete prostration. Clyde called, first alone and then with Larry, who had been given special permission to leave college for the purpose, only to be turned away by Titine the caretaker with the announcement that they had not once left their darkened chambers and that they were 'takin' on somethin' terrible.' However, within a week, Bassie, Titine's new husband, delivered a note at Cindy Lou, so deeply bordered in black that there was hardly room for the superscription. Inside, the brief message, written in French, was couched with great formality: if M. Batchelor would make allowances for the outbursts of grief which they might not be able to control, and which they were sure he would understand in view of their recent great bereavement and the conflicting emotions awakened by the sight of their old home, Mme Vincent and Mme la Marquise de Chanet would be glad to receive him at five the following afternoon.

Clyde's mouth twitched slightly as he read this communication, and when he had dressed in the black suit which he almost never wore nowadays, but which had been taken out of mothballs for the funeral rites, he winked at himself once in the mirror before starting downstairs. Sugar and Spice had been appropriately covered with tasselled black netting before they were harnessed in the cabriolet; and Nappy, proudly wearing a long-disused black livery, was in the driver's seat, holding a whip which had been adorned with a large black ribbon bow of watered silk. In fact, everything had been prepared in the most approved fashion for a *visite de condoléance*. When Clyde was ushered into the drawing-room at Victoria, he found, as he had expected, that the shutters were closed and the furniture shrouded with coverings. It seemed rather a pity, when he had taken pains for years to see that the house should be kept properly aired, that it should now be stifling. However, he recognized the pattern.

Mrs. Vincent and Armande came into the room together. Their elegant *crêpe* dresses were cut after a fashion which had not yet reached the river road, with underskirts so narrow at the bottom as to make walking awkward and difficult, and overskirts so voluminously folded as to give the false effect of enormous hips. They both wore onyx jewellery and carried black-bordered handkerchiefs. Clyde, who had not seated himself while awaiting their arrival, went forward with becoming gravity and Mrs. Vincent extended her hand at a level which indicated she expected him to kiss it, not shake it; Armande followed suit. Clyde had never overcome his aversion to hand kissing as a social gesture, but he decided that on such an occasion as this he would do well to respond in the manner expected. However, when Mrs. Vincent began to speak to him in French, he shook his head and answered courteously but firmly:

"I'm very sorry, madame. Of course you've forgotten, but I never knew how to speak French and I can't follow more than a few words of it. I'll have to ask you to talk to me in English."

"It's so many years——" Mrs. Vincent said, with a deep sigh. She glanced around the shrouded room, touched her eyes with her black-bordered handkerchief and seated herself on a small sofa, signifying that she wished Armande to sit beside her and that Clyde should take an armchair near by.

"Yes, it is a great many years. I am very sorry it has been so long. And of course sorrier still for the reason. I shall always think of Lamartine as one of my best friends."

"One of the best friends, one of the best husbands, one of the best fathers——"

Mrs. Vincent glanced for confirmation toward her daughter who, as yet, had not spoken at all. Clyde gathered that Armande's natural taciturnity had increased with time. At all events, she disregarded the implied suggestion that she should join in the conversation, and Clyde concluded that he had better pursue it without her assistance.

"You know I want to do whatever I can to help you," he said. "I hope you've found everything in good order here and that the servants are making you comfortable. As I've written you, some of the older ones have died since you went away, and I have not thought it was necessary to replace them, because Titine married and there was so little work to be done. I don't need to tell you that until your arrival she and Bassie have been merely caretakers. But if you require more service, I can send either Delphie or Ivy over from Cindy Lou. Belle has died, too, and of course, in my opinion, there will never be another cook like her. But she taught Ivy all she could, and Lucy found Delphie fairly satisfactory as a maid. She does not do quite so well without feminine super-vision, but you could supply that—which I can't."

"I really do not have the heart to attempt it. I find that these younger Negroes make very poor substitutes for their fathers and mothers, and the Grim Reaper has taken those faithful souls, just as he has taken their masters." Mrs. Vincent paused, with such a deep catch in her breath that the sigh seemed likely to become a sob. But she recovered herself and went on, "Titine and Bassie leave much to be desired, of course. But as you know, we have our own excellent French maid Leonie with us, and since our stay will be so short——"

"Will it? I had hoped, now that you are here——"

Mrs. Vincent raised a slim white hand in protest. "You must remember that Armande has children. It did not seem best to interrupt their studies, or to subject them, while they are still so young, to the ordeal of such a melancholy journey. Of course their grandparents give them the greatest care, and the *princesse* and the *baronne* both assured us that they would make frequent visits to Monteregard during our absence. Even so, a mother's heart——"

"I understand. But since Pierrot and Janine are so well cared for, surely you don't need to worry about them. And you haven't seen anything of Larry yet. I think you'll be very pleased with him, very—very proud of him. He's a fine boy."

"Oh, yes, Larry." Mrs. Vincent glanced at Armande again and again Armande disregarded the signal. "I must see him, of course, before I leave. I know you brought him here, the other day, but it was really too soon. Perhaps some day next week——"

"It would have to be a Thursday or a Sunday, and then as a special concession, because of the circumstances. The college is pretty strict about giving leave of absence, and of course Larry's had some already, for the funeral and the first call. But if you'll tell me which day would be agreeable, I'll ask the president. I'll tell him you feel you can't stay until the holidays. That is, if you're sure."

"Oh, perfectly sure!" For the first time Mrs. Vincent spoke with animation. "So shall we say next Sunday? I'm sure the president of the college will not make any difficulties, when you tell him how important it is that I should return promptly to France. And certainly I should see Larry before I go— once, anyway. Meanwhile, speaking of Larry——"

She paused again, but this time, though she did draw a deep breath, it was also a quick one. She neither sighed nor sobbed, but went on quite briskly.

"Since my time is so limited, I think we should not waste it. I think I should talk to you at once about my husband's will. It was his wish that Larry should inherit as much as would have normally gone to poor Savoie, if Savoie had survived him. That is, a fourth of all his property. I am sure you will agree this is a very generous apportionment."

"Yes, madame, I surely do."

"As to the other three-fourths"—for the third time, Mrs. Vincent glanced at Armande, who stirred slightly, but who still made no other response—"Armande and I are agreed that we would like to keep our house in New Orleans," Mrs. Vincent went on. "I do not foresee any likelihood of wishing to return there. But of course there is always a possibility, and it does not involve much expense for our caretakers, Patsy and Amos, and taxes and occasional repairs. I should be grateful if you would continue to look after such details for us in the future, as you have in the past. And it has occurred to us that you might be willing, as Larry's guardian, to waive his rights in a share of that property, if he were given, by way of exchange, a larger share in Victoria. If I am not mistaken, this would be comparable to the arrangement that was made in regard to his inheritance of Cindy Lou."

"I'd be very glad indeed to do both, madame—glad to continue my supervision of the New Orleans property and glad to exchange Larry's rights in it for a larger share in Victoria," Clyde answered, without making any comment on the latter part of her speech or even feeling any curiosity as to how she had learned of the arrangement between himself and Miss Sophie.

"I am delighted to hear it. And since that point has been settled so easily and so quickly, we can go straight on to the only other which seems to me to require adjustment. I do not care to retain possession of Victoria and neither does Armande. Would you like to buy our rights in it for Larry?"

So it had come at last, the opportunity for which he had worked and waited so long. There was no room for doubt in Clyde's mind: Mrs. Vincent had guessed how greatly he coveted this plantation for Larry and she drove a hard bargain; in order to close with her, he was forced to offer far more than the plantation was worth in dollars and cents. She laid aside all pretence of grief as she haggled and revealed herself simply as an avaricious old woman, intent on wringing all she could from him. But it was worth the sum on which they finally agreed, in other ways than money; and he had the dollars and cents ready and waiting for her demand. When she went back to France with her silent daughter, two weeks later, Larry was the undisputed owner of Victoria.

Meanwhile, accompanied by Clyde, he had paid his grandmother the one stiff Sunday visit which she stipulated. The shutters had been opened by this time and the furniture uncovered; but she and her daughter entered the drawing-room in much the same manner that they had before, and made no effort to put the boy at his ease. Clyde had warned him in advance that Mrs. Vincent and Armande would expect him to kiss their hands, and was proud of the lack of embarrassment with which Larry performed the unaccustomed rite. Clyde had also told him that his grandmother had become very French and very formal, and that his aunt, who had never been talkative, was now noticeably silent; perhaps it would be well for him to begin by addressing Mrs. Vincent as madame, and wait to see whether she herself would suggest grand'mère. Though she did indeed make the suggestion, she did this belatedly, as if it were an afterthought. She designated a small bench opposite her sofa, as Larry's seat, and asked him a succession of questions, without drawing either her daughter or her second visitor into the conversation at all.

"So you are my other grandson, Larry. I think you are

taller than my French grandson Pierrot. Of course, you are about six months older. But you seem to me very large for your age. Have you been told that before?"

"Yes, madame."

"And you look more like your mother than your father, even if you do have his straight black hair instead of her golden curls. I suppose you've been told that, too."

"Yes, madame."

"It is very sad that you should have lost both your father and mother when you were a baby, that you can't even remember them."

"Yes, but then I've always had Daddy."

He turned to glance at Clyde, his eyes lighting with unabashed affection. In fact, nothing about the call seemed to be causing him any embarrassment. He sat erect but easily on the stiff little bench, his feet crossed, his hands clasped in his lap and, except for that one glance at Clyde, he kept looking straight at his grandmother. He did not fidget and he did not stare around the room. Clyde, who was aware of the inherent shyness which Larry had never wholly overcome, had dreaded this interview for the boy. Now his relief was mingled with pride. If he were not mistaken, Larry was sizing up Mrs. Vincent quite as shrewdly and swiftly as she was appraising him, and it was evident that he was not overawed by her and that he saw no reason why he should be.

"Daddy?" Mrs. Vincent inquired, as if she were puzzled by the designation or thought it unbecoming. "Oh—you mean your grandfather! I didn't grasp, immediately, to whom you were referring. But I suppose, under all the circumstances . . ." She shrugged her shoulders slightly, and it was then she bethought herself that Larry should not be addressing her as madame. "Of course you and your grandfather must decide between you what you are to call him," she said, condescendingly. "But I am going to ask you not to call me madame. That is most inappropriate. After all, I am your grandmother."

"What would you like to have me call you? *Grand'mère*?"

"Yes, that would be entirely proper. Do you know some French?"

"Yes, *Grand'mère*."

"Enough to carry on a conversation with me?"

"I think so."

"Well, let us see. *Vous étudiez quoi, à present?*"

From there on, Clyde was able to follow only in a general way. He realized that Mrs. Vincent was asking Larry about his studies and his schoolmates and what he did in the way of recreation, and that Larry was answering adequately, though not expansively. Then he saw the boy's face flush with sudden colour and, for the first time, heard a hesitant answer. Something had obviously gone amiss after all; he would try to find out, later, what it was. Fortunately, just then Titine came in with coffee and little cakes, and Mrs. Vincent suggested that Larry might like to pass them. As he handed Armande her cup, he smiled and spoke on his own initiative.

"I'm sorry Pierrot and Janine didn't come with you, Aunt Armande. I'd like very much to meet them."

Evidently Armande found something persuasive in his manner, for she broke her long silence. There was not much warmth in her voice, but she spoke agreeably.

"Thank you, Larry. It didn't seem best to bring them to Louisiana. But perhaps you'll come to see us some day, at Monteregard."

"Well, I don't know whether that would be best, either. Daddy doesn't care much about travelling any more. We don't even go to New Orleans, except once in a great while."

"You could go to Monteregard without me, you know, Larry," Clyde said quickly. "I'm too old to travel myself now. But I'd like to have you accept your aunt's invitation. I'd be glad to have you see something of your cousins. And you'd enjoy the trip."

"Not unless you went, too."

He was still completely courteous, but his words were conclusive. Clyde recognized the stubborn streak which, like the streak of shyness, was still there. He knew it would do no good to insist but, taking the initiative in his turn, he said he would be pleased if the ladies would come to dinner or supper at Cindy Lou, some day before their departure. Larry, unfortunately, could not be there. But perhaps they would like to see the old house again.

Before Mrs. Vincent could voice formal regrets, Armande,

surprisingly, said she would be very glad to go, and that possibly evening would be the better time, since they were very busy during the day, sorting and packing the personal belongings which were not included in the sale of property. Clyde answered that he quite understood and how about Wednesday at six-thirty? He was suddenly relieved that Armande had chosen evening; by candlelight the shabbiness of Cindy Lou would not be so apparent as in the more revealing light of day. It was a long, long time since any renovating had been done inside the house. Not since Lucy had died. Many of the rugs were worn, much of the upholstery dingy. And the house had not been painted outside, either. It had begun to have a weather-beaten look, very different from the resplendency which had characterized it when Armande was a girl. Well, now that Victoria was bought and paid for, he could begin to make the superficial improvements which would restore Cindy Lou to its erstwhile elegance, both inside and out. Until now, he had limited himself to essentials in the way of repairs and replacement. The roofs had been kept tight, the timbers sound. There had been better and more machinery on the place all the time, better and more wagons, better and more livestock. The outbuildings were in first-class condition, the Negro cabins exceptionally comfortable, the land well drained. But nothing had been done in the way of embellishment.

These thoughts darted through his mind as the call came to an end. When Larry approached Armande to bid her good-bye, she leaned over and kissed his cheek. After that, Mrs. Vincent could do no less; but she said nothing about hoping to see him again. She thanked Clyde for bringing her grandson to visit her and said she was gratified to find him in such obvious good health and to learn that he was making so much progress in his studies; but she confessed that she was slightly disappointed to find that he had left the locality so little and that he seemed to have formed so few close friendships. Evidently Larry's quick blush had been occasioned by some reference to such lacks. On the ride back to Convent, Clyde asked Larry, as casually as he could, whether the boy felt like telling what all that jabbering in French had been about.

"I don't mind. She asked a lot of questions—whether I liked Latin, whether I had any talents——"

"Had any talents?"

"Yes. Whether I had a good voice, or whether I could play any musical instrument or paint pictures. I told her I could sing in the choir, at a pinch, and that I could strum on the piano a little, but that I didn't care about either one and that I couldn't draw anything to save my life. I told her I got along all right in Latin, because having French, too, helps, but that I'd be glad when I was through with it. So then she asked me what I did like."

"And you said——"

"I said I liked to read and to ride. And she said those were both apt to be rather solitary occupations—those were the words she used. She seemed to think I ought to be in a crowd all the time. I told her I hated crowds. And then she said she wasn't talking about crowds, she was talking about society."

"What kind of society?"

"Why—parties and stuff like that. She seemed to think I ought to be going to dances—where there were girls."

So that was what the sudden blush had meant! Like most children raised in the country, Larry had learned a good deal about sex, as he had learned something about death, from observation of the animals on the plantation. But he had never asked many questions about it or revealed any special curiosity. As far as Clyde had been able to discover, his attitude was still that of a child rather than that of an adolescent; and in view of the confidence which existed between them, Clyde thought it unlikely that the boy could be specifically inquisitive or emotionally disturbed without revealing the fact to his grandfather. The man was annoyed, almost angry, because Mrs. Vincent had raised such an issue inopportunely, even if she had done this unconsciously. He tried not to show this irritation, but to continue speaking casually.

"I suppose some of your schoolmates have parties given for them at home. I suppose boys and girls both go to such parties."

"Yes, I suppose so."

"You could have a party at Cindy Lou, you know, any time you wanted."

"I don't want a party at Cindy Lou at all. I see all I want to of the other boys at school, Daddy. I've told you that before.

And I don't want to see any girls. If I had wanted to, I'd have told you that."

Clyde realized that it would be futile to press the matter and the rest of the ride took place in silence as well as in darkness. But he was deep in thought. Looking back, he remembered that he had been very little older than Larry when he had first spoken to a girl in the street and afterward gone to her wretched room with her. He was thankful that it was going to be different now. Larry would be older and more selective when he had his first experience with sex. Clyde did not even try to visualize what form this would take; but he felt sure that it would not be premature and that it would not be sordid.

The little supper party went off as well as could be expected. Clyde invited Mrs. Surget to join the other ladies and asked her to superintend Delphie beforehand, in getting out long disused linen, china and silver and in opening, airing and cleaning the closed drawing-room. There were still a few dusty bottles of sound old wine in the cellar, and Clyde himself made a careful selection from these. Ivy's supper was creditable, even though it was not especially imaginative, and the wines and service gave it a certain distinction. After supper, before conversation had a chance to lag, Mrs. Vincent suggested that since there were four in the company they might play bridge whist—personally, she did not feel that a quiet game of cards, among friends, was incompatible with mourning. Neither Clyde nor Mrs. Surget had ever played bridge whist, though they had heard of it, and Mrs. Vincent did not attempt to conceal the satisfaction she felt through telling them it had been played in France for years already; in fact, that many persons now referred to it as auction bridge, omitting the outmoded word 'whist' altogether; but one could hardly suppose that in provincial Louisiana! . . . A card table was set up in the drawing room and two packs of cards brought in. Mrs. Vincent expressed surprise because these were the large, old-fashioned type, outmoded, too; and she presumed they would have to use home-made score cards. Then, with still greater condescension, she began to explain the principles of the game. She thought it would be hardly fair to cut for partners; this might result in putting Armande and herself together. It

would be better if each of them took one of the beginners. . . .
Well, she said, three hours later, when the home-made score
cards showed that Armande and Clyde were considerably
ahead of the other two, she had always realized that her
daughter was a good player—evidently an even better one
than anyone in the De Chanet family had imagined. Bridge
was part of the daily schedule at Monteregard, but unless she
were needed to make up a fourth, Armande frequently
excused herself. It was ridiculous, when she could play so
well.

As Clyde gathered up the cards, he happened to glance at
Armande and was startled by the expression on her face. She
had been caught off guard and there was something in it very
like desperation. Up to then, he had been merely annoyed by
her persistent silence; now, for the first time, he wondered
what might lie behind it. She had been a pleasant, friendly
girl, even if she had lacked animation; but her only evidence
of kindliness, in the entire course of her recent stay at Victoria,
had been in her farewell to Larry. And she had not only
failed in graciousness; she had not once joined in her mother's
complacent comments about Monteregard, she had never
spoken of her husband's relatives or of her husband himself.
Of her husband. . . . Clyde met her eyes again and suddenly
thought he had found the answer to the riddle: she was a
wretchedly unhappy woman and her husband was the cause
of her unhappiness. Her reserve was not, like Larry's, caused
by contentment and self-sufficiency; she had withdrawn into
herself because she did not intend to be hurt any more than
she had been already. Her silence was her protective
armour. . . .

Clyde slid the old-fashioned cards back into their cases and
followed his guests from the drawing-room. Mrs. Vincent
and Mrs. Surget were walking ahead, absorbed in an
animated discussion of the relative merits between whist
and auction bridge. Clyde fell back a step and spoke in a low
voice.

"I'd like to give you something that belonged to Cary," he
said. "She was very fond of you, Armande. I know she would
have wanted you to have a little keepsake to remind you of
her. Of course, most of her personal possessions were—

destroyed. But there were a few trinkets that she never took away from here—they didn't have much value and she thought they were too childish looking to wear after she was married. But some of them are rather pretty—a small locket set with turquoises and pearls, for instance. If it would mean anything to you——"

"It would mean a great deal. And it means even more that you've offered it to me."

"Well, could I bring it to you tomorrow? What time would be convenient?"

"If you don't mind, I'd rather come here and get it. While *maman* is resting."

He nodded and stepped forward again. He was just in time. Mrs. Vincent was already extending her hand for his kiss.

"Such a delightful evening, my dear Clyde. Really, no one can take the place of old friends, after all. It makes me feel very sad to think that the time is drawing near to part from them again."

If he had thought she was speaking sincerely, he would have been much concerned, for the final papers had not yet been passed, assuring Larry's possession of Victoria. But he knew such expressions were only part of her pose. The more he saw of her, the more he despised her for her shallowness, her artificiality, her pretentiousness. He knew she had always possessed these qualities to a certain degree, just as she had always had a false sense of values; but they seemed to have been intensified through her residence abroad. Lately he had discovered that she had also become avaricious; and now he began to wonder how great a share she might have had in her daughter's unhappiness. If Armande's marriage had been a failure, then surely her mother should have been the first to shield and support her, even, if necessary, to remove her from the scene of her misery. Instead of that, she had so obviously revelled in the prestige of prerogatives and rank that she would have sacrificed almost anything else to retain them. The more he thought of it, the surer Clyde became that she had sacrificed her daughter.

Armande had not mentioned the time of her mother's siesta, but Clyde took it for granted that this was probably in the afternoon, directly after dinner. He told Delphie to dust the drawing-room again and to have the coffee service ready; and immediately after his own dinner, he changed from the clothes he had worn during his rounds of the plantations that morning and this time, when he looked in his mirror, he did so with a certain degree of satisfaction. His figure was still spare and his alpaca coat was carefully tailored, fitting his wide shoulders and lean flanks flawlessly. His colour was still fresh and his hair abundant as ever, though it was now silvery white instead of ruddy gold. The heavy brows over the deep-set eyes were white, too, and so was the sweeping moustache. Clyde raised his hand to this and brushed it, first left, then right, into the merest suggestion of a cavalier's twirl at the points. His fingers were bony and his seal ring was loose between the knuckle and the enlarged joint, but his carefully tended hand still suggested the dominance that had always given it virility.

Instead of going to his office to work on his accounts, as was still his habit every afternoon, Clyde awaited his guest in the drawing-room. The trinkets which Cary had left behind at the time of her marriage were all together in a small carved wooden box, and he had decided to let Armande take her choice among them, instead of simply giving her the locket. There might well be something else she would prefer and, in any case, the offer of a gift had been merely a pretext to give her a chance to talk with him, if she wished to do so. He thought she understood this and that she did wish to do so, or she would not have suggested coming to Cindy Lou, instead of receiving him at Victoria. But the afternoon wore on and she did not appear. Clyde sat fingering the little wooden box, toying with its quaint golden clasp and lifting its lid; then taking out the ornaments it contained, one at a time, spreading them on the table beside him and putting them back again in a new arrangement. It was true that none of them had much value; but as he turned them over and over, he could see how they had looked on Cary when she wore them in the radiance of her youth. Besides the locket, there were also ear-rings, bracelets, a brooch and a ring, all set with turquoises and pearls; he remembered that these stones had been favourites of hers, at a certain stage of her development, and that every time he came home from a trip he had added another match-

92

ing ornament to those she already had. He was almost sorry he had told Armande he would give her one of them; whichever she took, the set would no longer be complete without it. And he had kept it so all these years. He would never see it in use again himself, but perhaps some day a daughter of Larry's would wear it. Or if Larry should happen to fall in love, very young, with a very young girl, he could offer it to her. Sometimes boys like Larry, who were girl-shy longer than most boys, did fall in love very young, and when they were finally smitten, it was suddenly and hard and their first love might be their last.

Well, it was too late now to change his mind. He had offered Armande the locket and, if she wanted it, he would have to give it to her. But he wondered what had become of her. He restored the trinkets to their proper places, closed the clasp and, setting the box aside, took out his watch. It was after five o'clock. Something must have detained Armande or prevented her from leaving the house. Possibly she had even changed her mind about wanting to come. At any rate, it was too late for her to do so now. He would go to the office and work on the ledgers until suppertime. In fact, as he was so late in starting the accounts for the day, he would go on with them, straight through the evening. Telling Delphie that she might put away the coffee service, but that he would like sandwiches later on, in the office, he descended to the ground floor.

There was thunder in the air and darkness had closed in early, though it was pierced by occasional flashes of lightning. Presently, rain began to fall. Clyde made sure that the windows and doors were tight, brought his books within the radius of the lamplight and settled down to his accounts. The results of his ciphering were gratifying. Even after paying the unreasonable sum that Mrs. Vincent had extorted from him as the purchase price of Victoria, and allowing for the loss of his salary as its manager, he and Larry would still be in comfortable circumstances. He had never mortgaged his crops again, since Lucy's death, and the mortgage on the house had long since been paid off. Any further hesitancy about improving the appearance of the place would represent parsimony. He would get hold of a painter the next day, and it was also high time that the plumbing was expanded and modernized. He would consult Amy Surget about restocking the linen closet, replacing threadbare upholstery and turning out the store-rooms. The grounds, too, needed attention. There was no reason why he should not have a good gardener. Lucy's camellias required expert care and he had not the strength to look after them properly any more; none of the coloured hands on the place was capable of doing so. The gardens as well as the house must be revitalized.

He became so absorbed in his figures and his plans that he failed to notice the increasing fury of the storm. The rain had been falling in torrents for some time; now it was streaming against the windows and gushing from the overflowing gutters. The wind was rising, too; not with the death-dealing suddenness which had cost Lucy and Savoie their lives, but with steadily increasing momentum. The window panes and blinds were rattling harder and harder, and above the noise they made came the racket of a door blown open with violence. It was not until the wind swept into the room through this opening that Clyde realized it was his door which had been forcibly unclosed and sprang up to shut it. Then, instinctively, he recoiled. On the threshold a veiled figure, robed in dripping black, was standing with arms outstretched.

CHAPTER SEVEN

THE RECOIL was only momentary. Armande had not thrown back the veil, which she had stretched out her hands to raise, before he recognized the identity of his sable-clad visitor. He hastened toward her, his own hands extended.

"My dear child! Whatever are you doing, out in this storm? I gave you up hours ago! You must be soaked to the skin. Come, let me take you to Delphie. She'll find something dry for you to put on and make you a hot drink."

"Please don't bother. I've got to get back as soon as I can and——"

"*Get back!* You won't stir out of the house, not while this storm lasts. In fact, I think you'd best let Delphie get you straight to bed. As soon as the rain lets up, I'll send a message to your mother."

"Please, Mr. Batchelor! As soon as the rain lets up, I must go myself. I don't want my mother to know I've come out at all. That's why I couldn't get here sooner—she didn't take a siesta today and she wouldn't let me out of her sight. It was almost as if she'd guessed. But she went to bed early, because of the storm. She's terribly afraid of storms and, for some reason, she imagines she's safer in bed. She's got Leonie in the room with her and I've bribed Leonie not to tell. It isn't the first time. But I'd rather none of your servants found out. You know how these Negroes gossip among themselves. Please!"

She took off her dripping veil and, leaning over the hearth-stone, wrung the water from it. Then she unfastened her cloak and shook it hard. Clyde was relieved to see that it was fairly heavy and that therefore it must have given her a certain amount of protection. But her long hair, which had come unbound, hung in wet, black waves around her shoulders and he knew that her shoes must be soaked. She would certainly be chilled through and through; she might even contract a serious illness unless he could persuade her to accept help. But the same look of desperation which he had caught on her face the day before had come into it again and he hesitated to insist.

"Won't you at least take off your shoes and dry them in front of the fire?" he asked gently. "I can have one going, you know, in no time at all." He took the napkin from the tray which Nappy had brought in some time earlier, but which was still untouched, and handed her the large square of linen. "Here, take this and get some of that rain off your hair. And you won't refuse to take a drink and eat a sandwich with me, will you? I haven't had my own supper yet."

Without waiting for her to answer, he busied himself with the wood and soon had a cheerful blaze burning. Then, going to the cellaret, he filled two glasses. Armande took off her wet shoes and, lifting her narrow skirt a little, sat down near the fire with the drink in her hand. But she shook her head when Clyde offered her a sandwich.

"No, really. I don't want to eat anything. I just want to talk to you."

"I thought perhaps you did. But you could have waited until tomorrow, just as well. As I told you, I never dreamed you'd come out in this storm."

"Tomorrow *maman*'ll keep me beside her all the time, just as she did today. The number of things she's packing to take away—well, I suppose it's all right. I suppose you don't care about china and silver and linen and things like that, as long as you get the house and the land for Larry."

"Not much. Not enough to make an issue out of them. But after all, some of those things are Larry's by rights, and others I'm paying for. When your mother spoke of keeping personal possessions, I thought she meant little ornaments and family photographs that had a special significance for her. I didn't think she meant valuables and furnishings."

"No, I didn't believe you did. Just the same, unless you're willing to have the sale delayed—and possibly fall through— I—I wouldn't make any objections, if I were you. That's one of the things I wanted to tell you."

"Thank you, Armande. Well, I'll think over what you've said. I don't like the idea of being cheated by anybody—if you'll excuse me for referring to your mother as a cheat. I've never let anyone get away with chiselling yet. But perhaps this time . . . yes, I'll think it over. That wasn't all you wanted to say to me though, was it?"

"No. I wanted to tell you things I've never had a chance to tell anybody and that I might never have a chance to tell anybody again. Things that have been—well, choking me for a long time."

"I'm very glad you felt you could confide in me, Armande."

"I'll have to go back a long way—to the time I got engaged to Pierre. I knew he was in love with Cary and still I accepted him."

The look she turned on Clyde now was not only desperate, it was imploring. He answered her even more gently than he had spoken before.

"Do you want to tell me why you did that, Armande?"

"Yes. Yes. That's just what I want to tell you—first. I was afraid I was going to be an old maid. I hadn't had a proposal in a long while. I wasn't grieving for my first love—the boy who died of yellow fever—any more; I hadn't for years. That was just a legend of *maman*'s, to explain why I didn't accept suitors—suitors who didn't exist."

As vividly as if it were yesterday, Clyde recalled Lucy's summary of the situation—a summary which was almost word for word the same as the one Armande was giving him now.

"Every other girl I knew had been married," Armande went on. "Even Cary, who took so long to make up her mind— because she had so many suitors she got confused. And then she chose wrong. I don't mean there was anything the matter with Savoie, except that he lacked force, just as I do. Perhaps it's a family failing, a failing in lots of families like ours. But he wasn't the man for her. If he had been, it wouldn't have taken him so long to get her and he wouldn't have lost her so soon. Pierre was the man for her. She knew it the minute she saw him and so did he."

"She didn't meet Pierre until after she was married to Savoie, Armande. And she—she pulled herself together. She wasn't unhappy and she made Savoie a good wife. He never guessed. I don't see how you did. I don't see how you guessed I knew, either."

"The last was *just* guessing. You and Cary were so close to each other, I didn't see how she could keep anything from you. But I knew how Cary felt because I knew how Pierre felt—almost right away. It was one of those things that you can't help knowing, that's so powerful it demands recognition. I knew he'd come here, hoping to get her for his mistress, since it was too late to get her for his wife. I knew he took me, out of pique, when he couldn't. I knew it, and still I accepted him. And not just because I didn't want to be an old maid, either. I really loved him. I loved him with all my heart and soul. I really thought that perhaps, after a while, he'd love me."

"I'm very sorry, Armande, that it didn't turn out like that. Sorrier than I can tell you."

"But I didn't deserve to have it turn out like that. Because there was still another reason why I accepted him. I accepted him to take him away from Cary. I thought it was quite a triumph to do that. I—I gloated over it. You see, she'd had so many suitors, and I was so close to being an old maid, that I thought, in the end, to get the man she wanted and who wanted her——"

Clyde leaned over and took Armande's hand. "Love's a strange thing, my dear," he said. "It does strange things to all of us sometimes. If you really cared for Pierre, you shouldn't blame yourself too much."

"I really cared for Pierre, but I was a false friend. I knew that Cary was suffering and I wasn't sorry. I was glad. And she was magnificent. Will you ever forget her, at my wedding? I never shall. . . . No, I didn't deserve to be happy. But somehow I don't believe I deserved to be as unhappy as I have been."

"Why don't you leave your husband, Armande? Why don't you come home?"

"I—I can't. I can't leave my children. And I couldn't take them away. I couldn't bring them with me, even for a short visit. You don't know what pressure can be like, from a French family. And I'm a Frenchwoman now. I lost my nationality when I married Pierre. I lost my real home. And then my mother. . . . I think my father would have helped me, if he could. But he couldn't even help himself. My mother was too strong for him, too. She's the only strong one among us. She seems fragile, but she's got an iron will."

"Do you want me to try to get you your freedom, Armande? Because, if you do——"

She shook her head and, as she did so, her long locks of black hair fell over her face, concealing it for a minute. Then she lifted her hand and brushed it back.

"No," she said. "What would be the use? You couldn't do it, even if you did try. I just wanted to talk to you. Now that I've done that, I feel better."

"I'm very glad, my dear. But I still wish there were something——"

"There isn't. And I mustn't give you the idea that Pierre—maltreats me. He doesn't. He's very polite to me—most of the time. Painfully polite. But when Cary died—well, it was an awful shock to him, of course, especially—especially happening the way it did. He—he lost control of himself, he told me she was the only woman he'd ever loved. Afterward, he apologized. He never told me so again. But I can tell that he wants to, every time he's annoyed with me. Every time I don't come up to his stiff French standards of what he thinks

98

his wife and the mother of his son ought to be. Every time he imagines I'm disrespectful to his mother."

There was a long silence. At last Clyde asked, huskily, "Are you disrespectful to his mother, Armande?"

"I don't mean to be. At least I don't mean to show it. And she isn't at the chateau much any more, she's in Paris most of the time. So it isn't hard—not nearly as hard as it used to be . . . but I don't respect her. You met her when you bought this house, and later, when she came to Victoria to visit. Did *you* respect her?"

There was another long silence. For the first time in more than forty years, Clyde thought, fleetingly, that the moment had come when he could permit himself the comfort of full confession, in a way and in a quarter which he never could have foreseen. But almost instantly he knew that it had not come after all, and that it never would. Even on the chance that he might help Armande, he had no right to give her more than the briefest of answers.

"No," he said at last. "But you mustn't ever tell anyone I said so. Least of all Pierre."

"I won't. And I won't ask you but one more question. It would help though, if you'd answer that. Do you know what it's like to live with a secret and to feel that it's your fault you have to?"

It was not until after the storm had abated and Armande had gone out into the night again that Clyde remembered he had not given her the pearl and turquoise locket after all. It still lay, nestled among the other ornaments that matched it, in the little carved box which he had left upstairs. . . .

He did not see Armande alone again and, when he took her and her mother to the station, she was once more the silent, elegant French lady of fashion who treated him almost like a stranger. It was hard to believe that she was the same woman who had come to him, in secret, through a storm, and who had sat dishevelled and distraught by his hearthstone, as she poured out her heart to him. And it was not until Larry came home for his summer vacation that he and Clyde went through the house at Victoria together and rode over the land. There had been no previous opportunity to do so since Mrs.

Vincent's departure, because Larry had used up all the leave of absence which he was able to get; and though they had often surveyed the plantation in the past, they had never before been able to do so with the consciousness and the pride of ownership. Both eagerly awaited the occasion.

They rode past the mule barn and the quarters into the sea of standing cane that stretched away before them to the dark line of trees where the swamps took over. Clyde was handsomely turned out in freshly laundered linen riding breeches and polished, handmade boots; and despite his years he sat his bay gelding easily. From beneath the wide brim of his finely plaited Panama, he shot a swift glance at the slim, tall youngster on the sorrel stallion beside him. What a world of difference there was between this boy and the gamin who had clawed and battled his way from the barrel-house dives of St. Louis to the proud position of a landed proprietor! Larry would never need to fight for a place in the world, never need to assume a virtue he did not have; he was really to the manner born. And now Clyde Batchelor was taking his beloved Lucy's grandson out to show him the domain which that erstwhile guttersnipe, that erstwhile river gambler, that erstwhile profiteer, had won for him.

The two trotted along in companionable silence between walls of green and purple cane until they came to the heavy gates which led to the fenced lane which divided the land of Victoria from the land of Cindy Lou. Larry slipped swiftly from the saddle to open the gates for his grandfather, leading his mount across the gaps.

"No need to close them, Larry," Clyde said. "Matter of fact, I could have had that fence taken down the minute the act of sale had passed. No sense, with all the wagons and teams going back and forth, making the hands stop to open and close those gaps every time. I just kind of felt I wanted you to be with me when we finally opened them for keeps."

"Thanks, Dad. For waiting, I mean. That's swell of you. It makes me feel like—well, I reckon you know what I'm trying to say."

"Yes—and there are things I want to say. Things I want you to look at, too, closer than you ever have before, because now they belong to you. Suppose we go up on the old Indian mound, where we can get a good view and rest awhile."

The Indian mound to which he referred had long been a favourite objective of theirs. There was none on Cindy Lou and there was no other on Victoria; but it was one of several similar elevations in the vicinity, which had presumably been built by aborigines, so that they might have the security of high ground when the river flooded the lower land in the spring. Arrowheads and skeletons had sometimes been unearthed from their depths; and the Negroes insisted that strange lights, which looked like balls of fire, played over them at night, as a warning for white folks to keep away. Larry had a few of the arrowheads, which he treasured greatly, but he had never been scared by the stories; in fact, the mound, shaded as it was by pines and moss-hung magnolias, had always seemed to him a pleasant spot for a breathing space on a warm day, quite aside from the fact that it afforded the best possible view of the surrounding countryside. Now he fell in readily with his grandfather's suggestion. They slipped forward in their saddles and the horses obediently broke into a brisk trot that covered the distance between the lane and the green elevation in a matter of minutes. Alighting and tethering their mounts to a hackberry sapling, they climbed the steep slope. As they reached the crest Clyde dropped an arm casually about the boy's shoulders.

"As you know, over there's the main part of the fields," he said, pointing. "But don't pass up that woodland on the far side. One of these days, when cypress gets scarce, there's a real fortune waiting for you there. Frank Williams, over in Patterson, is close to being the richest man in Louisiana, and he came there as a sawmill hand not too many years back. Cypress did it. And his cypress isn't going to last for ever. As the rest of it is logged out in other places, here's where they'll have to come for more. And don't you be in any hurry to sell. Wait till . . ."

"I'll wait till you sell it, sir," Larry said in his newly acquired baritone. He had never before called Clyde anything but 'Daddy' or 'Dad.' Yet Clyde found the 'sir' strangely warming.

"I'm not going to be here too much longer," he told the

boy placidly. "No, never mind about that"—as Larry seemed about to interrupt—"I'm in no hurry to go, and I propose to hang on as long as the good Lord'll give me leave to stay, getting a bit crankier and peskier with the years, maybe. On the other hand, I'm well past the threescore-ten the Bible talks about. I'll be seventy-eight years old pretty soon. So we've got to face facts. That's why I'm talking to you about all this, because one of these days, no matter if it's soon or it's late, the whole thing is going to be your responsibility. I'd kind of hoped to have it for mine, and to head up a great big—well, call it empire—she's all of that, now; better than eight thousand acres, and there's places in Europe where you'd need a passport to come into or leave a chunk of land that big. But it's too late for me to make it, now. All I could do was get it together, and you're bound to know who I got it together for. So I'm showing it to you. Your empire. The fields and the cypress over there. The sugar mill close by the levee, because one of these days there'll be barges bringing you cane to grind. The big house you've got to keep in prime condition, because one of these days you'll have a daughter or a son to turn it over to for a wedding present. Naturally, I'm hoping you'll keep Cindy Lou for yours. No gates between them any more. It's one place—one empire—and it's yours. . . ."

He paused, too moved to say anything more. Indeed, it seemed to him, at first, that there was nothing more which required saying. Then, as Larry remained silent, too, he added, "Is there anything else, Larry, you'd especially like to have? I mean anything I haven't told you about, while we've been talking these matters over. Because if there is, I wish you'd ask me for it. There's probably no reason why I shouldn't give it to you now, and it would please me a lot to do it."

"All right, Daddy. I'll tell you. I'd sure enough like a dog. You know I've never had one."

A dog! Yes, it was true, there had never been a dog at Cindy Lou. Oh, of course the overseer and the manager of the sugarhouse had their hunting dogs and the Negroes had their feists! But there had never been a dog, a pure-bred, in the Big House. Now that Larry mentioned it, Clyde could not understand why Cary had never asked for one, why he and Lucy had never been conscious of such a lack, why he had not offered one to Larry long ago. A dog would not only mean a great deal to the boy; it would also mean a great deal to him, in those long periods which inevitably lay ahead, when Larry would be gone and he himself would be alone at Cindy Lou.

"Why, of course, Larry. Of course you ought to have a dog. Of course you should have had one long ago. We'll start looking around for one tomorrow. Have you thought what kind of a dog you'd like?"

No, Larry had not gone as far as that. They discussed, at some length, what kind of a dog they should get, without reaching any decision, and concluded there was no hurry about that, anyway. Tomorrow would be plenty of time. However, Clyde asked another question.

"When I said I wanted to know if there were any special thing you'd like to have, Larry, I wasn't thinking of something like a dog. I don't mean that a dog isn't important— that it can't be, anyway. But I was thinking of something that might mean a really big investment, something that might affect your future. Is there anything of that kind?"

"Well, yes. I don't know whether it's the sort of thing you meant, but sometimes I've wondered——"

"Yes, Larry?"

"About the boats. Yours, I mean. They were all gone, you know, before I can remember. There've been nothing but pirogues around—at least that had any connection with Cindy Lou. But I've been watching the river. There are more and more towboats on it all the time. Have you noticed, too? If we could have some of our own, you and I. . . ."

CHAPTER EIGHT

"I DON'T know that we could begin on the river, Larry. It would mean huge investments and uncertain returns, because it's paralleled by the railroads—damn them!—along most of its major branches and tributaries. By highways, too. And those are getting better and better all the time, thanks to gravel."

"Where could we begin then?"

"On the bayous. They run through swamp country where year-round roadways can't be maintained and where wheeled traffic—other than rail, of course—is feasible only during the dry seasons."

"I see. Well, whereabouts would we start on the bayous?"

"I'll tell you what I've considered and let you say what you think of it. I've heard that a small stern-wheeler, the *Palourde*, has sunk in Lake Verret. Of course the wreck's for sale cheap. I thought I might make a deal with the Teche Lumber and Planting Company whereby I'd purchase the wreck, raise it, repair it and operate it if they'd give me a contract to haul sugar cane for them from Bayou Aux Chenes and other small waterways of the countryside to Franklin. Our boat would be just doing the towing, you understand. If the Teche Lumber and Planting Company'd agree to furnish the barges and pay seventeen cents a ton, and we could move around seven hundred tons a day, between early October and early January, I think we could gross nearly—well, let's see."

Clyde swung around in his swivel chair and, facing his desk, began to figure. Larry, who had been sitting close beside him, rose and leaned over his shoulder, watching with absorbed interest.

"A hundred dollars a month for the captain—and I think I know just the man for the job. Clovis Bourgeois, his name is. I ran into him first at Morgan City, which used to be quite a shipbuilding centre for bayou boats—he was the man who generally took new boats out on their trial runs. But there haven't been any new steamers built in nobody knows when—and Clovis has been living in Madisonville, where there's a shipyard turning out small tugs and shrimp boats and such as that. He'd sell his eye teeth for a chance to take hold of the spokes of a wheel again, and he'd know where to pick up a pilot—he and the pilot could stand twelve-hour watches, and so could the rest of the crew. The pilot would get seventy-five dollars, two oilers sixty each, two firemen forty-five each, a cook the same, eight deck hands thirty each, a cabin boy fifteen." Clyde added up the figures rapidly. "That seems to

104

total $685.00. It would cost about $250.00 to feed that many men and the fuel—wood—could run to another ninety. Well, allow a little leeway and, say, a grand total of about $1,050.00 for expenses per month. At that, we ought to net about twenty a day."

"That's pretty good, isn't it?"

"It's damn good. Even if I had to borrow against the contract, in order to salvage the *Palourde* and put her into condition, we ought to be able to pay for her within a year, because at the close of the sugar season we should be able to get another contract."

"For what?"

"For hauling rafted cypress logs from Bayou Boeuf and other forest waterways to the sawmill at Patterson, hard by where Bayou Teche empties into the Atchafalaya."

"You said 'even if you had to borrow the money.' Do you have to borrow it?"

Clyde began to figure again. "Not if we cut some corners here. I'd meant to do a little fancying up, at Cindy Lou, now that Victoria's paid for. But if we put that off——"

"Why on earth did you want to fancy up Cindy Lou?"

"Well, it's getting pretty shabby. Nothing's been done to it for a long while—seventeen years, to be exact. I had a run of bad luck about the time—about two years before your grandmother died. We had to figure pretty close for quite a spell—and I couldn't have pulled through if it hadn't been for her. She was wonderful—about that and everything else. There never——" Clyde checked himself. He had been on the point of saying, "There was never anyone like her before and there never will be again." If he had, Larry might very logically have asked, or at least wondered, if his mother hadn't been equally wonderful. "After your grandmother died, of course I didn't care, for a long time, how things looked," Clyde went on. "And it didn't seem to matter, anyway, with just you and me here. It's different when there's a woman— a lady—in the house than when an old man and a small boy are living by themselves."

"Yes, I suppose it must be."

"Then after I began to realize it was a shame, in a way, to let the show place of the river road get so run-down at the heel, I'd also begun to wonder whether I couldn't get hold of Victoria for you. And it seemed more important to save ahead, in the hope of doing that, than to spend money in—well, in fancying up."

"I think you were right, too."

"And now, if you and I are going into partnership——"

"I'd rather have the boat, Dad, than the trimmings. I'd rather have it than anything else in the world."

His voice broke with earnestness. His black-and-white setter Nuffy, who had been lying quietly on the rug near by, with his head between his forepaws, looked up with an expression of anxiety in his great liquid eyes, and wagged his tail intermittently, in a manner that suggested troubled inquiry rather than unquestioning joy. Nuffy, who had been named Sure Enough, because of the way Larry had asked for him, but who had quickly been nicknamed, had been a member of the household for only a few weeks, but he was already attuned to his master's moods. He knew, from the tone of Larry's voice, that portentous matters were under discussion, and he was not altogether sure that they were progressing satisfactorily. Clyde leaned over and patted the dog on the head. It was understood, of course, that Nuffy belonged to Larry; Nuffy knew this and so did everyone else. But there was also a strong bond of friendship between him and Clyde. The night after the dog's arrival at Cindy Lou, he had raised his head and howled dismally several times. This had then been attributed to his natural feeling of strangeness and loneliness in his unfamiliar surroundings; but when the habit of intermittent howling persisted, in spite of his appearance of general contentment, some other cause was sought and eventually found: Nuffy's mournful cries always coincided with the passage of trains over the 'Valley' or the L.R. & N. tracks at the rear of the plantation. Why these distant sounds so distressed him, when others left him unmoved, no one had been able to discover. However, Clyde insisted that Nuffy was only giving vent to feelings about railroads which a man like himself, while endorsing, must perforce conceal, whereas a dog could properly give tongue to them. In other words, Nuffy was his mouthpiece as well as his kindred spirit.

"It's all right, Nuffy," he said now, pulling the dog's ears gently and giving him a final pat. Then he straightened up. "If you really feel that way about the boat, Larry——"

"I really do, Dad. I don't know that I'd like Cindy Lou fancied up. I like it the way it's always been, even if it is sort of shabby. It won't suffer in any way, will it, if you buy the boat?"

"No, it won't suffer. At least, I suppose I ought to have some painting done, not so much for looks as for preservation. But I'll keep it at a minimum. And I won't try to do anything in the way of interior decorating or landscape gardening. I still don't feel things like that matter very much without—just for you and me. And since you like it the way it is. . . . But we'll buy the *Palourde* and put it into action. I'll get in touch with Fred Banks at the Teche Lumber and Planting Company right away. If he and I come to terms, we ought to be ready to start operations this fall."

So it came about that more than ten years after he thought he had left the river for good, Clyde Batchelor was back on it again. The first contracts for hauling sugar cane from various waterways to Franklin, and rafted cypress logs from Bayou Boeuf to Patterson, were followed by other contracts still more profitable: for towing gravel barges from Profit Island in the Mississippi, just above Baton Rouge, to Morgan City on the Atchafalaya: for hauling granulated sugar from Glenwild landing near Charenton, and rough rice from the Teche country to New Orleans; for hauling general merchandise on the return trips. All this was done with the reclaimed stern-wheeler. Then came the proud moment when Clyde told Larry that the time had come for them to expand, to charter barges themselves, and bring loads of cotton down from the Ouachita River country, after having taken groceries, dry goods and other such commodities as far north as Camden, Arkansas, on the upstream leg of the journey.

By this time, Larry was nearing the end of his high school course and all for coming back to Cindy Lou to stay. His marks had continued to be good, but this was due to a combination of pride and intelligence, rather than to any special love of studying; and though he was well liked both by his teachers and his schoolmates and had made some real friendships among them, he still preferred his grandfather's company to any other. He could not see the slightest sense, he said, frequently and vehemently, in putting up with the restrictions at Jefferson four years more. It was ridiculous to expect that he would be satisfied any longer with those stiff, short Sunday and Thursday visits—as if he ever had been really satisfied with them!—with getting home only once a month in term time, and with only two vacations a year, one of them so short that it hardly counted! He was even more vehement when Clyde suggested that it might be a good thing for him to have a complete change from Louisiana and go to one of the big eastern colleges. The last thing he wanted was a complete change from Louisiana—he had never said he was not satisfied with *that*! What he was after, as he thought he had made clear, was not more separation from his grandfather, but less. If Dad was sincere in saying that he wanted Larry to relieve him, increasingly, of the plantations' management, if they were really partners in the new C. & L. Navigation Company, then the place for him was Cindy Lou.

It was with the greatest difficulty that Clyde persuaded him to accept Tulane as a compromise. If Larry went to college there, Clyde pointed out, he would have more freedom of action than at Jefferson; though New Orleans was so much farther away than Convent, he could actually get home from there oftener and stay longer at a time—in fact, he could come as often and stay as long as his scholastic standing would permit. It was true that Clyde was more than ready to relinquish the reins of management on the plantations; but when he did so, he wanted to be sure that Larry was properly prepared, in every way, to take hold of them. He would be far more capable of handling such a task at twenty-one than at seventeen—not merely because he would be more mature and could assume authority more convincingly; but because during the interval he could learn many things, both at college and elsewhere, which would help him to be a good manager. What, for instance, Larry wanted to know. Well, there was sugar chemistry, for one thing; not that Larry would be a sugar chemist, of course; he would hire those. But it would give him a great advantage to have all the fundamentals of this and other phases of sugar processing at his finger tips; he would not be like those planters who were obliged to accept the reports and conclusions of their subordinates. By the same token, he should study business administration, enough law to cover the question of contracts, warehousing, import and export shipments, and enough about accounting practice so that he would not be dependent on such rule of thumb bookkeeping as Clyde himself had been obliged to use. Then there was something else, and it was very important: Larry should not confine his studies at the university to those subjects which would be immediately and directly of use to him in his work and his business. Clyde had never realized how much he himself had missed, through lack of acquaintance with the classics, until Larry's grandmother had brought Alexander Peyton's library to Cindy Lou from Virginia. It was true that Larry had always had the run of this, and had profited by its availability and by his natural taste for reading, as well as by the courses he had taken at Jefferson; it was also true that an awareness of great literature and an acquaintance with languages did not help a man to buy supplies for a steamboat or to purchase the best sugar mules. But such breadth of knowledge not only increased the respect in which he was held as a member of a cultured community; it enriched the counsels he could thus contribute to discussions of men and affairs and it deepened the enjoyment he took from life as he lived it. With the guidance he could get at the university, Larry would be able to widen immeasurably the horizons he had only glimpsed through his great-great-grandfather's library and through his high school course.

As far as the partnership was concerned, of course it was a real one; but Clyde was beginning to foresee further contracts, even more profitable than those they had had in the past, but very different in character; he did not feel too sure that he himself had the knowledge to deal with these changing and expanding markets, so Larry must acquire it. What changing and expanding markets, Larry inquired. For oil, Clyde told him. Maybe that was not so important now, but it was going to be. Petroleum would certainly replace wood and possibly some day even coal as fuel for boilers, just as in a few short years it had already driven whale oil out of the market as fuel for lamps. His next towboat would have oil burners under her boilers—and think of the time that would be saved by not having to transfer cordwood bolts from wood flats to his own decks, and the labour that would be saved in stoking the furnaces! Ever since that man Heywood had made his strike near Jennings a dozen years before, more and more oil had been discovered in Louisiana—all west of the Mississippi so far, to be sure, and there were those who said that would always be the boundary line of discovery. But Clyde did not believe it. He thought that one of these days it might be found almost anywhere or everywhere in Louisiana, when men developed a surer way of looking for it in the flat country. An enormous refinery was already in process of construction, unit by unit, in Baton Rouge. And there was one commodity— oil, that is—where the railroads, damn them, could never compete with the river. A tow of three barges, say, could carry as much oil as seven trains of sixty tank cars each—and think of the time to be saved in loading those barges! Only three couplings to make. One man could do the whole thing in twelve hours. On those seven trains more than four hundred couplings would have to be made and unmade, and you couldn't load more than a dozen cars at a time on any single spur anyway, so it would take a week just to fill the tank cars and another week to empty them when they got to their destination. Yes, indeed! Oil! That was the thing to bring back the river to its glory. One of these days he and Larry would take a trip to that Evangeline field—in fact, if there were no more of this talk about leaving school for good, they would take it that very summer, as soon as Larry had finished high school. Clyde had met young Heywood in Morgan City one time, and they had developed a mutual interest in the idea of transporting petroleum in barges. Of course, it was impossible to take oil from Jennings to Baton Rouge by water now; but one of these days it might not be, one of these days there might be canals. That was what Heywood had predicted; and people were already talking about an intracoastal canal that would run from Brownsville in Texas all the way to the Mississippi River at New Orleans. . . .

Admittedly, the prospect of the trip had more effect on Larry's decision than the good advice about courses in sugar chemistry and the comments on the advantages of familiarity with the classics. Clyde recognized this, but he did not greatly care, as long as he had secured the desired results. The trip took place and, all in all, was a great success. Moreover, as Clyde wisely timed it toward the end of the summer, its after-effects were such as to start Larry off to college without too much protest. Another one of its many good results had been to overcome much of his adolescent diffidence and reserve. At Tulane he continued to do well in his studies and to make his mark in athletics; but he also mingled more willingly with his classmates than he ever had at Jefferson; he even joined a fraternity and began going to dances. Though he established no David and Jonathan friendships and singled out no one girl or succession of girls for special attention, Clyde felt the boy was making progress in the normal—and therefore in the right—direction.

This progress was facilitated and expedited by the unawaited appearance of Armande de Chanet on the scene. Mrs. Vincent had recently died and Armande arrived in New Orleans alone —except for her maid Leonie—opened their long-closed house on Elysian Fields and settled down, apparently for an indefinite stay. She offered no explanation to the acquaintances whose curiosity was aroused by this procedure, beyond stating briefly that there were certain matters, in connection with the settlement of the estate, to which she thought she could attend more satisfactorily in person than through corres-pondence. When pressed, she added that her son Pierrot was in college, her daughter Janine at the Sacré Coeur and that neither of them needed her at the moment; therefore it seemed a good one for returning to her old home, which she had always hoped she might occupy again sometime. Having said this much, she politely but adroitly withheld further information, and it was soon obvious that she had no intention of giving any. She did not seclude herself, but made visitors welcome, in a somewhat impersonal way, and returned, with becoming promptitude, the calls that were made upon her, using a very handsome turnout for the purpose, and dressing, almost invariably, in black velvet with touches of ermine which, as everyone knew, was not really mourning at all. She also went to Mass at the cathedral and to meetings of the

Athenée Louisianais and accepted the invitations to informal soirées, extended with some hesitancy because of her recent bereavement, but with hopefulness that in course of time she might become more communicative. Though these hopes remained unfulfilled, she gave distinction to any gathering she attended because of her elegant attire, imposing presence and polished, though guarded, conversation. Moreover, she seemed quite conscious of the fact that if she accepted invitations she would be expected to return them, and inaugurated a series of quiet dinners and small bridge parties which were recherché in every sense of the word. By this time she had reorganized the dormant household staff and expanded it, taken the family silver and other valuables out of storage, and given such fine feminine touches to the double drawing-rooms as to make them seem more generally inviting; and long before she became recognized, to any extent, as an experienced and charming hostess, she had taken pains to let Larry know that he would be most welcome at her house whenever he felt like coming there, and that she also hoped he would feel free to bring his friends.

Her first note, asking him to come and see her, reached him before he was even aware of her presence in the city, and he responded to it with a promptness and politeness not characteristically collegiate. He had been genuinely attracted to her during the course of their one meeting, at Victoria, and had felt vaguely sorry for her, without knowing quite why. Later he had spoken to his grandfather about this and Clyde, without saying enough to betray Armande's confidence, had told the boy he was right, that his aunt's life was not a very happy one and that, unfortunately, there seemed to be nothing they could do to help her—which was all the more to be regretted because much of her unhappiness was not her fault. Since then, Larry had thought of her fairly often, considering the number of other things which were on his mind, and had hoped that his grandfather was mistaken, that some day they might be helpful to her after all. It was with this in his thoughts that he went so promptly to see her; and he was both relieved and surprised to find that she did not seem nearly as sad as she had before, and that evidently, far from needing or expecting help from him, she was eager to do everything she could in the way of contributing to the pleasures of his life at college.

"She said maybe I'd like a standing invitation for Sunday night supper," he told his grandfather when he went home over the weekend. "Not just for myself, either—for as many people as I'd like to bring to her house. I told her I still didn't care much for crowds and, from the way she smiled, I could see she remembered that awful call at Victoria, just as well as I did. But all she said was that I'd probably be getting over such a feeling, almost any time now, and that meanwhile I could come alone, or with one or two other fellows, just as I liked. I told her I nearly always came to Cindy Lou for Sunday, and she said all right, any other night then. She made me feel she'd really like to have me and I began to feel as if I'd really like to go."

"I'm very glad. And look here, Larry, you know you don't have to come to Cindy Lou every Sunday. You know——"

"I know we've hashed that all over before and that we're not going to again. Aunt Armande and I settled on Wednesdays. I'm going to supper this coming Wednesday and Blaise Bergeron and another fellow I like, named Gus Gallion, are going, too. I didn't say I'd go every Wednesday, but it's understood I can if I want to. Aunt Armande's looked up my godparents, and she says they've told her they're going to get in touch with me; if they don't, pretty soon, of their own accord, she'll invite them to supper, too, some Wednesday when I'm there. She's even offered to fix up some rooms that I could call mine, or to let me do it—a bedroom and maybe another room, too, where my friends and I could play cards or rough-house or do anything else we wanted. She says she's just rattling around, alone in that great house. It *is* a great house, you know—as big as this one."

"Yes, I know. Your grandmother and I used to visit there, quite often." Clyde might have added that he was rattling round alone in a great house, too, but he did not. He sat still, stroking Nuffy's head, and listening to Larry as the boy rambled on with an unusual degree of expansiveness.

"Aunt Armande said that she remembered when you and my grandmother used to visit there. She said she hoped you'd come and visit there again."

"Well, I don't know, Larry. It's a good deal of an effort for me to go anywhere these days—you know that. And now my partner's off at college, of course I'm pretty busy with that navigation company of ours, let alone the two plantations."

"Aunt Armande realizes you are. I told her about the new navigation company and she was very much interested. But I think she really does hope you'll come to visit her, Dad. I hope so, too."

"All right then, I will, one of these days, after grinding's over."

"She especially told me to give you her love, Dad. And she asked me to tell you something else. She said she brought back a lot of stuff with her from France—stuff she says really belongs at Victoria. I didn't understand what she meant, but she said you would."

"Yes, I think I do. I'll tell you about it some time, Larry. Well . . . that's very thoughtful of your aunt, very thoughtful and very fair. I've been thinking, even before you told me about all this stuff, as you call it, that we ought to put Victoria at your aunt's disposal. Maybe she'd like to come there for week-ends—or longer, if she's going to stay on."

Clyde was not among those who had plied Armande with importunate questions. He had waited for her to take her time about getting in touch with him, and he was really moved by the way she had chosen to do so. Now he would have been glad to know something about the underlying causes for her sojourn in New Orleans and about her future plans.

"I guess she must be intending to stay quite a while," Larry went on. "She said she was going to take a *loge grillée* at the opera house through the season, and I don't suppose she'd be doing that if she didn't mean at least to spend the winter. She said I'd be welcome to bring friends to the *loge*, too, any time, if I'd just let her know beforehand, so that she wouldn't have it filled already. She said maybe you'd like to go to the opera again—she thought it was a long time since you had."

"She's right. It is a long time since I have. But when your mother was a young lady . . . I'll never forget how she looked the night of her début. She wore a white tulle dress, looped up with lilies of the valley, and she looked like a fairy princess. I wanted your grandmother to wear white, too—white satin and pearls. But she said one white dress would detract from the other and she was right, as usual. She wore old rose moiré and cameos set with diamonds and she—well, she looked like a *queen*! They sat side by side in the front of the *loge* with your mother's bouquets heaped all around them—we always had a *loge ouverte*, because that was what your mother preferred, but of course we'd have had one for such a special occasion anyway. Your father came to the *loge* between every act and so did his various rivals—Valois Dupré, I mean the younger one, and Nial Stuart and Andres Santana, and I don't know how many others—not that they ever got very far, against your father's persistence, but they all tried to get in a word edgewise." Clyde paused and Larry remained silent, realizing that his grandfather was never happier than when reliving those golden days—realizing, too, that the old man did this more and more frequently all the time. "Well, of course I can see that a *loge grillée* would be more suitable for your aunt than a *loge ouverte*," Clyde said at last, in a tone that suggested he was reluctant to return to the present, but that he realized it must be done. "After all, she's more or less in mourning, and she can keep the grille closed, if she wants to. Naturally, I'd feel very honoured to act as her escort. But I must see about some dress clothes if I'm going to start going out on the town again, mustn't I? And by the way, what about *your* clothes? The next thing you know, your aunt will be talking to you about white ties and tails. As if I didn't know. . . ."

Subsequent events proved that he did, indeed, know; and it was a proud moment for him when he and Larry, equally elegant and equally immaculate in their beautifully tailored new evening clothes, stood back for Armande, superbly gowned in royal purple, to sweep into the *loge grillée* before them, on 'French Society' night, when the Creole population of the city turned out in full force to crowd the great opera house, which was properly decorated with flags and bunting. The fourth member of Armande's party—a well-connected young girl, pretty enough to pass, but not sufficiently striking

115

to detract from the effect produced by Armande—did not really count. Neither did the opera itself, which was a very fine performance of *Thaïs*, with Mlle Savarenne singing the title rôle; and neither did the fact that at the end of the second act Mme Dalcia, who took the part of Albine, stepped before the drawn curtains, robed as La France, and sang the 'Marseillaise' with magnificent effect. What counted to Clyde was that he and Larry were going out together now, as two men, and that they were fitted, in every way, to do so, not only when they rode the crops or went to see an oil field; but also when they were the chosen companions of a beautiful woman at a spectacle where all the world would be made aware of her choice.

His satisfaction over the turn things were taking was so great that he was persuaded to prolong his stay in New Orleans for several days, to act as host at one of Armande's *soigné* little dinners and to make a fourth at bridge whenever she was inclined to have the card table set up. She made him feel that he was flattering her by his presence, which naturally had the effect of increasing the sense of flattery inspired by her hospitality; but it was not until the last evening of his visit, when her other guests had left after prolonged expressions of appreciation for a delightful evening, that she abandoned the rôle of accomplished hostess for that of a confiding friend.

With the exception of Leonie, who always awaited her mistress in Armande's bedroom, to help her prepare for the night, the servants had gone to bed, after leaving the double drawing-rooms in perfect order, mending the fires and setting out drinks and sandwiches. Armande did not object to the smell of smoke herself, and apparently felt no apprehension lest this should cling to the draperies and upholstery, for she encouraged Clyde in the enjoyment of his cigars. He sat smoking contentedly while she excused herself to change from the black velvet dress, which she had worn for dinner, to a *robe d'intérieur*, in which she could be more at ease. When she returned, her appearance was quite as elegant as before, but it was definitely less formal; and she made a charming picture in her négligé of snowy chiffon fastened at the throat, the waist and the wrists with grosgrain ribbon bows. Its full bishop sleeves fell softly over her arms and its pleated skirt spread out like a fan when she seated herself. She had taken down her hair, and her long sleek braids were also fastened with white ribbon. Clyde realized, poignantly, that he had not seen a woman's hair, plaited for the night, since Lucy died, and that it was one of the loveliest and most intimate sights which could be vouchsafed a man. Of course Armande's raven locks could not compare, in beauty, with Lucy's golden tresses —or Cary's, either, for that matter. But then Cary had never wanted to bother with braids. Before the girl's marriage, Lucy had insisted upon them as part of a proper ritual, like prayers; and in Cary's last dreadful illness, she had lain unprotesting while her grandmother or Amy Surget brushed and combed the long strands and arranged them neatly. However, Clyde knew that Savoie had encouraged her to leave her golden curls unbound, and that her husband had loved to see her lying with them spread out all around her, on her white pillow, as Clyde did himself. Sometimes when she was riding, too, they escaped from their knot and their net; Clyde wondered if this had ever happened, in the woods at Monteregard, and what Pierre de Chanet had said, or done, if it had. . . .

Clyde went on puffing at his cigar, glancing every now and then with continued appreciation at Armande's filmy dress and sleek hair. He no longer found her silences oppressive, as he had when she came to Victoria with her mother. He found them companionable—not to the same degree, of course, that he so found Larry's, but to a very pleasing extent. This time, however, Armande spoke fairly soon after she had effectively disposed herself and her white draperies in the chair facing his.

"This isn't much like the last time we sat together, by ourselves, on either side of a hearthstone, is it, Uncle Clyde?" she asked with a smile.

He had still been thinking about Cary's beautiful unbound curls, and all the potentialities connected with them, when Armande broke the silence. As so often happened nowadays, it required an effort to bring himself back to the present; and this would have taken him still longer had it not been for the words 'Uncle Clyde' at the end of her question. The designation was new and very, very pleasing to him. It helped to rouse him from his reveries.

"No, my dear, it isn't," he agreed. "The weather's unusually mild and pleasant, for this time of year, and there was a wild storm that night, as I remember."

"Is that the only thing you remember about it, Uncle Clyde?"

"No. I remember being very much afraid that you'd catch a bad cold. Did you? I never heard. You were dripping wet—you never should have been out on such a night."

"But I wanted so much to see you that the storm didn't matter. And no—I didn't catch cold, I very seldom have a cold. However, I was desperately unhappy, I wanted to confide in you. Do you remember that, too?"

"Yes, I remember that, too."

"Well, I'm not desperately unhappy now, but I'd like to confide in you again. Do you mind very much? I've tried to wait for just the right time."

"My dear, of course I don't mind. Of course I'd be honoured by your confidence. Naturally, I felt rather curious. But I haven't wanted to question you."

"You're about the only person who hasn't. That's one reason why I feel like telling you of my own accord. Not the only reason, of course. Another reason is that I'm very fond of you."

"I'm honoured by that, too. And it's a sentiment I fully reciprocate."

"We could go on paying each other compliments for a long while, couldn't we? And the best part of it is that they'd all be sincere. . . . But what I really wanted to tell you is that I've left Pierre at last."

"I'm very glad. You know I asked you why you didn't two and a half years ago."

"And I told you I couldn't then—at least I didn't see how I could. But *maman's* death made everything much simpler for me. I don't need to pretend, to you, that this loss was a blow to me, and I don't want to pretend, to anyone else— that's why I don't discuss it. I heard someone say, a long while ago, that old age is the great test. The majority of persons are at least reasonably pleasant and reasonably upright when

118

they're young. Then, at middle age, latent faults and failings begin to show, if there are any; and by the time a person's elderly, those faults and failings are either overcome—or intensified. An old man or an old woman who's really fine is about the finest creature there is, just as one that's handsome or beautiful at eighty is about five times as remarkable as one who's handsome or beautiful at eighteen. *Maman* couldn't meet the great test. She grew more and more shallow and snobbish every year, more and more hard and grasping, too. Her association with the French aristocracy didn't help, either. She tried to copy a sophistication and pretend to a tradition that were natural to the people she met, but that she wasn't equal to assuming. And she got the idea that more money would help—which of course it doesn't, in that particular milieu, unless you've got the other qualities to go with it. So she was disappointed and embittered and she took out her disappointment and her bitterness on me. I'm afraid she took them out on poor Papa, too, and he was even more helpless than I've been. . . . Well, we won't speak of her again—I feel justified in doing it this once, so you'd see the whole picture. But now, let her rest in peace. At least she got her final wish—a magnificent Parisian funeral and burial at Père-Lachaise, with a marble monument that's the marvel of all beholders. I'm thankful she didn't want to be brought back to Convent. I should think you'd be thankful, too. I shouldn't think you'd like to get the feeling that whenever live Vincents reappeared on the scene, they were accompanying a corpse."

In spite of himself, the corners of Clyde's mouth twitched. He did not attempt any reply.

"So with *maman* magnificently interred, everything began to seem simpler," Armande went on. "The children are both in boarding school now, and French vacations are very short. Pierre and I reached an amicable agreement about those: after this year, Pierrot and Janine will come to the United States for a little while every summer, or I'll go back to France, just as seems best, until Janine's grown up. Meanwhile, I'll look around for a suitable apartment or small house in Paris and when Janine's old enough to go out in society, she can divide her time between my *pied-à-terre* and Monteregard. There haven't been any dramatics at all between Pierre and

myself—in fact, it's only fair to say that he's made no difficulties for me. Of course he never was a fortune hunter—he
has more money than I have and I've got plenty. We'll
appear together whenever it's necessary, and we'll be very
careful to see that nothing is done that could jeopardize a
suitable marriage for either or both of the children. Of course
Pierre wouldn't have been so reasonable if he'd cared about
having me stay with him."

For the first time, her tone was bitter—while she was
talking about her mother it had been merely hard. But very
soon she went on more lightly.

"I think the person who really did the most to make it all
seem easy, though, was Pierre's niece Josephine de Courville.
She and her husband Jehan agreed to disagree long ago. She
made me see how simply it could all be done. Of course the
de Courvilles have only one child—Louise—and that made
things less complicated than if there'd been two, especially
as they've always left Louise at Monteregard a great deal,
and she prefers being there to staying with her grandmother,
the Princesse d'Ambly. That's natural, for she hasn't any
cousins, except Pierrot and Janine, and no brothers and
sisters. She's in boarding school, too, now—at the Sacré
Coeur, in the same class with Janine. They're really inseparable."

"Well, that does seem a logical arrangement all around."

"Yes, doesn't it?"

"Logical, but not especially loving."

Armande rose, adjusting her beautiful white draperies.
"Uncle Clyde, do you know what you are? You're an old
sentimentalist. You like to pretend you're tough and you're
just as softhearted as you can be. Of course I have to admit it's
no wonder—you did have a happy marriage, I mean *really*.
But it's the only one of the kind I've ever seen. You know
perfectly well that Cary's—no, I won't say it. However, let
me tell you something else: you're one of those few who *have*
stood that old-age test I was talking about a while back.
You're the most magnificent old gentleman I ever saw. If I
weren't afraid of running up against something in canon
law I don't know about, I'd set my cap for you. Can you
marry uncles if they're just make-believe uncles? I don't

120

know! There . . . you know I was only joking. But I do love you a lot. Larry, too. Good night, Uncle Clyde."

More and more Armande became a recognized member of their small family group, from both Clyde's viewpoint and Larry's. She agreed, without making any stilted speeches to the effect that of course it was not really her home any more, to spend frequent week-ends at Victoria; and gradually the mansion there, like the one on Elysian Fields, showed the excellent effects of her inhabitance. She went often to Cindy Lou as well, and continued to make Larry and his friends welcome at her town house. When the spring semester ended at Tulane, she told him he must bring them to Victoria instead, and he was glad to do so; for the first time, he also had frequent guests, quite voluntarily, at Cindy Lou. Throughout July the old plantations teemed with young visitors as they had not done in twenty years. Theoretically, Clyde was delighted; but after his long years of seclusion, he found the constant tumult unexpectedly wearing; he longed for solitude and for Larry's unshared company. The servants also showed signs of strain. As Clyde had told Mrs. Vincent, the efforts of Titine and Bassie, for a long while, had been confined to the comparatively easy task of caretaking; and though Armande brought Patsy, Amos and Leonie from New Orleans, there were occasional mutterings about extra washing, late hours and unexpected arrivals. At Cindy Lou, no attempt was made to increase the household staff, but neither Clyde nor Larry heard as many complaints as Armande. Tudie good-naturedly accepted pointers from Leonie about waiting on young ladies, and helped Nappy serve in the dining-room, the drawing-room and the gaming-room; Delphie got through a good deal of chamber work and dusting because none of it was done very thoroughly; and Ivy patiently cooked on and on. However, the results were a far cry from the days when every guest had a body servant, and afternoon tea was a ceremonious occasion in the terraced garden. Fortunately, none of the youngsters who now came to the plantations expected much personal attention or gave so much as a passing thought to afternoon tea. On the other hand, boys and girls were constantly dashing back and forth between the two places, more often in Model T Fords than on horseback nowadays; there were swimming parties in the old barrow pit, excursions up and down the river, shrimp and beer suppers on the *batture*, fish fries in the largest grove, tennis on the lawn; and every night, and many afternoons as well, there was dancing in the ballroom to a gramophone and on special occasions to the music of a Negro band. The multicoloured lights were as brilliant and kaleidoscopic as ever; but they played over dances very different from the polkas and schottisches of former times, and the only waltz in favour was called the 'hesitation,' and was generally danced to a tune entitled 'Mighty Lak a Rose.' More favoured were the one-step and the fox-trot and such intricate, exotic dances as the tango and the maxixe, which only the more experienced and skilful did really well. Armande was a beautiful dancer and a willing exponent of the new steps. Larry and his rapidly increasing 'gang' learned more from her than they ever had from each other, and there was not a boy among them who was not pleased and proud to have her for a partner. But she did not lack partners of her own age, either. Any number of personable men in their late forties and early fifties seemed to be perpetually about; and though they played more bridge than the collegians—who were by no means at a loss when it came to cards, either—they also wedged in considerable dancing. Clyde could not imagine where they all came from, how they happened to have so much leisure and why they still seemed so comparatively young. If Armande had lacked attention as a girl, she certainly had plenty of it now—so much, indeed, that Clyde began to wonder whether her many admirers were under the impression that she was a widow. It was his first encounter with an unattached, middle-aged, married belle and he found it vaguely disquieting. Nobody else seemed to be worrying much about chaperons, for the mothers of the girls who visited assumed that Armande was fulfilling this role; but he pressed Mrs. Surget into more and more constant attendance and made a point of being present in the ballroom himself.

"You ought to be dancing, too, Uncle Clyde," Armande told him one night, as she sank down breathlessly beside him after a lively turn. "You know Rodney Ashe, of course?" she added, almost as an afterthought, as she indicated her partner. "Rodney, do get me some punch. I'm simply parched." And when the dapper, urbane gentleman had gone to do her bidding, she added, "Everyone's doing it now."

"It really looks that way," Clyde answered a little dryly. "Still, at eighty——"

"Why, you don't seem eighty! You could pass for sixty any day. And lots of sixty-year-old men are having the best time they've ever had."

"Maybe, though I doubt it. Be that as it may, if they are, remember they're *really* sixty, not passing for it."

"Not always," Armande answered, nonchalantly. "And not that it matters. Truly, Uncle Clyde, I'd love to dance with you."

"It's very hard to resist such a tempting invitation. But I think I'd better."

"You used to dance, didn't you?"

"Yes. I danced the Viginia reel with my bride, at our wedding. And while we were coming down the river, on our honeymoon, we used to join in a square dance called the 'pawpaw patch'."

"I think that sounds fascinating! Won't you teach it to us? I'll clap for attention and then everyone——"

Hastily, he put up a warning hand and, at the same moment, double deliverance came: Rodney Ashe returned with the punch and the Negro band struck up 'I'm on My Way to Dublin Bay.' Armande, apparently forgetting that she was simply parched, was on her feet just in time to avoid being swung from her seat by her next partner. Clyde noticed that she was not affecting even half mourning any more. She had on a pale green satin dress with a full white lace overskirt and transparent lace sleeves that did not reach halfway to her elbows. It was not cut unduly low, but somehow it seemed to be very revealing; and suddenly Clyde realized that this was because Armande did not have on very much underneath it. He looked around the ballroom, with new clarity of vision, and suspected that the same thing must be true of practically all the girls in the room. Apparently, they did not wear corsets—at least not the kind with which he had been acquainted—any more; there was no sign of rigidity about their clothing; and though this, in itself, was perhaps an improvement, their figures, slim and supple as these were, had lost some of their femininity, for with the larger waists had come smaller breasts and thighs. Possibly it was this very lack of beautiful bosoms and curving hips that made these modern maidens less seductive in his eyes than those of his own time; and doubtless it was just as well that they should be, dancing the way they did, so close to their partners that it would have been hard to get a sheet of paper between them. And as for the costumes in which they went bathing! . . . Yet Larry, as far as his grandfather could tell, was either quite unconscious of this daring lack of discretion—not to say modesty—or quite unmoved by it. Clyde wondered. . . .

Armande's birthday was late in July and, when she spoke of celebrating it at Victoria, Clyde asked her if she would not let him have the pleasure of giving a party at Cindy Lou instead. She seemed to hesitate.

"That's sweet of you, Uncle Clyde, and I do appreciate it. But it won't hurt your feelings, will it, if I say you seem the least bit old-fashioned when it comes to parties? I want this one to be really gay and——"

"We'll have it as gay as you like, Armande. You haven't hurt my feelings. I'll admit I like the old ways better. This seems to me an era of restlessness rather than an age of elegance, and I enjoyed the elegance and the—well, the refinements that went with it. You—you remember my wife?"

"Of course I remember her. She was the loveliest lady I ever knew."

"Yes. Well, of course there never could be anyone like her again. But somehow I didn't suppose——"

"That the change would be so much for the worse? Perhaps we aren't as different, inside, as you think. Perhaps the change is just in our figures and in our habits." Armande laughed and Clyde smiled, indulgently if not altogether approvingly. "And perhaps there'll be another change, later on, for the better," Armande continued. "Anyhow——"

"Anyhow, I hope you'll let me give you that birthday party. We'll have a band up from New Orleans, gin as well as champagne, plenty of places for sitting out. Whatever you say."

"All right, Uncle Clyde, if you really want to. Because you *are* sweet, you know."

If he could have passed for sixty, in her opinion, she could easily have passed for thirty, in his. And obviously he was not the only man who felt that way about it. He was sure that several, Rodney Ashe among them, were seriously smitten, and that a number of others were dangerously close to it. Clyde had made inquiries about Ashe; it seemed that he was very well thought of, besides being very well off; he was a banker, of Carolinian extraction, who had made quite a place for himself in Louisiana. Clyde felt sure that Ashe must have made inquiries, too, that he must be aware Armande was not a widow. But his conduct was certainly that of a declared suitor and there was nothing in Armande's attitude to give the impression that she was trying to discourage him. He was a constant and obviously a welcome visitor at Victoria. . . .

The birthday celebration was gay enough to fulfil Armande's fondest hopes. It was primarily her party and though Larry, of course, was present, Clyde had suggested that on this occasion his aunt's friends, rather than his, should be their guests; and Larry had said sure, that was all right by him, he could have his gang any other time. Clyde was a little sorry, at the last moment, that he had never done that 'fancying up' at Cindy Lou, which he had had in mind when Larry and he decided to have the barge line instead. But after all, as he had reflected before, the worn places on the upholstery and the faded streaks in the draperies did not show up much at night; and he doubted whether the assembled company was much interested in upholstery and draperies anyway. There was dancing all night, to the jazz music of a New Orleans band, and there was a great punch bowl whose well-spiked contents were frequently renewed. Armande wore a turquoise chiffon dress, beaded in gold, with a wide gold belt, a matching band of gold around her black hair and long pendant earrings. She was still as fresh and as gay, when she came to say good-bye to Clyde at four in the morning, as she had been when she arrived at eight the evening before; and as she went down the grand staircase he could hear her laughing and jesting with Rodney Ashe. . . .

The next time he saw her she came into his office with a blanched face and asked him if he had read the paper that day.

"No, not yet," he answered. "I'll have to confess I've been

feeling a little tired since that party of yours, so I've been taking things easy. I've spent most of the day rereading some of the letters Cary wrote her mother and me while she was on her honeymoon. I want Larry to read them, too. I want him to go to the same places that she did, because I believe that's what Cary would have wanted. Even—even to Monteregard. Since you say there isn't any strain between you and Pierre, perhaps you'll renew the invitation you gave the boy the last time you were here. Sit down, Armande, and have a julep with me. It's a warm day."

"You read about the murder of that archduke in Servia, didn't you? Before, I mean? You knew about that?"

"Yes, but that was just another of those Balkan outbreaks. There was one two years ago. Those people actually seem to enjoy killing each other."

"Uncle Clyde, you don't seem to realize what I'm trying to tell you. France is at war—at war with Germany. I've got to go back—I've got to get home as fast as I can."

Neither of them noticed that this time she had spoken of France as 'home.' Clyde struggled to his feet—it was harder and harder for him all the time to rise from his chair—and tried to speak comfortingly and reassuringly. But words of fright and horror came tumbling from Armande's lips and she did not even listen to him.

"Pierre's in the reserves, he'll be called out immediately. After all, he is my husband, after all, I do love him. I always have, even though I've tried to pretend that I didn't. I wouldn't have left him if I hadn't known he didn't care whether I stayed with him or not, that he never had, really. Pierrot's only seventeen, he won't have to go to war right away, but they'll be after him presently and meanwhile I don't know where he is, whether he'll be safe. Janine, either. If there were a siege of Paris, like the one in the last war with Germany, if there are battles like Sedan . . . Uncle Clyde, you will help me to get home right away, won't you?"

Larry and Clyde both went to New York with her, because the ships that went from there were faster than the ones that went from New Orleans. She had no difficulty in getting immediate passage—most people were hurrying west, not east,

126

across the Atlantic in those days. Larry and Clyde saw her comfortably settled in an excellent *cabine de luxe* on a Cunarder, the *Lusitania*, that stopped at Havre, and told her they were sure there was no reason why she should worry: everyone said the war would be over in three months: Pierre and Pierrot and Janine and all the rest of the family would certainly be quite safe in the meantime.

Like most of their fellow Americans, Clyde and Larry proved very poor prophets. Gilles de Lorne was killed in the first Battle of the Marne and his wife Isabelle, in Paris, when a shell struck the Church of St. Gervais, where she had gone to pray for the repose of his soul. Jehan de Courville was sent on a military mission to Washington, and on his return journey to France his ship was torpedoed. His widow Josephine, far from being inconsolable, promptly married a cabinet minister, with whom she had for some time been on admittedly intimate terms. Pierre de Chanet was slightly wounded and his son Pierrot severely wounded at Ypres; though the boy made the better physical recovery of the two, he suffered so acutely from shell shock that he was confined, for months, to a base hospital in Brittany before he could return to the front. Armande visited him as often as she was permitted to do so and, meanwhile, carried the full responsibility for the maintenance of Monteregard, the welfare of the women and children on the estate and in the neighbouring village, and the supervision of her daughter Janine and her niece Louise— for the cabinet minister had made it quite clear that he did not care to be encumbered with a stepdaughter. Pierre's mother had remained in her Paris apartment; apparently she was not suffering any hardships or deprivations, but neither was she mitigating those of anyone else. The two girls were helping Armande as best they could. Of course their education had been interrupted and they were having no diversions. The young men whom they would have normally been seeing by this time were all at the front, if they had not already been killed. And, something less than three years after Armande's return to France, Larry came into his grandfather's office, late one April afternoon, and told Clyde he had just heard the United States had entered the war and that he was about to start off to enlist.

CHAPTER NINE

He had come home the day before for his Easter vacation and, as this was Good Friday, he had gone to church in Convent. After the services were over, he had stopped in at the Valley station to see if the new bearing for a water pump, which had been delayed in transit, had finally arrived, and the telegrapher had given him the news as it was ticked off the wire.

"De kaiser, dat species of h'animal, him, he goin' find out, yes, he made a bad mis-take when he ain' satisfy, no, he already fight de Fr-r-r-ranch an' de h'English, he got to fight us, too, him, yes," the operator had sputtered in conclusion.

"And of course that means I'm going right back down to New Orleans to enlist," Larry added, in repeating this to his grandfather. "Some of the fellows have already gone in, you know, with the Canadians, and even one of the professors has been driving an ambulance."

Clyde nodded in apparent agreement. The proverbial Easter cold snap had come, and he was settled in his armchair before the fire, a cheering glass in his hand and a pile of old letters beside him.

"Of course you're going to enlist, Larry," he said. "You wouldn't be much of a man if you didn't do your duty. But it doesn't make sense to rush off blindly. I . . . I know what I'm talking about. Let's find out first of all where you're needed most."

"Now look, Dad, if you're going to tell me how important it is to raise crops and how I'm more needed at home, it won't go. I'm not a jelly bean, hanging around drugstore corners. I'm a man, and the Army needs men."

"That's right. But look at it this way. War is a disaster, like a levee break or a steamboat wreck. If the levee breaks and everybody who wants to help rushes off to do the same thing, nobody's going to accomplish anything. If a steamboat hits a snag and everybody rushes to the rail or to the lifeboats, the result is panic. Somebody has to direct the efforts to make them effective. You know that. All I want you to do is wait until we hear what our leaders in Washington want."

"But we know they are going to want men."

"But we don't know where. For instance, you spoke of the Army. But maybe men are needed more in the Navy right now. Our first job is going to be to get an army across the seas and to supply them after they get there. We're going to have to feed half the world, too. And all the sugar that is being raised everywhere—here, Cuba, the Philippines—everywhere, isn't going to be enough. It's too late for this year's crop, but by next year we ought to turn a lot of the tobacco fields into cane—it's going to be a lot easier to do without perique than without sugar. That's the sort of thing I mean. All I'm asking you to do is wait, before you join up. Wait to see what Washington wants. A few weeks won't matter. And by that time you'll have your degree."

"What's a degree but an insignificant old piece of parchment?"

"It isn't insignificant. It's a visible and tangible proof of what you've been and done before you could get that piece of parchment. I never got one—because I'd never been or done any of those things. Do you remember my telling you once that I'd hoped I'd rule—well, a sort of empire some day? And that I couldn't, because I didn't have what it takes to do that? But I got it ready for you to rule and you will have what it takes by the time you're a little older, if you keep on the way you're going."

Larry, who had been standing by the hearth, kicking at a log which had fallen forward, turned just as his grandfather attempted to rise. The effort was obviously even greater than it had been at Christmastime. Then he had made only one false start, supporting himself meanwhile on the arms of his chair. Now he made two. But Larry knew he did not want any help, that it hurt his pride to acknowledge his increasing stiffness and lameness. He finally struggled to his feet and put his hand on the boy's shoulder.

"I don't often bargain with you, Larry, but I want to this time," he said. "If Washington hasn't spoken by the time you graduate, and you still feel the way you do now, I'll say go ahead and enlist. I really think, though, that this is a case when you should follow the leader—not in any game, either."

Washington spoke, unmistakably, the following month, with the passage of the Selective Draft. However, Larry did not bring up the question of enlistment again until he was safely in possession of the 'insignificant piece of parchment.' But on their first evening at Cindy Lou, after the commencement exercises, Larry handed the rolled degree to his grandfather, saluted solemnly and then stood before him, grinning.

"All right, all right," Clyde said, grinning also and laying the degree carefully on the desk beside him. Then he opened a drawer of his desk and took a cigar box from it. "Go tell Nappy to bring us some coffee, will you, Larry?" he asked. "We might as well be comfortable while we talk."

"But there isn't anything to talk about this time. You said——"

"I know what I said, and I always aim to keep my promises. If you want to enlist now, I'm not going to try and stop you, like I did before. I can see how you'd feel a lot better if you did, instead of waiting until you're called, in the fall, after you're twenty-one. But I do want to have one more talk with you. So, as I said, if you'll just go and tell Nappy to bring that coffee——"

Rather abruptly, Larry left the office. It was easy to see that he was closer to being angry with his grandfather than ever before in his life. But Clyde watched his departure imperturbably. When he returned to the office the old man's cigar was burning evenly, and he was leaning back in the swivel chair whose arms, long since denuded of varnish, had been worn smooth through constant use during many years.

"I want to ask you what you think about enlarging the kitchen garden," he said, puffing comfortably. "Food is going to be mighty important, with sugar and flour rationed already, and we could raise a lot of cabbages on a small piece of our cleared black land."

"Food may be important, but I still can't see what cabbages have got to do with winning the war," Larry said, almost sulkily.

"Cabbages are only a starter. I'm saying that, because what isn't eaten can be brined into sauerkraut and provide food all through the winter. Up north they can have root cellars for potatoes and beets and such. We can't. Our winters aren't cold enough. . . . Well, here's the coffee."

For a few moments they sipped the fragrant beverage in silence. Then Larry looked up.

"I suppose that after cabbages are harvested, the same rows could be planted to sweet potato slips, Dad," he said hesitantly. "And there's certainly no better eating for man or beast than yams. I don't need to tell you that the vines make prime hay for the mules and the milch cows, and we could turn a couple of shoats into the field to glean the roots that aren't big enough to stack away."

"That's sound thinking." Clyde put down his cup and took up the cigar he had momentarily laid aside. "Larry, ever stop to think that I'm eighty-three years old—be eighty-four this coming winter if I make it?"

"Shucks, Dad, that's only on the calendar! You're the youngest man on the place for real. Everybody knows that. Old Dumaine was saying only yesterday you'd walked his legs down to a nub and weren't even drawing a long breath, when he was looking for a hole to fall into."

"Granted that I've still got the use of myself, eighty-three is old bones and we all know it. Ordinarily, when a young man goes off to war the question is whether he'll live to come back. But when you go off. . . . Well, after all, we don't know how long this man's war is going to last, do we? We made a pretty big mistake about that once before when we were seeing your aunt off on the *Lusitania*. So the question this time is whether I'll be here until you come back. I once made up my mind I'd be bound to live till you were old enough to fend for yourself. I've done that, now. But whether I live or don't live until you come back from the war, I can't carry the whole load of the two plantations any more."

"I should say not, Dad. And nobody expects it of you. Not that you aren't still worth more than any three of the rest of us. You certainly are. But there's plenty of help on the place for you now."

"Plenty of help to do the things I say I want done, yes," agreed Clyde. "But not to do the saying—and the thinking. That's what you've been doing. Maybe you don't realize it, but you practically ran the plantations all through your last summer's vacation. A body doesn't have to draw a whole blueprint for you. Just a suggestion here and there, and you don't actually need even that. Like when I talked about the cabbages: you were right there with the sweet potato project that made the whole deal worth its salt. And there's nobody else here could do that."

"Septime would have been a whip, if he'd only stayed."

"Maybe yes, maybe no," Clyde answered with continued imperturbability. He did not fail to catch the note of envy in Larry's tone. Septime Prudhomme, the swarthy strapping young Cajun who had formerly been the overseer at Cindy Lou, had hastened to become a marine at the first opportunity, and he, Larry Vincent, was still on Cindy Lou Plantation. Dumaine, the paunchy, middle-aged incumbent of the same position at Victoria, did not hesitate to say that he doubted whether this action had been prompted wholly by patriotism; there was a girl Septime had been going with, who was threatening to make trouble for him, and he was tired of her. But after all, Dumaine had been obliged to take over many of Septime's duties, so under the circumstances, allowances were made for his caustic remarks. Clyde answered Larry from still another viewpoint.

"Of course, Septime was a college man," Clyde went on, "studied agronomy or whatever at L. S. U., and he was a good first mate. I don't know how he'd have made out as pilot or captain, and I don't need to tell you we need someone who knows the river as well as the plantations."

This was still another phase of the situation, and one which they had failed to discuss in their previous conversation on the subject of enlistment, but which Larry was bound to recognize as extremely important. An organization known as the Commercial Solvents Corporation had been formed, not long after the outbreak of the war in Europe, to utilize molasses, as well as grain, for the basic fermentation in the manufacture of acetone. Both Louisiana molasses and West Indian molasses were pressed into service and were now being used for the manufacture of munitions by some factories near the upper reaches of the Mississippi River in Illinois. The West Indian molasses was brought by ocean vessels to New Orleans and there pumped into barges—the barges belonging to the new C. & L. Navigation Company among these—to be taken upstream to these munition plants, along with the

Louisiana molasses. Far from hurting the river, the war was helping to bring it back to its day of glory as a trade artery; and what was even more important, in the light of the present discussion, was the fact that the barges were making a mighty contribution to the war effort.

"However, Captain Bourgeois can help on all that," Clyde went on, as he saw that Larry was pondering the last remark. "Matter of fact, he can run that part of the show now. And Dumaine's son Georges can learn enough to give me the rest of the assistance I'll need, even if he is only seventeen, provided you'll stick around this summer and train him. They won't call you until you're twenty-one and that'll be in October. We'll be grinding by then or soon thereafter, and Old Man Dumaine, with Tregre to superintend the sugarhouse, can take over. I won't say you won't be missed . . . but you could be spared. So it's up to you. I won't say one more word to stop you if, after what I've just explained, you decide to go ahead and volunteer anyhow."

Larry cleared his throat. "You're right—and it wouldn't be the first time or the last, Dad," he conceded. "Of course I do want to go charging off to New Orleans and tell the recruiting officer, 'Hey, give me a gun and a bayonet, so I can kill us a few Huns.' But we'll let the Kaiser and Hindenburg draw a breath of relief by sending them word that Larry Vincent isn't going to join up until October."

It was long before daybreak, on a chill November morning, that Larry reported at the Convent Courthouse for induction, having duly registered two months earlier and subsequently been passed as 'sound as a nut and twice as strong' by Dr. Doussan, who acted as medical examiner for the draft board.

About twenty other registrants from St. James's Parish reported at the same time to Sheriff Dornier, the chairman of the local draft board, and Larry knew several of them—in fact two, besides Blaise Bergeron, had been his schoolmates at Jefferson. One of these was Tracy Dixon, a tall, blond and rather vague young man, whose father was an official in the offices of the Colonial Sugar Refinery at Gramercy; the other was Henri Laburre, an automobile repairman in a garage at Lutcher. Tracy had stayed at Jefferson for the college course, and had received his bachelor's degree the previous June, having completed a number of courses in both moral and natural philosophy. Henri, short, stocky and already wearing a heavy moustache to make himself look older, had been obliged to drop out of his class when his father, a sawmill foreman, had been killed in a mill accident. Henri had been working ever since to help keep a large family intact. His mother was doing needlework and an older brother was clerking in a store. Always passionately fond of mechanical things and a wizard at bringing cars back to operational status, Henri hoped to own a big garage of his own, one of these days, and was already fishing around for a sales agency. Larry knew that he was not too happy about being drafted; on the other hand, he knew it never would have occurred to Henri to ask for a deferment or to declare himself a conscientious objector. . . .

Larry was also acquainted with Tony Mangiarino, a sleek-haired, good-looking chap who was very much the ladies' man and who had been captain of the Lutcher High School football team. His father was a very successful truck farmer, who sent his cabbages, cauliflowers, spring onions and other vegetables in season to the French Market in New Orleans, and who was now branching out into what was fast becoming a very important agricultural development in the Florida parishes—strawberries. Tony was one of nine brothers and sisters; but in spite of the demands inevitably made by such a clan on its principal provider, the boy appeared for draft induction wearing an expensively tailored suit, and was driven up to the courthouse by his father in a shiny, seven-passenger touring car. With Tony was Fletcher Trumbull, the English teacher at the Lutcher High School—a small, spindle-shanked man in his later twenties, who wore pince-nez glasses hooked to a loop of gold wire by a fine gold chain. He was the only one of the group who appeared to be frightened—not bewildered, but really terrified; as he raised his right hand to take the oath, it trembled, and his voice broke at several points in repeating the words: "I, Fletcher Trumbull, do solemnly swear that I will bear true faith and allegiance to the United States of America; that I will serve them honestly and faithfully against all their enemies whomsoever; and that I will obey the orders of the President of the United States and the orders of the officers appointed over me, according to the Rules and Articles of War." When his arm dropped to his side again, the signet ring which he wore— and which was too loose—slipped from his finger and fell, clattering, to the floor; as he stooped to pick it up, he trembled all over.

The next man to approach Sheriff Dornier did not act as if he were frightened, exactly, but it was obvious that he was bewildered, and it presently transpired that this was because he did not understand or speak English, and that therefore the sheriff would be obliged to repeat the oath of allegiance in French for his benefit. He was short of stature, with brown eyes, red hair and a freckled nose. Larry, who had never seen him before, set him down as a farm boy from one of the brûlées back of Vacherie, where his forebears had probably burned off a section of the woodland to clear it for planting. He had a singularly pleasant face, and Larry took an instant liking to him; somehow he got across the notion that in spite of his ignorance he was willing and intelligent, and that he would be glad to do whatever was expected of him whether or not he understood, at first, what it was all about. After him came another non-English-speaking chap from the back country—a sullen-eyed, unkempt, jeans-clad swamp man. There was also a gap-toothed, whiskery specimen, who might have been a shrimp fisherman during the season, and who seemed to be very dim mentally. He was powerfully built and walked as if his shoes bothered him, which Larry thought they probably did. The last of the individuals before the sheriff was so undistinguished looking that he would have been passed over in almost any crowd, except for the cannon ball shape of his head and his large protruding ears. Larry could not seem to identify him with any special trade or locality. . . .

When the oath had been administered to all the men reporting for induction, Sheriff Dornier led them in a straggling walk, which did not even remotely resemble a march, from the courthouse to the little railroad station. It was almost time for the arrival of the Gulf Coast train, which had left Houston the night before and which used the Valley tracks into New Orleans.

"Just remember, all of you," the sheriff said as they walked along, "you're in the Army now, as much as you'll ever be. We're starting you off on your way to Beauregard by yourselves. But if you strike out on your own in New Orleans, you won't be just strays—you'll be deserters. Now, as soon as we get to the station, I'll call the roll once more and give each of you his own ticket."

When the tickets had been duly distributed, the men drifted apart. Rather forlornly, those whose kinfolk had not been able to accompany them to the station, like the sullen-eyed swamp man and the red-headed farm boy, clotted into a special group of their own. Tony was soon the centre of a family circle which ranged from a worshipping small brother and a beautiful dark-eyed sister to his father, who was obviously torn between pride over this fine man-child of his and pain over the impending separation. Henri's mother was trying desperately hard not to cry, but she clutched a damp handkerchief in her needle-pricked fingers, and every now and then she blew her nose and dabbed at her eyes. The lump in Larry's throat grew bigger every time he glanced at her. He slipped his arm through his grandfather's, drawing the old man as far as possible away from the others.

"There's a lot I'd like to say, Dad, but somehow it won't come out," he began, in a low voice.

"Forget it," Clyde answered abruptly. He was standing very erect, with his head held high and his shoulders thrown back. "If we had to put everything we want to tell each other into words, we'd be wasting a lot of good time."

"I know. But somehow I'd like to say it. I mean about my not having any father or mother, and yet having so much more than any of the boys I know that did have fathers and mothers. I mean you've been more to me, you mean more to me, I mean . . ."

"Look here, Larry," Clyde interrupted, "you're a man, going off to war, and I'm a tough old he-coon that's too mean to die when his time comes. So let's act like it—if we can."

"You a tough old he-coon!" Larry scoffed. "You're an old fraud, that's what you are. But you're something else, too—you're everything my grandmother and my mother thought you were and we both know what that was. Now you've got to promise me you'll take care of yourself, you hear? None of this getting up to ride the crops in the chill of the early morning and staying until all hours in that office. You've got plenty of men to do the leg work now. Isn't that why I stayed home all summer? To see that you would have? You take it easy."

"Say, which one of us is going out to get shot at? You're the one that's running into danger. And don't you go taking any reckless chances. I'll do my best to hang on until you get back, but all I want in this living world is to hand the whole shebang over to you to run and to worry with, while I sit on my scrawny old hind-end and look at the river and our barges on it. So don't you be too long winning this war. And if you need anything, you let me know. By the way, here's some money I forgot to give you before we left the house."

He pressed some bills into Larry's hand and the boy took them mechanically. Then, as he glanced down at the sizable sheaf, he said hurriedly, "Thanks, Dad. Thanks a lot. But you shouldn't have. My new boss pays off regularly and feeds me, doctors me, clothes me, teaches me—does all the things you did for me. I'll just keep this to buy you a nice present in Berlin."

"That'll be fine, if you can spare the time from the beer gardens. Meanwhile . . ."

A headlight winked at them out of the morning fog, far down the tracks, and a mournful, yet curiously impatient, whistle was borne faintly across the distance. The Mangiarino tribe began to swarm around Tony, almost overwhelming him. Henri's mother flung her arms around his neck, sobbing unrestrainedly now, and he hugged her in return, while some of the other men, who had been accompanied by girls, clasped them in long-drawn-out embraces. Larry swallowed hard, but managed to grin at his grandfather as he held out his hand, gripping the other's bony fingers in his own and striving not to let the sudden realization of their shrunken flesh show in his expression.

"No matter what happens, Dad, I'll always love you better than anyone else in the world," he said chokingly. Then he turned and swung aboard the steps of the day coach. One at a time, the others were hustled aboard. Some of them were encumbered with musical instruments—guitars and banjos, even, in one case, an accordion; some were carrying paper parcels containing clothing which they did not realize they would have to send back as soon as they were outfitted. A few had old satchels and only Tony a handsome new suitcase. The coat of a very young-looking boy had a strange bulge to it and muffled sounds came from within it. When they had all gone up the steps, a flagman waved his lantern and the train chuffed into motion. A grey smudge was beginning to show along the eastern horizon, but the area beyond the lighted platform was still dark and into this darkness Clyde strode steadily. It did not matter now that his shoulders were no longer thrown back and his head was no longer held high. He was thankful to think that Nuffy would be waiting for him at Cindy Lou.

CHAPTER TEN

"MORNING—especially this early in the morning—is one hell of a time to be getting to a place like New Orleans!" It was Tony Mangiarino speaking. "The way I hear it, they'll grab us off right at the damn station and hustle us right to the damn barracks."

"You shoulda been like we were, Blackie," gibed one of the group that had been put aboard the train at Baton Rouge. "We gave the gals a good time last night. I mean a *good* time. I don' know have I got enough man left in me to pass no army test."

"Aw, hell, you don't get no tests till they send you to Beauregard or Houston or wherever they ship us. By that time we got enough food and stuff so your manhood don't have to worry you none—if you really had the manhood to start with."

"Don't you worry none about my manhood, or we can take it from there any place or any time or just as far as you want."

"Aw, save that for the Krauts, and for Christ's sake, shut up. I want to sleep."

In the rear of the coach a group began to sing:

"You're in the Army now,
You're not behind the plough,
You'll never get rich, you son of a bitch,
You're in the Army now."

Larry wondered what it would be like. The L. S. U. boys would know, of course. They had a cadet corps there. It had been fun to kid the L. S. U. 'dogs' about their hayfoot, strawfoot chores and their uniforms, but most of them would be made officers straight off. Like Septime Prudhomme, the erstwhile overseer at Cindy Lou, who had enlisted in the Marines to get away from a girl and was a second lieutenant already. How did anyone who had no military training at all go about becoming an officer? Left to himself, Larry would have applied for the first officer training school at Fort Logan H. Root in Arkansas, as some of the other Tulane boys had done. But he had promised his grandfather to wait until he was drafted, and now it was too late; now he would have to peel potatoes and clean latrines—well, there were worse things. At least he'd be doing a job in the Army.

". . . and so she gives me the eye. Well, she was wearing those plaid stockings and I said . . ."

Larry had been shoved into the same red plush seat as the man with the protruding ears and the head shaped like a cannon ball, whom he had not previously been able to identify. This fellow draftee now volunteered enlightenment: his name was Jules Robinaux and he was a refinery worker from Baton Rouge, whose family home was on the river road near Paulina, where his people had always raised perique. But the bigger wages offered by the refinery had lured him away and he hated the idea of exchanging these for thirty bucks a month. He had been saving up to get married. . . . The whiskery specimen, who was in the seat behind and who had leaned forward and listened with interest to this information, now volunteered some of his own: he had been dragged back from Manila Village in Barataria Bay, where he had stayed hoping to escape the draft; but the authorities had found out where he was and had sent a deputy to bring him back to St. James. According to his story, he had accompanied this official with-

139

out protest, his attitude having apparently been that you couldn't blame a guy for trying, and that being a member of Santo Bajo's seine crew was a helluva lot better than being in the Army. Besides, you could get rousing drunk at Myrtle Grove, when you had the money. However, as long as they had sent to get him, okay, let them tell him what to do next. . . .

The group in the rear of the coach was singing again:

> "It's a long way to Tipperary,
> It's a long way to go.
> It's a long way to Tipperary,
> And the sweetest girl I know.
> Good-bye Piccadilly, farewell Leicester Square,
> It's a long, long way to Tipperary,
> But my heart's right there."

The train jolted over the interlock at Kenner, went past a vegetable packing shed and so on to its stop at Carrollton. The bright sun was throwing long shadows to the west as the cars rumbled through a slum section of littered tenements and stopped with a jerk in a grimed, red brick station where a sergeant with an outjutting chin and rakishly tilted hat was waiting at the steps of the coach and snapping, "All you snot-nosed draftees over there by that post." Behind Larry there was a murmur of resentment.

"Who does that mother-lover think he is? Take that uniform off him and I'd goddam well show him whose nose needs wiping and I don't mean maybe, either." But the murmur was discreetly low and the draftees obediently headed toward the designated post, while the other passengers —the ones Larry suddenly realized were merely civilians— filed down the platform with their baggage. When they were gone, the sergeant held up his hand for attention.

"Now get me, guys," he said sharply. "Some of you may have been big shots in your home town. You may have been used to telling other people what to do. But you're in the Army now, and the first thing you learn is to do what *you're* told. There's trucks waiting outside. We're going in them to the barracks."

"Hey, when do we eat?" asked a taunting voice from an unidentifiable source in the crowd.

"I'll answer that this once. You eat as soon as you get to the barracks."

"Eat hell, when do we drink?" called another voice, but less loudly, as though the owner were anxious not to be identified by the eyes of authority. General laughter followed. They had emerged on Rampart Street, and across the way were many saloons and package houses, quite a few of the latter frankly announcing that they would send liquor into dry Mississippi, or other dry territory, for a reasonable fee.

"Say, is this the Rampart Street I been hearing so much about?" inquired the refinery worker. "Those don't look like no whore houses to me."

"Hell, no. This is Rampart Street all right, but it's South Rampart. The district is all on the far side of Canal Street." Tony Mangiarino, the cosmopolite, was explaining. "Anyway, what the hell do you care? Who'd want to go there this time of morning?"

"Any time's a good time if you got your nature," chuckled one of the waiting group.

"All right, all right, button them lips," the sergeant shouted. "Listen to me now. When I tap you, climb into them trucks and don't drag it. You're in the Army now."

"You mean we got to stand up in them things?" inquired the young-looking boy with the bulging coat, as the first of three olive-drab trucks wheeled up the cobbled esplanade in front of the station.

"Yes, you'll stand up in them things," replied the sergeant in a mincing falsetto. "You'll stand on your head if I tell you to, and you'll . . . Say, what the hell you got under your coat?"

"N-n-nothing, sir. I got nothing——" stammered the luckless youngster.

"Nothing my behind!" The sergeant yanked the lapels back. "Well—I'll—be—a monkey's—uncle!" he exclaimed, grinning, as a nondescript, bright-eyed mongrel puppy was brought to view, cowering trustfully back toward its master's armpit. "What the hell you scared of, anyway?" The sergeant woolled the puppy's ears. "Get in that truck, now, before I boot you into it," he added goodnaturedly.

The truck ride was uncomfortable as they rumbled along

St. Claude Street towards the river front, and into the shelled driveway of Jackson Barracks. There they passed the armed sentries at the entrance and drew up before a long wooden building in whose shadowy interior breakfast was spread on long tables flanked by benches.

"Go ahead. Climb out of those trucks and eat," came the next order, "but stay put until you're through."

Breakfast was plentiful and surprisingly well cooked. There were platters of ham and of fried eggs, bowls of grits, mugs of coffee, all the butter and spread anyone wanted to eat. "Say, this isn't bad," commented one of the rooks. "I can go for this chow any time, me."

"Better not hit the Java too hard though," advised the man who had said it did not matter to him what time they reached New Orleans. "They tell me it's got saltpetre in it. They put it in to take away some of your nature, else maybe you'd go over the hill after you were in camp awhile."

"Aw, that sounds like a lot of crap to me. Don't you ever think about nothin' except your nature?"

"It ain't too bad to think about and I'm only tellin' you what they say. Me, it'd take more than a little saltpetre to take my mind off what I got my . . ."

"All right, everybody out and line up, now," barked a voice from the doorway. "Come on, you rooks."

This order was preparatory to a march which took the men to a distant area where they were told to walk around picking up all cigarette butts, all matches, fragments of fallen leaves or anything else in the way of trash. After having been kept thus occupied until dinnertime, they were herded to the mess hall once more for a meal of roast lamb, green peas, mashed potatoes and coffee, brought to them by mess attendants as they sat at the tables, commenting on the general situation.

"I thought you had to hustle your own chow . . . this isn't bad at all. I'm beginning to like this man's army if they got people to wait on you. . . ." "Well, I d'know, a man couldn't work on that much food, you got to have more in you than that to do a day's chopping in the woods. . . ." "D'you reckon we could be let go to town tonight? I been hearing about those cabbyrays, all my life I been hearing about the . . ." "No dice, boy. Tonight they ship us off to Beauregard. . . ." "Aw, how the hell would you know? . . ." "Okay, boy, okay, you wait and see."

Surprisingly enough, the prophet proved right. After an early supper the recruits were once more put aboard a train— a troop train, this time; and while they waited in the station, elderly, buxom ladies, in Red Cross garb, passed apples, cigarettes and chocolate bars in through the car windows. Larry found himself beside the youngster who still had his nondescript puppy with him, and who did not want to reach out of the windows, so he passed his share of gifts to the boy. He wondered, as he did so, whether any women who were young and slender and pretty ever came to troop trains in Red Cross uniforms. He could visualize the possibility that some might look rather fetching in such a garb. . . .

An impromptu quartette, with a couple of banjos and a guitar as accompaniment, had been organized and was bearing down heavily on the harmony of 'There Are Smiles That Make Us Happy' and 'There's a Long, Long Trail A-winding.' This quartette was soon augmented into something like a glee club, with almost everyone joining in the chorus. Larry did not take part; he was thinking about his grandfather, as the train moved on through the night, and when it lurched thunderously over the Blind River Bridge, he realized that they were passing behind Cindy Lou, and that Nuffy would be howling.

The train stopped at Baton Rouge in a sparsely settled section of the city, then headed toward the ferry on which it was carried across the Mississippi, to the accompaniment of switchmen's dancing lanterns and the hoarse blaring of steamboat whistles. The songs in the car had stopped. At the forward end, a dice game was in progress; at the rear, a huddled group of men told an endless succession of droll tales, which they punctuated by loud guffaws. Larry joined in neither the game nor the stories; and somewhere beyond Morganza he dozed off, not to wake again until almost daybreak, when he was roused by the jolting of the cars as they were switched back and forth in the Alexandria yards for the transfer to the seven-mile spur ending at Camp Beauregard.

The sun was just rising when the train stopped for good and bellowed commands to "Tumble out there! Get the lead out, you're in the Army now!" summoned the men from the coaches. Outside, they were lined up in four rows, one behind the other, where they stood shuffling their feet and feeling self-conscious, even among themselves. A truckload of men, wearing blue denim fatigue suits and equipped with shovels, rumbled by and began to jeer, "Lookit the *ears* on 'em! Lookit the *ears* on 'em!" Meanwhile a sergeant—a tall, wide-shouldered, flat-stomached man with a seamed face—was snarling at the newcomers. His hatbrim looked as stiff as if it had been cut from metal, the sleeves and yoke of his serge shirt were sharply creased and his canvas leggings scrubbed to near whiteness. His voice was a harsh, hoarse rasp.

". . . and while I've seen some lousy rooks in my time, you buckwheats are the sorriest bunch of misfits anybody was ever expected to make soldiers outa. . . . SHADDAP THAT TALKIN' in the ranks; those guys hollering at you are on a garbage detail because they didn't shaddap when they were told. What the hell do you want to pay attention to bastards like that for?—old hands that have been soldierin', man and boy, for two whole weeks. Now you rooks pay attention to me, or I'll have somebody on the end of a shovel cleaning out a latrine. No use tryin' to learn you anything yet, so just face the same way I'm facing, that'll mean left from the way you are now, if you know your left hand from your right, that is, and follow me."

In a shuffling, awkward column of fours, the men straggled off toward a raw, wooden building, where batteries of clerks sat behind long plank tables. At these, the recruits were enrolled, given papers to carry and passed along to a door at the far end of the building, where they were divided into smaller groups, which were herded off toward different company streets in what Larry soon learned to call 'the casuals'. Eight were assigned to each of the pyramidal tents that lined these streets and were told to deposit their belongings on the steel cots there; then, within a matter of minutes, they were summoned out again, lined up and marched off to one of the supply buildings, where mess kits and canteens were issued to them and instructions given in the use of these. Next, holding a pannikin in one hand and a cup in the other, with knife, fork and spoon clasped against its handle, they filed down the long mess line for breakfast, which was eaten at top speed. As soon as it was over, the men were shown first the huge receptacle into which any food remnants on their pannikins should be scraped, and then the three GI cans of hot water in which they were to wash and rinse their mess kits and herded back to their respective tents, only to be summoned forth almost immediately again and marched to a bare, tunnel-like building. Here they stripped for a searching physical examination, much more brisk and businesslike than the one which old Dr. Doussan had previously given Larry. "Breathe in—all right, let 'er out—pull up your left foot behind you, now the right one. All right—over there!" came the barked commands. Visual and auditory tests followed and after that the quick look at the teeth, the prodding fingers at the groin and the order, "Now cough—all right, bend forward."

Some sort of segregation was obviously in process as the line flowed steadily by—one group for dental treatment, one group with blue tickets, for venereal segregation, one group back toward the starting point. Occasionally a medical officer would growl, "You'd think they wouldn't send us a man with a heart valve like that of an old flivver," or, "If the kaiser could see this line-up, he'd laugh himself to death and the war'd be over." Between the file of recruits and the exit gate toward which they worked their steady way, a group of medical corpsmen stood waiting, apparently in gleeful anticipation, to pounce upon their hapless victims. One of them seized Larry's left arm and scratched two parallel vertical lines on it with a needle before rubbing a glass rod dipped in smallpox vaccine over these; another corpsman seized his right arm, pinched up the skin just below the shoulder, sent a hypodermic needle deftly into the tissue and pressed home the plunger of his syringe.

"Get out there and put your clothes on, Slim," a bored-looking corporal directed. "And make it good, because you won't be putting civvies on any more for a long while."

As Larry complied, he heard the thud of a falling body and turned to see a strapping, muscular figure crumped on the floor and the corporal shaking his head. "Looks like it's always the huskies that faint at the sight of a needle," one of the corpsmen muttered. "Some soldier, believe you me!"

"Isn't anyone going to pick him up?" Larry asked the bored-looking corporal.

"Hell, no! He's all right. And don't hold up the line. Get going, you! You're in the Army now!"

Larry went back to the bench where he had left his clothes and tried to hurry, not very successfully, as he put them on, for his sense of strangeness was developing into a state of general bewilderment. When his detail was reassembled, Larry noted that there were several absentees—the youngster who had played the accordion and the sullen-eyed, loose-lipped man from the marsh country, who spoke no English, were not among the others as they were marched to the Quartermaster's Building, where they filed along the counter and were issued various articles of clothing: cotton socks, long drawers, long-sleeved undershirts, breeches, khaki shirts, a blouse, a hat, a blue corded hatband, a webbing belt, denims, a blue barracks bag and three pairs of shoes, one of them hobnailed. As soon as they were back in their tents the men were told to change, and there Larry saw the accordion player and the sullen-eyed swamp man for the last time. They had been given tickets back to their homes. "Lungs," explained the swarthy little musician to no one in particular. "Ain't that a hell of a note? And I never had no idea. Me— a lunger!" It was not through calloused lack of feeling, but because they could think of nothing to say, that none of his tentmates replied. The swamp man said nothing and no one asked for an explanation.

The men were all in uniform, after a fashion, when the hard-bitten sergeant's whistle called them once more into the dusty company 'street' before their own particular row of pyramidal tents. "All right, men," he barked. "Here's where you're going to be for two weeks, in the casual section, until after you've had your third typhoid shot. Now listen to me: there's an outfit over in the next street that thinks they're something, and they've sent word they got some good boxers. Any of you men know anything about fighting, you come and give me your names after mess.

"Another thing: we ought to have some kind of a company fund, so we can get a few extras for chow, maybe a baseball mitt or a football, stuff that you don't get in this man's army. You'll be doing it when you get into your permanent outfits after you leave here, and you might as well start now if you want to. Say every man puts up about ten cents a day—and you can pick anybody you want to for treasurer. The supply sergeant would be a good guy, because usually he'd know where to get hold of some grapefruit maybe, and things like that—you'd be surprised at how much you can buy when a lot of men put up a thin, slick dime apiece. But anyway . . ."

The sergeant's harangue was interrupted by a tinny crash, as a man, one Larry had not noticed before, fell unconscious to the ground, his mess kit clattering into the dust.

"All right, all right," rasped the sergeant. "Two-three of you guys that are in the same tent with him carry him back and lay him on his bunk. That's only the typhoid shot; it gets some and it don't get others. He'll be as good as new in an hour or two—and the rest of you wipe them goddam smiles off your pans. You're liable to be the next ones to get it, or if you don't get it this time, maybe you will after your second shot, or your third. . . . Now about your bunks, the way they're supposed to be made up . . . and each tent picks one man to get up and light the fire in that Sibley stove in the mornings . . . you can take turns. . . . Fatigue details will be posted. . . ."

At various times in the lecture, other tinny crashes interrupted the talk. But finally the sergeant said, "Now, for Christ's sake, see if you can stand up straight, and see if you can face left, for once, and we'll march off to chow like we were gonna be soldiers some day. . . . Tai-ai-ain-SHUN! Lay-yufft FACE!"

Neither of the first two shots bothered Larry, though he felt a sudden queasiness after the third one and took to his bunk for an hour or so. He was wretchedly homesick, but physically he had never been better in his life; and he adapted himself readily to camp routine, feeling neither resentful nor distressed that all hands were required to 'police the company street' or that he was frequently assigned to the latrine-cleaning detail. He was, however, appalled by the hit-or-miss fit of his uniform and made several visits to a camp tailor before he was reasonably content with the appearance of his blouse; and he occasionally experienced a pang of envy when other men received sheaves of mail and boxes of goodies or other presents. Clyde and Father Le Grand were the only two persons who wrote him regularly, and Mrs. Surget the only one who sent him presents. For the first time, he was dimly conscious of his lack in not having a sweetheart; and this sensation was not assuaged when he heard his tentmates joking about home-knitted articles: socks that did not fit, sweaters with no sleeves and—God help us—pulse warmers. He knew that such gifts, like the fudge that was hard and grainy and the cookies which were broken to pieces by the time they arrived, had been made by someone who cared in a way that no one cared for him; the fact that this was his own fault—for he had continued to maintain an unusually objective and diffident attitude toward the opposite sex, despite numerous golden opportunities to do otherwise—did not help, either. He wished, now that there was nothing he could do about it, that he had not neglected all those golden opportunities.

This vague and intermittent discontent, however, in no way interfered either with the efficiency or the eagerness with which he did everything required of him—and often a good deal more; and his general attitude won grudging praise from the sergeant in charge of his group, when Larry suggested that he might be useful in one of the mule lines of the artillery, because of his long experience with these animals on Cindy Lou and Victoria.

"Now get me, Slim," the sergeant advised him earnestly. "If you really got a yen to be a mule nurse, tell the guys in your new outfit you was a church choir tenor, or a he-milliner or a baker. Then they'll assign you to the farriers. Tell 'em you been working mules all your livelong life and they'll make a typist or a dental assistant outa you."

"But why?"

"I dunno. That's just the Army for you. Take me. I was in since long before the Mexican border business—I made expert rifleman, I been shootin' a gun since I was knee high to a wart hog, so I'm stuck here to teach rooks how to clean a latrine. . . . Say, do you realize that four batches of buckwheats I helped to break in are in France already, or at least England, and I'm still at Beauregard?" His voice rose an octave. " 'Grampaw, tell us about what you did in the great war.' That's what I'll be asked one of these days. And what'll I say? Why, I'll tell 'em how I fit the battle of the Bentley Hotel—I wish I had all the brass hats in Washington here with no holds barred, I'd have every one of them shoved down into it as far as the Adam's apple. . . . In this man's army there ain't but one God-damned safe rule. Keep your mouth shut and your bowels open, and don't never volunteer for nothing."

The day after this conversation Larry was transferred to Company M of the 156th Infantry. Then came four months of rugged training. Gradually, he acquired more equipment: his overseas pack and entrenching tools and the webbing with which to put them about him; his rifle and bayonet; long woollen spiral puttees to supplant the canvas leggings; and finally, an overseas cap in place of the campaign hat, which was saved for special occasions. Each day started with 'monkey drill'—callisthenics, in which the rifle was later used, too. Then came close order drill, first by squads, next by platoons, finally by companies. He had become a corporal by the time they reached the stage of battalion practice marches. Meanwhile, there had been rifle training and endless drills in constructing all sorts of complicated entrenchment systems, with braided willow-withy fascines to hold the parapet and the parados in place, and *boyaux* for machine gun emplacements. Larry's instructors in these manœuvres were a French lieutenant, who demonstrated the use of the machine gun which had been developed from the French cavalry carbine, and a British sergeant-major, who was bayonet instructor and who also trained the recruits in the use of gas masks. Larry enjoyed most of the manœuvres; however, for some reason, bayonet drill irked him. He could not have told clearly why the endless repetition of parry, lunge, thrust and jab became a form of inquisition. But it did; and it was not in the least relieved by the British sergeant-major's exhortation, before sending them against the six-foot cylinder of tightly bound sticks suspended from a cross-frame that represented "the bloody 'Un," to "call 'im a son av a 'ore, call 'im a bleedin' barstid, call 'im wotever the flyming 'ell will make you believe that bundle o' faggots ryped your sister an' stick that gun-knife in 'is guts like you wanted to scoop 'em out o' 'is bleedin' belly."

He would certainly be thankful when he knew he would never have to hear all that again, Larry reflected—by no means for the first time—one afternoon when Company M was marching back from bayonet drill, with the loose, easy stride of toughened muscles and heightened co-ordination. Larry had never felt so well in his life; such a thumping big— he searched for the right word—such a hunk of man. He ate like a horse, slept like a log, rejoiced in the life that surged through all the tissues of his hard young body. If this was a fair sample, and war was hell, Larry decided he would have to lead a much more sinful life to assure himself of a pleasant future!

The column swung around a sharp detour to the left, still in route step, so as to skirt the outer edges of the grenade area, where trainees were learning that a Mills bomb could not be thrown the way a baseball was tossed from player to player. There could be no wrist snap, or the thrower would soon have no further use of a lame arm. A long, circular sweep of the fully extended arm, like that Scottie in the kilts had shown them—that was the trick. Once you got on to it, it came easy. But a few of the men never did quite master the knack; they could not unlearn the ball-tossing technique with which they had grown up in special scorn against the stiff-arm motion 'like a girl throws a ball.'

The boys were using live bombs this afternoon, Larry noted. They were bursting beyond an earthen parapet which shielded the surroundings from flying fragments. Then suddenly there was a frenzied, high-pitched scream, and an explosion from within the trench where the practice squads were stationed. Instinctively, the men of M Company started to break ranks and run to the spot.

"Company, halt!" shouted the lieutenant. "Hold your ranks, there. I'll shoot the man that moves. Sergeant, take a detail of four men and find out what's happened, and whether we can be of assistance."

The sergeant called for "Slim, Whitey, Ted and Sam—on

the double." As Larry sprinted across the ground, ground that thousands upon thousands of heavily shod, marching feet had denuded of its grass, he saw a motor-cycle roaring away from the spot where the bomb had burst. By the time they reached the scene, a siren's wail heralded the approach of an ambulance. But there were few fragments that could be picked up, and none of these were recognizable as parts of an individual.

"It was Captain Foss," explained a frightened-looking corporal. "He was trying to explain the throw to one of the boys, and told him to go ahead and pitch his pineapple. The guy reached back stiff armed, and knocked his hand against the back of the trench and dropped the bomb. The pin pulled out when it fell. Cap. came charging along the trench and knocked the guy a dozen feet away, and then fell on the bomb and rolled himself into a ball over it, like he was trying to hug it right into his belly, and that—that was it. They won't find much of him, but nobody in his outfit got more'n a scratch. That man had guts, believe you me. What a guy. . . ."

The corporal's eyes suddenly widened, tears welled out from them; his face became a weeping grimace as he turned away.

"Come on, you guys," said the sergeant. "Let's get back. There's nothing we can do around here." He clapped the weeping corporal heavily upon the shoulder as he turned away. "Happens to the best of 'em, buddy," he murmured. "Looks like the better they are, the more apt they're to be tagged."

Larry rejoined his company with dragging footsteps. The catastrophe, which had reduced the finest officer at camp to bloody, quivering fragments, had made the boy recognize, with hideous suddenness, that war *was* hell, after all, that soldiering was fraught with peril and that he himself was now a soldier. His present training, sometimes monotonous, sometimes stimulating, was merely a preparation for facing danger, mutilation, agony and sudden death. The realization was terrifically sobering.

Because he was young and healthy, because he worked hard and slept soundly, Larry was able, eventually, to overcome the depression which engulfed him after the tragic death of Captain Foss and to carry on as usual. But he could not help asking himself why, if such catastrophes were inevitable, they must 'happen to the best of them' as the sergeant had said. Everyone at the camp had admired and respected Captain Foss; many of the rookies had referred to him affectionately as 'a regular prince,' and even Nyagolski, the Socialist, who came from the sawmill country near Urania, who used to spit when he talked about the ruling classes, never bitched about Foss. Larry felt a deep compassion for the clumsy trainee who had dropped the bomb. The poor kid must be ready to cut himself a piece of throat—his own. Larry thought that even Father Callahan, who never seemed to feel any load was too hard to handle, might find it a pretty hard job to bring that boy back to normal everyday thinking.

Next to Captain Foss, Father Callahan was the man whom Larry had admired most at camp from the beginning. A wonder, that priest, Larry mused. A real soldier of the Cross. Had his football letter from Notre Dame, built like a wrestler, realized the boys couldn't seem to talk right without cussing some, now and then, could organize a boxing tournament like nobody else could, and yet—Larry had heard it from some of the convalescents—tender as a woman with the boys in the post hospital during that frightful Spanish 'flu siege. And Larry knew something else, too. He had the story from Private Nathan Friedberg himself. Friedberg, an engraver, was a Halstead Street product who had bummed his way down to New Orleans, where he had found work at his trade. He was an artist at cutting likenesses of the St. Louis Cathedral into the bowl of a silver teaspoon, for example, but he was given to boasting about his prowess. Consequently, when an accurate representation of a latrine was found graven in the bowl of some tablespoons at the general's own mess, it didn't take the M.P.s long to find the culprit; nor was it long after that before he was tossed into the guardhouse to ponder upon the vice of defacing government property. But it was Father Callahan who realized that the sentence carried over into the high holy days of the Jewish calendar; and it was his threat to consign some very brassy hats to purgatory, despite the fact that the words were accompanied by a warming Irish grin, that secured for Friedberg a furlough from the clink and thus enabled him to attend Yom Kippur services in the temple at Alexandria.

Larry couldn't think of any other officer, or any other Catholic, for that matter, who would have known about such things, and who would then have acted on the knowledge. Except maybe Frank Waddill, a master sergeant whose name had already gone up for promotion to lieutenant. Frank and Larry had met at Tulane during the course of a warm winter evening when they walked along Walnut Street to the river and sat in a tavern garden, drinking a few goblets of beer, while the mellow peal of ships' bells and the hoot of steam whistles proclaimed the shuttling of ferryboats between New Orleans and Westwego. Frank was specializing in sonar research and was always looking for a listener to whom he could talk about this subject. "An echo bounces back the way a tennis ball does when you toss it against a wall; it bounces back from anything solid. You make a sharp, clicking sound, and if you've got the timing equipment and the detectors that are delicate enough to catch the rebound, you can tell from the elapsed interval how far away the thing is that the sound bounced back from. Like in ships, for instance. Heaving the lead to take soundings at sea used to be a slow job, and not much more accurate than if you'd sent your mother's seamstress down a rope to do it with her tape measure. But you can take an echo sounding in less than a second."

"Yeah?" Larry had inquired, without much enthusiasm.

"Yeah," Frank replied, warning to his theme. "Now it's my idea that if you'd hitch your detector to a pencil of some kind, you could make a continuous record of what the bottom of a river looked like, and think what that would mean in controlling Old Man Mississip' in flood time, all the way from Vicksburg to Port Eads. The way I figure. . . ."

Gradually, Frank had roused Larry's interest and they had become fast friends; it had been more or less of a habit for them to go to the tavern garden to drink beer and talk about sonar research. Then, for a time they had lost touch with each other, without losing any of their mutually friendly feeling. Larry was delighted when he ran into Frank again at Beauregard, though he felt that of course his friend should have been sent to the Navy. Seeing Frank on the dusty parade ground, Larry could imagine just what sort of comments his first hard-bitten sergeant would have made back there in the casuals:

"Like I say, that's the Army for you. He shoulda told them he was a guy who never done a thing in this world outside of make gates ajar funeral pieces with flowers. Then they'd sent him to sea, and everything . . . SHADDUP THAT TALKING back there!" Larry hoped that even after Frank was made an officer, with cordovan puttees and a gold-braid hat cord, they would find ways of having long talkfests some evenings; and Frank eagerly accepted Larry's invitation to visit Cindy Lou after the war and see what might be done about modernizing the sugarhouse operation at Victoria. . . .

In his tentmates, also, Larry found satisfying companionship. Among these was the farm boy from the brulée, who was proving quite as adaptable, willing and intelligent as Larry had expected and whose progress was all the more amazing in view of his original handicaps. The youngster who had smuggled his puppy on to the train from Convent to New Orleans was another tentmate; and the puppy, which had now reached the gangling stage of its growth, far from being kept under cover, had achieved the proud position of company mascot. His presence was a constant reminder of Nuffy, and made Larry doubly homesick for his own dog; but he shared the general pride of the tent in having contributed 'an extra' to camp life. His former fellow student Tracy Dixon was a tentmate, too, but Tracy continued to be vague and self-absorbed. His greatest ambition was to continue his studies along the same lofty lines he had pursued at Jefferson, and he seemed to regard the war as an ill-timed interruption of the cultural pursuits which would eventually lead to the possession of a master's and then a doctor's degree. This attitude kept him aloof from the rather earthy atmosphere created by most of the others.

Toward the end of Larry's training period—he was company supply sergeant by that time—he and other noncoms could leave camp late in the afternoon, almost any day they pleased, as long as they were back in their barracks and had reported in before taps. The first time that Larry availed himself of this privilege, he was accosted by a woman who hailed him as 'Soldier Boy' and announced that she would like to adopt him. She was a female of indeterminate years, with a middle-age spread, and there could be no doubt of either her complete respectability or her excellent intentions. She quickly became voluble on the subject of her home-cooked chicken dinners, the nice, wholesome girls to whom she would be glad to introduce him, and her close connection with the Y.M.C.A. Larry escaped from her grasp as soon as he could, murmuring something about being late for an appointment; and after a second experience of much the same sort, he guiltily gave his would-be benefactress a fictitious name and address and announced to his companions that he was through with Alexandria. It required a good deal of ribbing, on the part of his special cronies, to get him back there a third time. After all, he wasn't such a bad-looking number, they told him—he'd got to expect some pickups; and as long as he didn't go for the other kind, why not see if the nice, wholesome girls wouldn't fill the bill? Larry shrugged off these importunities with a good-natured retort that, even if it did seem to be taking him quite a while to find a girl he wanted, he still preferred to do his own choosing; and eventually his friends prevailed upon him to accompany them again, after he had extracted from them a mock solemn promise that he should never be left unguarded in the future.

Sometimes they left early enough to eat supper at 'the Greek's', a small restaurant just across from City Hall, two blocks after crossing the Red River Bridge into Alexandria proper. At other times, they merely wandered about the streets in groups, or attended a dance at the Elks' Club. Most of the sergeants in Larry's company were older than he, and married; their wives roomed in 'Aleck', and these married noncoms would leave their fellows as soon as they reached the city. The others did not visit any of the tawdry brothels in a group, nor did any of them say to the others, "Well, I'm going down the line tonight." If someone failed to go to Alexandria with them, but met them at the corner of Second and Murray streets in time to join in taking a jitney back to the camp, it was tacitly assumed he had been with a woman. But hardly anyone ever boasted of such excursions, not even by such indirections as a smirking, "Well, it comes high, but it's worth it." There was, however, one curious story which was bandied about more or less freely: a certain schoolteacher, who seemed at first glance to be the personification of primness, had proved amazingly responsive to the advances of one of the earliest trainees, though he had not expected to be taken seriously in making them. When he left Beauregard for Dix, his inamorata had amazed him still further by presenting him with a Testament for a farewell present. The first astonished philanderer had been followed by an equally astonished successor, who had received the same spontaneous welcome and the same farewell present. After that, word had got around, and there had been less and less astonishment. The Testaments were always respectfully preserved. . . .

By the time regulations permitted the outings in Aleck, the men no longer looked much like the nondescripts who had scrambled aboard the trucks at New Orleans station. How long ago was that? Larry asked himself. Four months? Five? Yes, sir, going on five. There was a rumour in every company street that the 156th was about to move out for Camp Dix, and was going from there overseas. And certainly most of the men he knew were receiving furloughs to visit their families. He had been told that his own would begin the next week and could think of nothing but how grand it would seem to be at Cindy Lou with his grandfather again.

The next night he and his first sergeant Pete Spofford and regimental sergeant major Jack O'Bierne of the 114th Engineers went to the Bentley Hotel in Alexandria for dinner. The dining-room was famous both for its service and its cuisine, and Jack O'Bierne was a great buddy of the Irish head waiter's, whom he had known in New Orleans. Whenever a special celebration was about to be staged, any table Jack wanted was reserved for him, and apparently this was all on the house, for no one was ever told how the banquets were paid for.

So the three sergeants went to the ornate main dining-room and feasted on roast turkey and oysters and raspberry parfaits and coffee, and afterward, well fed, well content, they strolled about City Hall Square until it was time to find a jitney for the drive back to Beauregard. "This'll be about the last spread for us," Larry observed, as they jolted along. "The last one on the house or somebody else in Aleck, at least. My leave is next week and after that——"

"I got bad news for you, Slim," interrupted Spofford. "I

didn't want to spoil your good time by telling you before, but now we're headed back to camp you might as well hear the worst."

Fear clutched at Larry's heart. His grandfather . . . but no, they would have told him that before; and yet . . .

"You don't get any furlough, Slim," Spofford went on.

"No furlough?"

"Uh-hu. You ain't going to Dix with the outfit. How you did it, I don't know; in fact, I'll never know how a lunkhead like you could put it over on the brass hats. I got orders for you to go to Camp Merritt in New Jersey, as a cadet for officer training. But it's only a staging area, so you won't be there long, Slim. They'll shoot you across to la Belle France to finish your course—and if you're ever going to find a girl that'll suit you, you ought to do it there."

BOOK TWO

IN CASH AND IN KIND

Spring, 1918—Autumn, 1927

CHAPTER ELEVEN

On board ship,
Friday, April 26, 1918.

Dear Dad:

I am writing this as we are in the sub-zone somewhere off the coast of Spain. We expect to make port tonight or tomorrow morning. So far, there has been nothing sighted except a few battleships and a couple of empty lifeboats. I don't think we are allowed to say what ship we are on, but it is a large passenger boat and quite comfortable. We were fortunate enough to go second class, so had cabins. The ocean is wonderful and I have enjoyed every minute of the sailing, in fact I would like another week of it. I haven't been sick at all, although many of the men have. The weather has been warm and there have been very few rough seas. I would have liked to see a good storm for I love the motion of the boat. We sailed on the 16th around the middle of the night. There are about [here a small rectangular hole is cut in the letter, presumably by the censor] troops on board besides a couple of hundred doctors and Red Cross nurses. I have met quite a number of them and have seen quite a good deal of one nurse, an English girl who trained at the Massachusetts General Hospital and whose father is an English consul—or something. She is bound for Italy, so I probably won't see her again, although one never knows. We have had nothing to do except a few lifeboat drills and some callisthenics and have had the rest of the time to ourselves. All the crew of the ship are French, so we are getting quite a lot of practice in conversation. I find that my French is good enough so that I can get along fine. The O.T.C. from Oglethorpe—who are all southerners —are a good crowd, so if we are kept together I think we will have lots of fun. Anyway, I know I will always be glad I had the chance to come. We have got very little news on board, so have no idea what has been doing on the different battle fronts, but will probably hear as soon as we land. I never heard from you at Camp Merritt and wondered why. We have not been allowed above decks during daylight since yesterday morning and get pretty restless sitting around waiting for night to come and have some air and exercise. Everybody is rather keyed up just now and will be until we get out of this zone. They have dozens of men constantly watching and gun crews at the guns day and night. I left a postal in New York which the Gov. will mail just as soon as they get word that we have landed, so you will have that two or three weeks before this.

Later

Since I started this letter we have got close enough to land so that the water is green instead of blue, and we are getting some of the fog which they say is natural when near shore. Just a few minutes ago the whistle blew and as three blasts are a signal to get ready to abandon the ship, it startled a lot of the passengers and they sure moved some for a minute, although none of the soldiers that I saw jumped. I have spent quite a lot, so the money you've sent me will come in mighty handy, as I don't expect we will get paid for two or three months. I will write again very soon and tell you all I can and, in the meantime, please don't worry for everything is going to be fine.

Your loving grandson.
LARRY.

Cadet Lawrence Cary Vincent,
Officers' Artillery Training School,
American Expeditionary Forces (write in full),
France.

April 28, 1918.

Dear Dad:

We arrived at the debarkation camp [rectangular blackout, presumably cut by the censor] 11.30. We got into dock at 7 p.m. after a trip of about four hours on the boat up a river, the name of which I cannot give you. We came through some of the most beautiful country I ever saw and they tell us here that where we are going is just as fine. That river trip was really most awfully impressive and I shall never forget it. Everybody all along came to the bank and cheered us continually. We passed a U.S. construction job on the way up and the boys there sure gave us a hand and blew every whistle in the place. This country here is beautifully clean and green and with every bit of it like a well-kept park. We were told just after landing that we were chased the last night for three hours by two subs and finally dodged them in the fog. After landing, we marched for about five miles to camp and, having had very little exercise for two weeks and a full pack and overcoat, it was a rather hard trip. The people here are intensely patriotic and everybody is willing to talk to you. It is awfully funny to see some of the efforts at conversation. I can't take time to describe all the little incidents now, but when I get home I think I can amuse you for hours. We don't know how long we will stay here before going on to the school, but probably not for very long. We talked with some fellows just back from the front, also a French sgt., and from what they say, I think the Germans will soon have a most hearty respect for the Yanks, as everybody now calls us. (It sure sounded funny to me at first and the other southern boys I've talked to felt the same way, but we're getting used to it.) The Huns seem to be bearcats for fighting and don't bother to use their rifles, preferring a bayonet which has been well sharpened; so maybe that British sergeant-major at Beauregard was right when he egged *us* on, though he irked me a good deal at the time. Everybody also says that the war is not far from its end, but I hope to get a whack at it before it's over. Our quarters here are very good, but of course not like Beauregard. We are in a forty-eight-hour quarantine, but as soon as it is lifted I am going to have a fine time looking this country over. I took my first bath and changed my clothes for the first time in two weeks this morning. I don't think I would ever go dirty from choice. We have had lots of fun watching the people this afternoon. They have little two-wheeled carts and the whole family gets into one and is drawn by a little donkey not as big as a newborn colt. I saw a family stop to talk to some soldiers and the donkey sat down on his haunches for a rest while the conversation went on. I will write again soon.

Lots of love,

LARRY.

Saturday, May 18, 1918.

Dear Dad:

We finally arrived at school last Wednesday afternoon after a day and a half on the train. The ride was rather tiresome for we were pretty well crowded and had to sit up all night, but I enjoyed seeing the country in spite of it all. From the train I saw about fifteen airplanes all flying in a bunch and it surely was a pretty sight. We started work the next morning and were glad to do it for we had done nothing for a month and that gets monotonous. This life is going to be some change for we get much better treatment and accommodations than we have had before—and they use us as though we were men, not kids. The barracks are enormous, being built around a court and made of stone. We have rooms holding from four to eight with tables, chairs, bureaus, washstands and sheets and pillows. Also maids to care for the rooms. The food is fine— with all kinds of vegetables and soups and real dishes to eat it from, also waitresses. The work is on the same lines as at Beauregard, but much more thorough and with better instructors. I have just returned from riding and we have a French instructor in that. They surely know how to ride. The country around here is very beautiful—with a wonderful climate, I think, for it has been very warm and fair since we arrived. We are situated right in a city of about forty thousand. From my window we can see a good deal of it and only a short way from us on a hill is a large castle. We expect to get three months' instruction here and then probably go right to the front. I have heard no war news for weeks, so know very little of what is going on. I haven't got any mail at all yet, although some of the men have. We haven't been paid, either, and I would have been stone broke without the extra money you gave me. You spend more than it seems as though you could, for things, like underwear, that haven't been issued us cost a mint over here. I haven't seen anybody that I know, but expect to any time, for some of the fellows here have met men that they knew. Write me if they are shipping men from Beauregard yet. I wish Dumaine could see the way they work the ground over here and the crops they grow. There are no weeds and every inch is cultivated. The cattle aren't as good as what we breed, but you see lots of good horses. Please write as often as you can. I will be tickled to death to hear from you.

Love from

LARRY.

Cadet L. C. Vincent,
A. P. O. 718 S. A. S.,
American Expeditionary Forces,
France.

Sunday, May 26, 1918.

Dear Dad: I wonder if you have been getting my letters. I have not heard a word from you. The daily mail was just brought around and both of the men in my room got some, but I did not. Out of luck. We have had our rooms changed and I am in a room now with two Vermont boys. We are on a regular schedule and work from 7 a.m. until about 5.30 p.m. We have supper at 6.30 and can do as we wish until 9.30. We don't get our Saturday afternoons off here as we did in the States, only have the evening with taps an hour later and Sundays, so I haven't been able to plan any overnight trips —if I could have, I might have got to Monteregard, but that's out of the question, at present, anyway. However, some of us quite often go to a village about eight miles from here where there is a wonderful restaurant, run by two sisters who simply can't do enough for us. There's a fine view from the terrace and we sit there and look out on the river and eat and eat and eat.

We get a holiday Memorial Day and I think I will spend it in the country. Yesterday while I was out studying field service, I saw farmers cutting their first crop of alfalfa and it smelled pretty good to me. The equitation here is great stuff, for we have good horses and excellent instructors. We do our riding in a big hall and get all kinds of suppling exercises which cause a lot of falls. One of the men that went off yesterday fell under his horse and got kicked in the head, taking a lot of skin and hair off. So far, I have managed to stay on. We hope to get paid some time, though the Lord knows when that will be. Write as often as you can and make the letters long.

Your loving grandson,
LARRY.

Sunday, June 9, 1918.

Dear Dad:

I got a letter yesterday from you that was written the 10th of May. It was the first one and sure was welcome, even if what you said about the high water going down at last, so that they could start loading gravel at Profit Island, made me more than a little homesick. Incidentally, that idea about the steel barges instead of wooden ones sounds mighty good, but it would be my guess nobody would be able to get steel for that until after the war is over; they are even building those Hog Island ships mostly of wood, I understand. Over here, our training goes ahead. We went out to the range this week for the first time and fired and observed fire of the French 75. They are a great little gun and better than our own three-inch everybody says. That part of the work and the horses appeal to me much more than the mathematics, in which I am pretty weak. I believe we will go straight to the front from here. It looks to me as though the Allies were waiting for us to get a lot of men over with a preponderance of artillery before starting a big push and then settling the thing for good. There are a lot of wild rumours floating around today about commissions. Yesterday they collected all our recommendations and something is certainly happening which has got a lot of the men all haired up. Personally, I would much rather wait until I finish here and make good as a sergeant, then be commissioned, than to be busted after not finishing successfully.

Yesterday we went out into the country to make sketches and saw a lot of caves in the side of a big cliff. We were told these used to be occupied and I guess they were, for they had windows and doors big enough for horses and teams to pass through. We went up on top of an old mill to draw and though, as you know, I am not a Whistler by any means, I enjoyed it, for the mill was quite a sight, too. It was made of

163

rocks and divided into rooms, halls and stairways and was evidently hundreds of years old, for the stone steps were worn down as much as six inches where people had walked.

Thursday, the 30th—the northern Memorial Day—we had a holiday and all the American soldiers marched out to the cemetery with the French and decorated the soldiers' graves. There must have been about a thousand soldiers that marched out there and it surely was impressive. About one hundred and fifty had American flags and another one hundred and fifty carried bouquets. After we reached the cemetery and were lined up around the section the soldiers' graves were in, a French general and our commanding officer—a lieut.-col.— made short speeches. Then the band played while first the men with the flags filed in and each stood by a grave and then together stuck their flags in each one. After they filed out, those of us with flowers did the same. There was only one American grave, I think, and the French decorated that and it was piled high with flowers. The French people in town were awfully pleased with the whole thing. Yesterday I returned from a class just in time to see three Frenchmen given medals. That was quite a ceremony, too. One, an officer, received the medal of the Legion of Honour, the highest the French give. A civilian got two—the Medaille Militaire and Croix de Guerre. Then a private on crutches got a Croix de Guerre. They had a line of French and American soldiers who stood at 'present arms' during the whole thing. A lot of officers lined up and a general did the honours.

Yesterday noon, just as we were coming out of the mess building, a Yankee aviator flew over and evidently seeing the crowd under him decided to show us a few tricks. He cut very short corners, side-slipped, looped the loop, went way up and shut off his engine and took a long dive in which he just skipped the top of the school and skimmed along the parade grounds in front of it, then went up and away. It surely was pretty and we near broke our necks watching him. When he slipped off sideways and was dropping straight down on edge, there were several of us directly under him. We kind of edged back to give him plenty of room—providing he didn't change his mind and keep on coming. He changed it though, which was a great relief to us. I guess I have told you all the exciting news. The work goes well and outside of a hard cold and couple of raw spots caused by riding, I am very well.

Lots of love,

LARRY.

P.S. Just as I am finishing this, there are about a dozen of the most wonderfully toned church bells ringing all at once. Please tell Father Le Grand for me that there's a beautiful church very near the barracks—not to mention several others, one quite famous for its tapestries—that I've enjoyed seeing and that I go to Mass regularly.

June 24, 1918.

Dear Dad:

I received several letters from you this week. One of the letters you sent me while I was at Camp Merritt just came, but I have never got the package you spoke of. If there are any of Aunt Amy's cookies in it, that will be just too bad, even if it finally does get here. Of course things must have been moving right along at Cindy Lou since you wrote. By this time, you are probably cutting the perique. Anyway, the kids must have suckered the plants, and I hope you can get some of the high school boys to help bring the stalks to the drying sheds, during their vacation, for I know you are shorthanded. But the crop won't be nearly as big as usual this year now that you've put all that additional ground into cane. How long it seems since we first talked about doing that! I didn't write yesterday for I went out into the country during the day and spent the evening studying for an examination. Last Monday we went through a gas attack and saw weapons of that nature demonstrated. This morning we had lots of fun riding. Our instructor took us out to an old steeplechase course where we took jumps about five feet high and did so well he told us that next time we could take some higher yet. Up to now, we have had to ride without stirrups at all gaits, but only over low jumps. Sometimes your horse goes down or feels particularly good and starts bucking, but there are very few falls. I haven't been off yet, but am knocking on wood as I write this. We just had a talk by a major on the Headquarters Staff, telling us about some of the work they are doing over here and I

165

think the old U.S.A. is going to show them something before they get through, at that.

Your loving grandson,

LARRY.

Cadet L. C. Vincent,
U. S. A. P. O. 718,

←————————Form we have to follow.

American E. F.,
France.

July 5, 1918.

Dear Dad:

Just received a letter you wrote the 23rd of May, and of course you won't get this one until almost the 20th of July at the earliest, so it will be two months to make a round trip by mail between me and good old Cindy Lou, where the river shrimp must really be running by this time. Is Nappy setting out his sacks with corn meal for them? Don't forget to eat some for me. Well, yesterday was the Fourth, and of course we had a holiday and quite a celebration. At ten in the morning they had a review with about two thousand men in it. Then we were all addressed by a French general and after that there was a presentation of an American flag. In the afternoon there were all kinds of races. Sprints, jumps and that stuff and then races between mounted batteries who had to harness, gallop across the field and go into action. They had a mule race that was awfully good. A lot of men, each with a mule, had to lead it across the field, around a tree and then ride it back. It was a funny sight. There was some trick riding, like one man riding three horses, standing on the two outside ones; also riding bucking horses and lassoing a running horse with a man on him. In the evening the fellows gave a show which was awfully good. Altogether it was quite a day.

There really is no news I can tell you, only the little incidents that happen in the day's work.

Love from

LARRY.

P.S. Today, at dinner, they told us the water was not good. (Of course, we have been drinking it ever since the middle of May!) I am afraid I shall have to cultivate a taste for wine.

July 21, 1918.

Dear Dad:

I am now a lieutenant! We were commissioned Friday and I blossomed out today in all my regalia. We finish our course in one more week, so by the time you receive this I will be somewhere else in France, or perhaps in Italy. I don't know. The war news is very encouraging now and I rather anticipate getting in on a big push. Recently we conducted fire with an aero-observer who flew over the target and sent back reports by wireless. After we finished, he looped a few loops and landed. Last week about two hundred and fifty second lieutenants came in from the States and they were all men from the third camp. They were commissioned the 1st of June and we were, too, but our commissions were held up for some reason or other. At that, these men haven't had the experience we have and we figure we are a lot better off, after all. We have got them all scared to death by telling them what they have coming to them—study, hard work, etc. I am going out to supper tonight with a French family by the name of Detain and expect a wonderful feed. I have eaten there before and the mother and daughter are both marvellous cooks.

I have two problems to work out for tomorrow, so will stop now and get at them. Just as soon as I get located after leaving school, I will write again. Don't worry for I am well and happy and confident that I will see you again before very long.

Your loving grandson,
LARRY.

Lawrence C. Vincent, 2nd Lieut., F. A. N. A.,
U. S. A. P. O. 718,
American E. F.,
France.

August 7, 1918.

Dear Dad:

I landed here in Camp Meucon last Monday morning and have been too busy to write before. Meucon is about five miles from Vannes, which is near the coast, so you can look it up. I am once more in school and am kind of disgusted. I hope to goodness we finish this everlasting study some time and get to doing a little fighting. The country here is very rolling and

167

not as fertile as where we have been. It is in Brittany and the country people's dress is rather novel. The women wear all sorts of fancy white bonnets, some enormous, some tiny, and the men wear big round hats with ribbons hanging down their backs. The brigade we are attached to has not arrived here yet, but some of the officers have preceded it and are at school with us. We travelled down here in first-class carriages and eat at an officers' mess which costs us six francs a day, but it is real American food and the first I've had since we arrived in France. We had pie for dinner and it was good, but I would gladly give all the pie in the world for one dish of Ivy's gumbo. We will be here several weeks for it takes that long to train the men and officers, but then we go to the front. They sure split us up at school for the men were sent to join different outfits anywhere from the Swiss border to the North Sea. I hit my first real case of bugs here. We had a few at school, but they soon got rid of them for us, but here I am afraid we will be constant companions. The little devils bite me, but don't poison me much and really they bother me most by waking me up at night; but some of the fellows are badly poisoned by them and suffer quite a lot. They are just common bedbugs, but most awfully active and hungry. I may have to cash another cheque for, as yet, I haven't been able to get all my pay and it is imperative that I have more equipment before going to the front. An officer has to buy everything he has, even his own tent and dishes, so you see it costs some money. How is everything going at home? Fine, I hope, and I bet the war news is pleasing to you as well as us. I must close now, but will try and write again soon.

Lots of love,
LARRY.

Lt. L. C. Vincent,
U. S. A. P. O. 779,
American E. F.,
France.

August 26, 1918.

Dear Dad:

I have not written for some time, but have been so busy that when I got through work it seemed as though I could do nothing but go to bed. Things seem to be going well with me—meaning that I am giving satisfaction—and I expect to stay with this outfit probably through the war, though one never can tell. I will tell you my schedule today to give you an idea of what I have to do, although the schedule varies and some days I do a lot of firing and mapping. Reveille was at 4.45. After breakfast, which followed immediately, we got the cannoneers and drivers out, groomed and harnessed forty-eight horses and got the guns out to the range at 7. The drivers came back and I had charge of them and the stables for the day. I had to give infantry drill to about seventy-five men part of the morning, take them on a hike with our gas masks on for two hours and see that one hundred and sixty-four horses were fed, watered and cared for. After dinner, I gave the drivers mounted drill, then watered and sent them after the guns. After that, had the rest of the men work at the stables on the other horses. Wound up with retreat at 5.45. Now since supper, I have had a half-hour gas drill, attended a lecture on the organization and use of artillery and now have a stack of letters about a foot high to wade through and censor. All of this on top of a trick at guard in which I had to ride forty-four kilometres and take my few hours of sleep on the floor. Don't think from this letter that I'm feeling abused, because that's not true. I am contented and perfectly healthy.

Your loving grandson,
LARRY.

Lt. L. C. Vincent,
Battery E. 113 F. A.,
155 Brigade,
American E. F., France.

September 13, 1918.

Dear Dad:

I am taking a few minutes off tonight to write a little. We have been very busy the last few days getting ready to go. It is quite a job getting everything packed, lashed and ready to load so that the minute we detrain we can start on the road, for there is the possibility of having to detrain under shelling.

I am very limited as to space, because I can't take more than can ultimately be distributed over a horse. I know where we are going, but can only tell you that they have just started a big drive there, so we ought to hit it right in the midst of things. We leave here Sunday, the 15th, at 8 a.m. and travel about three days by rail. This brigade is part of the 80th Division, so perhaps you may follow our movements in the papers.

This letter is rather disjointed as I have been interrupted while writing it and have had to do it hastily, as I must also take time to write one in French to the Detains, thanking them for inviting me to spend my first leave with them. I should like very much to do that, so my visit to Monteregard may be still further delayed. Good night, Dad.

Lots of love,

LARRY.

September 22, 1918.

Dear Dad:

I haven't time or facilities for writing much, as all I have for a table is a small notebook and I am all curled up in a pup tent. We are camped in some woods just back of the lines and we move into position tonight. I cannot tell you where we are, but it is very famous for the battles that have been fought there during this war. From all indications, there is going to be another big one very shortly. I have seen several air battles and of course we can hear the firing here. I was out this morning doing some reconnaissance work and the Germans started shelling a hill just a short way off. They were very big shells and it kind of makes you want to duck when they come whistling over and burst close by. We are getting lots of rain and the mud is a foot deep, so we are nearly always wet and daubed with mud. We do all our moving at night, which is some job when it is pitch dark and no lights can show. I just got orders to see to the packing, so must stop now. Don't know when I can write again or when I will ever get any mail, but hope before long.

Your loving grandson,

LARRY.

Another change:
Lt. L. C. Vincent,
Battery E. 313 F. A.,
American E. F.,   O.K.,
France.   L. C. Vincent, 2nd Lt., F. A.

September 30, 1918.
8 a.m.

Dear Dad:

I have got a few minutes this morning while waiting for my horse to go out for all day on a battalion problem. I didn't write Sunday because I went to town Saturday night for my last crack at civilization. You would have laughed if you could have seen how I ended up. I had hoped to spend the night in one of those marvellous French beds, but found the town was filled up and not a room left. As there was no way to get out here to camp—it was so late when I finished hunting—I crawled off in the grass beside the road, curled up in my trench coat and spent the night. I slept until seven, then went to a hotel and washed and had breakfast. Coming out on the train, I ran into three more officers who did the same thing.

It sounds a good deal like the front as I am writing this, for there is a regiment in position about a thousand yards from here and they have been blazing away for over an hour. The brigade finishes its training here in about a week and then we move up to the big doings.

From now on, don't put any P.O. number on letters for we will be moving continually and won't have the same number. I must stop now for it is time to go.

Much love,
LARRY.

Lt. L. C. Vincent,
Bty. E. 313 F. A.,
155 Brigade,
American E. F., France.

October 14, 1918.

Dear Dad:

My last two letters have been necessarily brief, so tonight I am going to try and make this as interesting and descriptive

171

as possible. There is a little lull tonight which accounts for it. To begin, I am sitting in a little hole in the ground just big enough to lie down in and about two feet deep. Protection from splinters. I haven't had a bath since September 14th and have not had my clothes off since about the 20th of September. I have been four days without even washing my hands or combing my hair. The last two days have been rather warm in respect to scrapping—and I have several times been as close as is healthy to some of Fritzie's shells. The nearest was yesterday, about ten feet, and a big one, too. You sure would have laughed to see me lying sprawled perfectly flat in the mud while it was bursting. If you have time after hearing it coming to flop you are fairly safe. To tell you somewhat of how we do this job: we move into position about three thousand yards from Fritz at night and get set. Then for the next couple of days help the doughboys hold the line while our heavies, which are less mobile and slower to move, come up to two or three thousand yards behind us. Then, when all is set, everybody opens up at once and we shove the Germans back three to five miles. Sometimes it takes a couple of days to do it, but so far they have gone. In the meantime, as the Germans begin to locate us, our position develops more business. We receive 'em as well as send 'em. Thus far, our battery has been lucky and the casualties have been light. Some of the others in the regiment have not been so fortunate. I am knocking on wood as I write this, also I pause occasionally to scratch. I sure have them—and one of the greatest joys of my life is going to be a hot bath and a bottle of larkspur.

I saw a funny one the other day which gave me a good laugh. A plane came over and dropped out a small balloon—about like a Fourth of July one—which landed in a field. About twenty doughboys, who happened to be near, started as fast as they could to see what it was. When they got about twenty feet from it, some cautious bird happened to think that it might be a Fritz plane and some trick he was up to. So they all stood around for a few minutes, first looking at the plane which was by then a long way off, and then talking the thing over. Finally they all took off their helmets, put on their gas masks and one bold lad walked up and carefully looked the thing over. There was a carton of cigarettes hitched to it.

There is another side which is not so pleasant, but I will tell you a little of that. This morning I was walking across a field, chasing up some ammunition we needed, when a shell broke near by and I turned partially around to see if it would be better to change my direction. I stepped on something soft and looked down to find the head and shoulders of a red-headed American under my feet. The rest of him was near by and he had evidently been there two or three days. I had the poor boy buried. Enough of that.

I think one of the things that interests me most is to see what you can do with a horse before he drops dead from work and where one can go with them hitched to wagons and guns. I'll certainly know how to show our people what to do with mules when I get back to Cindy Lou. I have put the battery into position in the thickest of woods in rough country when it was so black you couldn't see your hand in front of you and so slippery with mud you could hardly stand up. The planes and balloons are mighty interesting, too, and nothing is more thrilling than a scrap between two planes. The figures they cut in manœuvring for position are marvellous and the final dive of the one that gets beaten makes your hair prickle all over you. I have seen quite a few of our balloons brought down in flames by the German planes—seen the observer in the balloon jump in his parachute and float down, and then seen our anti-aircraft guns get the plane before it was safely away. I would give quite a good deal right now for a good soft bed with sheets and things, for this ground is kind of hard, damp and cold, but I sure can sleep on it at that when I get a chance which is not awfully often. I am anticipating a good night's sleep tonight for we attacked this morning and drove them back six kilometres and then got orders not to move up tonight for some reason or other, so hope it will be quiet. The peace news is very encouraging and we all hope they will declare an armistice before long. I am hoping to be able to dodge 'em a little while longer, for it would be hell to get bumped off so near to the end of it all.

The beautiful countryside we are going through has not a soul in it but soldiers, and the little towns which must have been so pretty are in perfectly flat ruins. I think I had better sleep now for I don't know when I will get another chance

like this again. I hope this reaches you safely for it is the
longest I have written for a long time. I am very well—aside
from a little dysentery and a cold which go with all the rest
of this. Don't worry, for I think the fighting will stop soon
and then it can't be very long before I see you again. The
days and nights are pretty full, for this kind of warfare is not
like trench warfare—for when one is not fighting one is
moving.

Lots of love,
LARRY.

P.S. It's funny, since I have been up here I haven't got a
letter from you. Don't worry—I am *not* going to bring home
a French girl, although they are *wonders*.

Lt. L. C. Vincent,
Bat'y. E. 313 F. A.,
A. E. F., France.

Tours.
November 3, 1918.

Dear Dad:

I am sitting in a café in Tours writing this and hope that
the crowd around will furnish enough inspiration to make it
interesting. I came down here last Thursday to go to the
Observers' School after having answered a call for volunteers
at the front. This flying is great stuff and although I don't
think it furnishes more thrills than the artillery, one is sure
more comfortable. An observer's job is to locate all things of
military importance, to be a good machine gunner for the
fights—and must know how to handle a plane, too, in case
the pilot gets hit. I have run into about twenty-five Saumur
men I knew before who are here on the same work. It makes
it seem kind of like home for some of them come from Beauregard. I am sitting here writing with a lieutenant of Engineers
named Frank Waddill, who was one of my buddies there and
whom I also knew at Tulane, where he was hipped on the
subject of sonar research. He's going to modernize our sugarhouse when the war's over. Meanwhile, he and I have been

spending some nights rather wildly—but after six weeks at the front we thought it was due us. I also did Paris on the way here and it certainly is all it's cracked up to be. I had a little hard luck on the way down for every bit of my baggage, except toilet articles which I carried, has been lost. It is going to cost me three hundred and sixty dollars to get re-equipped and some more to buy my flying clothes. The govt. furnishes them now, but they are not warm enough for winter use. The Army sure uses an airman well for we have practically no discipline, the best of grub and quarters and short working hours. This is a great camp here—with lots of activity. There are usually forty or fifty planes in the air at once and the fellows have great fun after finishing their missions by chasing farmers out of the fields and scaring people on the roads. I rather doubt now if I ever see the front again, for it looks as if the war would finish "*toute de suite*" and I am sorry in one way for I would have liked to see it as a flyer. The war news looks awfully good, and if it ends soon I expect to be home shortly thereafter for, although I lost all chance of promotion by leaving the artillery, I am now detached. So I ought to be one of the first to leave. Am shy of paper, so will quit.

Your loving grandson,
LARRY.

Lt. L. C. Vincent,
2nd A. I. C.,
A. P. O. 717,
A. E. F., France.

November 12, 1918.

Dear Dad:

I want to write you now while everything is fresh in my mind. We got the news of the cessation of hostilities yesterday and all of France has gone wild. It is the greatest celebration I ever hope to see and a most wonderful change in a nation. I was in town Sunday and everything was quiet and the people very serious and sober as all French have been. Last night all lights were lighted, you could hardly get through the streets and everybody wild with joy and, for the most part, French and Americans both quite drunk. The Americans express their joy with wild whoops and yells, while the French scamper about singing and kissing and hugging everybody. I got my share. The city was decorated, everybody in their best clothes, and fountains playing that haven't worked for months. As for my part of the celebration, I got gloriously drunk and had for a companion one of the prettiest and most stylish girls you ever saw—a vaudeville actress who is showing here now. She got drunk, too, also insisted on paying her way. The last I saw of her, I recollect having told her I would take her to America with me and she commenced crying, with both arms around me and kissing me between each sniffle—all right on the sidewalk with a million people about. I was too exhilarated to be embarrassed, but nobody paid any attention anyway. I have a hazy recollection of her saying she would blow me to my Thanksgiving dinner. It seems very wonderful to think this grinding war is over.

I am getting along well here and am making lots of friends amongst the wildest bunch of men in the world. I haven't had any mail for ages, but hope it will begin to come through before long. Write often, please.

Lots of love,
LARRY.

November 17, 1918.

Dear Dad:

Now that the war is finished, I guess I can tell you more of what I have done and where I have been. I landed in Bordeaux—went from there to Ussel—from there to Saumur—thence to Vannes and from there to Verdun, where we went into the lines. We were on the west bank of the Meuse between the river and the Argonne Forest. It was one of the toughest sectors on the whole front. I have seen two hundred effective men reduced to fifty in less than thirty minutes and there was lots of that kind of stuff. We started with one hundred and ten horses and four weeks later had only twenty-four and our battery was no exception. I can't tell you all the things I saw for it would take reams of paper, but will when I get home.

I have just finished my gunnery course which consists of range work with machine guns and then aerial fire. Now I am starting the observation course which consists of taking photos, making maps, adjusting fire for artillery and liaison with infantry. The flying is fine and I enjoy it a lot, except that now it is getting pretty cold. The course here only lasts thirty-three more days and perhaps some of us will be sent home then. The celebrating has ended now and everybody has settled down again to work. It was great while it lasted though.

Loads of love,
LARRY.

December 16, 1918.

Dear Dad:

Once more I have moved and this time to the most desolate place in France. I am at Le Courneau, south of Bordeaux and very near Arcachon. They closed up the school at Tours and dumped us all down here, though we wanted to go to our own outfits. This country is perfectly flat and covered with scrub pine. I have no idea when I will get home, but hope to by spring at least. Haven't had a letter in ages.

Your loving grandson,
LARRY.

L. C. V.,
A. P. O. 778,
A. E. F., France.

January 1, 1919.

A. P. O. 778.

Dear Dad:

New Year's Day and it is most beautiful—warm and sunny, so I am celebrating by writing. I haven't written for some time for I have been on a seven-day leave, which I managed to stretch to twelve days. I meant to get to Monteregard, but after spending two days in Saumur, I went back to Tours and never got away from there. I had a wonderful time—saw some good shows, had lots of good stuff to eat and plenty of sleep. I am enclosing a picture of the lady who was kind enough to make all this possible. She is the daughter of a French officer who was the governor of one of the French provinces in Algeria and the widow of another French officer, killed near the Marne. She has a baby a year old, is well educated, plays the piano, has a good voice and has an independent income of her own and lives in a big house just outside of Tours, well staffed with servants. Incidentally, she is much prettier than the picture indicates and one of the few Frenchwomen I have seen who doesn't use make-up—she doesn't need to. We took a walk every day, went to shows in town and dined at the best hotel several times. We also went to Midnight Mass at the cathedral, the most beautiful service I ever saw. (Tell Father Le Grand that.)

No, she is not in love with me, although she did kiss me good-bye at the station in front of everybody, and I found that very easy to take, for I do like her a lot. While I'm not exactly in love with her, either, I can imagine that I very well might be.

They are closing up this camp now and getting the men all sorted into districts, so they are going back to the States very soon, but as for me, I don't know. I will probably draw some job on a dock or something for a year or so, but never mind, I'll get home eventually.

Your loving grandson,
LARRY.

A. P. O. 703, A. E. F.

January 27, 1919.

Dear Dad:

I landed here (Gondrécourt) last Saturday after taking six days to get here. I visited the lovely widow in Tours again and stopped off in Paris on the way, also lost all my baggage for the second time. The French system baffles me—I saw everything put on the train at Tours and when we arrived at Paris it was minus—it had been dumped off somewhere in between. It is rather inconvenient for I have no clothes except what I had on and they are my best ones and I don't care about knocking around camp in them. This is a reclassification camp —all officers who have lost their outfits go through here and are assigned new jobs according to their qualifications. Most of the work they are giving out now is special work like military police, railroad transportation, baggage department, labour battalions, prison camps, etc. This is all a great experience anyway and I ought to be able to do anything when I get home, which I hope will be by fall at least. Gondrécourt is just south of Bar-le-Duc and is an enormous camp. It was one of our forward camps during the war. Jeanne d'Arc's birthplace is only about ten miles from here and I hope to see it before leaving. I have hopes of being stationed somewhere soon and staying there long enough to get some mail.

Heaps of love,
LARRY.

A. P. O. 703.

February 11, 1919.

Dear Dad:

I got a letter of yours today dated August 11th. Outside of two or three letters all my mail has been like that. I got no Christmas boxes at all, but I wasn't surprised, for Aunt Amy was the only person I knew who went in for that sort of thing. It will seem queer not to have her around when I get back and I will miss her a lot. Of course she really was a very old lady though and you're right, we ought to be able to take losses like that in our stride, even if they do hurt. But it seems real silly to be answering what you wrote me 'way last August. By this time you're not only all through grinding, and then some; you've put the seeds for the new perique crop in the cold frames by now. Lordy, Lordy, what I wouldn't give to be there with you and to go with Captain Bourgeois to get that new hundred-foot steamboat at Zanesville. You didn't tell me what you'd named her or much else about her and I certainly would like to know more.

I am still in the same camp, but have hopes of getting out soon, for I have been living an awful existence for the last two months. Absolutely no work—nothing to do but eat and sleep. You can't even get drunk in this town to break up the monotony. Speaking of drink, you ought to hear the soldiers, officers and all, express their opinions of the folks back home who have passed the prohibition law. There is going to be an awful holler when they all get home. This place is horrible— mud a foot deep and rain all the time, so you get practically no exercise and simply sit around and cuss. No passes are given here except to the permanent personnel. I have run into some of the fellows I came over with who have been sent down here for reassignment. Most of them didn't get to the front at all, but got stuck in some camp, so maybe I was lucky after all, and I may get sent to Germany eventually. Anxious as I am to get home, I'd be glad to go if I thought I could be of any real use there. I don't feel that I am here.

Love,

LARRY.

April 30, 1919.

Dear Dad:

Well, at last I can write you in a somewhat more definite way and that means it will also be in a more cheerful vein. No doubt that will be a relief to you, for I know I've done an awful lot of griping lately and you must be sick of it. By some miracle I have succeeded in getting a ten-day leave and I suppose this means that afterward I'll be attached to a regular unit again. I may be able to tell you something more definite the next time I write.

Meanwhile, I can tell you right now that I'm going to take advantage of my leave by going to Monteregard. You're quite right, I ought to have done it before. But as you probably gathered, I had a pretty good time at Saumur and Tours from the beginning, so I couldn't resist the temptation offered in the persons of very attractive young ladies to get back to both places when I had the chance. Of course I realize by now that these attractions were just passing fancies, but they sure were pleasant at the time. Haven't you told me yourself that if I ever got started in the right—or even the wrong—direction, I might like girls better than I expected? Well, you knew what you were talking about, as usual.

I've been looking up train schedules and I go from here to Paris, which is fairly simple, then after several main line changes to a place called Saintes, where I change again to a local which takes me to the small village of St. Porchaire, very close to Monteregard. I am sure to find some kind of an inn there, where the food and the beds will both be good, because that seems to be true everywhere in France. I'm not going to write beforehand to Aunt Armande, because mails are still so uncertain that I'd probably get there before the letter did and anyway, I think it would be more fun to surprise her. If she's really glad to see me, and I guess she will be, I can easily move over to the château from the inn. I only hope I won't lose my baggage again, for I'd hate to get there looking like a tramp. I suppose there may be some attractive girls in that vicinity, too, I mean besides Janine, who, of course, doesn't count.

Well, that will be all for now, as I'd better start packing and be on my way to Dublin Bay. (How long it seems since we used to dance to that tune and how good it would be to dance to it again!)

Lots of love,
LARRY.

CHAPTER TWELVE

LARRY was hungry and the lunch was very good: sardines, cold sliced sausage and fresh young radishes for hors d'œuvres; then crisply fried sole, veal steak delicately browned, a green salad, cheese made from goats' milk; to top all this off, wild strawberries with thick cream. When he complimented the *patronne* on the butter, she answered with satisfaction that it was all very well for Normans to claim the best butter in the world was made at Isigny, but everyone who was really informed knew that it could not compare with Charentes butter. The difference was caused by the fact that in Normandy the cows were left out from morning until night, whereas, in the Charentes, they were carefully brought into shelter during the heat of noonday. And the cheese, another speciality of the region—did not M. le Lieutenant think it superior to Pont l'Evêque and Livarot? It was evident that she felt great pride in local products and Larry was glad that he could praise these wholeheartedly.

A carafe of red wine stood on the table and he had poured it out with a liberal hand; it was good sound wine that had a glow to it, and suited him. But when he praised this, too, the *patronne* looked apologetic. It was nothing but a common-place *vin de table*, not suitable to go with sole and veal; above all, not suitable for such a connoisseur as M. le Lieutenant was revealing himself to be. If she had realized in time, she would have brought him something better from behind the faggots—a vintage Montrachet, for instance, of which she happily still had a few bottles. She would make up for the omission at dinnertime. Meanwhile, M. le Lieutenant would of course have cognac with his coffee and that must be on the house. Oh, but she would insist! This was cognac country —and 1914 had been an especially good year. He could not decline to accept the country's hospitality on his first visit there!

By the time Larry rose from the table, he was so full of good food and good drink that the morning's urge for activity had materially slackened. He would have been quite content to sprawl out beside one of the little tin tables in front of the inn and bask almost drowsily in the sunshine. Not that he would be averse to passing the time of day with anyone who happened to come along; but he had no special craving for immediate companionship. It actually took a certain amount of will power to strike out for Monteregard, as he had originally planned, almost immediately after lunch; and he sauntered along, smoking a cigarette, instead of going at his usual smart clip. However, he had declined the *patronne's* friendly sugges-tion of a cariole and a driver who would act as a guide. The walk would do him good and he was sure he could find his way. If he had understood her correctly, he was to turn down the road which ran at right-angles to the inn and proceed about a kilometre. The first fields he saw would already be part of the Monteregard property; the forest lay just beyond them.

It did not take him five minutes to get past the twin rows of grey houses which fringed the village street and which were redeemed from drabness only by their blooming flower gardens; and once he had reached the meadows which men were busily tilling and the pastures where cattle and sheep were grazing, his drowsiness was dispelled by the freshness of the breeze which still retained the salty tang of the sea. The sunny landscape changed quickly in character: the open country was soon interspersed with wood lots and he saw less livestock and no workmen. Then, suddenly, the fields were completely engulfed by trees. With a quickening of senses, Larry saw them closing in upon him.

For this was a forest unlike any he had ever seen before. Dense as it was, it had none of the gloom which enfolded the swamps and groves of Cindy Lou. The sunlight filtered in through the verdant branches of ivy-wreathed trees and lay in bright patches on the moss and ferns beneath them. All about him was the radiance of gilded greenery. But it was strangely still. Though the sun had penetrated to its innermost depths, the breeze had failed to pass beyond its network of boughs and not a leaf was stirring. If birds nested within it, their song was silenced; if foxes burrowed there, they were withdrawn; if hares sometimes scampered through it, they had leaped away. Larry paused, and when the sound of his footsteps ceased, there was no sound at all.

All at once he remembered a letter, written on paper crackling and yellow with age, which his grandfather had shown him, and a sentence from it seemed to stand out as vividly as if it had been written in letters of flame and not in faded ink:

"You approach the château through a beautiful forest of ivy-wreathed oaks and there's something actually magical about the effect of the sun shining through their greenery."

The mother he had never known had been right. There was a look of magic about this place, a feeling of it, too. As this feeling grew stronger and stronger, Larry remembered, not quite so clearly, something else the letter had contained: something about roads branching through the forest in every direction and about a little grassy plot, with ancient stone seats in it, which could be reached by one of those roads, though it was so well hidden that this must have been done on purpose, in order that the plot could be a secret trysting place. And suddenly he knew he would never be content until he had explored the roads of the forest, until he found this place of which his mother had written and which had been so carefully concealed from curious eyes. He was no longer in a hurry to reach the château or to meet his aunt and his cousins. He wanted first to find the hidden enclosure.

At the moment, only one road stretched out before him. It was straight and wide and level and was obviously designed to lead directly to the château. However, he had not gone much farther when he saw another, branching off to the right. He took it without hesitation, but almost at once decided that, though narrower than the first, it was also too straight and open to promise romantic possibilities. He had not pursued it very far before discovering that his surmise had been correct. An enormous kitchen garden surrounded by outbuildings, came into view; and though Larry was still at some distance from it, a couple of workers in it raised their heads and stared at him in a way which showed they felt he was an intruder. He turned again and, after regaining the highway and walking a little farther on, saw another road branching from it, this time to the left. Its condition showed that it was less travelled than those he had seen before and it led more deeply into the woods; but when he came to a circular open space, he found it neatly clipped, ornamented with flower beds and dominated by a white marble column, for which he could see neither rhyme nor reason. Nothing about it bespoke secrecy or antiquity; evidently, for some inexplicable reason, it was a place in which the De Chanets felt a certain pride and on which they lavished a certain amount of attention. But it had no special attraction for him.

Larry would have been glad, then and there, of a stone seat, moss-grown or otherwise. He had evidently walked farther than he realized or else the afternoon was actually warmer than he had supposed, for he was hot and tired. But he was still determined to go on with his search; and after a moment he saw that the road by which he had entered the cleared circle, though it was the only one leading directly toward the high way, was not the only one branching out beyond the clipped lawn and the flower beds. There were others, radiating like spokes from a wheel. They were all very narrow and they all apparently led deeply into the forest; there seemed to be no special differences among them. If he guessed wrong more than once, as to which would take him where he wanted to go, the afternoon might very well be almost gone before he could rectify his mistake. He finally made his choice in favour of one which had a slight slope to it and which soon dwindled to the size of a path. It was thickly bordered by underbrush and the branches of the trees met and interlaced overhead. Presently Larry found that he would have to skirt large stones in order to continue on his way; then, that the branches above him were bending lower and lower. As he stooped to avoid being brushed by them, he was aware, for the first time, of a sound which was not made by his footsteps—a very slight murmuring sound, such as might be caused by the gentle flow of a small stream. Then he heard another—and it was the sound of a human voice, quickly mingled with a second one. Both were fresh and vibrant, suggesting youth, and one had a musical quality that went straight to his heart. He plunged forward, no longer mindful of impediments. The trees parted suddenly and he saw in front of him the secret place he had sought.

On an ancient stone seat before him sat two young girls, who were holding a book between them, and whose heads were bent over it. One was dressed in white with black ribbons and the other was dressed in white with green ribbons. One had very sleek black hair, parted in the middle, and the other had unruly golden-brown curls which were not parted at all. That was all he had time to observe before they sprang up and he saw that one was pale and the other rosy. They stared at him in amazement, but not, he was relieved to see, in fright. Then one of them spoke so quickly that he had not been able to think of anything to say which would explain or excuse his intrusion.

"Monsieur has lost his way," she suggested. "If he will retrace his steps to the column which marks the circle from which he must have come, he will have no trouble in getting from there to the main road."

It was the pale girl with the black hair and the black ribbons who had addressed him. Now the other one spoke, too.

"Perhaps he didn't lose his way," she suggested. "Perhaps he wanted to come here all the time."

She smiled, and her smile had the same effect upon him as her voice. And he no longer had any trouble in framing an answer.

"You are right, mademoiselle," he said. "This was the very place I set out to find. Only I didn't expect to be so fortunate as to discover that it was peopled with wood nymphs."

"Well, you must have had some good reason for wanting to find it."

It was the brown-haired girl who had spoken again. She was still smiling, and the more she smiled, the lovelier she looked. The other girl seemed much graver and, though she did not speak discourteously, there was a marked coolness in her manner.

"Possibly you had in mind a visit to the grottoes. But those are best reached by another route and, in any case, the public has not been admitted to them, since the war. I am sorry to say that there can be no exceptions made to this rule. I must repeat, monsieur, that you will find it easy to reach the highway if——"

"I don't care about visiting the grottoes just now. This really was the place I wanted to find. And I don't particularly want to go back to the highway, either. As a matter of fact——"

"Monsieur——"

"Why don't you let him finish, *chérie*?" asked the brown-haired girl.

"Thank you, mademoiselle. As a matter of fact, I hope you won't feel I'm an out-and-out intruder, though I realize I should have gone to the château first and introduced myself properly. But please let me do that now. My name's Larry Vincent and I think one of you must be my cousin, Janine de Chanet."

He looked hopefully from one to the other. The black-haired girl, though her expression was still slightly severe, appeared to relax a little; while she regarded him silently, as if willing to believe him, but somewhat doubtful as to whether she should, the brown-haired girl laughed outright.

"If you're Larry Vincent, Janine *is* your cousin," she said. "So she ought to be the first to welcome you to Monteregard. But I can't wait any longer for her to make up her mind, so I'll do it. My name, in case you're interested, is Louise de Courville, and the relationship's very complicated—in fact, it doesn't exist at all, as far as you're concerned. But I'm very glad to see you, just the same."

Even though Janine had not been the first to welcome him, her greeting was now wholly courteous; obviously she was the *jeune fille comme il faut* of fond French tradition. She was sorry she had not realized Larry was her American cousin; but, as he himself had said, if he had only come first to the château and presented himself to her father . . . She could understand his wish to see their beautiful woods, but after all, there would have been plenty of time for that afterward. And naturally, she had been slightly surprised that a stranger . . .

"You mean there'll still be plenty of time," Louise interrupted. "So why not all go up to the house together, right now?"

As if it were futile to discuss the matter further, she turned in the direction of the path. It was so narrow, until they came to the circular open space, that they could not walk two abreast. But when they reached that point, she suggested that Janine should continue to lead the way and fell easily into step beside Larry.

"You probably wondered about that column," she said, answering his unspoken question. "There are four of them on the property—one at each of the cardinal points of the compass. They're not very old. Uncle Pierre had them set up and surrounded with flower beds. I've never quite understood why. They don't seem to me especially important."

"They provided an agreeable occupation for him," Janine remarked turning. "I don't think you should speak so slightingly, Louise, about Papa's activities."

"I didn't mean to speak slightingly. I've always been puzzled, that's all. . . . Didn't the column puzzle you, Larry?" she added.

"To tell the truth, it did. But I'm still more puzzled about this question of relationship. Evidently, my uncle Pierre is also your uncle Pierre. But you said——"

"I said it was very complicated, and it is. Also that the relationship didn't exist at all, as far as you and I are concerned. Would you like to have me explain?"

"Very much."

"Well, you knew that my uncle Pierre's father—let's call him the old Marquis de Chanet, for the sake of convenience—was married twice, didn't you?"

"It seems to me I did. I'm not sure. My grandfather's tried to explain, but——"

"I'll probably have to draw you a plan, in the end, to straighten you out. But I'll do the best I can now. His first wife was the Princesse de Herbemont. She died when her only child, Asceline, was only a few weeks old and the marquis didn't feel competent to take care of a baby. So little Asceline was raised by the De Herbemonts. When she grew up, she married Etienne d'Ambly and had two daughters herself—Josephine and Isabelle. Josephine married Jehan de Courville and Isabelle married Gilles de Lorne. I'm Josephine's daughter. So the old Marquis de Chanet was my great-grandfather. Is that all clear so far?"

"More or less. I don't know whether I can take in so many strange names, all at once, and connect them to the right people and get all the various relations straight. But I'll try."

"And I'll help you. I told you I'd draw you a plan if you wanted me to. But if you'll listen carefully——"

"I'm listening all right."

"Well, a long time after the death of the Princesse de Herbemont, the old marquis married again—a lady we always think of as an American, though actually she was French by birth, too. Her name was Dorothée Labouisse and she also had a baby—Pierre. So he's my uncle Pierre—my great-uncle rather, because he and my grandmother are half brother and sister, though she's old enough to be his mother."

"I see."

188

"I'm not sure whether you really do, or whether you're just being polite about it. But anyway, Pierre de Chanet grew up, and went to the United States with his mother, the former Dorothée Labouisse, and met a certain beautiful Miss Vincent, who really was an American, and fell in love with her and married her."

"And that lovely young lady was my aunt Armande—my father's sister!"

"You're right. You see, it really isn't so complicated after all. The present Marquis de Chanet is my uncle Pierre and your uncle Pierre, just as you said. But just as *I* said, you and I are not related at all!"

Louise laughed, as if there were something amusing in their lack of relationship. Larry laughed, too. For no special reason, he was inclined to agree with her.

"I've been looking forward a lot to meeting my cousin Janine," he said. "I didn't know that at the same time I was going to meet a cousin of hers who wasn't a cousin of mine, but who'd add a lot to the pleasure of making her acquaintance. If I had known, I'd have looked forward to it a lot more."

Louise laughed again and her laugh, like her voice and her smile, seemed to go straight to Larry's heart. However, it quickly occurred to him that he ought not to have spoken about anticipating the pleasure of meeting Janine without saying that he was anticipating an equal amount of pleasure in regard to meeting her brother.

"I mean, of course, I'd been looking forward a lot to meeting both my cousins—in fact, the whole family, and to seeing Aunt Armande again. I hope everyone's at home?"

Janine turned again, and this time the look she gave him was not merely reproachful, as it had been, more or less, from the beginning; it was surprisingly stern, for the expression of so young and beautiful a girl, and it was also very sad. Larry realized that somehow he had erred, even more gravely than through his intrusion; and, though he had not been much concerned over his first offence, this time he was suddenly appalled.

"Evidently you did not know that you were coming to a house of mourning," Janine said chillingly. "If you had inquired——"

189

"Probably he hasn't been any place where he could inquire, Janine," Louise interposed swiftly. "We don't know yet where he has come from, or when. He hasn't had time to tell us. We haven't even asked him. It isn't any stranger that he shouldn't know about us than that we shouldn't know about him." She laid her hand lightly on his arm, and Larry realized that she had sensed his distress. "We ought to have told you right away," she went on gently. "But there didn't seem to be just the right moment to do it and of course it's very hard for Janine to talk about it. I don't talk about it, either, if I can help myself. I try to talk about—well, cheerful things, as much as I can. I hope you will, too. But Monteregard *is* a house of mourning, a house of—of great desolation. You see, just the day before the Armistice, when everyone was so happy because it seemed certain that the end of the war was in sight——"

Janine had not turned again or spoken again. But quietly, collectedly, Louise told Larry how Pierrot had met his death: a German battery of heavy artillery, far behind the lines, had one shell left and decided to fire it in the general direction of the west before dismantling or crippling their gun. The shell landed in a ruined field, beside what was left of an old stone farmhouse, and a jagged splinter of metal, ricocheting off the stones, had struck Pierrot in the temple. . . . "It was more than his mother could bear, after four long years of anxiety," Louise went on. "Pierrot had been badly wounded twice before, once at Ypres and once at the Meuse. Aunt Armande—well, you can understand that she'd been through a terrible strain all through the war."

"And what happened?" Larry managed to ask. But his mouth was very dry, because he thought he knew already.

"Of course, it may have been an accident. She may just have slipped. Or she may not have noticed where she was going. Because she really was distraught. Not that it wouldn't have been very, very sad in any case. . . . You've heard of the Blue Pool at Monteregard, haven't you?"

Again it seemed to Larry as if he were holding in his hand that letter, yellow with age, which his grandfather had shown him; again it seemed as though he were reading those words which were so vivid, though they were written in such faded

190

ink. "Pierre . . . told me the legend of the Blue Pool which the river widens to form at the foot of the caves. According to this legend, a De Chanet lady who lost her lover flung herself into this pool several hundred years ago and ever since then, a spring has bubbled up from the place where she was drowned. Of course, it's just a silly superstition, but just the same——"

"Yes," he answered, speaking with still greater difficulty, "I've heard of the Blue Pool."

"The day after we had the news of Pierrot's death, Aunt Armande stayed in her room for a long while, with the door locked. Afterward, we discovered that she'd been writing most of the time, and though she'd torn up practically all the notes into tiny pieces and thrown them into the fireplace, one was still lying on her desk. It read, 'I haven't lost my lover, for I never had him. But I have lost my only son and that is worse.' I told you she was distraught—the note goes to prove it. She didn't lose her lover, as you know. She married him."

"It seems to me I've heard she was engaged when she was very young to a man who died of yellow fever. Perhaps she was referring to him."

"Perhaps," Louise said doubtfully. He knew she did not think this was the case, and it did not surprise him, because he did not really think so himself.

"Besides, it can't be worse to lose a son than a lover," Louise said thoughtfully. "At least, I don't think so. I think if I loved a man, I'd feel the worst thing that could happen to me would be to lose him. Not that I'd commit suicide if I did."

"I think you would feel that way." Larry did not know why he spoke with such conviction, but it was very deep. "I'm sure you wouldn't commit suicide, either."

"Well, we mustn't talk about me. I must go on telling you about Aunt Armande. She finally left the château without saying a word to anybody. But Justine, our portress, saw her pass through the Gate of the Lions and leave the avenue for the woods. No one ever saw her again after that, but there were footprints on the path that goes by the caves—the path that's been closed ever since. And by the edge of the Blue Pool was a scarf."

This time Larry did not even try to answer. They had left the forest now and gone through a marble portal, adorned with sculptured lions, to an inner avenue where wide lawns dotted with scattered statues stretched out beyond the trees. There was a thatched cottage just inside the portal and, as they passed it, an aged man came hobbling to the door and stared out at them, mumbling something that seemed to have no meaning. Almost instantly, a sturdy woman whose thin hair was strained back from her ruddy face and who was dressed in dingy black, appeared beside him and spoke to him soothingly before saying, "*Bon soir, m'sieu-dames,*" to the passers-by. Janine acknowledged the greeting with an inclination of the head and a murmured "Good evening," but keeping at some distance ahead of the others, she walked straight on toward the huge entrance gate surmounted by a great tower. Louise paused, her hand still resting on Larry's arm.

"Good evening, Justine," she said pleasantly. "It *has* been a lovely afternoon, hasn't it? I do hope your father's rheumatism will be much better, now that he will be able to get out in the sun again." The woman smiled, and though this smile revealed the sorry condition of her mouth, which contained only a few blackened and broken teeth, it also changed her look from one of anxiety to one of great goodwill. It was not hard for Larry to guess that the old man was in his dotage, and that his daughter was grateful to Louise for disregarding this and referring only to his rheumatism. "As you see, we have a visitor, Justine," Louise went on. "This is M. le Marquis' American nephew, M. le Lieutenant Vincent. You will, of course, let him in and out of the grounds without question, at any time."

"But of course, mademoiselle. It goes without saying. M. le Lieutenant must be very welcome at Monteregard."

She nodded, smiling more broadly and toothlessly than ever, and Larry felt unaccountably warmed by her friendliness. He had been so shocked, and so stirred, by what Louise had been telling him, that he was grateful for any sign of cheer. Evidently Louise was aware of this, for she looked up at him and smiled, too, and her smile was very lovely.

"We must not speak any more of these sad things," she said, "and you must not think about them too much, either.

You had to know them, because otherwise you would not have understood. But please do not think that Uncle Pierre will feel you have intruded. I believe he will be very glad to see you—very grateful for your company. He is so terribly alone. I do not think he and his mother were ever very close to each other, and now she stays in Paris all the time. She has always preferred that to Monteregard and she never comes here any more. She says it gives her a creepy feeling, that it is like a tomb. I hope you will not feel that way about it; and even if you do, I believe you can help to make it seem more like a home again. I do the best I can, but of course that isn't much."

"I should think you would make almost any place seem like a home," Larry said thickly. "But if I can help——"

"Of course you can help. I'm counting on you."

Louise quickened her pace, evidently hoping to overtake her cousin. But Janine had already disappeared when the others entered the great courtyard. A high wall, jutting out from the watchtower, met the château on one side and enclosed the raised garden which bordered it on the other. A row of red-tiled dependencies faced the entrance; these, in turn, adjoined the château, which flanked the entire left side expansively between its two majestic turrets. The courtyard was vacant, and there was something overpowering to Larry about is severity and its immensity; even the greenery of its triangular garden seemed dominated by the flights of stone steps which led from one terrace to another and the great stone jars which adorned them. There was no sunshine in the place, as there had been in the forest; there the warm light had filtered through the ivy-wreathed trees and here, where he felt the stones should have been bathed in it, there was none. Everything about the place was fortresslike and forbidding and there was an emptiness to its grandeur. Had it not been for Louise, Larry would have been tempted to turn away without going farther. As if she guessed what was passing in his mind, she slid the fingers which had been resting so lightly on his arm into his hand and pressed it.

"I think Janine's already told Uncle Pierre you're here," she said. "I think she hurried ahead, on purpose. Please don't be disturbed because she didn't seem very glad to see you. Pierrot's death was a terrible shock to her, too—they were much closer to each other than most brothers and sisters. She's had any number of suitors and they haven't meant a thing to her. She never wanted a sweetheart—just Pierrot. He felt the same way about her. And now she's talking about going into a convent. If that happened, it would be still another blow for Uncle Pierre. She's all he's got left, of his own. Of course he's fond of me, but it isn't the same, it couldn't be."

Just as she finished speaking the front door opened and, as it swung slowly back on its heavy hinges, Larry saw that a tall, slender man, dressed in black, was standing in the embrasure. His hair was iron grey and there were deep lines around his mouth, but he was strikingly handsome and carried himself with great distinction. Louise pressed Larry's hand again and then detached her fingers and hurried forward.

"Uncle Pierre," she began. But the man in the doorway shook his head slightly as a signal of interruption and came toward them, looking Larry straight in the face in a way she had never seen him look at anyone else before.

"Come in, Larry," he said, holding out both hands. "You are very, very welcome at Monteregard. I should have known you anywhere for Cary Vincent's son. No one else in the world could have had eyes like hers."

CHAPTER THIRTEEN

As CLARITY of thought gradually overcame delicious drowsiness the following morning, Larry was aware that sunshine was streaming into his room. Since this was the case, he speedily assured himself, his first impression of the château as cold and gloomy must have been erroneous. He lay still, revelling in the warm light—and in the astonishing and glorious realization that he was head over heels in love.

What a fool—what a fatuous fool—he had been, not to come to Monteregard on his first leave, and at every possible opportunity thereafter, instead of wasting precious time at Saumur and Tours! Why, if he had only followed his grandfather's advice, he and Louise might have been engaged by now, they might actually be preparing for their wedding! And he could be making this visit in the role of an accepted suitor—or even a prospective bridegroom! In his blissful state, he did not stop to consider that there might have been obstacles to a whirlwind courtship. After all, nothing could have been kindlier or more moving than the welcome he had received from the marquis. As for Louise, her instant acceptance of his presence, her unquestioning cordiality, her disarming confidences and the candour with which she returned his gaze of admiration, already quickening to ardour—all these combined to convince him that he had found favour in her sight, almost as swiftly and surely as he had looked on her with eyes of love.

Janine was nowhere to be seen when her father, linking his arm into their guest's, had drawn him into the entrance hall the evening before, and she did not reappear until just before dinner. Meanwhile, after inviting Louise to join them, Pierre had taken Larry straight through the drawing-room to his private study, rung for refreshments and told the servant who promptly brought pinaud and cookies that M. le Lieutenant's luggage was to be fetched immediately from the inn and placed in the *chambre charentaise.*

"I think that is the one you will like best, Larry," he said, turning back to the boy. "It faces east, so you will get the morning sun there; and it overlooks the reflecting pool and the surrounding gardens, which to my mind form a pleasanter view than the courtyard where you entered. I shall give orders, immediately, that we must have the fountains put into play again, in honour of your visit, and tomorrow night we will have them illuminated. But I believe there is a moon, and they are very pretty, by moonlight, without any artificial illumination. Am I right, Louise, about the moon?"

"Yes, Uncle Pierre. It is almost full."

"In that case, perhaps after dinner you and Larry would enjoy strolling in the garden for a little while. . . . And now, my dear boy, I want to hear where you have just come from and how long we may hope to have you with us at Monteregard. Later, if you feel inclined, I hope you will tell me what you have been doing ever since you arrived in France. Not that I expect you to go into details. But I should like very much to know about your experiences, in a general way."

The first two questions did not take long to answer. Then Pierre and Louise interrupted, almost simultaneously, with the protest that ten days were far too few for a leave, and Larry found this objection unexpectedly heart warming.

"Perhaps you'd let me come again sometime," he said a little hesitantly. "That is, if——"

Again he was interrupted. Of course he was to come to Monteregard as often as he could and stay as long as he wanted. There was no immediate prospect, was there, that he might be sent home?

"I don't think so. But that's just guesswork. The rule for dealing with soldiers seems to be a lot like that for dealing with reporters: 'Catch 'em young, treat 'em rough, tell 'em nothing'."

They laughed, as if he had said something witty and original and, encouraged by their friendliness, he began to talk about Saumur, the riding school and the kindly people, the sparkling wines and the beautiful countryside. He did not want to talk about the weeks at the front and he thought they guessed this, for they did not press him to do so; and he checked himself, when he was on the point of talking about Armistice Day at Tours, remembering that for them it had been a time of such personal tragedy that this must still overshadow all feeling of patriotic rejoicing. When he paused, Pierre asked him a few questions about the observers' course and the camp near Bar-le-Duc; then he rose, saying that he would show Larry the way to his room, that the luggage must be there by now and that perhaps a bath before dinner would feel good. Linking his arm through the boy's again, he went with him up the great marble staircase with the balustrade of wrought iron, down a long corridor hung with family portraits and beautiful old engravings, and threw open the door of a large chamber hung with soft chintzes. Finally he led Larry over to the casement windows, which he flung open.

"Look!" he said. "Don't you agree with me that this is a charming view?"

Larry's gaze followed the sweep of his host's arm. Beyond a great parterre, studded with flower beds and small conical trees, lay a silvery expanse of water, in which the wide colonnade, the great façade, the sloping roof and the twin towers of the château were reflected with such clarity that the effect was one of superb duplication. Flagstone walks, bordered with verdure, enclosed this magical mirror and met at its farther end near the base of a tiered fountain, surmounted by a marble maiden, where the water fell in shimmering sheets from one brimming basin to another. Except for the sound that this made, the place was still with a stillness akin to the silence of the enchanted forest. . . .

"Do I think it's *charming*?" Larry asked, after a long pause. "I—I think it's the most beautiful place I ever saw in my life!"

"That is what your mother thought, too," Pierre de Chanet answered in a strange voice. And he closed the casement and turned back into the room.

It was only a moment before, speaking quite naturally again, he called Larry's attention to the *dressoir* which stood in one corner, and which was adorned with quaint pottery plates, set in carved racks above a wide shelf, and deep drawers with ornamental handles. It was an old custom, in Charente-Maritime, to have such *dressoirs*, which resembled buffets, in bedchambers; but Larry must not think for a moment that they were intended to supplant the large sideboards which he would find in dining-rooms! Incidentally, dinner would be in an hour or so and the two girls would meet them in the drawing-room beforehand for an *apéritif*. Perhaps, given the ingredients, Larry would prefer to mix a cocktail himself. Or would he rather leave all such responsibilities to his host?

Much rather, he replied. And when Pierre had left him, after telling him again how very welcome he was at Monteregard, he went back to the window and reopened it. In the soft twilight, which merged into darkness so much more slowly in France than in Louisiana, the surface of the water seemed even more silvery than it had before, the greensward a deeper emerald, the flowing fountain more limpid. As Larry stood watching, the first gleams from the rising moon widened into radiance behind the marble maiden; and he saw that between the fountain and the pool there was a stone seat, not hidden away, like those in the forest, but openly placed, as if inviting rest after a stroll along the flagstone walk. Was this really where he and Louise would be coming, after dinner, he asked himself unbelievingly. It must be, from what his uncle had said to her in the study—"Perhaps after dinner, you and Larry would enjoy strolling in the garden for a little while." Yet it was hard to realize that before the end of the day, when he had found Louise in the secret bower, he would walk with her beside these moonlit waters.

The music of chimes, followed by the striking of a clock, sounded above the flow of the fountain and served as a summons to leave the window a second time and make haste with his preparations for dinner. A bathroom, less suggestive of ancient and honourable custom than the *dressoir*, adjoined the *chambre charentaise*; and, having hastily showered and dressed, Larry raced through the long corridor and down the stairs. The drawing-room door stood open and, as Larry entered, Pierre looked up with a smile from the drink he was mixing and told his guest to help himself from the tray of canapés that stood near by. The marquis had changed from his black clothes to a striking uniform and there was a row of ribbons across his breast—obviously he had received almost every kind of decoration which a grateful government could bestow. The two girls were seated side by side on a sofa, and it was Janine who was wearing black now. Larry could not help feeling that she was trying to emphasize the family mourning with all the greater insistence because her father had made an effort to lighten it; but the dress was beautifully cut, and the sheer chiffon of which it was fashioned softened the effect of her plainly parted hair and the slight stiffness of her carriage. Louise was in chiffon, too, a pale grey shot with silver, and with this she was wearing a long chain of moonstones. Looking at her, Larry felt as if she were telling him something, too—telling him that she had chosen this dress and these jewels because they were suited for a walk in the garden and that she wanted him to know she was eagerly awaiting the moment when they could wander beside the water.

Dinner was announced while they were all still sipping their drinks and Janine put down her glass at once. It was still almost full, Larry noticed, and she had hardly spoken at all.

Pierre, on the other hand, had taken the lead in pleasant and easy small talk; now he motioned the servant away and assured Larry there was no hurry, nothing would spoil if they had refills. Despite his preoccupation with Louise, Larry had not failed to be conscious of their uncle's extraordinary charm, and to sense, beneath his grace of manner, a deep underlying sadness which bore no resemblance whatsoever to his daughter's parade of grief. He spoke to her very gently, as if he were sorry for her and were trying to spare her feelings in every possible way; but somehow it did not seem to Larry as if she were as close to him as Lousie, to whom he kept turning with obvious affection and without restraint of any kind. Perhaps that was part of the tragedy of Pierre de Chanet's life—that his niece was really dearer to him than his daughter and that he would have been happier if he could have claimed the nearer relationship. But it could be only one part, of course —the terrible dual loss he had sustained in the death of his only son and of his wife would account for a great deal more. Not everything, though. Larry did not know why he felt so sure of this, but he did. Perhaps Pierre had hoped for several sons, which would have been quite natural; perhaps he had not only been deeply disappointed because there was only one, but unable to rise above the realization that, had there been three or four, it was improbable that he would have lost them all. Larry did not hazard any further guesses. But, inconsequentially, he remembered that Pierre had spoken twice of Cary Vincent—and that each time, brief as the comment had been, it had been deeply moving.

As if he divined that Larry was thinking about him and wished to divert these thoughts, Pierre remarked that perhaps they had better go in to dinner at the end of the current drink —after all, this was an occasion that called for champagne and they must not dull their taste for that. So they left the drawing-room and passed through the hall into the great library, which Larry had not seen before, and from there to the original kitchen which, for the last few generations, had served as a dining-room. An enormous hooded fireplace covered all one side of it; and, close to this, a small refectory table had been drawn up, leaving the centre of the room spaciously open. A fire, kindled from small, neat pieces of wood, was burning on the hearth; and the great copper utensils, with which the remaining three sides of the room were hung, caught and reflected the light from this and from the sconces interspersed among the burnished basins and skillets and saucepans. An arrangement of spring flowers, in a large copper bowl, formed the centrepiece of the table and two smaller bowls, correspondingly filled, stood near either end. The service plates, similar to those Larry had seen on the *dressoir*, were more noticeable for quaintness of design than delicacy of texture; but the silverware was massive and crested and the crystal finely etched. Two decanters, which matched the goblets in pattern, were filled with wine, ruby coloured in one case, topaz coloured in the other; and as Pierre asked Larry his preference, he remarked that both were the product of the Monteregard vineyard and that he hoped his nephew would feel like sampling both—if not that evening, then all in good time.

"I am sure you had sole for lunch, and veal," he remarked. "So we have tried to vary the menu a little tonight, and let you begin with our own favourite *pot-au-feu*, in whose concoction we think our aged Alphonsine excels, and then go straight on to our duckling, of which we are also rather proud. Therefore, the red wine is quite in order, from the beginning until the salad. Later there will be a soufflé, for which we may have to wait a few minutes—Alphonsine can take no chances on the length of time we may talk; but I believe you will feel it worth waiting for. The champagne will come on with that and afterward, of course, the cognac—that is inevitable in these parts. Incidentally, it might interest you to go to the city from which this most noble of liquors takes its name. It is not far from here—just far enough, in fact, to provide a day's pleasant outing. Yes, decidedly, we must arrange such an excursion. I have several friends among the manufacturers and I really believe you would enjoy visiting both their homes and their factories which, for the most part, adjoin each other, in a row facing the river. Some of them date back to the time of Francis I and many have lovely gardens. Ah—here is the *pot-au-feu!* Now tell me frankly what you think of it, Larry, and if it is not to your taste, we will find you something else."

200

Indeed it was to his taste, Larry answered, feeling the reply inadequate. He felt the same way about his praise of the glowing wine, the crusty bread, the succulent duck, the frothy soufflé—in fact, everything he mentioned. He felt even more strongly about the things he did not mention—the fragrant flowers, the warm fire, the soft candlelight, the gleaming copper; most strongly of all about the growing attraction which Pierre de Chanet had for him, and the tenderness, fast becoming a tumult, which Louise had awakened. Of course nothing could ever be quite perfect, he told himself; and this time it was Janine's attitude which disturbed his sense of well-being and brought a little bitterness to his brimming cup of happiness. She had crossed herself and murmured something, presumably a grace, as she sat down, and the action might have been a touching one if it had been differently performed; as it was, Larry could not help feeling that it was a deliberate rebuke to her father's conviviality, just as her exaggerated mourning had been a rebuke to his full-dress uniform. Once seated, she had kept crumbling her bread into little pieces, occasionally putting a morsel into her mouth. She tasted her soup, but she ate almost nothing else; and when her father asked her, solicitously, if she were not feeling well, she reminded him that it was a long while since she had had any appetite. She did not decline to drink a toast when the champagne was served, but Larry felt she might almost better have done so, for she raised her glass unsmilingly and barely touched it with her lips. Then, soon after coffee and cognac were brought into the library, she asked her father if he would excuse her, this time with the reminder that ever since the beginning of Lent, she had spent every evening at prayer in the chapel.

"I had thought that perhaps, since this is Larry's first night here——" Pierre began, in the same gentle, almost careful way that he had spoken to her right along. But Janine interrupted him.

"I shall, of course, include Larry in my prayers. However, with your permission, *mon père*——"

He rose, kissed her forehead and stood watching her as she accepted, without returning, an embrace from Louise, and bowed to Larry. When she left the room, instead of sitting down again immediately, Pierre glanced from his niece to his nephew, and then let his gaze rest affectionately, first on one and then on the other.

"You must both make allowances for Janine," he said. "The young—especially the female young—do not know how to make a companion of grief. They treat it like an enemy and so, of course, it becomes one. Fortunately, you do not know any of this from experience, as yet; but take my word for it. Janine is really suffering and I am afraid this makes her seem a little self-centred. Well, we will not talk about that any more—in fact, I do not think that you two should remain here any longer, chatting with a dull old man who prefers a comfortable fireside to a moonlit garden. Get yourself a wrap of some sort, *chérie*, and then take this *mauvais sujet* out of my way, so that I can read some naughty novel in peace."

"But you will tell us the name of the naughty novel, so that we can read it ourselves at some time, won't you, Uncle Pierre?" Louise inquired archly from the threshold.

"Perhaps. If you will promise not to read it aloud to each other. That I could not countenance. You must admit that I have already shown myself very broad-minded, in suggesting an evening stroll."

Lousie laughed and ran off to get her wrap. Larry stood very still for a moment, studying the deep-cut motto above the stone mantel. It read:

FIDE—FIDELITATE—FORTITUDINE

He was conscious of Pierre's eyes upon him as he did so and then of the older man's arm around him again.

"We have our standards, too, you see," he said, "though I'm afraid we don't always live up to them."

"Does anyone?"

"Perhaps not. But some of us come closer than others. And all of us come closer than if we were without any—even the worst of us."

"Uncle Pierre," Larry burst out, "you don't know what it's meant to me—having you welcome me the way you did, making me feel like one of the family. I've been away from Louisiana a long time and—well, I guess I must have been getting more homesick than I realized. Anyhow——" He stopped, swallowing hard. "And now, letting Louise go out with me," he managed to add, "I—I know it's very unusual, in France, for the guardian of a girl like her to—to——"

"It's not unusual, in France or anywhere else, for a man of average intelligence to see straight enough to size up a given situation," Pierre answered. "Probably I don't need to tell you that this will be the first time Louise has ever been out alone with a man. But we have an old saying, '*Bon grain fait bon pain*'—good grain makes good bread. Well, I didn't need to translate—you speak French almost as well as I do. I knew your—I knew both your parents. I knew your grandmother and your grandfather, too. No, I don't need the reminder I know you'd rather not give me that Clyde Batchelor really isn't your grandfather. You're the child of his spirit, and sometimes such a one counts for even more than a child of the flesh." He paused, and again Larry thought of the impression he had received earlier in the evening that it was Louise and not Janine whom Pierre loved best in the world. "I know that you and Louise will be very happy together in the garden, this evening," he said. "And I know, too, that she will be as safe there with you as she would be here, with me. Later— some other day, I mean, of course—you will probably visit the grottoes together. But even then——" He dropped his hand and turned. "Ah—there you are, my dear. A very wise choice, that little grey fur cape. It is still chilly, after the sun goes down. I shall sit here, reading my naughty novel, till you come in, and then perhaps we may all have a nightcap together. But do not stay out too long. The aged need more sleep than the young."

That was the way it had been and now Larry lay thinking about all this as he watched the sunlight come streaming through the casements, flooding the room with its warmth and its brilliance. He was quite content to stay where he was—for the time being. Of course before long he would want to get up and go downstairs and find Louise. But first he wanted to relive every moment they had spent together from the time of their meeting in the forest to the time when they had bidden each other good-bye in their uncle's study.

They had not meant to stay in the garden so late. But somehow the stroll from the colonnade to the fountain had taken longer than they expected. Then they had sat down to rest a few minutes, not because they were tired, but because it seemed the natural thing to do. Once they were seated, there seemed to be many, many things that it was natural they should want to say to each other; and by and by, it seemed natural that their hands should meet, and that they should sit with their fingers intertwined, not talking any more, but in an even more blessed communion of silence. Finally, Larry, looking into Louise's eyes, knew that he wanted to kiss her— more than he had ever wanted to do anything else in his life; knew, too, that she wanted to have him do so. But because she was what she was and what he wanted her to be, and not merely because Pierre had trusted her to him, he also knew that he must not do that until he had told Pierre, before he told Louise, what she meant to him and had asked for permission to marry her.

So they had come back to the study, not thwarted through the consciousness of that unshared kiss, but happy in the promise of it, and in the mutual understanding, which neither had put into words, of the reasons why it was still a promise and not an actuality. Pierre had laid aside his naughty novel, and looked from one to the other, and Larry had felt certain that their uncle not only knew how it was with them, but that he had known, from the outset, just how it was going to be. He did not reproach them for staying out so long; but he said he had found, when it got close to midnight, that he was growing thirsty, so he had had his drink without waiting for them, and now perhaps they had all better be saying goodnight. He would go to Larry's room with him again, to make sure everything had been prepared for his comfort; and when Larry protested, Pierre had said nonsense, he was going up anyway, for it was high time old men like himself were in bed. So they had all mounted the marble staircase together and, when they reached the top of it, Louise had thrown her arms around Pierre and hugged him hard, instead of standing solemnly before him, waiting for him to kiss her forehead, as Janine had done. Then, before she turned and ran down the long corridor, in the opposite direction from the one Pierre and Larry were taking, she had given Larry her hand and looked into his eyes again, and the promise of the kiss shone in her gaze, even more brightly than it had before.

After that, Pierre had paused at his own doorway and told Larry to come back and knock on it, if he found that everything was not all right in his room. Then Larry knew that his uncle was not going on with him, after all, because, in that case, they would have started to talk about Louise, and they had already said as much as they should to each other, for one evening, especially the first evening they had ever spent together. But Larry knew it would be all right to talk to Pierre about Louise the next day, in fact, that Pierre was expecting him to do so; he went on to bed and quickly to sleep, in spite of his joyous excitement. Now he had slept for hours and hours and it was morning again and the sun was streaming into his room and he was head over heels in love and it was a wonderful world.

CHAPTER FOURTEEN

LARRY was still rapturously daydreaming when there was a knock on his door and Léonard, the houseman who had served dinner the night before, came into the room, flourishing a tray.

"M. le Marquis felt sure M. le Lieutenant would wish to have coffee and crescents in his room," he observed, setting down the tray even more jauntily than he had carried it. "Especially as such service is not too customary in the Army," he added with a broad grin.

"You're right, it certainly isn't. . . . I take it you've had some military experience yourself."

"As what able-bodied Frenchman has not, *mon Lieutenant*! Ah, well! The bad years are over now and good ones ahead— or at any rate, so we may hope!" Léonard moved the coffeepot slightly to one side, bringing a vase into better view. "Alphonsine prepared the breakfast, of course, but Mademoiselle picked the flowers and placed them on the tray," he remarked objectively. The grin had disappeared and his manner was now entirely impassive. "I thought possibly it might be of interest to M. le Lieutenant to know this. And I was almost forgetting: M. le Marquis told me to say that he hopes M. le Lieutenant will enjoy his breakfast at his leisure. But later in the morning, M. le Marquis would be very pleased to see M. le Lieutenant in the study."

"Thank you, Léonard. Tell him I'll be there inside of an hour."

So he guessed immediately, Larry said to himself, as Léonard, grinning again, saluted smartly and marched away. *Well, I'm glad he has. There's no time to lose—two days out of ten gone already, and I've got to allow another to get back to camp. Why, that gives me only a week here!* It was all very well to talk about breakfasting at leisure, but his feeling of lazy contentment was gone now. He swallowed the coffee and bit into the crescents almost unmindful of their excellence, then shaved, showered and dressed at top speed. It was well under an hour when he presented himself at the door of the study and Pierre, who obviously had not expected him quite so soon, was deep in conversation with a thickset, black-bearded man whom he introduced to Larry as Robert Sabadelle, his head forester.

"No, don't go," he said, as Larry, somewhat confused because of his involuntary intrusion, murmured an apology and turned to leave. "Robert and I had finished with almost everything that required discussion, in any case. Incidentally, it might interest you to go out with him some time and see him in action. The beauty of our woods is not wholly accidental—we must give him credit for part of it." Then, when the forester, beaming with pride at this praise, had bowed his way out of the room, turning his soft hat round and round in his ruddy hands as he did so, Pierre went on, "We have eight families living in cottages on this place, besides a few unattached bachelors who are quartered in the tower. We try to keep the unattached spinsters quartered in the château proper, but sometimes the younger ones stray—well, that is neither here nor there. What I started to say was, that what with foresters and gamekeepers, gardeners and vineyardists, shepherds and stablemen, all needing to see me, or imagining that they do, I'm on call most of the time. Fortunately, Louise is very adept at running the house, considering her youth, so at least I do not have the cook and the butler and the rest of the domestic staff charging in and out of here early and late, and I have given instructions that you and I are not to be disturbed. . . . I trust you slept well?"

"Very well, thank you."

"Which goes to show you are young, healthy and essentially an Anglo-Saxon, in spite of your Creole heritage. Otherwise you would have been much too excited to sleep, judging from appearances when you came in last night—or did I misjudge them?"

"No, of course you didn't. You knew I'd fallen in love with Louise at first sight. But I wasn't so much excited as— uplifted. And I hope that doesn't sound like a silly thing to say, because it happens to be true."

"No, it doesn't sound like a silly thing to say and I know it's true. Sit down, Larry. You and I've got to talk this over, you know."

"Yes, I know," Larry answered, obeying instructions. "I was going to ask you if we couldn't, but you got ahead of me, by sending for me before I had a chance. I'm sorry. I did sleep like a top last night, but this morning, while I was waking up, I did a lot of lazy and very pleasant daydreaming. I didn't realize it was so late until Léonard came with the coffee and your summons."

"It wasn't a summons. It was an invitation—an invitation for you to ask Louise's hand in marriage, if that is what you want to do."

"You know it's what I want more than anything else in the world."

"Well, the idea isn't displeasing to me, either. If it had been, I wouldn't have sent you and Louise out into the moonlight together." Pierre paused and smiled so engagingly that Larry who, up to that moment, had spoken with the utmost seriousness, could not help smiling back, his heart warming more and more toward his host. "However, I think I should warn you that I am not the only person to please," Pierre continued.

"But I honestly believe that Louise——"

"There isn't the slightest doubt of it. In fact, she has told me so already—she succeeded in getting to me before Robert." Pierre smiled again, and this time Larry's heart seemed to turn over in his breast. "However, Louise is not of age and I am not her legal guardian—only a sort of foster father to her. I think you know—at any rate you should—that her mother—my niece Josephine—remarried shortly after the death of her first husband, Jehan de Courville. Louise's stepfather, Paul Carrere, has never shown much interest in her so far. But he is sure to reveal some, when the question of her marriage arises. In fact, I'm under the impression that he has been making some plans for her himself, and he is a very powerful person—which means that he would like to have still more power. It never fails. The right alliance for his stepdaughter might give it to him."

"But you wouldn't sacrifice Louise to the ambition of some revolting old man!" Larry exclaimed, his happiness suddenly engulfed in horror.

"Not willingly. Not without a struggle. But I am warning you that there may be a struggle. And probably, in all fairness, I should add that Paul Carrere is not a horrible old man. He is very personable and very gifted and he is about my age, like Josephine. Those two marriages of my father certainly made our family relationship very confusing. . . . Speaking of my father's marriages, my own mother is still living. In a sense, she is the matriarch of the family. The wishes of a woman in that position carry great weight in France."

"But surely there couldn't be any reasons why she should raise objections! I should think it was a lot more likely that she'd be very pleased, too. After all, Cindy Lou was her home once. If Louise married me the marquise might feel that it was coming back into her family, in a way. At least——"

"At least, it looks like that to you. But unfortunately, my mother and yours were not especially congenial. Not that I am blaming either, you understand. It was just one of those things."

"Why, Dad showed me the letters my mother wrote when she was visiting here and she said she admired the marquise very much!"

"Yes, I believe she did—then. Or perhaps she was in a mood to admire almost everyone and everything. She was on her honeymoon, you know." Pierre picked up a paper cutter and began to balance it on his fingers. The gesture did not seem like an indication of restlessness; on the contrary, like everything else about him, it betokened the ability to give the impression of ease under almost any circumstances, the refusal to permit grimness or even grief to engulf urbanity. He was now wearing grey tweeds, with only a black tie and a black arm band as concessions to mourning custom, and his face was less drawn than it had been the night before; even the lines around his mouth looked less deep. "However, later on, when my mother and I went to Louisiana, the spring before you were born, she and Cary apparently rubbed each other the wrong way, on one or two occasions," he went on casually. "I wasn't present, so I don't know exactly what happened. My mother never told me and naturally I didn't ask."

"My mother didn't tell you, either?"

"No. Remember I never saw her after that spring, Larry."

"But surely you don't think merely because my mother and yours weren't congenial, as you put it, the marquise would object to my marrying Louise!"

"I don't know. I hope not—though I believe the sort of alliance Paul Carrere has in mind would have more appeal for her. In any case, we shall very soon find out."

Pierre laid down the paper cutter and straightened the big, leather-bound blotter on the desk. "It is not very often that a well-brought-up French girl attempts to circumvent her father," he said. "But Janine has done exactly that. She visited me this morning, even earlier than Louise, and informed me that she had written her grandmother, who, as usual, is in Paris, and Josephine, who is also there, urging them to come here at once. She sent these letters off by the first post, before she told me about them. It seems she was very much shocked because you and Louise stayed in the garden so late."

"*Very much shocked!* Why, there wasn't a word we said or a thing we did that——"

"I know, Larry. And I think, down deep in her heart, Janine knows it, too. But she is in a very strange—a very sad state. My poor wife was also subject to such periods of depression. If she had not been . . ."

209

Pierre left the sentence unfinished and Larry did not attempt to complete it for him or to answer him. If Armande had not been the victim of acute melancholia, of course she would not have committed suicide, Larry realized that. Probably she would never have left her husband, either, if it had not been for a distorted outlook on their relations to each other and on life in general. Yet it was hard for the boy, who remembered her only as kindly and beautiful and pleasure-loving, to visualize her in the same light that he saw Janine. However, Pierre apparently saw them both clearly and turned the same unflinching gaze upon himself.

"I am afraid these periods of depression have been largely my fault. I have not been very successful, Larry, either as a husband or as a father. That is, I certainly did not make my wife happy, and I have not made my daughter any happier, though it was different with my son. He and I spoke the same language. We were very close to each other." Pierre glanced down at his desk again, and Larry saw that his eyes were fixed on the photograph of a fair boy, who looked too young to be a soldier, though he was in uniform, and whose expression, like that of Louise's, was singularly candid and cheerful. "When I say the same language, I am not thinking about French and English," Pierre continued. "Of course we are all bilingual, and even if we had not been, that would not have made much difference. I doubt whether there would ever be any difficulties between you and Louise, even if you had begun your acquaintance without the benefit of a common tongue. I had something else in mind."

"I know you did," Larry answered. Momentarily, his sympathy for Pierre had engulfed his dismay at the unexpected prospect of obstacles to his suit.

"Well, Louise and I speak the same language, too," Pierre said, turning away from the picture. His first words had been obviously spoken with an effort; but as he went on, his voice sounded quite natural again. "And I'm sure that everything will come out all right in the end. Meanwhile, I must give you two reminders, which will probably seem to you con-tradictory: first, you and Louise are not engaged, nor can you be, until there has been a family council on the subject; second, my mother, my niece and my niece's husband, the cabinet minister, will probably all be arriving here within two or three days, and after their arrival your style will be very much cramped—to borrow a good American expression. There is nothing, as far as I am aware, to cramp it in the meantime—except your own sense of the fitness of things. I have told Janine that I am greatly displeased by her lack of cordiality to a guest and a kinsman; I think you will find her less antagonistic from now on, especially as she has done, or tried to do, all the harm she can for the present. I shall not use up your time with any more long talks, and Louise tells me that she has unlimited leisure on her hands. I think, if you look for her, you may find her in the library, and as she is not an especially avid reader, she will probably be very glad to take a short walk before lunch. And, by the way, you might give her this—from me, of course."

He picked up a small box, covered in threadbare velvet, which lay beside Pierrot's picture, and handed it to Larry. "If I am not mistaken, the heart-shaped brooch inside this box belonged to a very distinguished ancestress of yours," he said. "At all events, the tale told of it is that it was given to such a lady by the King of England when she went with her young husband, as a bride, to claim a royal grant in Virginia. It was handed down, from one generation to another, until it came to your grandmother. Then, with great generosity, she gave it to my fiancée, instead of keeping it for her own daughter. Now I should like to give it to Louise rather than Janine, and I think my poor wife would have felt the same way, or of course I should not do so. Who knows? Perhaps it will prove to be a luck piece, and that some day your bride will wear it at Cindy Lou, which is where it belongs."

CHAPTER FIFTEEN

PIERRE was right: his mother, his niece and his niece's husband all arrived at Monteregard within three days.

The marquise was the first to put in an appearance, as the cabinet minister was detained in Paris by an important meeting, and she was not willing to await his departure, which, as a matter of fact, his wife did most reluctantly. As soon as the marquise was settled in the apartments at Monteregard which were always kept in readiness for her, though she so seldom occupied them, she sent for her son and subjected him to a tirade which became increasingly vehement when he listened to it with the air of detached indifference which had always infuriated her. After she could think of nothing more which could possibly be said to Pierre, she demanded that Larry be brought into her presence and, after inspecting him through a lorgnette, as if he were some kind of a repulsive curiosity, she began to bombard him with questions, most of them entirely superfluous.

"So you're Cary Vincent's son?"

"Yes, madame."

"And you've lived at my beautiful old home all your life?"

"Well, not quite. I wasn't born there. I was about six months old when my parents died. Since then I've lived with my grandfather, except, of course, this last year and a half, when I've been in the Army."

"You don't mean to tell me that your grandfather is still living?"

"Yes, I'm thankful to say he is."

"He must be a terribly decrepit old man by now."

"He's over eighty, but he's not in the least decrepit. He still rides around the plantations every day—at any rate, he was still doing so when I went to camp in the fall of '17 and he's never written about having stopped."

"He probably doesn't want to tell you. Or perhaps he can't. Senility sometimes sets in very suddenly."

"I'm sure that if anything like that had happened, Father Le Grand would have written to tell me about it."

"Father Le Grand? Who, pray, is Father Le Grand?"

"He's the priest at Convent who married my father and mother and baptized and confirmed me. He and my grandfather are great friends."

"I thought your grandfather was an atheist. I can't imagine a priest being friendly with him."

"Well, he is."

Larry's tone was even and his manner civil, but both gave the same impression of detachment and indifference which

212

had so infuriated the marquise on the part of Pierre. As a matter of fact, the principal effect she had produced on Larry had been one of deep disgust. He had expected to be somewhat overpowered by her; instead he saw nothing awe-inspiring about her—a wizened old woman, with too much rouge on her withered cheeks and too many rings on her clawlike hands, whose fussy dress gaped open to disclose a shrivelled neck and whose curly black wig had slipped a little to one side, revealing wisps of mousy hair underneath. She was a great one to talk about decrepitude and senility—why, she must be getting on toward eighty herself, and she certainly did not carry her years with either vigour or dignity! When Pierre had spoken about the 'matriarch of the family' Larry had visualized someone quite different—a stern, forbidding sort of woman, but a person to be respected as well as feared. If he and Pierre and Louise among them could not get the better of this vapid old hag, they did not deserve to. But of course they would. . . .

"So you came here hoping to marry my granddaughter?" the marquise inquired sarcastically, rousing Larry from his brief reverie.

"No. I came here to see my aunt and meet my cousins and my uncle. I hadn't heard about Aunt Armande and Pierrot. Of course if I had, I wouldn't have barged in so unceremoniously. But I'd have tried to come, sometime before I left France, to see Janine and Uncle Pierre. I didn't know about Louise beforehand—that is, I must have heard about her in a vague way. But as she and Uncle Pierre both admit, the various relationships in the De Chanet family are awfully confusing to an outsider. I never paid much attention when I heard them discussed."

"Well, you hope to marry her now, I understand."

"Louise de Courville? Yes, I do. But she's not your granddaughter, is she? I think I have got relationships straightened out enough now to know that."

"To all intents and purposes, she is my granddaughter—quite as much as you are Clyde Batchelor's grandson."

"Oh! Well no, I didn't realize that."

"Which is quite natural, because she isn't," Pierre remarked equably.

"I'm not talking to you at present, Pierre. You and I have finished our conversation. In fact, I do not see that any useful purpose will be served by having you remain in the room any longer."

"As far as that goes, I don't see that any useful purpose will be served by having Larry remain any longer. You already knew the answers to all the questions you've asked him and you know the answers to those you still intend to ask him."

"No, I do not. No one has told me what Larry has to offer Louise—if anything. So far I'm forced to conclude that he's been presumptuous as well as precipitate."

"I'm not sure I understand just what you mean, madame—that is, about being presumptuous. I'll admit I was precipitate. But my leave is for only ten days."

"And you imagined you could leave Monteregard, at the end of ten days, as the accepted suitor of Louise de Courville?"

"Why, yes, I did. In fact, I've been encouraged to think I might."

"*Encouraged!* By whom?"

"By Louise."

"And by me," Pierre interposed quietly. "I'll admit I haven't given much thought to practical matters. They haven't greatly concerned me. But since they concern you, *ma mère*, I wouldn't say Larry's prospects were so bad."

"I suppose you mean he'll be his grandfather's heir. Well, I haven't forgotten about the paltry sum he paid me for Cindy Lou. No doubt it's worth more than that now, just as it was then. But it isn't worth enough to make Larry Vincent a desirable *parti*."

"Perhaps you've forgotten about Victoria, madame. That's mine already. My grandfather gave it to me on my twenty-first birthday. And he and I own a steamboat line together."

"A steamboat line! *A steamboat line!* I thought Clyde Batchelor sold that, after it nearly bankrupted him."

"He sold one, but now we've got another. And it's doing very well indeed. Of course I couldn't surround Louise with the magnificence she lives in here. But after all, this doesn't belong to her, does it?"

"The places you're talking about won't, either. I know that much about Louisiana law. They'd be your separate and

214

paraphernal property, because you owned them before your marriage."

"I don't own Cindy Lou yet. I hope I shan't for a long time after my marriage. Because when I do, it'll mean my grandfather's dead. But then it will be community property."

"Bah! The next time you hear from Clyde Batchelor, it'll probably be indirectly, through his executor."

"I don't agree with you, madame. But if you really think there is any such danger, why not consent to an immediate wedding? As I just pointed out, any property I acquired after my marriage would belong to Louise as much as to me. So if we married before the end of my leave, she would be completely safeguarded from the financial point of view and you could be quite easy in your mind."

Pierre laughed outright. "*Touché, ma mère!*" he said lightly. "I think Larry has you there. What do you say? Shall we set the wheels in motion at once? Of course there are certain formalities. But what is the use of having a chapel under your own roof, if these cannot be expedited, on occasion?"

"I think you must have lost your mind, Pierre. And between you and Larry, I am completely worn out. I feel the need of a long rest and shall not come down to dinner."

"You certainly won that last round," Pierre observed to Larry, as they went down the corridor together. "And I imagine you are not feeling very sorry that you were at least partly responsible for my mother's exhaustion. But do not be too hard on her. When she was young, an extremely small waist was considered a sign of great beauty—a wasp waist, it was frequently called. To achieve it, a lady went through all kinds of tortures from tight lacing, which compressed her inner organs. In the process, her disposition sometimes suffered also and became waspish in its turn. I am afraid that is what happened in this case."

"I can't for the life of me see why a small waist should be considered beautiful."

"Of course you can't. But that is because the girl you are in love with wears dresses as straight as a chemise from shoulder to hem, and thus sets your standards of the female form divine. What is more, the hemline is sufficiently high to permit a very satisfactory view of her shapely legs, which I assure you would not have been the case in the days of tight lacing—you would have been lucky if you had caught sight of anything above the ankle, before your marriage. What is more, if you tried to take your fiancée in your arms, you would have encircled stiff stays, you would instantly have been repulsed and you would have been able to get very little feeling of a warm, vital body underneath. I am told that now, even in quite conservative circles, young girls of unimpeachable character permit their accepted suitors to embrace them—with discretion, of course."

Larry did not answer. To his chagrin, he realized that he was blushing, for he could feel his face and neck growing hot. But at least it was not the heat of anger. He had been furiously angry before the session with the marquise was over, but he had managed to conceal this—or at any rate believed that he had. If he had been obliged to choose between the two, he would much rather have betrayed slightly guilty embarrassment than rage.

"However, as I reminded you before, you and Louise are not engaged yet," Pierre went on serenely. "What is more, if my mother accepts your challenge, you never will be, for you will be married before there is any time for an engagement. Well, I suppose we must await the arrival of Paul and Josephine before we go any further into this matter of marriage. But that gives you another twenty-four hours' reprieve from dismissal, at all events."

M. and Mme Carrere arrived the following afternoon and, from lunch time on, Larry waited in his room, expecting a summons as prompt as the one he had received from the marquise. But hour after hour passed, while he strode impatiently up and down or stared almost unseeingly out of the casements, and still no one sent for him. He tried to read and could not; but at last he managed to focus his gaze, if not his attention, on a beautiful white swan which was gliding over the reflecting pool, followed by her cygnets. He had not noticed them before, but that was no sign they had not been there; after his first breathless glimpse of the gardens, he had been far too preoccupied with Louise to be conscious of other attractions.

At last, when he had waited so long that he had begun to

imagine all sorts of unlikely calamities, Léonard brought him a note on a crested tray. He tore it open and read it avidly.

Dear Larry:

You will be wondering if we have all stabbed each other in the heat of argument. It is not quite as serious as that, though from your point of view, I can well understand that the elimination of everyone but Louise—with the possible exception of myself—from the scene might appear an unmitigated blessing. Unlike *maman*, Paul and Josephine wished to talk first with Louise. They did not invite me to be present at this interview, but after they had dismissed her—I think in well-concealed despair—they sent for me and I was able to form a pretty fair idea of what had just taken place. My guess that Paul already had some sort of alliance in mind for Louise was correct—a very wealthy and well-born young diplomat, Raoul de Bonneville, just now attached to the Foreign Office on the Quai D'Orsay, but scheduled for a post at Rome in the near future. I am sure they imagined that Louise would find such brilliant prospects irresistible, and that they were as much surprised as chagrined by her complete lack of appreciation, and her stubborn reiteration that if she could not marry you she would not marry anyone. Their attitude toward me was one of cold courtesy and even chillier criticism; they blamed me for inviting you here in the first place and for aiding and abetting your suit afterward. I hope you will not feel I failed you when I tell you my reply: that I did not invite you here, and that your suit needed no aiding and abetting from me, since you and Louise fell in love with each other so fast that everything was as good as settled between you by the time you emerged from the woods and reached the château. Of course I added that, though I did not expect you, your visit was the most welcome one we had had in a long while, as far as I was concerned, and that I whole-heartedly supported your proposal of marriage. So now you and Louise and I are all in the bad graces of the Carreres together, as we are in my mother's. But you need not fear that you are in for another scene, such as you had with her. Paul and Josephine will be exceedingly polite to you,

217

because it is part of their code to be civil, even when they have murder in their hearts, and I do not think they have quite reached that stage, even yet. You will find us all assembled in the drawing room for drinks before dinner, as usual, and if you will take my advice, you will act as if you were a kinsman, taking his reception for granted, rather than an uneasy swain. Have patience, I still believe *tout s'arragnera*, though not tonight.

Yours, with affection,
PIERRE DE CHANET.

So everything would arrange itself, would it, though not tonight? A likely chance! Never had the complacent French phrase, which Larry had always hated, seemed so irritating and so misleading. And how in heaven's name was he to have patience—with five days of his leave already gone and only five more ahead of him, the last of which must be spent in getting back to camp? Pierre knew better than to give such assurances and advice! Yet, as Larry re-read the letter, he was increasingly and ungrudgingly aware of the kindliness with which it was permeated. 'Yours, with affection, Pierre de Chanet.' Yes, there was no doubt about it, his uncle was his friend, and his best chance of success lay in following the lead that had been given him. Since nothing had been said about presenting himself sooner, Larry gathered that he was not expected to put in an appearance until just before dinner and that, above all, an attempt to see Louise alone would be very unwise at this juncture. Glancing at his wrist watch for at least the fiftieth time, he saw that he still had another hour of involuntary seclusion and, sitting down beside the window, he scribbled one of his half-punctuated, unparagraphed letters to his grandfather. It was longer than usual, partly because he had not written at all since he had left camp and was suddenly and guiltily aware of this; partly because he really wanted to tell Clyde everything about his visit at Monteregard, including his newborn love for Louise; and partly because he felt the driving need of occupation. He was still writing, at last absorbed in what he was doing, when Léonard knocked at his door again and said that M. le Marquis had sent word to say that drinks would be a little earlier than usual, because, with more of the family present, more time would be required to enjoy them before dinner.

Grateful for the warning, Larry pushed aside the sheets on which he had been scribbling, washed his hands and went downstairs, reaching the drawing-room just as Pierre entered it from the study, but not before the marquise, who had evidently recovered from her exhaustion, was already ensconced in a thronelike chair. Far from giving her regal aspect, this made her appear more artificial, more shrivelled and more venomous than ever. She barely acknowledged Larry's cool, "Good evening, madame"; but when M. and Mme Carrere came in, accompanied by Louise, they shook hands with every appearance of cordiality and at once entered into animated conversation with him. Even though this was only surface courtesy, it was infinitely better than the unveiled animosity of the marquise; and if Larry had not realized that, at heart, the new arrivals were quite as hostile as she was, he would not have been too unfavourably impressed by them. Mme Carrere was beautifully turned out, and her fine figure showed off her perfect clothes to great advantage; and though her complexion and her hair had unquestionably both received expert touching up, her colouring still retained much of the same quality that made Louise's so lovely. M. Carrere's dinner jacket was a little too tight for him, and he did not wear it with the careless grace which Pierre managed to effect, whatever he put on; but, on the whole, the cabinet minister, though not as tall as his wife and considerably broader, carried himself well; and his geniality, if assumed, was an excellent imitation of the real thing. Janine, who was the last of the family to arrive, was accompanied by a plump priest, whose appearance was actually jolly. The marquise, after acknowledging his presence with scarcely more ceremony than she had Larry's, beckoned to her son and spoke to him in a stage whisper.

"I thought this was to be a family party, Pierre. You did not tell me that you had invited outsiders."

"Oh, but M. le Curé is hardly an outsider, *ma mère*! I thought it would be pleasanter to have an even number at dinner . . . also, that possibly our good priest might tell us whether he could waive some of the usual formalities, in the event that Larry and Louise should decide to get married at once."

"In the event that *Larry and Louise* should decide! Really, Pierre, you are becoming more and more insufferable every minute! This boy must have you bewitched, just as his——"

Larry had caught most of her speech. But the end of it was suddenly muffled, almost as if a silencing hand had been placed across her hideous painted mouth; and though of course nothing of the sort had happened, Larry saw that Pierre had bent over her and, while his face was hidden, something about the quick gesture seemed to bespeak threatening anger. At all events, her sharp words became an incoherent mumbling and presently trailed away into silence. Before anything else could be said, Léonard opportunely announced dinner.

The small refectory table, cosily drawn up before the hearth, had been supplanted by a large round one, set in the centre of the room, the peasant pottery by fine porcelain, adorned with the family crest. The tablecloth and napkins were also crested, and the latter were so large that as Larry unfolded his he thought at first a mistake must have been made somewhere along the line, and that this was also a *nappe*, not a *serviette*. The marquise was duly seated at the head of the table, with her son opposite her, the cabinet minister at her right and the priest at her left. Larry, securely wedged in between Josephine and Janine, thought she seemed in a somewhat chastened mood; and this gradually mellowed into something approaching urbanity, possibly because her dinner companions were extremely gallant in their bearing toward her. Janine, as usual, spoke very little and never on her own initiative; Josephine, on the contrary, chatted along in a merry, effortless way, and again Larry was conscious of an underlying resemblance between her and Louise. Twenty-five years before, she must have looked and acted much as her daughter did now; what, besides age, he wondered, had brought about such a change in her? Then suddenly he thought he knew; she had not married for love, but for 'practical reasons,' and these had not been cogent enough, after all, to keep her and Jehan de Courville together; they had drifted apart, just like Armande and Pierre. He remembered another letter, one of those that his aunt had written after her hasty return to France, in which she spoke of Josephine's second marriage—'to a cabinet minister with whom she had long been on very good terms.' Well then, she had probably been Paul Carrere's mistress before she became his wife, and that sort of furtive relationship must inevitably have had a corroding effect on a type of beauty—and of character—in which candour and single-heartedness were predominating factors. Her small talk, her chic, her faultless manner all lost their attraction for him; he understood why Louise preferred to spend most of her time at Monteregard. . . .

Alphonsine had prepared a perfect dinner and Léonard, wearing livery instead of a white coat and aided by a second houseman whom Larry had not seen before, served it with silent skill. There were no awkward pauses and Larry was obliged to admit to himself that he had no sensation of strain. This dinner, he supposed, was a fair example of what *savoir-faire*, combined with good breeding, could do to save a situation—though as far as the marquise was concerned, nothing could ever persuade him that she had been to the manner born; he was convinced it was in spite of her, rather than because of her, that everything proceeded so smoothly. He was beginning to feel an aversion for her which amounted almost to antipathy. It was no wonder, he told himself, that she and his mother 'had not been congenial.' How could there have been congeniality between Cary Vincent and the erstwhile Dorothée Labouisse, whom he had never once heard extolled in the locality where she had long lived? He decided that when he reached home again he would ask a few questions about her. Why, his grandfather should be able to answer them! After all, Clyde Batchelor had bought Cindy Lou from her. He must have seen something of her, and heard more, in the course of this transaction. . . .

Despite the absence of strain, Larry was relieved when the marquise gave the signal to leave the dining-room and Pierre, rising with her, said that, with her permission, the gentlemen would take their coffee in the library and join the ladies later in the drawing-room. Since he could not be alone with Louise, and since he knew that even an attempt to talk with her lovingly in the midst of such a gathering would have been a dismal failure, Larry welcomed the prospect of being in a group of men, rather than in mixed company. After all, he had been raised by a man; he had gone to a boys' boarding school and, even before he entered the Army, he had felt more at ease with men than with women. Perhaps he would get on better with Paul Carrere and M. le Curé than he did with the marquise and with Josephine. It was certain that he understood Pierre much better than he did Janine. Louise was the one glorious exception to his lack of understanding, when it came to women—his first real love, as he felt sure she would be his last. . . .

He was soon reassured by the general tenor of conversation, which ranged from political to military subjects, with no reference, for a long while, which could possibly be construed as personal. Pierre encouraged the cabinet minister to talk about crises, real and potential, in the government, and Carrere seemed quite willing to do so. Eventually, shifting adroitly from one topic to another, Pierre began to question the priest, whose name had belatedly been disclosed as Robineaux, about conditions in the parish, to which—so Pierre said—he feared he had not paid as much attention as he should of late. Then, remarking that of course all this was to be regarded as confidential, he asked whether, in the opinion of M. le Curé, Janine really did have a vocation, or whether he thought she was merely going through a phase, like so many girls and even some boys. The priest answered guardedly; certainly Mlle Janine was very devout, but he did not need to tell M. le Marquis that this was not enough for a vocation. To be a successful nun, a certain type of disposition was also desirable, if not actually requisite. A cheerful girl, whose own character was above reproach, but who viewed the shortcomings of others with charity, even with tolerance, was really more fitted for the religious life than one who was more morose and critical. The great Teresa herself— a pattern of austerity if there ever was one—had prayed to be delivered from gloomy saints. And, if M. le Marquis would forgive him for saying this, Père Robineaux felt that Mlle Janine was so inclined to see the dark side of things that perhaps . . .

222

"I could not possibly be more in accord with your views," Pierre said heartily. "In fàct, I'm inclined to believe that Janine would derive far more benefit from a love affair than from a postulancy. Do you think I could possibly be right, M. le Curé?"

"Yes indeed, quite possibly."

"She would have to be taken by storm, of course," Pierre went on, apparently warming to his subject. "But once all her false defences were down, she might surrender very quickly. You have known of such cases, haven't you, M. le Curé?"

"Yes indeed," the priest replied again. "In fact, the surrender is—ah—apt to be almost too rapid, if I may say so. Especially in unsettled times, like the present ones."

"Exactly. I think we must be prepared for such a contingency. Now if Janine should decide, very suddenly, that she wished to be married——"

The cabinet minister made a small clicking sound, to which Pierre paid no attention. Instead, tapping the arm of his chair by way of emphasis, he leaned eagerly toward the priest.

"Let us assume, for the sake of argument, that I, as her father and legal guardian, would have no objections to this marriage and would give my wholehearted consent to it, even though my daughter were under age," he said. "And let us also assume that I would have approached M. le Maire, and found that he was disposed to be most co-operative in regard to hastening the civil ceremony. Would you, as the priest of this parish, be equally co-operative? Supposing the young man in question could not, for instance, immediately produce a baptismal certificate, would the cabled assurance, signed by the priest who performed the baptism, to the effect that he was in possession of such a document, satisfy you? Would you be willing to do away with banns? I understand that a special dispensation is sometimes given to foreign nationals who are soldiers or war workers, and who cannot be absent, for any length of time, from their posts. Of course I may be mistaken, but——"

Father Robineaux glanced hastily in the direction of Larry. He thought he was beginning to understand the drift of the marquis' comments and questions, which at first had been somewhat puzzling to him. The cabinet minister made another little clicking sound, but his fellow guests, like his host, disregarded it. Larry and M. le Curé were now smiling at each other and, though the reasons for their smiles were different, mutual goodwill lay back of both.

"The church should of course co-operate with the state in every reasonable way," Father Robineaux said emphatically. "And in the case of our brave allies, who have done so much to rescue beautiful France from the detestable invader, the clergy, like the laity, must never lose an opportunity to show its gratitude. Of course it is also the purpose and policy of the church to—ah—safeguard young love with the proper sacraments. You may depend upon me, M. le Marquis, to serve you and yours in every way I can."

CHAPTER SIXTEEN

"Paul is very much annoyed with you, Pierre, and I am, too! You had no business leading M. le Curé on the way you did, giving him the impression all the time that you were talking about Janine."

"It's not my fault if M. le Curé leaps to conclusions. All I did was to present a hypothetical case. Possibly the next time Larry comes here to visit he will bring a friend with him; in that event, Janine might become as much attracted to such a friend as Louise has been to Larry. It is always well to be prepared for contingencies; as Janine's father, I naturally have her interests at heart."

"You were not thinking or talking about Janine and you know it. You were thinking and talking about Louise. You have put Paul and me in a very awkward position, Pierre."

"I am sorry. I did not realize you were so easily upset. I credited you with more *savoir-faire*."

Pierre de Chanet had risen politely when his niece came into his study the morning after her arrival at Monteregard, but he had immediately resumed his seat and remained entrenched behind his desk, while regarding Josephine with a calmness not untinged with slight mockery. He now picked up his paper cutter and began to play with it, a gesture which added to her fury. Still standing upright, she confronted him.

"And I credited you with more sense," she said angrily. "If I hadn't, I wouldn't have allowed Louise to come so completely under your influence."

"Excuse me. I thought the reason you were willing Louise should spend so much time at Monteregard was not because of my good sense, but because of yours. You realized, while poor Jehan was still alive, that a *ménage à trois* is not the best sort of home for a young girl. And after he was so opportunely killed, you realized that Paul's preferences should be your first concern—also that a grown daughter constitutes something of a give-away, as far as her mother's age is concerned. I have always admired your good sense very much, Josephine —in fact, I have often told you so. This is the first time you have ever mentioned mine. I did not suppose you thought I had any."

"I did, but I don't any more. Or any manners, either. How dare you say such things to me?"

Josephine's voice was becoming shriller and shriller. The more angry she became, the more composure Pierre displayed.

"Have I said anything that was not true?" he inquired calmly.

"It is no part of *savoir-faire* to talk the way you have been doing, whether one is telling the truth or not. You had better not mention that quality again. And since you realize that Paul's preferences are my first concern, you had better tell me how you think I'm going to meet them, in regard to this De Bonneville's marriage, now that you have made it so difficult for me to do so."

"I'm not going to tell you how I think you should meet them. I'm going to tell you, most emphatically, that I think for once you should disregard them, if you are not sufficiently adroit to change them tactfully." Pierre put down the paper cutter and his manner suddenly became stern. "Listen to me, Josephine," he said, almost harshly. "You will never get Louise to marry De Bonneville now. In fact, I doubt if you could have persuaded her to do so, even before she met Larry. I think she has somehow acquired the fixed idea that love is one of the requisites—perhaps even the main requisite—

for a successful marriage—possibly since she has seen one or two that were not very successful because they lacked it. Besides, I do not think that De Bonneville's type would ever have appealed to her—he is altogether too smooth a specimen to be quite real and Louise likes sincerity. Be all that as it may, she is now so deeply in love with Larry Vincent that you could not get her to so much as look at another man. If you and Paul will not let her marry him until she is of age, she will do so the day she is twenty-one."

"He may not be able to get leave the day she is twenty-one."

"Very well. Let us say for the sake of argument that he will not. I will amend my statement and say that Louise will marry him as soon after her twenty-first birthday as he is able to come for her. But I assure you I shall be very much surprised if there is any great delay. I think that at the first opportunity after his return to camp he will tell his commanding officer that he wants to get married, naming the earliest date at which his fiancée can arrange for the ceremony. And I think he will contrive to join Louise on or before that day. He is also very much in love and I think he has enough persuasive power to present his case so eloquently that no reasonable military superior of his will put obstacles in his way."

"Then the only hope you leave me is that he will encounter one who is unreasonable. Meanwhile, Paul and I will return to Paris tomorrow, taking Louise with us. I wish we were not dependent on the unspeakable train service. If we had come by car, it would have taken us longer to get here, but we could also have left as soon as we had sized up this deplorable situation."

Josephine flounced out of the study, slamming the door behind her. Pierre lighted a cigarette and, while he smoked it, pondered the situation which Josephine claimed to have 'sized up.' He did not consider that she had done so, and what was even more unfortunate, from his point of view, he did not feel at all sure that he could cope with it himself. However, after a few minutes' thought, he rang for Léonard and sent him to Larry with a message. When Larry appeared, in prompt response to this summons, Pierre chose his words

226

with extreme care, while endeavouring to avoid any semblance of undue concern.

"I'm beginning to feel as though this study were the *mise-en-scène* for amateur theatricals," he said. "You know, the kind where the different characters keep coming in and going out by the same door, in such a constant stream that you do not see how they can possibly avoid bumping into each other. At the same time, the opposing forces are not supposed to have the least idea what their antagonists are up to. Well perhaps it is not quite as bad as that but, as you know, there was a series of conferences here yesterday and now Josephine has just left and you have appeared."

"You sent for me, didn't you?"

"Yes, I sent for you, and I tried to make sure that Josephine, for whom I did not send, would be out of the way before you came through the drawing-room. I was speaking figuratively rather than literally. You didn't bump into her, did you?"

"No. But I suppose I should ask to see her, shouldn't I? That is, she and her husband are expecting me to do that, aren't they?"

"They are fearing that you will and they will be indignant if you do not. In the former case, they could not very well refuse to give you a hearing, which they wish to avoid, and in the latter, they would feel you had been remiss in not asking for one. I really think your best course would be to write a very formal note, requesting permission to pay your addresses to Louise, and then to wander off in the forest somewhere and not return until just before dinnertime. Alphonsine will give you some sandwiches to put in your pocket and a canteen to sling over your shoulder, or you can take a small knapsack, if you prefer."

"But then I wouldn't see Louise all day! And I have so little time left!"

Pierre picked up his paper cutter again. "I don't think it would be wise for you and Louise to disappear simultaneously," he said. "But if you will do as I have indicated, I will try to create the opportunity for her to join you after lunch. Don't ask me now just how I shall manage. My alleged mind is already overtaxed by all this manœuvring. However, no doubt I shall think up something. Meanwhile, by way of

227

further suggestion to you, I may add that the grottoes, especially the largest one, which we call the cathedral, have many times proved extremely satisfactory for rendezvous."

Larry remembered Janine had said, when he finally found his way to the little grassy bower, that the caves were 'best reached by another route,' and he thought it was quite possible that there was one which had been cut through since his mother's time. However, he also remembered Cary's description of tethering her horse to a stone seat and walking down a narrow winding path, bordered on one side by the river, 'thickly fringed with underbrush,' and on the other by 'a series of prehistoric caves, which keep getting bigger and bigger the farther you go.' Moreover, he remembered the sound he himself had heard as he approached the bower—the slight murmuring such as might be made by a stream or, in other words, by the river of which his mother had written. Since this was so, the grottoes could not be far from the secret enclosure. In any case, he was glad of a pretext to revisit the spot where he had first met Louise.

He went toward it without haste, but without bewilderment. He had a reasonably good sense of direction, and he experienced no difficulty in retracing his steps. But though the forest had lost some of its mystery for him, it had lost none of its magic. Since his arrival at Monteregard, one beautiful day had succeeded another, and the sunlight which filtered in through the branches of the ivy-wreathed trees had the same golden quality as when he had first seen it, the mosses and ferns beneath the same gilded verdure. When he reached the bower, he sat down and basked briefly in the midday warmth; then he plunged down the path which he had not previously taken.

It was even more overgrown than any he had found already and, at times, he could not hear the murmuring of water because of crackling twigs, unless he stopped and listened. Then its sound came to him, all the more alluring because it was so faint. Gradually he became aware that a rocky wall formed the background of the greenery at his left and glimpsed, at intervals, the rippling stream beyond the underbrush at his right. He was, perforce, going more slowly

228

now, because the path was almost impassable, and he began to wonder whether, after all, he had made a mistake in trying to reach the grottoes by this route. Then suddenly he saw a cleavage in the rock and a clearing in the underbrush. On one side of him was a low opening, overhung with dead branches, which looked all the darker because the stone which enclosed it had a glaring quality. On the other side of him was a limpid pond, surrounded by sedges and shaded by bright foliage.

So he had not been mistaken after all! Unquestionably, he had arrived at the first in the series of famous caves. The one he now saw was not large enough to enter, nor did it offer any temptation to do so. But in no time at all he would have reached his destination—the one which had a lofty vaulted top and long passages leading out of it in several directions. Meanwhile, under his very eyes, in deadly serenity, lay the Blue Pool.

For a few moments he stood gazing at it, fascinated in spite of himself. At first he could not see a single ripple on its smooth surface. But as he watched it a tiny bubble appeared near its centre and then another and another. Afterward, as surprisingly as they had come, they disappeared. However, Larry had seen enough to realize that under the seeming serenity was a whirlpool, and that once a hapless victim had been sucked under by it, rescue would be impossible. The story of the luckless lady who had lost her lover, centuries before, and who had cast herself into this pool because of the loss, might well be sheer fantasy; but the insidious force of the legend, combined with the insidious force of the water, had been strong enough to lure Armande to her death. Involuntarily, almost unconsciously, Larry crossed himself and, turning away from the Blue Pool, hurried farther down the path.

He did not stop to count the caves as he went by, but it was his impression that he passed five or six, each larger than the preceding one, before he came to the grotto which he instantly realized must be the cathedral. He believed he could easily have stood upright in two or three of the others; but he had felt no inclination to put them to the test, partly because the spell of the Blue Pool was still too strong upon him, and partly because it was only the cathedral that he was really eager to explore. It did not disappoint him. As soon as he entered it, he raised his arms as far as possible above his head and found that he could not reach the top even by doing this; and though he could not immediately adjust himself to the change from shimmering sunshine to comparative gloom, he realized that a good deal of light must actually be penetrating to the grotto because one of its immense sides was entirely open, and soon he was able to discern the vaulted formation above him and the tunnels which branched off at the rear. To his surprise, he saw that a fire, built of small neat pieces of wood similar to those used in the dining-room, was carefully laid in one corner. It must have been prepared years before, since no one had been allowed to picnic in the caves since the beginning of the war. But when Larry lighted a match and poked it under the sticks, these kindled almost instantly and suddenly the cave was transfigured by radiance.

It was not a rosy light; on the contrary, the dome above him seemed whiter than ever, the encircling walls more deeply green; but both were now dazzling in their brilliance and this brilliance was not confined to the cathedral. It suffused the openings of the passages leading out of it, at the rear, giving them an almost mystical quality of allurement. Larry found himself gazing toward them in fascination. Then, telling himself that it had been senseless enough to succumb to the spell of the Blue Pool, without doing anything so preposterous a second time, he resolutely looked away. . . .

Some flat stones had been arranged to form crude benches on either side of the fire and Larry sat down on one of these, smoked a cigarette and ate the excellent lunch which Alphonsine had prepared for him. Then, unexpectedly overcome by drowsiness, he lay down on the ground, using his knapsack for a pillow, and was almost instantly asleep.

He woke with a confused sense of strangeness and could not identify his whereabouts. At first he had a vague impression that he was again on the roadside near Vannes, where he had curled up and slept, because every hotel in town was full. Then he realized that the surface of the ground on which he was lying was much harder than the grass had been, that there was not open country but enclosing walls around him and that he was in a place where he had never been before. Next he began to remember what had happened that morning: he had waited and waited for Pierre to send for him, just as he had the previous day; and when he finally went to the study, he had been told to write a formal note to M. and Mme Carrere and then to go off for the day. He had been reminded that the cathedral had 'many times proved extremely satisfactory for rendezvous' and had gathered that he should wait for Louise to join him there. . . .

Well, he had waited and waited and still she had not come. In spite of the fact that his eyes were now accustomed to the dim light, he felt certain that it was darker in the grotto than when he had first entered it. He glanced at his wrist watch, whose radium dial gleamed in the gloom, and saw that the hands pointed to a quarter to five. With a one o'clock lunch, lasting an hour, Louise would have had all kinds of time to reach the cathedral, even if she had not been able to make a quick getaway; and after all, Pierre had not made any promises. He had only said that no doubt he could think up something. Perhaps he had failed to do so—or perhaps the failure had lain, not in his lack of resourcefulness, but in the execution of his plan. Larry had great confidence in Pierre's capability, when it came to meeting and overcoming difficulties, but he was under no delusions as to the amount of opposition which must be overcome. He would not even have put it past Mme Carrere, in her present frame of mind, to lock Louise in her room and keep her there until she could be swept off to Paris. . . .

That was absurd, he told himself next. Eventually Louise would come, thanks to Pierre's manœuvring, and she would have some logical, probably some rather commonplace, explanation for the delay. After all, there were still nearly two hours of daylight, out of doors. It had been senseless enough, the day of his arrival, to appraise the courtyard of the château as grim and cold, merely because he had first seen it at a time in the evening when the sun could not possibly strike it, except in midsummer. It was even more senseless to imagine that nightfall was near, merely because he was in a cave. Nevertheless, all this waiting was beginning to get on his nerves. He should have put a pack of cards in his pocket, or some writing paper, or both. He could have sat outside, near the entrance to the cave, and played solitaire or gone on with his letter, and that would have passed the time until Louise came. . . .

Failing such diversion, he cast about in his mind for some other. Fleetingly, he considered a swim in the near-by stream and as quickly dismissed the idea. He would no sooner get out of his clothes than Louise would come; that was the way such things always worked out. Suddenly he remembered that, according to his mother's letters, the tunnels leading from the caves also had some kind of a story connected with them, no less than the Blue Pool, though what the former was she had never learned. Perhaps, by investigation, he himself could find out. The idea had hardly taken form when the passages beyond him again seemed to assume a beckoning quality.

The fire he had kindled was out. He rebuilt it from stray sticks, scribbled a note on the paper in which Alphonsine had wrapped his bottle of wine and, propping up his knapsack against one of the stone seats, slipped the note under a strap. If Louise arrived while he was engaged in exploration, she would know that he had found their trysting place and that he would soon be returning to it. But he thought it most unlikely that she would get there before he came back. After all, he probably could not go far. It was merely that his curiosity had been so impellingly aroused that he had no choice but to satisfy it.

There were three apertures at the rear of the cave, superficially all much alike. Larry entered the centre one, which had a little more height than the others, and where he had no trouble in standing upright. But he had gone forward only a few yards when he was confronted by solid wall: the tunnel had come to an end so abruptly that when he turned to leave it he instantly saw the light from his little fire penetrating the gloom. The second aperture did not end so suddenly; but the stone formation overhead sloped downward in such a way that he found he could make no further progress, even on his hands and knees. Again he turned, worked his way back to the fire and went outside to look and listen for Louise. There was still no one in sight, no sound except for the rippling water and the slight crackling of the fire. He strode back into the cave and entered the third tunnel.

He was again able to walk upright, though he had less leeway than in his first experiment, and as he went forward he was soon obliged to stoop a little. Complete darkness enveloped him, but as he stretched out his arms he found that they no longer reached the sides of the tunnel. He stopped, lighted a match and saw that the passage had widened into a small low chamber, and that from this, in turn, two more tunnels branched out.

Since luck had come to him on the left before, after futile attempts in the centre and on the right, he decided to take to the left again. He progressed without difficulty and with increasing excitement; though he had a slight sense of eeriness, he had absolutely no feeling of fear. When another lighted match revealed a second low chamber, fairly gaping with openings, it did not occur to him to pause, as it had when he reached the clear circle dominated by the columns. There his good judgement had told him that if he chose the wrong path, among those which radiated from the circle like the spokes of a wheel, the afternoon might well be gone before he could rectify his mistake. Now he did not stop to reason; he thought only of going farther and farther into the cavernous depths. He hastened toward another tunnel, tingling all over with the thrill of adventure.

He was stopped, as he had been on his first attempt at exploration, by the abrupt ending of the tunnel. This did not discourage him. After all, it was only one of half a dozen which led from the second chamber; the next time he would have better luck. He felt his way back, lighted another match and surveyed his surroundings preparatory to making another choice. Only then did he realize that though he could indeed choose among several openings to continue his explorations, he had no idea by which one he had entered the chamber. They all looked exactly alike. He could go forward, as fast as he chose; it might take him hours to get back to his starting place.

He stood very still, trying to orient himself by remembering whether the tunnel by which he had entered the chamber had been opposite the one whereby he had left it and, if not, on which side of it. He could not do so. The sense of direction on which he had always prided himself had failed him, and in his haste he had acted with great foolhardiness. Now, all too tardily, he would have to pay the penalty for this, perhaps by hours of delay. Meanwhile, Louise would be waiting for him. Soon she would be worrying about him. Not, of course, that there was any reason to worry. . . .

He took off his jacket and laid it down by the opening of the tunnel from which he had just emerged. At least he would not make the mistake of going into that one again. If his next reconnoitre proved futile, he would lay something else beside the opening to the next tunnel he tried. On the other hand, if it led him back to the first chamber he could easily return for the jacket, because by this time he would have familiarized himself with his route. Resolutely telling himself that of course everything was all right, he entered another passage.

For some minutes he went cautiously along, again stretching out his arms to gauge the width of the tunnel. He still had plenty of matches left. Nevertheless, it was probably better to conserve them. He found, by feeling, that the walls still allowed him ample space; but for the first time his hands encountered moisture and the ground was slimy underfoot. Reluctant reason told him that he could not be headed toward the first chamber, for if these conditions had existed in the passage by which he had entered, he would have noticed them before. He swung around, determined to get out of the damp hole with the least possible delay. As he turned, he slipped; then his feet shot out from under him and he went down. When he regained his foothold he felt, instinctively, for his matches. They were no longer in his pocket.

It did not take him long to find them, but when he did so it was in a small crevice where water had formed. Frantically, he tried to light them, one after the other, in the desperate hope that at least a few might have escaped damage. Every one had been ruined.

He groped his way back to the second chamber and slumped down, engulfed in merciless and menacing darkness. By feeling for his coat, he knew which of the passages he had already explored because it lay between them. But there were still three or four other passages which he had not tried, besides

234

the one by which he had entered. There was no telling how long it would take before he found deliverance—if he found it at all. And he might very well pay for his recklessness with his life. Probably that was what had happened in this labyrinth before: some other rash fool had rushed in there, just as he had, and that was the last that had ever been seen of the hapless man. The reason Cary Vincent had never been told the whole story of the cave was because, after the story of the Blue Pool had been revealed, no one had wanted to heap tragedy upon tragedy in her hearing.

Of course he was not going to lie there like a log, conjuring up horrors. He would pull himself together and make a fresh start. Perhaps he would hit the right passage with the very first try. It would take a long while to find out whether he had or not, because he would be able to tell only by feeling when he reached the first chamber—if he did. Why, there was no if about it. Sooner or later, he was sure to find it. But it might be later rather than sooner. So there was no time to be lost. His search must begin right away. No, not right away, either. There was something else he must do first. Drawing himself to his knees, he began to pray. . . .

Prayer had been a habit for him, ever since he had learned the 'Our Father' and the 'Hail, Mary' from Tudie in his early childhood; from the time of his association with Father Le Grand, it had been something more than that. But he had regarded religion with reverence and with the feeling that it was part of the natural order of things, rather than with unquestioning faith or devout fervour. Even at the front, he had never prayed for safety. Indeed, he had regarded with a certain amount of contempt the men who prayed for their lives when they never prayed for anything else; what sort of a God was it they thought they believed in, he had asked himself more than once, if they approached His throne only to ask for favours and never in thanksgiving or praise or worship? Now, for the first time, he prayed with all his heart and soul that he might see the blessed light of day again—not because he was afraid to die, but because he could not bear the thought of dying until he had proved himself a man of mettle and not merely a foolhardy boy, not until he and Louise had shared the full experience of life and love. . . .

He was still on his knees when he heard her calling to him. The sound was faint and distant. But there was not even a momentary doubt in his mind that it was her voice he heard and that she had come to deliver him. As loudly as he could, he called back, "Louise! Louise!" The name took on new meaning and new music as he shouted. Her answering call came back to him instantly and it was louder now. He thought she might have reached the first chamber and since only two passages led from that, it would be only a matter of minutes before she could reach him, if she took the same one that he had taken. He called. "The left! The left!" But he did not know whether the words had carried, because all that came to him in return was something he could not distinguish. He tried again, in French, "*A gauche! A gauche!*" But the results were no better. Once more he heard the indefinite murmur and then there was silence. He realized that Louise must have taken the wrong passage.

A long period of blankness followed, but it did not trouble him. In one way or another, Louise would discover her mistake, return to the first chamber and try the other tunnel. He was so sure of this that he felt no anxiety, and was impatient only because the joy of reunion must be so long deferred. He waited with infinite eagerness but comparative calm, and when he heard Louise calling him again, he knew she had returned to the first chamber and that this time she would come unerringly toward him. Presently he heard her movements, as well as her voice, and then the striking of a match. There was a quick flash of light. The next instant they were in each other's arms.

CHAPTER SEVENTEEN

IT HAD become increasingly difficult for Clyde to write letters. This was partly because the physical effort of doing so was now very great; it was hard for him to sit upright at a desk. But it was even harder for him to make the mental effort of focusing his thoughts on a central subject and getting them on paper. More and more he was inclined to lounge in a comfortable armchair with Nuffy beside him—on cool days, close to his office fire; on warm days, under one of the great oaks that shaded the garden. Stretching himself out at ease, he would reread old letters which required no answers and, putting them back in their envelopes, close his eyes and relive the pleasant past which they evoked. Soon he would begin to grow drowsy and he seldom knew, nor did he greatly care, where his waking dreams ended and those which came with sleep began.

He was not lonely any more. The anguish he had suffered through the loss of Lucy and Cary, the poignancy of his parting with Larry, were sorrows of the past; one untroubled day succeeded another, with little or no variation. He was not annoyed when Dumaine or Tregre came to consult him about something on the plantations; they presented no serious problems for his consideration and they never stayed long. Since they said little or nothing to worry him and since their visits were brief, he enjoyed their company; but he almost never sent for them any more. Every Saturday, before Father Le Grand began to hear confessions, he came to see Clyde, and the old man looked forward to these visits. Less regularly and frequently, Dr. Doussan and Valois Dupré dropped in. Clyde enjoyed these visits, also. But Father Le Grand's were the only ones he would have missed if they had ceased.

He had stopped riding. But once a week Nappy drove him in the old cabriolet to the cemetery, so that he could put flowers on Cary's tomb. When he was not too tired, he stopped at Victoria, on his way back to Cindy Lou, and took a look around the Big House, to make sure everything was as it should be there. It always seemed to him as if it were. Other days, he made the rounds of the garden at Cindy Lou on foot, leaning more and more heavily on his cane. When he reached the enclosure where Lucy lay, he sat down to rest. It was a peaceful place, so peaceful that he often went to sleep there. When this happened, no one disturbed him unless rain set in or a sudden chill came to the air; then Nappy tiptoed up to him and waked him gently and helped him back to the house.

Once or twice it crossed his mind that perhaps he should let Larry know he had stopped riding, that the only parts of the plantations, except the houses and grounds, which he saw nowadays were those he could reach in the cabriolet. It was easier to get in and out of this than in and out of the Ford—and besides, it seemed more like old times to take a horse-drawn vehicle than an automobile. The roads which transected the plantations were good, as such roads went, and he could get a fair idea of how things were going without leaving his seat. But of course it was not like riding the crops. Yes, perhaps he ought to let Larry know. . . .

But he never did. The boy was already fretting at the long, senseless delay which kept him idle in one army camp after another. If he were suddenly sent home he would see for himself how things were, soon enough, and he would have everything that needed attention remedied in no time. On the other hand, if he were detained indefinitely overseas there was no point in worrying him about conditions which he could not correct. Besides, it really *was* a great effort to write letters, in any detail or at any length.

Because he was essentially honest, Clyde admitted to himself that this was one of the reasons why he did not write Larry that he had stopped riding. But it was a minor reason; he honestly did not want to worry the boy, either about an old man's failing faculties, which were real enough, or about deterioration of the property and its equipment, which might be merely imaginary. There was only one aspect of the situation at Cindy Lou of which he deliberately avoided mention: he had received a disturbing letter from the chairman of the Levee Board that he had never answered and, since then, some army engineers had been doing surveying in the neighbourhood. If the levee really were moved back, and the grounds at Cindy Lou were materially altered by such a move, it would be a shock to Larry to come home and see them changed, unless he were prepared for such a difference in them. But perhaps the levee never would be moved back, at least in such a way as to affect Cindy Lou. Clyde had not heard further from the chairman of the Levee Board and the engineers had not reappeared. Again, he decided against writing anything beyond the brief notes which he could scribble with a pencil while lounging in his armchair. . . .

And then he received a letter from Larry which roused him from his torpor and sent him to his desk with a clear head and a steady hand.

It was a very long letter, written in two main sections, and after these came a brief, hurried postscript. The first section told his grandfather about his arrival at Monteregard, his repulse by Janine, his welcome from Pierre and his immediate love for Louise de Courville. He had obviously been interrupted while writing it, and the next section had been written several days later. Meanwhile, the Marquise de Chanet and M. and Mme Carrere had all arrived at Monteregard and had all vehemently opposed his suit, which Pierre had continued to support. Acting on Pierre's advice, Larry had written a formal note to the Carreres, asking for Louise's hand; then, still acting on Pierre's advice, he had gone to see the famous caves and to wait for Louise in the largest one. There he had played the fool by trying to explore the dark tunnels which led from this; he might not have found his way back for days, he might even have lost his life, if Louise had not come to his rescue. When they returned, very late at night, to the château, they were both in disgrace with everyone but Pierre, and even Pierre could not and did not defend Larry's folly. The Carreres had taken Louise off to Paris early the next morning without even giving Larry a chance to see her again; and though Pierre had tried to smooth things over, the marquise had succeeded in making life at Monteregard so insufferable for Larry that he had decided to start back to camp at once. The postscript had been written after his arrival there. He had found his orders waiting for him: he was to proceed at once to Coblenz, where he would be attached to the cavalry unit of Headquarters Staff. There was no telling when he would have leave again, when he would see Louise, when he would get home. . . .

Clyde read the letter through rapidly once and twice more slowly. Then he sat for nearly an hour thinking it over, before reading it a fourth time. He did not grow drowsy or weary as he did so; on the contrary, his thoughts came to him with increasing clarity, and he felt a renewal of strength such as he had not known for months. He rose from his easy chair under the shade of a great tree and walked into his office with a firm step. Sitting down at his old desk, he drew several sheets of paper from one of its pigeon-holes and began to write.

Cindy Lou,
May 25, 1919.

My dear Larry:

Your letter begun on May 7th and finished May 11th has just reached me and I am hastening to reply.

First, let me say that I am glad your tedious period of inactivity is over and that you have ahead of you the prospect of interesting work in an interesting place. Under the circumstances, you certainly do not want to come home until the various complications of which you write me have straightened out, and certainly you do not want to stay at Gondrécourt any longer, either. It seems to me that Coblenz may very well be the happy medium between the two.

Next, let me say I am gladder still that you have found your true love—for, from what you tell me, I do not doubt for a minute that Louise *is* your true love and that you will have many years of the same complete happiness with her that I had with your grandmother. Do not allow yourself to doubt this, either. A girl with the courage she has revealed, first in refusing to permit herself to be browbeaten and second, in going heroically to your rescue, at the risk of her own life, will not permit minor obstacles to keep her from the man of her choice. And that you *are* the man of her choice is certainly self-evident. If you cannot go to her, she will come to you. Remember that she did so in the cave; if she could do it there, she can do it anywhere.

I am not surprised by the unfriendly treatment you have received in certain quarters; there are things which I have never thought best to tell you—and which I do not intend to tell you now—that would explain this treatment; but you may take my word for it that they exist and have long existed. Nevertheless, I am not especially alarmed by the situation, though I deplore it. Even if she had opposition on all sides, instead of on all sides but one, I am sure Louise would overcome it, as I have just said; and she has a very

240

powerful ally in her uncle. I am greatly impressed by what you have written me about him; to tell you the truth, I did not suppose that he was so much of a man. Now I see that I may have done him an injustice. I hope I may have a chance to tell him so in person some day, but at all events, I shall write to him at once, to say how much I appreciate the confidence he has shown in you. Of course I shall also write immediately to Louise, telling her how very welcome her presence will be at Cindy Lou.

I shall ask Father Le Grand to arrange for a copy of your baptismal certificate and also, since he has easy access to all such records, of your birth certificate, your parents' marriage, etc., etc. Perhaps you do not need all these documents, but it will be better for you to have them in your possession, in case you do. On the other hand, if you require more, let me know and I will see that you have them promptly. I think it also may be helpful to you to have a letter from me, formally stating that your marriage has my full approval and that you are my heir. (Which reminds me: my will and all my other papers of importance are in order. Since I am writing you anyway, it is just as well to mention this, though of course you do not really need the information at present.)

I gather from your letter that you are very low in your mind, not only because of your discouragement about Louise, but because you have played the fool, as you put it. I agree that you did a senseless thing in trying to explore the tunnel; and I know you must feel all the more strongly about this because Louise was endangered, as well as yourself. But a man is not a fool because he does one senseless thing—or even a great many. I had so much to live down, when I first met your grandmother, that I did not see how I could ever justify myself in her eyes. What is worse, I played the fool, as you put it, even after I met her—and in a far worse way than you have ever done or ever will do. Yet somehow, because of her, I found the way to rise above my sins rather than to live them down. I happen to know that Pierre de Chanet has also, in many ways, been a sinful man, and that he was saved from even greater sin only because the woman he loved was stronger than he was. Yet, from what you tell me, I know that he, too, has risen above his sins. You have no sins to live down or rise above. You can go to Louise with a clean slate and a clear conscience. Think of that, instead of dwelling on a single act of folly, and be thankful for it. It is a reason for greater thanksgiving than you now realize, though you may do so some day.

With this letter goes my abiding love. Men do not often speak of that in connection with each other. You tried to, the day you left for camp, and I silenced you. I have been sorry since that I did. But I know what was in your heart to say. Now I am saying what is in mine. You have been the light of my life, as your mother was before you and—in a different way—your grandmother before that. Without the light you have given me, my old age would have been passed in the shadows. You made it radiant. God bless you, Larry, and make you as happy as you have always made me, and as I know you will make Louise.

Devotedly, your grandfather,
CLYDE BATCHELOR.

Clyde read the letter through and hesitated. It did not sound like the way he usually talked, or wrote, either. Perhaps for this reason, it would seem to Larry that the words lacked sincerity. Then Clyde realized that it was *because* he was so utterly sincere, because he felt so deeply and was so determined Larry should know this, that it had been possible for him to express himself with more than usual eloquence, almost as though someone more powerful than he were helping him to do so, or speaking through him. He folded the letter carefully, placed it in an envelope, sealed and stamped this. Then he laid it to one side and reached for another sheet of paper, still conscious of no weariness of either mind or body.

My dear Louise:

My grandson Larry Vincent has written me of his meeting with you and of his love for you and yours for him. I am hastening to tell you how happy this news has made me, in many ways and for many reasons.

242

Larry writes me that even before he saw you, the music of your voice came to him through the silences of a forest. Many, many years ago, as I was walking along a street in a city ravaged by war, I heard a voice beyond a garden wall and my whole life was transfigured because of this. I know it will be the same with Larry. I could mention many other instances of experiences which he and I seem to have shared, and which, therefore, I can appraise at their full significance; but I know this one will suffice to show you what I mean.

I believe that Larry will have both the will and the power to make you happy. When you leave the place that has so far been your home, and come to his, your surroundings will seem strange to you at first. But soon they will become familiar and then dear because you will be living here as his wife, and his heritage and his hearth will be yours, too.

I also want you to know how warmly I welcome the thought of your presence at Cindy Lou. For more than twenty years now it has been without a mistress, and a house is only half a home that has no woman in it. You will make this house wholly a home again. I thank you beforehand because you will do this, and because of the joy and fulfilment that you will bring to the life of my grandson, who is dearer to me than any other human being.

Yours, with gratitude and affection,
CLYDE BATCHELOR.

Again he read his letter through, this time without hesitation, folded it and sealed it in its envelope. He was now beginning to be aware of physical fatigue. But his thoughts still came quickly and clearly and there was one more letter that he wanted to write. He drew another sheet of paper toward him.

My dear Pierre:
The receipt of this letter will be a surprise to you, but my reasons for writing it are so strong that I trust it will not seem intrusive.

243

Larry has written me of your great kindness to him and of your sympathetic understanding of the problems that have arisen in connection with his courtship of Louise de Courville. No doubt you were drawn to him partly because of his own personality; at the same time I realize there were other powerful reasons why you were disposed in his favour. I will not go into these; I have no desire to do so and I am sure you would not wish it, either. But I feel impelled to tell you that when death was very near, Cary called for you by name, and that these were her last words:

"It's terribly dark in this passage, isn't it? Of course, I was warned that it would be, that I shouldn't go beyond the great chamber of the cave. It's a little frightening, isn't it? At least it would be, if I were alone. But since you're with me at last, dearest . . ."

Her passing was peaceful and even happy because she believed you were with her. I should be everlastingly grateful to you for this—and I am.

Besides writing me about your kindness, Larry has written me about his foolhardiness. I know that if it had not been for Louise, he might have lost his life in the dark passages leading from the grotto, beyond which his mother never actually went, but where, in her last moments, she believed herself to be. I was a gambler once and, like most gamblers, I held to certain superstitions. I thought I had outlived them all and I have, as far as the old ones are concerned. But to me there seems something fateful about these occurrences in the cave, something linking not only mother and son, but you and yours with me and mine, almost as if the hand of God were uniting us. It is in the hope and with the belief you will share my feeling that I have written this letter.

Faithfully yours,
CLYDE BATCHELOR.

He was very tired now. When the third letter was ready for the mail, he rang for Nappy and told him to start for the post office at once. But when Nappy asked whether he should get the cabriolet ready, Clyde said no, Nappy could take the

Ford. That would be quicker, and he was not going to the post office himself. He was going out to the garden.

When Nappy came to report that the letters were in the mail, he did not find his master under the great shady tree, so he went on to the enclosure which was Lucy's resting place. As he expected, Clyde was seated beside her grave, sleeping quietly. It was still warm and sunny, so Nappy made no effort to waken him. It was a long time before the faithful servant realized that this was the deepest and most tranquil sleep of all.

CHAPTER EIGHTEEN

THE TRANSPORT *St. Mihiel*, sailing from Antwerp to New York with returning troops, was not as comfortable as the liner on which Larry had gone to France. At least, that was the way it seemed to him. But he realized that the impression might well be erroneous because, on the eastbound voyage, he had not expected to be comfortable and had not cared very much whether he was or not, and this time he was concerned about Louise.

Not that she had said or done anything to cause him anxiety; quite the contrary. She could have had a berth in quite a good cabin, on one of the upper decks, if she had not insisted she would prefer to share one with him, which meant she would be put practically in the hold. That was where they were now, in a stuffy little hole in the wall. The sea was very rough and Louise had been sick. Larry was terribly distressed by her sickness, but Louise did not seem to be distressed at all, except because of Larry: she said she did not see how a man could keep on being in love with a girl who kept getting sick. As far as she was concerned, she had been expecting to be sick, ever since she had known she was going to have a baby. Most girls were. However, she had not expected to be sick in his face, so to speak. . . .

It was all very well for Louise to joke in this way, but Larry knew that she was sick because of the stuffiness and the roughness and not because of the expected baby. She had known for nearly two months that she was going to have a baby, and she had not been sick a minute in Coblenz or in Antwerp or on the train between the two, though that had been very crowded. She kept urging Larry to go up on deck and get some air, and he continued to sit stubbornly on the little folding canvas stool, which was the only kind of a seat available, and for which there was barely room between the berths and the opposite wall. Fortunately, she slept a good deal between the sudden attacks of seasickness which woke her up, and while she was sleeping he sat looking at her with eyes of love and marvelling—as he had many times before—that anyone as wonderful as Louise should have loved him from the beginning and should have continued to love him as much as he loved her. . . . .

Though he had left Gondrécourt with a heavy heart, the change of scene and the satisfaction of being on active duty again had done much to raise his spirits; merely the sight of the Stars and Stripes, flying from the mast above the Ehren-breitstein—the great fortress which dominated the merging waters of the Rhine and the Moselle and the city which crowned their union—never failed to give him a feeling of triumph. But the news of his grandfather's death, which reached him when he had been in Coblenz less than three weeks, was a shattering blow. The cable from Valois Dupré announcing this, of course arrived long before Clyde's last letter; and Larry had hardly recovered from the first impact of grief when his grandfather's moving message poignantly revived it.

He was writing daily letters to Louise, addressing them to Monteregard, and not infrequently he wrote to Pierre, also. From the beginning, he had found release in the composition of these letters and, from the time of his grandfather's death, it brought him even more assuagement to know that the unrestrained outpourings of his grief would be received with sympathy and understanding. When he learned that Clyde had written to his beloved and to his uncle, as well as to himself, and that these letters had meant a great deal to them, his sense of shared sorrow and, consequently, of solace became infinitely greater. Louise sent him a copy of Clyde's letter to her, which Larry read and re-read almost as often as he did his own. Pierre did not quote at all from the letter he had received, but the one he wrote to Larry was the direct result of it, though Larry never knew this.

My dear boy:

Perhaps you will let me call you this, since I now have no son of my own, and since I believe I could not care for you more greatly if you really were my son.

I have been trying to think of something I could say that would help you through these next hard weeks, and I have not been able to do so, as far as any expression of condolence is concerned. I have never yet heard one myself that gave any real comfort and I am incapable of devising one. But perhaps I can say something on another subject that will serve to cheer you, at least a little.

It is this: I am more and more convinced that you and Louise were meant for each other, and that you should marry as soon as possible. If Paul and Josephine do not come to their senses—and it would not be true kindness to tell you I think they will, for I do not—I will see that Louise has a modest *dot*, a proper trousseau and a suitable wedding—in fact, I should be very pleased to have the marriage ceremony take place in my private chapel. Louise will be twenty-one in August, and I think we should allow her mother and stepfather that much time to change their tune, if only to save their faces—such face saving might be important to you later on. If by then they have not relented, I shall take action and I advise you to ask for leave, since I can be ready for you by the time you can reach here. On this you may count *with complete assurance*.

Devotedly, your uncle,
Pierre de Chanet.

Conscientiously, Larry had acted on this advice. But the months dragged by and still the Carreres showed no signs of relenting. In August, Larry applied for leave the first week in September.

The colonel of cavalry under whose immediate command he had been since coming to Coblenz had just been transferred to another post, and Larry had not seen the new C.O. until he presented himself at this functionary's office—or rather, until he had waited in the office for more than half an hour. During the course of this unwelcome delay, he noticed that the office had undergone a considerable change since he last reported there. It had previously been conspicuously bare; now, besides the necessary maps and other military props, it was adorned with various framed photographs, citations and diplomas, and there were flowers on the desk. Larry had just decided, out of sheer boredom, that he would inspect these ornamental additions, somewhat unusual in a milieu where great stress was laid on 'military atmosphere,' when a door opposite the one by which he had entered was thrown open and the colonel came in.

He was wearing a polo shirt with his riding breeches, and after casually returning Larry's salute he flung himself down in his desk chair and proceeded to riffle through some papers lying in front of him. Then he signed two or three letters and read a document of some sort, before giving more than a passing glance in his visitor's direction. During this interval Larry, whose patience had already been considerably taxed, regarded his superior officer with increasing distaste. The man was undeniably handsome, but he lacked the distinction which made Pierre's good looks so outstanding; curiously enough, the general effect he produced was not only un-military but unmasculine. His hands were too smooth and too white, his chin too rounded, his shoulders too sloping. He could not be overweight, or he would not have been a polo player; but there was a certain softness about him generally associated with superfluity of flesh. When he finally looked at his visitor long enough for Larry to study his face, the boy saw that there were dark circles under his eyes and that the eyes themselves lacked directness.

"I understand that you have come to apply for leave," the colonel said at last.

"Yes, sir."

"But apparently you had leave no longer ago than May."

"Yes, sir. Of course I should not have asked for it so soon again, if certain circumstances had not made it seem impera-tive for me to do so."

248

"I see. And these circumstances are . . . ?"

"I'm engaged to be married, and September is the most convenient time for the wedding, as far as my fiancée is concerned."

"I see," the colonel said again. "I take it then that your fiancée is an American girl, engaged in some sort of post-war work which puts limitations on her freedom?"

"No, sir. She is a French girl."

"Oh—a French girl! Then I should think it would be possible for her to arrange to be married at almost any time."

"Yes, sir, it would. Any time after August."

"And why not before August?"

"She won't be of age until then, and after that she'd need a certain amount of time to get ready for her wedding."

"But she can get married at any time, without waiting to become of age, provided that she is in possession of a birth certificate, that she can prove she has lived for at least a month in the *arrondissement* where the ceremony is to take place and that she has her parents' consent."

"Yes, sir, I know. But unfortunately she doesn't have her parents' consent."

"Why not?"

"Her father is dead. Her mother and her stepfather don't regard me as an especially good match."

"Why not?" the colonel asked a second time, in a tone less casual and considerably cooler than he had said, "I see," the second time.

"I think they had different plans for her. I don't know of any other reason. Her uncle approves."

"What is the name of this girl to whom you say you are engaged?"

"Louise de Courville. And I am——"

"Yes?"

"I don't mean to be disrespectful, sir, but I am engaged to her. I'm not just saying that I am."

"Yet you tacitly admit that her mother and her stepfather do not recognize any such engagement when you say they will not consent to her marriage with you. What is their name?"

"Carrere."

"And the friendly uncle's name?"

"Pierre de Chanet."

"Well, well! So Pierre de Chanet has entered the picture again."

"I don't think I quite follow you, sir."

"It isn't necessary that you should. What about his mother? Is she still living?"

"Yes, sir."

"And does she approve the match?"

"No, sir."

"And still you expect me to okay a leave in order that you may marry a girl whose entire family, with the exception of one uncle, is opposed to the match?"

"I hope very much that you will, sir."

"Well, I shan't. I think I should be doing the Marquise de Chanet and M. and Mme Carrere a great disservice by giving my consent—not to mention the girl herself. I have no doubt that the marriage which has been arranged for her is much more suitable. . . . That will be all, Lieutenant Vincent."

Larry bit his lip to keep from retorting, swallowed hard, saluted and turned to leave the office. He had almost reached the door when the colonel called him back.

"Lieutenant Vincent."

Larry swung around, a flicker of hope suddenly quivering through his despair.

"Yes, sir?" he said eagerly.

"Do you play polo?"

"No, sir," Larry answered, feeling very doubtful whether he was successfully concealing his angry disappointment.

"You've never played it?"

"No, sir."

"The general is very fond of polo. Perhaps you knew that?"

"I'd heard so, sir."

"But it's never occurred to you that it might be helpful if you played it?"

"No, sir."

"Well, it shouldn't be too hard for you to learn. I understand you're a good rider."

"Thank you, sir."

250

This time he knew he had spoken sarcastically. After all, there was no such animal as a graduate of the Cavalry School at Saumur who was a poor rider, and of course the colonel was fully informed, not only as to when his visitor had last had leave, but as to everything else connected with his military record.

"We could use another good player on our team," the colonel remarked nonchalantly. If he had noticed the note of sarcasm—and Larry did not see how he could have helped doing so—he apparently had not taken umbrage at it, or at least he did not intend to betray any such feeling. "Think it over, Larry." The colonel permitted himself a slight smile in answer to Larry's startled look. "I really do not see any reason why I should not call you by your Christian name when we are alone," he said. "In fact, you may call me Uncle Bushrod, if you like, under the same circumstances."

"It never entered my head that the new C.O. was my uncle," Larry wrote Pierre. "Colonel Page! . . . Why, there must be hundreds of Pages in the Army, dozens of them colonels, and he doesn't use his first name any more—it seems he's always hated it! He signs himself B. Harrison Page and all his cronies call him Harry—Colonel Harry Page, that was all I'd heard. And he'd only been here a week. Of all the cursed luck! I could have gone just as well to Kent, who was here before him, and who was a grand guy. But I waited, just as you thought I should. Not that I'm trying to shift the blame to you, of course you understand. It was just one of those things. . . . And why Page should take sides with the marquise and the Carreres, instead of with you and Louise and me, is just one of those mysteries, as our people say at Cindy Lou."

Yes, it was just one of those things, Pierre agreed in his reply, without making any answering comment on mysteries. And he was very sorry that *Colonel B. Harrison Page* should be so unreasonable, not to say so lacking in understanding. However, Pierre did not see why Larry's failure to secure leave should delay the wedding. Of course it was disappointing in some respects, that this could not take place in the chapel at Monteregard. But rather than wait on the vagaries of

Colonel B. Harrison Page, Pierre would bring Louise to Coblenz. He thought it very unlikely that, if he took this course, *Colonel B. Harrison Page* would go so far as to create further difficulties.

In this assumption, Pierre had been entirely correct; and before his arrival with Louise, Larry had revealed an aptitude for polo which was very gratifying, not only to the general, but to a number of other high-ranking players, and had also become something of a favourite among junior officers who were not polo players. So Colonel B. Harrison Page contented himself, for the time being, with having dealt one body blow and did not attempt another. In fact, he eventually recalled Larry to his office, now even more elaborately adorned than before, and said he thought that possibly leave could be arranged after all. But by that time all necessary formalities had been met for a marriage ceremony at the Liebfrauen Kirche and for a wedding reception in the palace garden. Larry wrote hastily to Pierre and Louise, telling them that if they would prefer a last-minute change of plans, he could meet it; both replied that they would rather let the existing programme stand. Louise did not go into any explanations as to why she felt this way, but Pierre gave his reasons in some detail: word had been widely circulated that Lieutenant Vincent could not leave his post at this time; it would cause confusion and needless curiosity if the information were reversed. Word had also been circulated that M. Carrere, both because of official commitments in Paris and because of the inevitably bitter feelings which still persisted between France and Germany, did not feel it best to go to Coblenz at this time. That would account quite logically for his absence and his wife's from the wedding, if it took place there. On the other hand, if it took place at Monteregard, in the face of his continuing hostility, this would make itself felt in the atmosphere, even if he attended the ceremony. At the last moment, he might very well decide to do so, rather than to give occasion for local gossip by his absence. But Pierre was not at all sure that this would have been an advantage.

"There would have been awkwardness either way," he told Larry, the first time they were able to talk quietly together after his arrival in Coblenz with Louise. "And then, there is my mother . . . of course a lady of that age could not be expected to travel any great distance, even if there were no question of national feeling involved, so you could be sure that she would not come here. But she has remained at Monteregard ever since you were there—the longest time within my recollection—and she does not seem to have the slightest idea of leaving. I think she would have contrived to make you very uncomfortable."

"She certainly did before," Larry said bluntly.

"Yes, I know. So I think it is just as well that she should not have another opportunity to do so. It affords me much more satisfaction to realize that you are having an opportunity to make *Colonel B. Harrison Page* uncomfortable—as you are undoubtedly doing."

"It affords me some, too. Not that I care much, one way or another. The only thing I care about right now is getting married. The place and the attendant circumstances don't seem to matter very much."

"It is quite understandable that you should feel like that. And believe me, my dear boy, things are better this way. . . . Now there is something else which we should have discussed before, but the right moment never seems to have arrived, up to now. That is the question of Louise's *dot*."

"It's not a question that interests me in the least. I can take care of Louise. If you're uneasy on that score, I can settle something on her immediately, so it won't be community property."

"I'm not in the least uneasy. . . . You are speaking rather abruptly this evening, do you realize that, *mon cher*? It is unlike you—but then, I suppose we must allow for a certain amount of edginess on the part of a prospective bridegroom. The reason I speak of her *dot* is not because I lack confidence in your ability to take care of Louise, as you must know—I should hardly be doing everything possible to facilitate your marriage, if I were. I speak of her *dot* because it is no more considered suitable for a French girl to marry without one than without a chemise . . . well, that is perhaps a slight exaggeration, but here is what I am coming to: I had thought, at one time, that I would be in a position to say she would have a rather handsome dowry—in prospect, if not actually in hand.

That was when I felt quite sure that Janine intended to enter a convent. Now I am not so sure."

"No?"

"No." The corners of Pierre's mouth twitched. "Your future mother-in-law was very much annoyed with my presentation of a hypothetical case to M. le Curé—a presentation which you heard," he remarked. "But there is solid basis of fact in the old saying that many a true word is spoken in jest. The Carreres insisted on having me invite De Bonneville to Monteregard. They were obsessed with the idea that if he and Louise were thrown together in romantic surroundings she would make a comparison that was unfavourable to you, and change her mind as to whom she wished to marry. The plot was a complete boomerang. Louise, who had never been ill before in her life, as far as I know, developed some sort of a sudden fever—that is, I did not take her temperature myself, but it was so reported to me. In any event, she hardly stirred out of her room during the entire course of De Bonneville's visit. Meanwhile, since time was hanging heavy on his hands, he naturally sought diversion— and found it with Janine, who apparently forgot all about a vocation from the moment she laid eyes on him. In justice, I must say that he is not unattractive, in his way, though it is a way that would never have done for Louise. Love at first sight seems to be very much the vogue. I think he and Janine are as good as engaged already."

For the first time in the course of the conversation, Larry laughed.

"Yes, it is rather amusing, isn't it?" Pierre went on, his smile widening. "Except in this respect, as far as you are concerned: if Janine had entered a convent, I should have made Louise my heir. So eventually, she would have inherited Monteregard and, as its future possessor, I should have felt it proper that she should have had a very considerable *dot* from me. Now, as things have turned out, I shall need that money for Janine's *dot*, for her wedding and the contingent expenses. So, at the moment, all I can spare for Louise, in the way of hard cash, is a small sum which, if well invested, should make her independent of you as far as pocket money is concerned—I have a very strong feeling that every wife should have that much independence from her husband. In addition, I should like to give her the house on Elysian Fields, in New Orleans. I am sure Janine will never want or need that and I certainly do not. I don't know what sort of condition it's in, or whether its location is still suitable for residential purposes. If it is in good shape, and if it would meet your needs and tastes, you might find it convenient to use as a town house. Otherwise, you might sell it, and add the sum you receive for it to the one I am giving outright."

"I think you're very generous, Uncle Pierre, to give Louise so much. I want you to know I appreciate it. But even if you hadn't given her a cent, I'd have felt you'd done a great deal for her—for both of us—already. And I meant what I said before—that nothing else seems to matter very much, if I can only marry her."

That was how it had seemed to him then and, throughout the three years which followed, that was how it had continued to seem. It did not matter to Larry that he and Louise were billeted, along with two other young couples, in a small, unattractive house on the Mainzerstrasse, instead of in one of the costly, commodious ones on the Rheinanlagen where his uncle lived in comparative luxury. It did not matter to Larry that his work was increasingly monotonous and increasingly meaningless. It did not matter that he was kept on and on in Coblenz, when everyone else with whom he talked on the subject succeeded in getting sent home. It did not matter that Colonel B. Harrison Page continued to needle him in small ways and thwart him in large ones. With Louise he found complete harmony and complete happiness. Why then *should* anything else have mattered all this time? But now that the sea was so rough and she was so sick, he was troubled. He began to think more seriously than he ever had before—though of course such thoughts had sometimes crossed his mind—about what their life in Coblenz must have meant to her. Not her life in relation to him—that, he felt sure, had been as rapturous, and as rewarding, as his in relation to her; but her life in relation to its general aspects. Hitherto she had always been lapped in luxury; she had had none in Coblenz. She had been the daughter of a nobleman, the stepdaughter of a cabinet minister and the niece of a man who treated her like his own child and whose name was illustrious, whose home was magnificent and whose personality was outstanding. In Coblenz, she was simply the wife of an obscure second lieutenant. No, that was not all, either. She was a Frenchwoman by birth, an unwelcome guest in the house of an hereditary enemy, and she had lost her father and a cousin who was like a brother to her in a war with this same enemy—a war whose gaping wounds were still unhealed. Over and over again she must have been obliged to stifle her sense of strangeness, of isolation, of hostility. But she had done this so successfully, indeed so completely, that she had never betrayed any such feeling and that Larry had never been conscious until this moment of its existence, at least enough so that it troubled him.

As he dwelt on all this, with increasing concern, Louise stirred slightly and opened her eyes. Then she smiled and held out her arms to him.

"I'm feeling ever and ever so much better," she said, in answer to the question which accompanied his kiss. "No, I don't feel like having anything to eat. I feel like talking, and I certainly haven't felt much like doing that these last few days."

"You certainly haven't. But I think perhaps you ought to try to eat something before you try to talk."

"All right, if you want me to. But I'd rather talk."

"All right, if you'd rather."

They laughed together. Larry forgot that he had been troubled.

"I want to talk about getting home," Louise said.

"That's a nice thing to talk about. I'd like to talk about it, too."

"We've got four more days at sea?"

"With luck, it might be only three."

"And you think we'll have to stay about six weeks in and around New York?"

"I'm afraid there's not much chance it would be any less, even with luck. It might be more."

"But not more than two months?"

"No, I shouldn't think so."

256

"And then you won't be Lieutenant Lawrence Cary Vincent of the United States Army any more? You'll be Larry Vincent of Cindy Lou?"

"Yes, thank God!"

"Free to start for Louisiana?"

"Yes to that, too—and thank God for that, too."

"It'll take two more days to get to New Orleans?"

"Yes—at least the train trip will spoil two days."

"And then we'll look at the house on Elysian Fields and decide what we want to do with it?"

"What you want to do with it. It's yours."

"It's ours. . . . Well, that shouldn't take us long, should it?"

"Not if it's in very good condition or very bad condition. But if it's somewhere in between——"

"Well, let's say four days. . . . And then we'll take the train to Convent—is that right?"

"Yes."

"Just an hour or two?"

"Yes."

"And Nappy will meet us at the station?"

"Yes."

"And we'll drive to Cindy Lou——"

"Yes, we'll drive to Cindy Lou."

"And it'll be wonderful, like everything else?"

"Yes. But that'll be the most wonderful of all."

They laughed again, secure in the certainty.

CHAPTER NINETEEN

NAPPY drove jerkily at best, slamming on the brakes whenever he wanted or needed to go more slowly. They were riding along close to the river, and when he turned abruptly to the left, with a sudden slackening of speed, Larry thought at first that this was simply preparatory to swerving around another curve in the levee, where the road was obscured. Then he realized that they were turning into a driveway and that a great square house was looming up ahead of them. But he did not grasp that this was Cindy Lou until Nappy came to a full stop.

The terraces, stretching spaciously out toward the road, were gone; and the unkempt lawn, which now divided this from the house, had so shrunken in size that the levee seemed almost upon it. The stately avenue, bordered by majestic trees, was gone, too; the driveway into which Nappy had turned was so short that it had not taken more than a moment to traverse it. And the house beside it did not merely *look* grey, because of the deepening dusk. It *was* grey, the grey of weather-beaten clapboards and pillars that had gone long unpainted; even the green shutters, which had once been so vivid against the brightness of white surfaces, had peeled to dinginess. Larry had meant to have the car stopped in front of the house, to walk toward it through the tiered garden and then to lift Louise triumphantly over the threshold, just as Clyde had lifted his Lucy. But the place was so changed that he had not known when they reached it, and now they were at one side of the great outer staircase, at the point where it looked least impressive, even at its best. And apparently much of its grandeur was gone anyway; its newel posts, its balusters, its handrails, were drab and dingy like everything else. . . .

He became aware that Louise was looking at him in a trustful but questioning way and that Nappy had already climbed out of the front seat and was opening the rear door of the car. Larry would have to say something quickly.

"We're home, darling," he told her with an attempt at a smile. Fortunately the dim light would prevent her from seeing just how unsuccessful the attempt was. "This is Cindy Lou. I—I didn't recognize it myself, at first. You see, while I was gone, the levee was moved back, and that did away with the terraces and the *allée*. Of course I'd heard about this, in a general way, from Valois Dupré, but I didn't realize what a difference all that would make. If I had, I'd have warned you. About the house, too——"

"I'm sure the house will be lovely, inside. It's sad for you, to find everything so changed. But remember I never saw Cindy Lou before, so I can't make comparisons. And I'm happy that we've reached here at last."

258

She leaned forward and kissed him. How like her that was, he thought, with a great surge of loving thankfulness, to show no self-consciousness, even though they were not alone, about giving him this spontaneous caress, which she knew would comfort him, and to behave as if the fact they had finally reached their destination was all which really mattered. But as he gave her his hand to help her alight and went up the stairway with her, it was she who went on chatting cheerfully, for he found he could not say anything to show his appreciation of her attitude. This was not because of the shock which the sight of the house had given him; he was beginning to recover from that. Now it was because he dreaded, unutterably, to reach the doorway and see it empty of his grandfather's welcoming presence. Always, before this, Clyde had stood at the top of the grand staircase waiting for him, and they had gone inside the house together. Even with Louise beside him, Larry found the entrance almost unbearably hard to face. He forgot, completely, that he had meant to lift his bride over the threshold; he turned his head away, trying not to look beyond the open door.

"Us sho' is proud to have you back, Mistuh Larry, you and Miss Louise. Us has waited de longes' for dis happy day."

It was Tudie speaking, Tudie the ever loyal, the ever kind, the ever capable. As if she understood that no one should stand at the entrance itself, since the old master was not there to do it, she had been waiting in the hall; but she came forward quickly and close behind her was Ivy. Both of them looked at Louise with eyes that were admiring and at the same time appraising; the thought passed through Larry's mind that they had wondered how far along she was and that now they thought they knew. Somehow the faint amusement which came with this realization helped to shake off some of his depression.

"I am glad to see you, too, Tudie—Ivy, too, of course. But where's Delphie?"

Tudie and Ivy exchanged embarrassed glances. "Us sho' sorry, but Delphie, she gone," Tudie said hesitantly. "But us gwine make out all right, me and Ivy. Us got everythin' lined up."

"What do you mean, gone?"

"She done leave Cindy Lou and go to work for some po' white trash nigh to Gonzales. Us never knowed she was all that triflin'. But don' you fret none, Mistuh Larry, me and Ivy got everythin' all lined——"

"All right, Tudie, all right. . . ." It was the first time, as far as Larry could remember, that any of their people had ever voluntarily left Cindy Lou. It had never occurred to him that one would do so. He had supposed there would be plenty of service for Louise—that, while this might lack distinction, it would always be forthcoming willingly, even eagerly. Now there would be only Tudie and Ivy in that great ark of a house and before very long Tudie would be needed for the baby. Well, of course Nappy could help, except that he was probably needed all the time outside; since there had been defection in Delphie's case, this was probably not an isolated one. But there was nothing Larry could do about this situation at the moment. Louise must be made comfortable at once; she must have some supper and get to bed.

"Do you want to look around a little, darling? Or would you like to go straight upstairs?"

"I think I'd like to go straight upstairs, if that's all right. If I could just wash and get out of these travelling clothes I've worn so long, I'd feel better. That is, of course I feel all right anyway, but——"

"But of course you want to wash and change. Come, I'll show you the way."

It was not until they had almost reached another threshold that he stopped again, once more appalled. He had given no instructions as to which room he and Louise should occupy. As far as he knew, the youth bed had never been removed from his grandfather's chamber; he had continued to sleep there, whenever he was at home, until he went to Camp Beauregard. The youth bed had been altered by replacing the original rails with longer ones, and he had never minded having it narrow. It would have no logical part in the new pattern of his life; but he would hate to see it standing empty and he would hate still more to see the room without it. Besides, he could not sleep with Louise in his grandfather's bed. He would constantly keep thinking. . . . Where would they sleep then? In the room that had been his mother's, across the hall? The spool bed she had loved was certainly not large enough for two persons. In the room of the uncle he had never known until they met at Coblenz? The furniture there was adequate, even very handsome. But he had always disliked it, for some reason hitherto inexplicable, but now linked to his resentment toward Bushrod Page. As to the guest-room, the one with the two convent beds, of course that was unthinkable. Except during the crossing on that unspeakable transport, he and Louise had always gone to sleep in each other's arms.

It was Tudie who saved the situation. "Us figured you would want to take you bride to you mama's room, Mistuh Larry," she said. "Miss Cary done have that fixed the way young ladies likes dey rooms, and now us got another young lady at Cindy Lou, us got to aim to please her." Tudie was already advancing toward the only open door on the second story and, as Larry looked beyond her when she paused respectfully on the threshold, he instantly saw that she had made a wise choice. The spool bed really *was* big enough; the fact that it did not have the great canopy and the carved framework of the Seignouret or the Mallard made it look smaller, that was all; its low headboard and complete lack of footboard did not affect its comfortable width; and an immaculate, embroidered linen sheet had already been turned down over the quilted coverlet in a way that seemed to invite restful slumber. Moreover, everything else about the room was attractive; the chintzes were not bright any more, but age had given added softness to their colour and delicacy to their design; the chaise longue, the easy chairs, the drawn curtains, all added to the general air of cosiness. A fire was burning brightly on the hearth and flowers had been lavishly used for decoration. Larry saw that Tudie was right; there was an air of femininity about this room which the others had always lacked; and while he was rapidly coming to the realization of this, Louise spoke in her warm, friendly way.

"You *have* pleased me, Tudie," she said. "It's exactly the kind of a room a young lady likes—this young lady, anyway! And everything's so complete—the bed turned down, the fire lighted, the flowers all around."

"Yassum, Miss Louise," Tudie replied, beaming with

relief and gratitude. "Us figured maybe you'd like to go straight to bed and have your supper on a tray. Mistuh Larry, he could eat his on a table right beside you. Ivy, she got a good gumbo made, same as Mistuh Larry used to like it, and she done her best with the rest of the supper, too, without she knowed your pleasure. She thought in the morning you an' her'd overlook the storerooms and such. But you must be tuckered for true tonight."

"I am a little tired. . . . Would you like to have supper here, *mon cœur*?"

"I think it's a grand idea." Larry would not have confessed, even to himself, that the reason he thought it a grand idea was not only because this room of his mother's had been made so inviting for the reception of his bride, but also because if they stayed here he could put off the evil moment of going into the rooms which he associated more closely with Clyde. "You've done fine, Tudie. There's just one thing lacking. I haven't seen Nuffy yet. I thought he'd be bounding out to meet me—at least, if he hasn't forgotten me, after all this time."

"Dogs, dey don' forget no more dan folkses, Mistuh Larry. But us got Nuffy tied up, 'cause us didn't know did Miss Louise——"

"But of course I want to see Nuffy! Of course I want him with us! Please go and untie him right away, Tudie!"

"I'll go myself. I don't want him jumping all over you, in his first excitement. Where is he, Tudie?"

He was in the kitchen, Tudie said, and he'd been restless all the evening, just like he knew something was going to happen. Ivy would go downstairs with Mr. Larry and she herself would stay and help Miss Louise unpack. Maybe draw a nice hot bath, too. Or would they be having supper straight off?

Again Louise consulted Larry before giving a definite answer, again he said he thought Tudie had a grand idea, this time in suggesting the bath, and again he knew in his secret heart that his reply was not wholly disinterested. Of course a bath would be refreshing to Louise, of course her supper would taste better to her after she had taken one and had been comfortably settled in bed; but he was also thankful for the chance of going to get his dog by himself. If Nuffy did remember him and greet him with barks and jumps of joy, then he would take the dog outside with him while he went to look at his grandfather's grave. He was not sure whether there was a moon or not, but the night was clear, the stars would be out, anyway. He would be able to see all right. And he did not want even Louise with him on his first visit to the little enclosure. But he would be glad to have Nuffy. Nuffy was still a link between himself and his grandfather. . . .

When he came back to his mother's room, with Nuffy trotting quietly at his side, Tudie had left everything in perfect order; Louise was already sitting up in bed, looking as fresh as a rose in her dainty *crêpe de Chine* nightgown. Larry leaned over to kiss her, and then put both arms around her and hugged her hard; but for the third time within less than an hour, he was prompted by conflicting emotions. Louise not only looked as fresh as a rose, she smelled as sweet as one. Her bronze-coloured hair was still damp around the temples and fell in a fragrant cloud about her neck; and the lace-trimmed nightgown, which was cut in a deep V and sleeveless besides, was at best a mere wisp of a garment, veiling, but not concealing, her beautiful body. From the first, their desire for the full experience of love had been mutual. Moreover, Louise had been instinctively aware that her husband's physical delight in her was akin to some other deep, almost tragic need and therefore had been all the more prodigal in her response to his passion. Unbelievably, however, Larry had taken her in his arms now only because he craved comfort. He had been to his grandfather's grave and had stood for a long while under the stars, looking at it. Then, when he had finally left the enclosure and had come back upstairs, Nuffy had bounded along ahead of him and had gone, not to the open door of Cary's room, but to the closed door of the room that had been Clyde's, and had turned to look at Larry with the piteous bewilderment of the faithful dog which grieves and cannot understand why his grief is not assuaged by the master who has never failed him before.

"Nuffy did remember me," Larry said at last, releasing Louise. "He did jump all over me, too, so it was just as well Tudie kept him tied up, until he got over his first excitement.

He'll be all right now, though. Come here, Nuffy, and meet your new mistress." Nuffy, who had been sniffing around the room, obediently approached the bed and Louise turned on her side to pat him and scratch his ears. Again his look was questioning and again his trustful brown eyes sought Larry's. But this time he seemed satisfied and, after a moment, he began to wag his tail, hesitantly at first, and gradually with more conviction of wellbeing.

"You won't object to having him here, will you, Louise?" Larry inquired. "He—he's always slept in my room, when I've been at home, ever since he was a puppy."

"Of course I won't object. Didn't you hear me telling Tudie I expected to have him with us? Is it all right for me to give him orders, or should all those come from you?"

"It's all right for you to give them to him. I don't know that he'll mind you, straight off. But he'll learn. What do you want him to do?"

"I thought I might tell him to go and lie down on the hearth, while we had our supper. It's getting very late, isn't it, darling? I suppose we ought to think of the servants."

She was right, of course; and though Nuffy did hesitate again, for a moment, and did again look questioningly at Larry, he obeyed the second time Louise spoke to him and lay quietly on the hearth while the two ate their supper. The gumbo was very good and so were the quail in brown butter and the stuffed mirlitons—all old favourites of Larry's. Louise was lavish in her praise of them, both to him and to Tudie, who proudly did the serving. She had decorated both the tray and the little table she placed beside the bed with a few early camellias; and when Louise once more voiced her admiration of these, Tudie spoke more happily than ever.

"Miss Lucy, she used to have camellias of every prescription. Us ain' got so many now as us used to have. But Ah specks you'll be takin' care of Miss Lucy's garden now, won' you, Miss Louise?"

"I'll try. I don't know much about camellias, but I can learn."

The reference to the camellias did not hurt Larry as much as most of the reviving memories. Clyde had endeavoured to see that Lucy's garden continued to have good care, from someone on the place, after her death; but the foundation of the new C. & L. Navigation Company had prevented him from spending the money to hire an expert to look out for them, as he had planned at one time. They had never been a subject of frequent discussion between him and his grandson, and their culture had not been among the activities which he and Larry had shared, for he had not known much about camellias himself. Larry was grateful to Louise for her expression of willingness to revive the garden and he reverted, of his own accord, to Tudie's suggestion about the storerooms.

"We'll look around the grounds together the first thing in the morning, if it's a pretty day—well, perhaps not the first thing. I suppose I ought to see Dumaine and Tregre as soon as I can. But some time before evening. Meanwhile, perhaps you and Ivy would go through the storerooms without me. I don't know much about those, anyway."

"Of course. Is there anything else I could do to be helpful?"

He was silent for a moment, thinking painfully again. "I suppose you'd better go straight through the house and see what condition it's in," he said at last. "Dad—my grandfather—and I never used the drawing-room much, except the summer Aunt Armande was at Victoria, just before the war broke out. That was the only time we had much company. We used the ballroom, too, that summer, but I don't suppose you and I——"

"No, of course we won't be giving any balls right away. But I will see that the drawing-room's ready to receive visitors. I suppose people will call, won't they? I mean, because I'm a bride."

"Yes, I suppose so. And you should always offer them black coffee and little cakes, when they do, the way pinaud and cookies are offered, when callers come to Monteregard."

"Thank you for telling me, darling. I'll try to do everything just as you'd like to have it done."

"I know you will. I suppose you ought to go through the linen and silver and china, too, in case we want to have people in for meals, later on. I've no idea what condition those things are in. Or the books. This climate's hard on books. And we never used the library much, either, Dad and I, after I was old enough to read to myself. Before that, we sat there every evening and he read aloud to me before I went to bed. I don't think he enjoyed it especially, but my grandmother always used to read aloud to my mother, so he thought it was the right thing to do. As soon as I could read myself, I took my books down to his office and to the gaming-room. Those open out of each other, on the ground floor, and he spent most of his time in them, after he got older. So I stayed there, too."

"Of course you did. As soon as I've been through the store-rooms, I'll go into the library and look over the books. If I think any of them need attention, I'll tell you, and we'll decide together what to do about them. But I'll leave the gaming-room and the office to you, at least until you ask me to help with them. Is that right?"

"Yes, that's exactly right. You always do the thing that's exactly right, Louise, you always think of it."

While they were talking, Tudie had unobtrusively removed the tray and cleared the little table. Then she had asked whether she should bring their coffee at any special time the next morning, or whether they would ring for it. When she had been told they would ring for it, she wished them good night and left them. As her footsteps died away in the distance, Larry rose and began to undress. He had progressed no further than taking off his necktie and unbuttoning his shirt when he realized he had said nothing to Louise about the other bedrooms.

"You'll probably want to look over this floor, too. The room across the hall was my grandfather's, and as soon as I got out of the nursery I always slept there, too, in a small bed beside his big one. We—we might leave that as it is for a while. One of the chambers at the rear has always been a guest room—it has twin beds in it, the kind that are called convent beds in Louisiana, because they were first used in nunneries. The only other narrow beds in general use were the sort I slept in—youth beds—and the accouchement beds that were put crosswise at the foot of four-posters. They look like what you call day beds in France. But in the old days here families were generally large and of course babies were all born at home, so these accouchement beds were kept handy."

"I see. A lady in bed with her husband was reminded all

266

the time what was ahead of her. I don't think that was exactly tactful, do you?"

"No, I'm afraid it wasn't."

He spoke very soberly and then realized that Louise might think he resented her light banter, whereas he was only remembering the stories he had heard about the horrors of plantation confinements, even in the most luxurious houses, and the number of times they ended fatally for mother or child or both, at the period when accouchement beds were in general use. Louise slid out of bed and came and stood beside him in her pretty filmy nightgown.

"Darling, you know I was only joking. If you'd like to put an accouchement bed in our room, it wouldn't trouble me at all. First, because I want you to make love to me, no matter what the consequences may be. I'm sure I'd die of a broken heart if you stopped now. And second, because I want lots of children, anyway. Don't you?"

"I—I guess I do. I haven't thought much about it. So far, I've only been thinking how much I wanted you."

They smiled at each other, the brief moment of constraint gone. Louise came closer to him and put her arm around him without waiting for him to put his arm around her.

"Are there any more rooms you want to tell me about before we settle down for the night?" she inquired.

"There are a whole flock of them on the ground floor, besides the wine closet and the storerooms you've already agreed to look over. The others were originally planned for the convenience of business visitors. In the early days, the planters and the shipowners kept their social life and their business life strictly separate—there's even a dining-room down there. One of the chambers was eventually converted into a schoolroom for me—there weren't any more business visitors by that time." He paused. "My grandfather taught me himself until I was twelve years old," he said at last. "I guess you might pass the schoolroom up, too, for the present, if you don't mind. But there's another chamber on this floor, opposite the one with the convent beds, that you'll probably want to look over. It's the one that was my nursery for a while —until I was old enough to move in with my grandfather. I believe it was mostly used as a second guest room in the old

267

days. But the servants always call it Mr. Bushrod's room."

"You don't mean your commanding officer at Coblenz, do you, Colonel B. Harrison Page?"

"Yes. You know he was my mother's elder brother—my grandmother's son by her first marriage. I believe it was understood, when she married my grandfather, that her children should share and share alike; so of course Uncle Bushrod was regarded as a member of the family at Cindy Lou, though as a matter of fact he never was here much, I believe, because mostly he lived with my great-grandmother in Virginia on her plantation, which he eventually inherited. But whenever he was here, that was the room he used. My grandfather always leaned over backward in his efforts to be fair—he made Uncle Bushrod a regular allowance, even after it was agreed that the value of his ownership of Sorrento and Amalfi more than offset the value of my ownership of Cindy Lou. That was before my grandfather got Victoria for me, however, so perhaps he figured Uncle Bushrod had something more coming to him. Anyway, you know Dad's will stipulated that Uncle Bushrod should get two hundred dollars a month for life, in spite of the fact that he's married to a millionairess. I told you about it, because I thought I ought to explain why you and I might be short of cash sometimes."

"Yes, I remember."

"Just the same, I have the impression he and my grandfather never got on very well together—of course, as you must have gathered, I didn't get on very well with him myself. And anyone who couldn't get on with my grandfather——" Larry paused again. "Anyway, I was so small the last time my uncle Bushrod came to Cindy Lou that I don't remember it," he went on. "And I don't remember hearing my grandfather speak of him, except in the most casual way. The servants used to talk about him a little more, but not much. I suppose it's conceivable that he might want to come here again, sometime. Perhaps I ought to ask him, anyway. As far as I know, he's the only relative, except Janine, that I've got left. I might like him better if I received him as an uncle, instead of being under orders to him as an officer."

"You don't mind too much, do you? About not having relatives, I mean?"

"No, of course I don't mind. How could I, when I have you, how could I miss anyone?"

The words were hardly out of his mouth when he was conscious of the lie he had told her. Only as long as he stayed in this one room, only as long as Louise prodigally gave him her love, could he forget the rest of Cindy Lou and close his consciousness to the great loss which had come with this great gain. But once he was out of this sanctuary, once he had left his beloved, it would be different. He would miss his grandfather with every turn he took, with every breath he drew. Nothing, no one in the world, could wholly compensate for that loss.

Belatedly, he realized that he had not returned her caress and, as he did so, his dormant desire wakened to urgency. He had been cheated out of lifting her over the threshold, but he would make up for that now. Without a word, he swept her from her feet and started across the room with her. She laughed and snuggled her head under his chin, kissing his throat. But almost immediately, she recognized the intensity of his mood and her own changed. He still needed her more than he wanted her and perhaps he always would. Since this was so, he required, more than anything else, the assurance of her compassionate understanding and her everlasting loyalty. A lighthearted response to his love-making was not enough, and it was not enough, either, that he should be able to take the unity of their yearning for granted; there must be something akin to dedication in her self-surrender. Her laughter trailed softly away into silence and she raised her head. Her lips were waiting for his to seal them as he put her down on their bed.

CHAPTER TWENTY

Louise was still sleeping peacefully when Larry waked the next morning. Army routine had tended to confirm the habit of early rising which the schedule at Jefferson and the normal requirements of plantation life had already formed; he still found it difficult to adjust himself to the later matutinal hours natural to his wife. After lying quietly beside her for a few moments, he became so uncontrollably restless that he was afraid he would disturb her; so he slipped out of bed, scribbled a note which he pinned on his pillow and carried his clothes to the bathroom. Once dressed, he took his shoes in his hand and tiptoed through the hall and down the stairs, while Nuffy padded softly along beside him. Ivy, who entered the kitchen at almost the same moment he did, looked at him in unconcealed surprise.

"You-all didn' ring, did you, Mistuh Larry? Us didn't speck you'd be up so early. An' Tudie said——"

"No, we didn't ring, and that *was* the agreement. Miss Louise is still asleep—you'll be hearing from her later on. But I was awake and I wanted to get out and see how the grinding's coming along. As soon as you can get some coffee made, you may bring it to me—in the dining-room."

"Yassuh, Mistuh Larry. Won' be but a few minutes. Will you have your grits now, too, or will you be comin' back for those?"

"I'll have those, too, as soon as they're ready—maybe with the second cup of coffee. And tell Nappy to saddle Black Jack for me, will you, when you get things started? Once I'm out, there's no saying just when I can conveniently get back—I don't want to make a special trip, just for grits. On the other hand, what about some eggs and bacon, while you're at the stove anyway?"

Ivy nodded, smilingly, and set to work; before the coffee was dripped, Tudie was there to serve it. The grits, the bacon and the eggs followed in swift succession; so did some tiny light biscuits and some fig preserves. Larry had not realized that he was so hungry; good as the supper had been the night before, he had not had much heart for it. Now his healthy young appetite was asserting itself again. He pushed back his plate with a sigh of satisfaction.

"Tell Ivy that's the best breakfast I've had since I left here. And, Tudie—I'm depending on you and Ivy both to see that Miss Louise has everything she wants and needs. She was pretty tired last night. If she still seems tired when you go to her, try to make her stay in bed. The storerooms and all that can wait."

"Yassuh, Mistuh Larry, Ah sho' will."

Black Jack was ready for him when he went out and he leaped into the saddle with rising spirits. He must do something about fixing up the house, of course, as soon as possible. But meanwhile the crops were his first consideration; and he was thankful they gave him a pretext for getting away from the desolate, battered bulk which bore so little resemblance to the resplendent mansion of his grandfather's pride, but which recalled so inescapably his grandfather's presence. The first sight of the fields stimulated him still further. The stand was fine. It would look beautiful from an airplane, Larry thought to himself, remembering his flights over Touraine— as if there were block after block of deep-piled green velvet. Dumaine was a planter's planter, for true. But Christ in the mountains! He was still trying to make a crop by the same methods as Etienne de Boré. Impatiently, Larry put Black Jack across a ditch. The big gelding made the jump easily enough; but as he landed on the far bank, a flock of doves rose suddenly and he bolted, rocketing off down the bank. At first Larry gave the horse his head, sensing that he was letting off excess spirits rather than yielding to the mad panic of a runaway. But presently Larry sawed on the bridle and brought his mount to a panting halt just as they approached a newly cut stubble field.

"Satisfied now, you old jug-headed son of a bitch?" he asked aloud. "Got it out of your system? If not, I'll give you a real workout, any time you say, the way we used to do at Saumur. . . ."

He looked across the stubble where, along the farther edge, men and women, swinging their cleaver-shaped knives, were cutting cane. Others followed in their wake to strip the leaves from the heavy, polished joints of the long stalks. Still others piled the stalks so that the creaking, two-wheel carts could pick up the loads and take them through the dusty lanes to the daily stockpile around the base of the sugarhouse carrier. All this was obsolete, Larry told himself with growing impatience. In the mill proper, Tregre would have everything going smoothly from carrier to centrifugals. But out here in the field were mule carts instead of trucks, mule-drawn ploughs instead of tractors. Hell, didn't anybody here realize yet that

271

a tractor didn't eat except when it was working, while mules had to be fed twice a day, the year round, whether they did a lick of work or not? Didn't anybody care that the land you used for mule feed couldn't produce a cash crop, whereas a tractor got its feed out of a tank? No wonder they'd had that knockout the year before when crops that cost four dollars to put in couldn't be sold for as much as three! The rice people had been hit worse, of course, but even so. . . . And those splintering old wooden bridges across the drainage canals and ditches! One team was kept busy just going around day after day replacing worn-out planks and stringers. Suppose cypress *was* cheap and labour didn't cost much? A good concrete culvert lasted practically for ever, once it was put in. There was not only plenty of work for him to do, there were plenty of changes he ought to make. He wheeled Black Jack around and cantered toward the cane cutters, whistling a rather jerky version of 'Where Do We Go From Here, Boys? Where Do We Go From Here?' and as he did so, he saw Dumaine, mounted on his walking mare, but relaxed 'slaunchwise' in the saddle, while he watched the progress of the work. He saluted Larry with a wave of his worn riding crop.

"It's good to see you out here again," he observed, pushing back his wide-brimmed hat and running a bright red bandanna over his brow. "After all, like your grandfather used to say, there's no better fertilizer for any field than the eye of the owner."

"I'd like to spend a lot of my time out here, and that's the truth," Larry answered. "But don't forget I've got a mill, some perique sheds, the tobacco fields and a towboat or so that all need looking after, too. And up to now, I've had a commanding officer to make the decisions. Learning how to do that'll take me a little time. However"—he pointed back to the headland along which he had just ridden—"one of the first jobs we've got ahead of us is putting in culverts, either concrete or iron, in place of those bridges, while we're cleaning out the ditch banks this winter. And as to our seed cane, from what he wrote me I gather Septime seems to think . . ."

"Oh, him!" shrugged Dumaine. "He's got a headful of book ideas, ever since he came back from the Army. You can't plant sugar out of those books, and what he says about our native seed cane being from a strain that's too old, and importing something that never did grow here before . . ."

"I know, I know," Larry interrupted. "Maybe you're right and he's wrong. But suppose you stop planting until we can all get together at the house some night—you and Tregre and Septime and all the rest—and decide among us what's best. That is, I'll do the deciding, because it's my responsibility. But I want to give everyone a chance to say what he thinks, first."

"Well, then, there's one thing I want to say right now," Dumaine declared with spirit. "What we really need most, to bring these fields back to where they ought to be, is mules. You know how it is yourself, Mr. Vincent. For sugar you need the youngest and strongest mules you can get. We didn't use to keep them after they got to be nine years old. Then we'd sell them to cotton planters, because they'd still be plenty young enough and strong enough to make cotton. But when the war came, the Army grabbed off all the mules there was, so nobody could get any. Then, after Mr. Batchelor died, we didn't like to bother you by writing you about it. But after all, we're using one hundred and eighty mules on the place, which is damn good for thirty-five hundred acres of cane— and at least a third of them are over age."

"So you mean we need at least sixty new mules, for a starter?"

"That's it."

"At a hundred and fifty each for low, that comes to—let's see, yes, sir, that's nine thousand dollars and we wouldn't get more than twenty-five hundred dollars for the old ones at best."

"But you've *got* to have mules for cane, just like you've got to have land."

"Like hell you have! Listen: new mules to be bought every year and at least one man to each pair of mules and the Lord alone knows how much acreage held out from sugar for corn to feed the mules. Why, you could do it all with fifteen or twenty tractors, run by fifteen or twenty men, with maybe two more men for a maintenance crew and with no acreage held back for feed. Don't you see we've got to run the place that way or go under? It won't be easy to find the money for the tractors, I can tell you. But at least when I've done it, I won't have poured it down a drain, as I would if I stuck to the old outworn ways."

"As far as the money goes," Dumaine retorted, "the cost of the mules wouldn't be much more than a starter. Just wait until you hear what Hermann Tregre's got waiting for you. And he's holding things down to what's needed most, such as shelling the mill. That hasn't been done since before the war and——"

"The whole mill? All nine cylinders?"

"Sure."

"But God almighty, that will come to at least ten thousand dollars!"

"Well, you're lucky a way's been worked out to slip those ridged shells, like sleeves, over the big grinding cylinder. Just think what it would have cost you if——"

"I know. But that isn't going to make it any easier to pull nine thousand or so out of a hat for your mules and then ten thousand more for Hermann to reshell the mill. Besides, I haven't heard yet what Septime wants in the way of improvements. And maybe you don't read the market reports. In case you don't know it, there was a bad break last year in commodity prices. All the clear cash profit we make out of this year's harvests we'll be able to put in our eyes and forget. The only thing that might keep us going, with luck, would be the perique, the way Septime's got it set up. I mean *lots* of luck!"

It was a good thing he had eaten a big breakfast, Larry reflected, rather grimly, as he turned home again at last; otherwise, he would have been almost starved, for, as it was, he was terribly hungry. He hoped dinner would be ready and, for the first time, he wondered how Louise had been getting along with her inspection of the storerooms—that is, if she had actually felt equal to beginning her rounds. As he approached the house, he saw that she was on the gallery, and she waved and called out to him in warm welcome. Instantly his irritation and sense of frustration about the plantation evaporated, for her presence meant that she was not exhausted, that she was ready and waiting for him, just as usual; since this was so, what did all Dumaine's griping—all Tregre's

274

stubbornness—amount to, anyway? Nothing at all—nothing, at least, that he could not easily cope with. But he had hardly reached this happy conclusion when he saw that Louise was not alone; a stocky, elderly man had come up behind her and the next minute he recognized Clovis Bourgeois. He tossed his reins to Nappy, who, for a wonder, was waiting for him, and rushed up the steps.

"Why, Captain! What good wind brings you here?" he exclaimed, wringing his visitor's hand. "This is the man I've told you so much about," he added, turning to Louise and giving her a hearty kiss. "If it weren't for him, the C. & L. Navigation Company never could have kept going all this time. Sit down, Captain, and tell me about everything while we have a good drink before dinner."

"It'd have to be a mighty long one, if I'm to tell you all about everything before we eat," Bourgeois answered, grinning. "So I hope some of my news can wait until afterward. But I will tell you, straight off, what brought me here on the double, the minute I knew I'd find you at home. We've had a steel towboat offered us by the Nashville Bridge Company, up in Tennessee, powered with a diesel motor, and complete. Listen, when I say complete, I mean *complete*. Put a couple of cans of beans and a ham in the galley, and you can step aboard her right this very now, and start for Council Bluffs or Wheeling or any damn place on any damn river you'd care to name. And you can pick her up for a measly twenty-five thousand dollars. She was built for some wartime outfit that busted up as soon as the war was over, and Captain Joe Chotin—I guess you'll agree he knows his ear from a hole in the ground when it comes to towboating—had the mate to her built for himself, and got a contract right away with the Standard Oil to tow their barges from Baton Rouge to Louisville."

"I like the way you say a 'measly' twenty-five thousand, skipper," Larry interrupted wryly. "Only it was just this morning I had them pick off all the dollar bills from the bushes, rake 'em in a pile and burn them. They were cluttering up the place something awful. So it will be anyway a week or ten days before a fresh crop of money grows back. . . . Meanwhile, I'm going to see about those drinks. I'm assuming Louise has already seen to the dinner."

His assumption was correct, she told him smilingly. In fact, she had some drinks ready, too—she had felt sure he would want one as soon as he got in, and Captain Bourgeois must be thirsty, too. Tudie had remembered how they used to like their liquor—so, well, here was Tudie now, with a tray. Both men pronounced the contents of the proffered glasses excellent and asked for dividends before they went inside for the dinner which obviously gave them an equal amount of satisfaction. But Bourgeois persisted in sticking to the subject of the new towboat, and it was soon evident to Larry that it would take plainer speech than table talk to divert his visitor. There was no help for it; he would have to take Bourgeois down to the office, which he so greatly dreaded to enter, and thrash matters out with him there.

"Where the hell do you think I'm going to snatch twenty-five thousand bucks without turning bootlegger?" he inquired, rather testily, when they were seated by the old roll-top desk. "I hear those boys are roping it in now that Washington is really trying to make the prohibition law stick."

"Mortgage the *Palourde* and the *Larry*, mortgage everything you've got, but raise that money, son," Bourgeois said earnestly. "You'll never get another chance like this. Listen to me, now: do you think the Standard is the only outfit that's going to be shipping barges of oil up and down this river? If you do, you're crazy. They're putting up a tank terminal at Good Hope; there's already a refinery at Destrehan and another at Norco, which I hear this big Dutch outfit, Royal Shell or something, is likely to take over and——"

"And what?"

"And one of these days there'll be oil fields right along this river. Mark my words, Larry."

"One of these days!" Larry burst out. "What'll I be doing with that diesel towboat while I'm waiting for one of these days?"

"Charter her, if you can't get a towing contract," Bourgeois replied unhesitatingly. "Betcha Joe Chotin would charter her, just like that. And if she's yours, you could name her the *Clyde Batchelor*. I've got a sneaking hunch he'd like that."

Larry rose abruptly and turning, looked out of the low window nearest him toward the truncated terraces. The

Clyde Batchelor! The return of that beloved name to the river! He could see the island, with its willow scrub and tall cottonwood, where once the *Lucy Batchelor* had been anchored and where she had sunk, at long last, to rest in the shallows. The island had been gradually formed as her upper works caught driftwood and trash in successive rises; new crests had been built up and the muddy water, checked by the obstruction, had deposited more and more silt there. The island was far out of the channel, and the members of the River Commission had let it remain there. They had, indeed, listened with favour to the suggestion Larry had made, while he was still overseas, that on their charts it should be designated as Batchelor's Island. And if there could be a boat by that name, too! . . . But twenty-five thousand dollars! With all the modernization for which the two plantations clamoured, with all the restoration needed at Cindy Lou, with the prospect of an increasing family and the expense which this would entail, he did not see how he could rightfully spare such a sum, even if he could beg or borrow it. Still, the temptation to try was too strong for him.

"I don't know how I can do it, skipper," he said at last. "But I'll go through my account books right away—of course I haven't had a chance to look at them yet—and then I'll go over Dumaine's and Tregre's and Septime's with them, to see exactly how we stand and what corners we can cut. After that, I'll let you know."

"But meanwhile that offer might go to someone else, who'd snap it up like we ought to and——"

"We could wire and get an option, couldn't we? If I stopped wishing—and talking—and settled down to those books, it wouldn't take me long to find out what I could do. Get along to Convent and send that wire and then come back and stay with us for a couple of days, anyway. Keep Louise company while I'm figuring. I need help to prevent her from trying to do everything that requires attention here, all at once. You see, we're expecting——"

"Say, that's great news. No man's really lived until he's paddled his son across the behind for being a wild young buck—like he was himself once."

"So I've heard . . . well, be that as it may, I know Louise

277

would enjoy visiting with you. I've told her a lot about you already. And maybe, if I get right to work, we can take the train to New Orleans tomorrow or the day after that and go into a huddle with Valois Dupré. He's better than I am when it comes to this high finance business. One way or another, we'll make strap and buckle meet."

The answer to the wire came promptly: the Nashville Bridge Company would be glad to let Mr. Vincent have a week's option on the new towboat. Without waiting for the telegram's arrival, Larry had settled down to his figuring, and by the following afternoon he was ready to talk with Dumaine, Tregre and Septime. In view of their first rather captious attitude and insistent demands, he had dreaded the interview; but he found them more co-operative than he expected. Sure, the old mules and the old machinery would go for a while longer, if they had to; crops had been raised without anything better before and could be again. Larry was reminded of men he had known in the Army, who griped when nothing much was the matter, but took it in their stride when a real emergency arose. . . .

He knew that next, in all fairness, he should talk with Louise. While he had been busy with his figures, she had been equally busy with the house. Before his first agitation over Bourgeois' visit had subsided, she had come to him with a little book, bound in red morocco and fastened with a tiny heart-shaped padlock. The hinges of its clasp had rusted with age and the padlock was, consequently, quite useless; but Louise was holding the book firmly between her fingers, taking great pains to keep it closed.

"Look what I've found!" she said excitedly. Larry, whose thoughts were centred on the new towboat, glanced at the little book without enthusiasm. However, since it was evident that Louise was thrilled by its discovery, he made an effort to show some interest.

"What is it?" he asked. "An old diary?"

"I think so. I haven't looked inside it, because I didn't know whether I ought to or not. You can see that it has a lock. I believe that in the days when ladies kept diaries, they used to write all their innermost thoughts in them. And I'm almost

278

sure this was hidden—purposely. It was in a secret drawer—I'd have never known there was one, in the desk where I found it, if there hadn't been one almost exactly like it in a desk at Monteregard."

Larry took the little book from her and turned it over. On closer inspection he thought Louise was right; it undoubtedly was a diary, but it was obviously a very old one and he opened it without hesitation. On the flyleaf was written, in faded ink:

Lucy Batchelor
With love from her devoted husband
Clyde Batchelor

Pittsburgh, Pa.
November, 1867.

The handwriting was his grandfather's, which Larry still found impossible to regard without a pang. He closed the little book.

"It does seem to be a diary," he said. "But I don't see any reason why you shouldn't read it, if you want to. It's probably just a record of rapture. My grandfather must have given it to my grandmother while they were on their honeymoon. I know she was blissfully happy, but I understand that in those days ladies were shy about saying, out loud, that this was the case, if their happiness had anything to do with their love life. Perhaps that's why they confided in diaries and hid those away. I'm sure glad times have changed. I'd much rather have you tell me—and show me—that you enjoy being married to me than to have you write about it in a book."

He handed it back to her with a smile. Her answering smile was warmly responsive. But she still fingered the diary a little hesitantly.

"You don't want to read it yourself?" she asked.

"Well, not right now, honey. You see, I'm pretty busy with all these figures. Maybe some other time. But you go right ahead."

He had not thought about the diary again for several days. Then he asked Louise whether she had found time to glance through it. He did not see how she could have, for apparently she was spending every moment when they were not together in making a thorough investigation of household supplies and a careful record of household needs. Still, she had obviously been greatly intrigued by the diary; she might have stolen a few moments, here and there. . . .

"I decided against reading it, after all," she answered surprisingly. "I know you said it would be all right and you and I usually agree. But this time I didn't agree with you. I felt sure that diary had secrets in it. As a matter of fact, I—I was so sure of it that I burned it."

"You burned it!"

"Yes. You don't mind, do you, Larry? You said you weren't interested in it, so I thought——"

"No, I don't mind," he replied, quite sincerely. Her action astonished him; it seemed both precipitate and extreme, and Louise was not given to extremes, nor had he ever known her to be precipitate, except when she fell in love with him. But he was not offended by what she had done and indeed he did not attach much importance to it. He had too many other matters on his mind and he also felt sure that by this time she must have all kinds of lists of things that she wanted and needed ready to submit to him. He had not suggested, before, that she should come to the office, but now he did so; and as she seated herself composedly beside him, he realized that this was very much as it must have been when his grandfather and his grandmother conferred together about ways and means. History certainly did have a way of repeating itself.

"I wanted to talk to you about this boat Bourgeois is so sure I ought to buy," he began. "You're my partner now and I think you should be consulted. It's this way——"

"Of course I am your partner—all good French wives are their husbands' partners," she answered. "And I think I understand already how it is, *mon cœur*. You want to buy that boat and you do not quite see where the money is coming from to do it. Well, of course I don't, either. But French girls are brought up to manage, as well as to prepare for partnership, you know, even when there's plenty of money in the family. And there wasn't much in mine. That is, of course, Uncle Pierre has a great deal, and he's always been very generous. But my father wasn't wealthy, and after he and my mother separated, she and I lived on what she had. Then when she remarried, naturally she felt she had to contribute toward keeping up my stepfather's position, and this meant there was still less for me. I explained that to you in the beginning, and I think Uncle Pierre did, too, because otherwise I would have had much more of a dowry, and we wanted to be sure you wouldn't be disappointed."

"Good Lord, I never thought about a dowry when I fell in love with you and you know it! In the first place, there wasn't time, because it all happened so fast. And in the second place, I'd have felt just the way I do now, just the way most American men feel, I think—that they'd rather support their wives than have it the other way around."

"It isn't a question of support, it's a question of mutual contribution in France," Louise said calmly. "I wasn't thinking of making any special contribution; I wouldn't, even if I could, unless there were an emergency, because I know you wouldn't like it. But I shouldn't think you'd mind having me show you how well I could manage, without spending much of your money, until you have more. Even if I didn't have a big dowry, of course I did have more linen and things like that than we could use up in a lifetime—that part of my *dot* was started as soon as I was born. I can replenish a great many household needs at Cindy Lou, without spending a cent— and I'll admit a good deal of replenishing seems to be needed! Don't forget we've got all the furnishings and equipment of the Elysian Fields house to fall back on."

"That's so. I'd forgotten about those."

This was quite true. So many questions—all urgently requiring immediate answers—had arisen since their arrival at Cindy Lou that the problem connected with the New Orleans property had inevitably been crowded out of his consciousness. The caretakers, grown old in the service of the family, had been faithful to their trust; the contents of the house, many of them beautiful, some of them valuable, were in as good condition as could be expected, after a long period of disuse in a hot, humid climate. But the house itself had deteriorated badly and the neighbourhood in which it was located had deteriorated still more. In order to make it habitable, a new roof, new plumbing and much other replacement would be necessary, besides extensive repairs; and even if all this were done, its surroundings, some of them almost slumlike in character, would have made it unsuitable as a residence of the kind Larry and Louise would require for themselves and their children. Neither of them had any sentiment about the house, and after their first disappointing inspection of it they had agreed that it should be either rented or sold as soon as possible. But they were in a hurry to reach Cindy Lou, and they had left New Orleans without coming to any definite decision about it nor had they brought up the subject since. Now Larry realized that Louise was right: whether the house was sold or rented, it should be emptied, as soon as possible, of everything that could be of use to them.

"I think we'd better decide, right now, to sell it," Louise went on. "Then we can take the money we get for it and apply that toward the purchase price of the *Clyde Batchelor*."

"I'm not sure that's fair. Remember Uncle Pierre said if we did decide to dispose of the house, the money we got for it ought to be added to your little capital and properly invested."

"But the *Clyde Batchelor is* a proper investment! If it weren't, you wouldn't be making it."

"Well, of course I've great hopes for it. Still, I'm not sure that Uncle Pierre——"

"I am. But we can consult him if you like. After all, the money won't be available for investment right away. But I think we ought to take whatever steps are necessary to make it available as soon as possible." As if that question were now settled, Louise went on to discuss others. "So we don't need to worry about household equipment at Cindy Lou, and I shouldn't think we'd need to worry about food, either. We can raise most of what we need, can't we? I should think we could. Even if we can't, another thing French girls know how to do is to set a good table without spending too much on it— we could do that before the war and we got better and better at it all the time. Naturally, Uncle Pierre would be sending us wine from his vineyards, if it weren't for this queer American law which says you mustn't drink it—*that* I don't understand very well. But I think I can learn how to make wine. And if Tudie and Ivy won't resent having me tell them a few things——"

"Never mind whether they resent it or not. Go ahead and tell them."

"No. Not right off and not that way, darling. They've been telling me how Miss Lucy used to do things—I've encouraged them to. And I'm learning a great deal. She must have been a wonderful housekeeper, and she was older and more experienced, even when she first came here, than I am, wasn't she? But after I've learned, gradually, all that I can from the way she did things, then I think maybe I could experiment doing things—well, perhaps more in the modern manner, inside the house, just as you want to experiment in the fields and the factory."

"Louise, I didn't suppose I could possibly be any gladder than I was already that I'd married a French girl. But if you go on talking like this, I think I shall be, at that. And I think maybe I can manage to get that boat. But I don't want to do it under any false pretences. We won't be able to go anywhere, we won't be able to do anything——"

"But why should we want to go anywhere when we've just come home? And why should we want to do anything that we won't be doing at Cindy Lou? I should think we'd have all we could possibly do, right here, this winter. And after the baby's born, we won't want to leave him, and it wouldn't be good for him to take him here, there and everywhere—now would it?"

So Larry told Captain Bourgeois to send another wire to the Nashville Bridge Company, and they went off to New Orleans together for a conference with Valois Dupré about high finance. And though, as Louise had said, there was certainly plenty for both of them to do on the plantations, Larry was obliged to leave fairly frequently after that, since it did not prove as easy a matter to put the *Clyde Batchelor* into actual operation as Caption Bourgeois had rather glibly intimated, in his excitement over the purchase. In spite of all the 'management' of which Larry and Louise were jointly capable, it was impossible for them to make an immediate cash payment for the new boat, and this was necessarily bought on the instalment plan. Then, after the act of sale had finally been passed, the arrangements for chartering the *Clyde Batchelor* to the Vicksburg & Bayou Sara Towing

Company required prolonged adjustment. It had been decided to operate her like a tramp steamer: hauling grain barges from Minneapolis and St. Paul for the big public grain elevator in New Orleans; bringing barges of cotton from Arkansas; automobiles from Ohio and loads of coal and steel from Pittsburgh. There was also the substantial hope that occasionally they might get a tow upstream, too, when there was more oil or gasoline—or both—to take north than the Chotin Navigation Company could handle in a single tow. But it took infinite time and patience, not to mention a good deal of tact, to make this hope a reality.

At last Larry started back from New Orleans on a beautiful spring day, fairly bursting with the good news that the final contracts had actually been signed, and that the decks of the *Clyde Batchelor* were really cleared for action. He had been summoned, unexpectedly, to close these last deals, and had driven down the river road in the old Ford, which he had decided would have to go another year, after all, when the question of 'management' for the *Clyde Batchelor* had arisen; then he had come pelting back again, the minute his business was finished, feeling more confident of impending prosperity than he had for a long while and correspondingly happier. He had just heard that the little island which owed its existence to the first boat his grandfather had built and owned had officially been given the name of Batchelor by the River Commission; the towboat *Clyde Batchelor* was indisputably his own and ready to begin operations, flying the C. & L. house flag; and within a few weeks now, there would be an even more important namesake for the man whom he had loved and believed he always would love beyond all others. Neither he nor Louise had ever doubted that the expected baby would be a boy—they always referred to it as 'him'; and the next time he went to New Orleans he would be taking Louise to the hospital, where the best available room had been engaged—for in this instance there was to be no economizing. The services of a specialist in obstetrics had been secured, too; and when this physician had last examined Louise, he had said that her condition could not possibly be more satisfactory; he did not expect complications of any sort, and she should be able to go home when the baby was two weeks old, if she took a professional nurse with her. Next, Larry reflected, there would be a gala christening which would be the first big party he and Louise had given, just as his own baptism had been the first to which his parents had invited their friends in their new house. It really was a pity that Cindy Lou had never been 'fancied up' to this day—such a celebration should have a more elegant setting than they could give it. But what really counted was that they had the boat and that presently they would have the baby. And they had each other. In that last respect, history was not repeating itself, but improving upon itself. Larry did not doubt that his grandfather's marriage had been an extremely happy one. But he did not see how it could possibly have been as happy as his own. Lucy Page had been a widow when Clyde married her, and that was not like having your bride come to you as Louise had come to him. And the other marriage had been childless, while the baby who was expected so soon would unquestionably be only the first of several. . . .

The nearer Larry came to home, the higher his spirits soared, as he thought of all this. Then, as he turned into the driveway, he saw the battered Dodge, belonging to Dr. Peter Mitchell—who long before had succeeded old Dr. Bringier as the family physician—parked near the grand staircase. Suddenly, cold fear swept through him. Neither Nappy nor anyone else was in sight and the place seemed curiously hushed. He tore up the steps, two at a time, and threw open the front door. The hall, like the yard, was empty, and there was no answer to his call. But when he was halfway up the second staircase, he heard the hushed murmur of voices and then a sharp, thin wail, which pierced him like a knife. The doors of all the rooms except his mother's, which he and Louise still shared, stood open; but no sounds were coming from them. They were vacant, too. It was behind that one closed door something was happening—that something had happened. The sickening smell of ether came from it; the murmuring grew louder and more confused and the wail penetrated it more sharply. Larry stopped abruptly on the threshold, tempted to rush in but somehow withheld; and, as he hesitated, the door opened and Dr. Mitchell, wearing a blood-spattered white garment, came out.

"Why, hello there, Larry!" he said. "This is a great time for you to be showing up."

There was no note of tragedy in his voice; it was almost bantering in tone. Larry seized his arm.

"What's happened?" he asked hoarsely.

"Why, just what we've been expecting—only we didn't expect it quite so soon." As he spoke, the doctor peeled off his rubber gloves, unbuttoned his blood-stained gown and tossed both nonchalantly on a near-by sofa. "We weren't very thoroughly prepared, but everything went off okay at that. Of course, I wouldn't be out here if it hadn't. You can go in pretty soon. Don't stay but a minute though. It's been rather a long pull. However, your wife's taken it like a Trojan— never saw anything to beat it—and she's fine now. So's the baby—a bouncer." He opened the door a crack. "Mr. Vincent's back. Let him know when he can come in, will you?" he said to someone Larry could not see. Then he closed the door again. "Well, I want to go and get cleaned up. So long."

He disappeared in the direction of the bathroom. Larry waited what seemed an eternity. He thought he could distinguish Louise's voice now, above the wailing sound, but he was not sure, for he had never heard it when it was so faint. Tudie came out with a big bundle of linen, holding it as if she were trying to hide the stains from him. But she was smiling broadly.

"We done cotched us de sweetes' baby you ever did see, Mistuh Larry," she said proudly. "It were a while befo' Miss Louise could turn dat child loose, but she done grand just de same. De nurse, she'll be out in a minute now and let you in."

Again the wait seemed endless. Finally the door opened once more, and a woman who was a complete stranger came out of it, but remained standing in such a way as to block Larry's passage. Her countenance was stern, her primly parted hair was surmounted by a stiff cap and her starched dress rattled with the least movement. She looked at Larry accusingly, as if she believed his past conduct to have been something close to criminal and also as if she had little hope of his future reformation. Then she spoke severely.

"After this, I cannot permit anything to interfere with Mrs.

Vincent's rest," she said. "But she has been asking for you, and Dr. Mitchell has overridden my advice and humoured her by consenting to allow you to see her now. I hope I do not need to warn you that you should not say or do anything which will upset her."

"Why in hell should you think I want to upset her?" Larry asked angrily. "But I do want——"

The strange woman raised a thin hand. "And you should not raise your voice, either. Noise of any sort is a very disturbing factor, at this stage. I shall return, in five minutes, with some nourishment for Mrs. Vincent. Meanwhile——"

"Meanwhile I'd appreciate it if you'd give me a chance to go to my wife, especially as she's asked for me."

He had not raised his voice this time, but something in it evidently warned the nurse that if she did not move of her own accord, he might thrust her bodily away. She stepped rapidly to one side and Larry strode past her.

The room was still permeated with the mingled scents of ether and blood; but as Larry crossed it, he became less and less conscious of these, more and more aware of the fragrance of clean linen and new wool, and of another fresh smell, which was unfamiliar to him, and which he did not instantly recognize as the unique sweetness that emanates from a newly born, newly bathed baby. The baby was not lying, as he had imagined it would be, in the curve of Louise's arm, but in an old wooden cradle that had been drawn up beside the bed; and, in a way, he was glad. At the moment he felt that he did not want even their child to come between Louise and himself. As he bent over her, he was horrified by her pallor; but though her eyes seemed preternaturally large in that white face, they were full of love as she looked up at him, and there was nothing about her smile which suggested suffering.

"I'm afraid you'll be terribly disappointed," she said. "I know how much you wanted a boy, so you could name him Clyde, but I love little Lucy already and I'm sure you will, too. Besides, next year, we'll give her a baby brother, won't we?"

CHAPTER TWENTY-ONE

IT WAS over two years, instead of only one, after all, before there was another baby and then it was a second girl.

It was true that Larry had been disappointed the first time. However, his disappointment had been swallowed up in his concern about Louise, and, as she had predicted, he quickly fell a victim to the charms of little Lucy, much as Clyde had fallen under the spell of Cary. But the second time, everything happened on schedule, in such a quiet orderly way that he had no cause for concern; and the second baby girl was not nearly as winsome as the first. There had been no name ready for her, because Larry had been so sure that this time the name would be Clyde; but after some hesitation and discussion, it was decided to call her Amy. After all, Mrs. Surget had left no child of her own, and Larry felt a certain debt of gratitude to her for her kindness to him during his childhood; it seemed as if he would be repaying this in some slight measure by giving her a namesake. Beyond this, he had very little feeling in the matter, anyway, for this time his disappointment was very deep. And it was not assuaged by Louise's hopeful prediction that the *next* one would be a boy.

"Perhaps we won't ever have another. After all, we didn't have Lucy right away or Amy very soon after that. And it certainly wasn't because of any preventive measures."

"No, and I'm glad that it wasn't. But I'm also glad we had those first years to ourselves. I wouldn't have wanted even a child to come between us then." She was putting into words what he had felt himself, at one time, but which he had never expressed. "And I'm glad Lucy and Amy weren't so near together that I haven't been able to enjoy them both and give undivided attention to them both. If they'd been only a year apart, I'd have had two babies at the same time— without even having had the excitement of twins. Please don't worry so, *mon cœur*. You'll have your boy yet, you'll see."

"I don't believe it. If we do have another, it'll be a third girl. We'll have a *drei Mädchen Haus*, as they say in Coblenz."

Perhaps if he had not been worried about many other things, Larry would not have worried so much about his failure to beget a son. But everything on the plantations seemed to be going wrong. The yield had been short and its sucrose content low; maybe Septime was right when he said cane got tired, and that after a certain number of years you had to try a new kind of seed to give it a fresh start. Then of course agricultural prices had really never recovered from the setback of '21. Besides, it had been absolutely necessary to replace more machinery than Tregre had indicated in his first surveys; and no one realized more keenly than Larry that his failure to modernize the entire equipment of the plantations was the principal source of trouble. Back of this failure, to be sure, lay his decision to squeeze from the turnip every drop of blood it held and thus buy the *Clyde Batchelor*. The money so spent could have been used to replace mules and carts with tractors and trucks; it could also have been used to modernize the mill, and so take advantage of the new deal everybody was talking about—making wallboard out of bagasse. The Godchaux at Raceland were already baling bagasse; but Larry couldn't swing anything like that at Cindy Lou or Victoria, because he did not have the money to shift his production line into new and more profitable channels.

He could not be thankful enough that he did not have a nagging wife, one who insisted on making a show, on 'keeping up with the Joneses', as people were beginning to say. From the outset, Louise had been a blessing straight from heaven. But now Louise was ill, and of course that was the worst trouble of all. It was all very well for the New Orleans specialist, who had been consulted this time, to tell him he needn't worry. How could he help worrying, for God's sake, when the dear girl was running a temperature, when she was steadily losing weight, when her erstwhile buoyant footsteps dragged listlessly and when her lovely laugh sounded less and less often? Where in hell she could have picked up that damned undulant fever was a mystery. The doctor had shrugged his shoulders when Larry told him every cow on the place had been tested. There was always a chance. . . . However, there was no cause for concern. Recovery was slow, but it was sure—practically sure, anyway. The doctor would admit, though, that it was a tedious business, for the fever was apt to recur over and over again, even after convalescence seemed assured, and a certain amount of pain did go with it. No one could expect women, especially young women, to be resigned to such discomforts. No, Larry said savagely to himself. And no one should expect a man who was trying to pinch a penny here and a jitney there to stop worrying when, in addition to his natural anxiety about his wife, he was wondering how to pay her doctors' bills. Louise was home again now, thank the Lord—the great gloomy house had seemed like a tomb without her; but the doctor had insisted upon having her at Touro until the nature of the disease was determined beyond any shadow of doubt. And that being the case, Larry himself had insisted on a private room and special nurses. You might economize on anything and everything else, but you didn't economize on your wife when she was sick. He hadn't changed his mind about that, either. However, this didn't alter the fact that payment had been required, in advance, for the private room, and every week for the nurses. And when the doctor's first bill—also very promptly rendered—had come in, Larry told himself grimly that it must be cheaper to run a steamboat line than a doctor's office.

Increasingly, he begrudged the monthly remittance which, under the terms of Clyde Batchelor's will, went regularly to Bushrod Page. Larry did not believe his grandfather could have realized how little his uncle needed it. Mabel, who had inherited millions from her father, the railroad magnate, had died, leaving her immense fortune to Bushrod; and Bushrod had promptly married again—a young and beautiful woman, who had no money herself, but who had considerable social standing and who had quickly presented her husband with an heir. So now Bushrod had everything: a substantial fortune, a charming wife, a proud position, and an assured inheritance. Somehow Larry, without knowing quite why he felt that way, did not believe his uncle deserved any of this, much less all of it; and he was consumed with rage when Bushrod, whom he had never seen since he left Coblenz and with whom his correspondence had been as brief and impersonal as was consistent with courtesy, wrote him a smooth letter, saying that henceforth the monthly remittance would be set aside as a 'nest egg' for the heir to Sorrento and Amalfi. Larry did not resent the belated arrival on the scene of the little boy whose birth deprived him of his own potential Virginia heritage; he himself was a Louisianian, through and through, as his Virginia forebears had believed he would be. But he felt there was no justice in a destiny which permitted his uncle to flourish like the green bay tree while he, Larry, struggled harder and harder to make both ends meet. Above all, it seemed to him like the irony of fate that he should be the one to squeeze out money to provide a 'nest egg' for the heir to Sorrento and Amalfi, when he himself was heirless.

But, as his grandfather had often reminded him, a promise was a promise; and the two hundred dollars did go every month to Virginia, no matter what that meant in the way of deprivation at Cindy Lou and, after all, griping about your troubles was about the only relief you got from them, whether it was in the Army or back home, Larry reflected morosely, as he sat over his accounts one fine summer day, when he would much rather have been out riding the crops. He had quickly abandoned the use of his grandfather's office on the grounds that, while he did not want anything changed there, he couldn't function efficiently with its antiquated equipment; he needed files, not pigeonholes, and a large, flat surface to his desk, not a roll top. This was the truth, as far as it went, but it was by no means the whole truth. He still missed his grandfather so poignantly in the surroundings with which Clyde had been most closely associated that he could not shake off the sense of loss; and he still instinctively looked for the old man, indeed sometimes still started to speak to him, before the swift realization came that it was tragically futile to do so. Larry thought Louise was aware of all this, although she had never voiced such awareness. The chamber which Larry and his grandfather had shared remained closed and unchanged, though they could have utilized that space now; and when Larry spoke to Louise about the inadequacies of the old office, she said of course he needed more modern equipment, and why not install it in one of those ground-floor chambers which were still unused? The schoolroom had better remain as it was, for who knew? They might be wanting that for Lucy and Amy and—she added unfalteringly —little Clyde some day, if not for lessons, then for games. To be sure, they were having business visitors again now, but not to the extent the builder of Cindy Lou had visualized, and probably they never would. Not that there would not be more business visitors than ever before. But the speed and ease of modern transportation had rendered long visits, for business purposes, superfluous. It was a simple matter now to leave New Orleans or Baton Rouge in the morning and return the same evening, having meanwhile settled any number of important transactions; there was hardly ever an occasion for an overnight stay, so another chamber could easily be spared for a new office. As to the cost of what Larry wanted and needed to equip it, he should not think of that; it represented an investment, not an expenditure. . . .

So Larry bought his big flat-topped desk and his files, secondhand, and they were duly installed, as Louise had suggested, in one of the rooms formerly set aside for business visitors, which still left several more available for that purpose; and Louise supplemented the new equipment in various ways. She had discovered a firm in Chicago which ground up old rugs and carpeting and made new floor coverings out of the material; so she had sent several of the most worn and ragged specimens at Cindy Lou to this resourceful and competent establishment, and the result had been one large and very presentable rug. She had also made chintz curtains out of some longer ones which she had found in a chest at Victoria, and which would bear shortening enough to do away with the worst parts; and the attics of both houses had yielded several pictures, in which Larry had seen no decorative possibilities whatsoever until Louise actually had them up on the wall, when he ungrudgingly admired them. So, taken by and large, the new office was a very cheerful, pleasant room— and a good thing, too, Larry said to himself, looking up from the discouraging figures to a shady corner of the garden, where Louise had taken the two little girls; if it had not been, he could hardly have withstood the temptation of strolling out to join her. The children were romping around her, but she was not romping with them, as she would have before she had been so ill. She was sitting in a big chair, watching them, and since she did not know anyone was watching *her*, the expression on her pale face was unguarded. Larry's heart smote him as he looked at her. He turned back to his books and, as he did so, Tudie knocked at the door of his office.

"Yes?" he answered impatiently, without raising his eyes from the figures.

"Dey's a gen'mun say he like to see you, suh," Tudie informed him.

"Tell him to go find Mr. Prudhomme or Mr. Tregre," Larry said abruptly.

"But he want to see you," Tudie persisted. "He say to tell you his name Mr. Waddle and the last time he see you it were in Two—or."

"Waddill! Frank Waddill!" Larry leaped up and, brushing past Tudie, rushed to the doorway. The next moment he and Frank Waddill were pummelling each other heartily and calling each other by such endearing terms as you old bastard, you, and you no-count lousy buckwheat.

"Come in, come in," Larry finally insisted. "Come in and park your carcass. What'll it be? Coffee? I can let you have some homebrew, too, that doesn't taste too God-awful if you don't look at the half-inch sediment of yeast in the bottom of the bottle. And I know there's still some prime old bourbon—pre-war, so help me!—back in Dad's cellaret. Give it a name, man."

They were soon seated in the office, with both coffee cups and tall glasses between them, talking about that café at Tours and the little black-eyed girls at the next table; about poor old Tracy Dixon, who had got his in the Argonne, instead of a master's degree at Princeton; and about the way some of those armchair soldiers were trying to grab off the American Legion. Then there was a brief pause, while Frank took a long pull at his glass and Larry glanced down at the sheet of paper on which he had been scribbling when his friend arrived.

"Hell, this reminds me," he exclaimed. "I expect you're about ready to make that survey of our sugarhouse over at Victoria. Boy, there's nothing I'd rather have or need more, too, I can tell you. But there isn't a god's blessed chance." He dropped his hand down on his discouraging notations. "I've just been telling myself the bad news. I mean bad. Now get me. I'm not going to sing the blues to you, but things have

293

just been breaking tough. I overextended myself in buying a towboat—but I'm not sorry—and I've been trying to piece out on the plantation the best way I could to make up for it. So anything that means putting up the frogskins is not for me; not now, at least. I was just sitting here, when I was told somebody wanted to see me. I was trying to figure things out. It's less than two weeks to my wife's birthday and if anybody ever owed anybody else a real present, I owe her one. But there's no way to make it; leastways not without opening a still back in the swamps and peddling out a choice lot of white lightning to the cash trade."

He paused and Frank held up a monitory hand.

"If you'd just give me a chance, stupid, I'd ha' told you I wasn't here to inspect your sugar machinery," he said. "You got bad news, you keep saying. Well listen, shavetail, maybe I got good news for you. Ever remember me telling you about that sonar stuff, that echo-bouncing business? Good Lord, man! That was while we were still in college, before ever we made the world safe for Democracy."

"Yeah, sure I remember. What was the name of that beer garden down by the ferry?"

"I forget. But it doesn't matter. This is what does: coming back from France, I ran into a navy officer name of Karcher. Listen, mah frien'. Karch started in on sonics about nine miles higher up than the farthest I got. That boy had it. And he had something else, too. He had a man name of De Gollyer. He was working on a plan to apply his sonar stuff to oil exploration."

"Oil exploration? Out in the water, you mean?"

"No. On land. Let me ask you. How much do you know about oil?"

"It's greasy, it stinks and it makes Osage Indians rich. Outside of that, precious little."

"Well, I won't try to give you a series of lectures on the subject this evening. I might later on, if you're interested then. But here's what might interest you right now: Karcher and De Gollyer have found a way for getting 'soundings' on land, similar to those the Navy used at sea during the war. They map out subterranean landscapes."

"Well, what of it?"

"Quite a good deal. In this way numbers of 'domes' have been discovered, in spite of the fact that the surface failed to indicate that there were mountains of rock layers where oil and gas could be trapped, thousands of feet beneath the top soil."

"And you helped develop this plan?"

"No such luck! But as I *had* done sonar research in college, I got in with one of the major oil companies, the Old Hickory Petroleum Corporation, and now I'm at the head of what they call their Exploration Department."

"That's fine. I'm sure glad for you. Maybe for me, too. When I'm even broker than I am now, I'll know who to hit for a fast loan."

"I can do a lot better than that for you. I'm going through this part of the country leasing exploration rights."

"Come again?"

"Let me get at it my own way. Probably you know that practically everybody in the oil business has been saying the deposits on the Gulf Coast were all west of the Mississippi River. I don't believe this. So eventually I sold my company on the idea of letting me run a shooting crew through the land between Lake Maurepas and the river. Never mind why I picked this particular area. It would take me a week to explain how we draw these underground maps from drilling logs, and fill in the blank spaces by guesswork. If our shooting crews—seismographic explorers, if you want to use the broad A—find nothing, we're not out much. If they do, we're first aboard the gravy train, with all the desirable spots under lease."

"You mean you want permission to make those bounce-back records on Cindy Lou and Victoria, and maybe find oil there? Hell, yes. Help yourself to the roasting ears."

Waddill threw back his head and laughed.

"Lord, but you're an easy touch!" he cried. "Lucky for you I won't take advantage of a partner who fought the battle of Murray Street with me in Aleck. How many acres have you got here?"

"Call it eight thousand and you won't be far wrong. Three thousand at Cindy Lou and the balance at Victoria, give or take a few hundred either way. It would need a survey to show whether the land outside our levees—the *batture*, you know—had been building up or eroding away."

"Good. Then here's my proposition. I'll pay you fifteen cents an acre for the right to make seismographic explorations on your land. That will be at least twelve hundred dollars cash on the barrelhead, here and now, this afternoon, if you sign the agreement. I've got copies of our standard exploration lease forms in my brief case out in the car. You get that much, win, lose or draw. . . . What's the matter?"

"Nothing's the matter. I was just thinking."

"All right, go ahead and think. Mind if I have another drink while you do it? This stuff isn't bad at all."

Without waiting for an answer, Frank refilled his glass. Larry, who had been staring at his friend, looked down at the sheet he had shoved aside and, picking up a pencil, scribbled on it again. Then he sat staring at the result.

Twelve hundred dollars! Twelve Hundred Dollars! TWELVE HUNDRED DOLLARS! Why, that would be enough for . . . for a gala trip to New Orleans during the last few days of Carnival and the right dresses to wear to Momus and Mystick and Proteus and Comus—perhaps an evening wrap as well. Or, if Louise would rather go to New York and see some shows, but have fewer dresses, that could be managed. Larry wouldn't feel any compunctions about using Frank's money for something like that, because it would be so much velvet and you didn't put velvet into necessities. You might even put it into jewellery, if Louise would rather have jewellery than a trip. He'd never given her any jewellery, not once since they were married. But now—well now, of course he still couldn't get her a bracelet with baguette-cut diamonds, or anything of that order, but maybe he could get her a sapphire clip or something like that. Or if she'd rather blow in everything on a party—the sort of party they used to have at Cindy Lou—they could give one of those, with an orchestra and champagne and everything. At least, he thought they could. He had never paid for that sort of a party himself. Perhaps it cost more than he thought. Besides, he remembered with a pang, maybe Louise wasn't well enough to give a party —or to go on a trip. Anyway, she had never seemed to be dependent on excitement of that sort for pleasure. Probably

she would rather redecorate one of the threadbare rooms—
or could she do more than one for twelve hundred dollars?
Even one room would be worth it. Then, with a less passing
pang, he realized that the twelve hundred dollars might have
to be used, after all, for more hospital bills . . . and that even
twelve hundred dollars might not be enough. . . . He looked up.

"And if there should be oil?" he asked quietly.

"If our shots show that there's a dome or some other
structure here, we'll make a regular mineral lease with you
that'll come to real money. Offhand, I'd say that if the
structure looked favourable, we might pay you a dollar and
a half an acre for the right to sink one or more oil wells on
your place in a year. If we hit, you're in the big time, because
an eighth of all the oil would belong to you, and that's no
chicken feed. If we don't, you'll be better off to the tune of
twelve hundred dollars, anyway. So what can you lose? Let
me get that lease form."

There would be only one way, Larry knew, by which he
could make Louise accept a present of any value. That would
be to put it beside her plate and let her find it there, when
they went in to supper on the night of her birthday. She would
pick up the little box and thank him rapturously, even before
she undid the ribbon with which it was tied or folded back
the tissue paper in which it was wrapped. As he had so
regretfully meditated, he had given her very few presents;
but she had always shown immediate and wholehearted
appreciation of every little thing. What mattered was that he
had wanted to make her a present; the form it took was
unimportant—at least to her. Larry did not feel that way
about it. He was immeasurably thankful that he could make
her a real gift at last.

He held back her chair for her and leaned over to kiss her.
They had decided that this should be a party, with all the
best silver and china and linen and all the things they liked
best to eat, and that they would dress up for it; but it would
be a party just for themselves. After Louise was seated and he
had kissed her, Larry lingered beside her, instead of going to
his own chair at the other end of the table. Louise caught
sight of the little box and picked it up.

"Darling, how sweet of you! I can't wait to see . . . but whatever this is, I'm sure it's lovely. Everything you give me . . ."

Well, it hadn't been true before, but it was this time, he said to himself, watching her as she undid the little package. When the tissue paper parted with a soft rustle, and Louise saw the word TIFFANY peeping out from between the folds, she looked up at him questioningly. The first box—cardboard covered with glazed white paper—enclosed a second one, made of velvet. She pressed the spring which controlled the lid and this flew open. Inside, formed like a tiny steamboat, was a diamond brooch.

"Larry—Larry! It's perfectly beautiful! But you shouldn't have! You know we agreed——"

"Yes, I know what we agreed and I know that agreement's got to be revised now." Purposely, he had offered no explanation of Frank's visit and she had asked for none. Now the words came tumbling out of themselves. "Our luck's turned, I know it has. This is your luck piece. Let me pin it on you, darling, and see how it looks."

The shot crews, as Larry soon learned to call them, arrived a few days later—a dozen or so brisk young men in four vehicles. One of these vehicles was a truck carrying a portable drilling rig. Another truck carried a mobile darkroom, within which Larry was shown a maze of instrument panels, recording devices and tiny, winking bulbs of vari-coloured lights, which meant rather less than nothing to him, apart from a general impression of bewildering intricacy. The third truck carried angry-looking red flags and startlingly lettered signs, with the single word EXPLOSIVES prominently displayed on each side. The fourth vehicle was the dust-covered, dingy Ford touring car in which the crew chief and his assistant rode.

From then on, the peace and serenity of Cindy Lou were shattered at intervals by thunderous explosions. Nuffy, who was old and irritable now, greeted each blast with an ear-piercing howl, as he scuttled for shelter. Nappy complained that he would have to send the cows away, for their milk was being soured. One of the field hands came to say that his wife insisted on being reimbursed for a setting of eggs that had been addled by a detonation close to their cabin. Tregre angrily demanded that Larry do something to prevent the explorers from jarring his sugarhouse machinery out of alignment on its massive foundations. Tudie muttered that no sooner had the children settled for their naps than the unearthly racket woke them up and that then they were fussy for the rest of the day. It was a task to keep the peace among all these malcontents. Larry tried his best to have the crew chief explain what was being done, but that lean and bronzed individual was singularly taciturn whenever he emerged from the mysterious fastnesses of his mobile darkroom.

"I hate to disoblige, Mr. Vincent," he drawled. "I sure do hate it. But a lot of oil people would give the teeth out of their jaws to know what's in these pictures. Don't mind showing you this, though, on account of even if you did understand them, just one wouldn't be of any help." He displayed a long strip of black photographic paper, on which white intersections were ruled, and on which crazy lines seemed to dance in wild confusion over the regular spacing. "But you can tell your people to rest easy from here out," he added. "We're moving back towards the swamps tomorrow, to make another set of shots around that gravel land—the Boisblanc part, I think is the name."

The Boisblanc part! The tract that had seemed so worthless to Valois Dupré that he had sold it back to Clyde Batchelor for one dollar! But that was also the tract where, from time immemorial, the plantation Negroes had claimed there was buried treasure—where Cary Page and, later, her son Larry had dug for it, because they listened to these legends and believed them. That was where Frank Waddill's crew was going to dig for treasure now—not pirate gold, to be sure, but black gold, desposited millions of years before by the death and decay of billions upon billions of billions of minute creatures of the sea, each so small as to be invisible, yet in the aggregate so rich as to make Ali Baba's cave look like a refuse heap. But treasure just the same.

When Larry went out to the Boisblanc tract very early the next morning, the exploratory shooting had already begun. After that, every night, messengers carried sheaves of photographic records to the express office where, under heavy seal, they were dispatched to Tulsa. There, figures and other data were entered from these records upon a master chart, which claimed more and more attention from a growing number of department heads and executives as it neared completion. When Frank returned to Cindy, he brought with him a thick roll of maps and a brief case bulging with blue-backed legal documents. This time, there was none of the jovial back-pounding and affectionate obscenity of their former reunion. Spreading his papers over the desk, Waddill came directly to the point.

"I'm not taking you around Robin Hood's barn," he said. "We've found a structure all right; that is to say, the geology sharps and the fossil boys and all the rest of our scientists back in the home office have come to the conclusion there's a dome somewhere under your Boisblanc acreage. Might be oil there, might not be; but it looks promising as all hell, and our geologists are excited no end. They say if it proves up, the whole industry will have to revise its concept of oil exploration and, for a starter, forget that business about no pools east of the Mississippi. Anyway, I'm ready to offer you not a dollar and a half, but two whole round iron dollars an acre to lease every inch of your land for oil drilling."

Larry started to speak, but Frank waved him off.

"Let me finish before you say anything. That's our top offer. The only reason I made it right away is for old time's sake. Naturally I was instructed to start by offering you a dollar, even when I told the boss I had already casually mentioned a dollar and a half. And, incidentally, I'm not driving such a hard bargain. Two bucks an acre makes a nice cosy sixteen grand for a guy I knew when he was pulling down thirty plasters a month."

This time when he stopped, Larry waited before asking, "Okay if I speak my little piece now, big shot?"

Waddill looked at him with a hint of uneasiness in his glance. "Shoot," he directed. "But where's the bunting and red carpet? I figured you'd greet me with at least that much when I dumped half the mint in your lap, or anyways offered to. What's itching you?"

"Nothing. Only you'd better sit down and hang on to

something before I let you in on what I got figured out. I don't want you passing out in the middle of the floor."

"I already told you I'd made you our top offer right off. Remember?"

"Surest thing you know. And instead of two dollars an acre, I want you to go back down to a dollar and a half."

"WHATTT?"

"You heard me. You aren't all that sunburned. A dollar and a half is the figure—*provided* . . ."

"Provided what?"

"Provided you also put into the contract that if you find oil the C. & L. Navigation Company, which is Louise and I, gets to transport it."

Waddill looked doubtful.

"That's out of my line," he said, hesitantly. "I'm in exploration and drilling. The transportation department . . ."

"Don't give me that applesauce, Frank!" Larry chuckled. "Sure, there's a transportation department. But here's the deal. If you hit oil, you'll have to put a pipe line to either the Valley or the Edenborn, or the I. C., and they'll have to build a loading spur for you. The most cars you can get on there at a time is eight—and think of all the time you'll lose loading your oil in tank car lots. Whereas you can build a pipe line straight across my land, on high ground—I'll give you the right of way for a cancelled two-cent stamp paid in advance—to the river, where you can run it into my barges in a fiftieth of the time and at a fiftieth of the cost, and I can move it, either to tidewater in New Orleans or to any riverside refinery you want. You folks have one of those refineries in West Virginia, haven't you? See what I mean?"

"Yes, of course. That's how Standard does it with the Chotins, from Baton Rouge, only they ship refinery products like diesel oil and gasoline."

"But they haven't got an oil well right alongside the river."

"No, and for that matter neither have we—though it looks good. Tell you what I'll do. Hold the offer open while I drive to Lutcher and make a phone call to Tulsa. Better yet, hold it open until tomorrow, in case it takes me longer than it should to get a call through. Incidentally, can you lay your hands on the equipment if they want to make the deal?"

"I already have a diesel-powered, all-steel towboat, the *Clyde Batchelor*. She's under charter to the Vicksburg and Bayou Sara people, but the charter can be cancelled, by either side, on thirty days' notice. The barges—and I'd need three of those . . ."

"How come you know all that—and the time-cost differential between barge and rail shipments so pat, anyway?"

"I learned it all from my grandfather, who knew more about the river than I'll ever find out." Larry paused. For the first time, the awareness of Clyde brought with it no grief. It was poignant still; but this was the poignancy of triumph, the exaltation of long-delayed fulfilment. As clearly as though they had been spoken only the day before, his grandfather's words came ringing out to him: "There's one commodity— oil, that is—where the railroads, damn them, can never compete with the river. A tow of three barges, say, could carry as much oil as seven trains of sixty tank cars each, and think of the time to be saved in loading those barges! Only three couplings to make. One man could do the whole thing in twelve hours. On those seven trains more than four hundred couplings would have to be made and unmade, and you couldn't load more than a dozen cars at a time on any single spur, anyway. So it would take a week just to fill the tank cars and another week to empty them when they got to their destination. Yes, indeed! *Oil!* That's the thing to bring the river back to its glory! . . ."

"I wish he could know what's cooking here, today," Larry said to himself. "Well—perhaps he does." Larry looked across the desk at Frank. "About those barges," he said steadily. "I can get the mint to finance me on buying them if I have a contract with you and a producing oil well in my back yard. There's a friend of mine, incidentally, a salty old steamboat captain named Bourgeois, you'll want to meet one of these days. He's in command of the *Clyde Batchelor* now. My grandfather trained him . . . but never mind about that. Sure. Go make your phone call. I think we both know what the answer's going to be."

302

PAYMENT RECEIVED

Summer, 1930

EVERYTHING connected with the preparations for dedicating the Clyde Batchelor Community Centre seemed propitious.

In the first place, the Big House at Cindy Lou lent itself far more easily than had been expected to adaptation for the purposes planned. On the ground floor, the gaming-room and Clyde's office remained unchanged. The gaming-room, it was agreed, should be used exactly as it had been throughout Cary Page's girlhood, for almost any sort of recreational purpose; if more persons wished to play cards, dominoes, checkers or chess than could be readily accommodated at one time, it was understood that they might set up folding tables in the adjoining office. Larry's schoolroom underwent only such minor alterations as would make it suitable for night classes in handicrafts, bookkeeping and English composition, with special emphasis on letter writing. These would be open to anyone who wished to take advantage of such instruction, not only at the terminal, the oil field and on the plantations, but in the general locality. The office which Louise had helped Larry equip was kept exactly as they had arranged it on his return from war and as he had used it in his capacity of terminal superintendent. The head stenographer, who also acted as his private secretary, was installed in the next room; and this still left plenty of space for the other clerical employees, after providing offices for the harbour master and the engineer. The huge antiquated bathroom had been divided into separate washrooms, complete with showers, for men and women. The old racks in the wine closet were not removed; but coolers for Coca-Cola and cigarette and candy vending machines were set up beside them and supplemented by general utility cupboards, a porcelain sink and a small gas range, where coffee could be dripped continuously. It was easy to visualize the adjoining room, where business visitors had formerly been given their meals, as an attractive setting for self-service snacks.

The main floor had required even less adjustment for the

needs it was now intended to meet. True, the books which had originally belonged to Alexander Peyton, and other volumes of special significance and value had been removed to Victoria; so had the more precious silverware, porcelain and ornaments. But to the casual observer, the dining-room and the drawing-room looked much as they had in their best days. However, a trained librarian had been installed, subscriptions entered to leading magazines and newspapers and numerous weighty books of reference purchased; nor had the wider appeal of light reading gone unconsidered; books of fiction could be borrowed, or they could be read on the premises. In the drawing-room and dining-room, meetings could be held or parties given after reasonable notice to the capable manageress, who was another recent addition. She and the librarian were friends and were already sharing the chamber with the convent beds. It was understood that Bushrod's old room and Cary's old room were generally to be used for such guests as wished to 'rest their wraps,' but that occasionally some especially favoured visitor might spend the night there. Nothing had been said, as yet, about Clyde's old room; but it was also understood that, for the time being, it would continue to remain closed. The ballroom was to be used again for small dances, though large ones would continue to be held, as such functions had been for some time now, in the pavilion at the real estate development known as Batchelor's Village.

It was astonishing how rapidly this had come into being. The Old Hickory Petroleum Company had hastily run up a few temporary buildings, near the Boisblanc tract, to shelter the first few men they sent to Cindy Lou. Then, as soon as it became evident that an oil field of considerable extent—and not merely an isolated pool—had been tapped, the personnel was enlarged to include a field superintendent, a drilling superintendent, an engineer and assistant engineer, a driller and assistant driller and a crew of twenty-four 'roughnecks,' who worked in two twelve-hour shifts. Very shortly thereafter, the advisability of further expansion was indicated; and more or less simultaneously, Larry found that the dock, pipe line and railroad spur of which his terminal had originally consisted now needed a machine shop, a general power plant and a tank farm; also that a correspondingly increased number of employees was required for effective operation. At this point, he was approached by a realty corporation, first with tentative suggestions and then with definite plans for a settlement where executives and employees of both the field and the terminal could be permanently domiciled: individual houses for the married men, a large boarding-house for the bachelors, some kind of a commissary. Possibly the lane which had once divided Cindy Lou from Victoria might be made into a good road, leading to such a development, the realtor said persuasively; and there could not be a better location for the development itself than one close to that old Indian mound. . . .

Larry consulted Louise and neither was hard to convince that such a settlement would prove a great advantage to all concerned. So presently, the place was swarming with carpenters, masons, plumbers and painters; and little by little, the neat bungalows with their well-tended lawns; the big, bare-looking boarding-house which was so surprisingly comfortable inside; and the commissary, which provided everything from needles to lawn mowers, were supplemented by other buildings to meet the requirements of a community which numbered nearly five hundred persons: a small school and a small bank; a doctor's office, where a young physician began a promising practice; a newspaper office, where an elderly reporter, tired of taking orders, became his own boss; even a beauty parlour, where an operator who had never found success in a competitive city environment discovered it in this receptive rural atmosphere. The beauty parlour opened its doors at about the same time the dance pavilion was finished and, from the first, its business was brisk. As to the pavilion itself, that was also well patronized; and the older men, some of whom had daughters of marriageable age, were not displeased to see that the bachelors were less prone to wander off on Saturday nights to distant dances, where they frequently met girls who caught their fancy, than before this attraction was so accessible. Weddings occurred more and more often and a new crop of babies came along in their wake. The young doctor began to talk about an office nurse, the schoolteacher said she needed an assistant and the elderly reporter who had turned editor said he would have to get himself a leg man. As to the beautician, she married, became a mother and advertised in the paper for a helper!

Gradually, the incredulous amazement with which Larry and Louise at first viewed the sudden improvement in their fortunes changed to a sense of security, and with this came also an increasing awareness of responsibility. Larry had been brought up in the tradition of a planter's accountability to his 'people' and Louise had received somewhat the same training in respect to the peasants at Monteregard; but the present situation was different. There was no question, here and now, of dealing with individuals or groups who were ignorant or dependent; not a few of the men at both the oil field and the terminal were college graduates or had gone to good technical schools; their wives, in some cases, had benefited by similar educational advantages. But there were many instances where the persons were city bred, to whom life in the country was admittedly monotonous. Several who had come from cooler climates suffered in the torrid summers to the point of actual disability, and several others found the change from the surroundings to which they had been accustomed a real deprivation. Louise knew there was nothing she could do, she told Larry regretfully, for the man from Montana whose prickly heat had become a real problem, for the boy from the Bronx who did not 'feel natural' where there were no sidewalks, or for the woman from Colorado who was pining for her mountains. But she could not get away from the conviction that there should be some way in which she could help the girl from New Hampshire who had assumed that of course there would be a local library, because she had never heard of a village without one. . . .

"I told her she was welcome to come here whenever she wanted to," Louise went on, glancing toward the well-filled shelves behind her chair. Like Lucy, she preferred the library to any room in the house, and she and Larry frequently sat there now, after supper. "But this girl—Myra Dale, her name is—said no, she'd always be afraid of intruding. It wouldn't be like going to a public library; and anyway, she couldn't get any satisfaction out of a book that she couldn't read at her leisure—especially at night, after she'd gone to bed. I told her

she was welcome to borrow our books and she said no again—
she wouldn't like the responsibility of doing that, even if we
were willing she should. She was brought up on the theory
that one book should never be taken away from the place
where an entire set is kept, because if anything happened to
that one book, then the whole set was spoiled."

"We've got plenty of books that aren't in sets. We could
lend her those."

"Ye-e-s. But I see what she means. She wants to feel free
to go into a little library and browse around for a while.
Next she wants to leaf through several books whose looks she
likes, and finally she wants to take one home with her. She
doesn't earn enough to buy all the books she wants and she's
hungry for them. There are some people to whom books come
next to bread. She's one of them."

"Is she terribly plain?"

"No, she's quite pretty—in an earnest sort of way, if you
know what I mean."

"Yes, I know what you mean. Well, there's a young
engineer, graduate of Massachusetts Tech., who's just come
on the field, and I think we'd better ask him and this girl—
what did you say her name was?—to supper some night. I
hear he's homesick, too. It's the food he can't take, of all
things—probably hungry for baked beans! I have a hunch
they'd like each other. Then maybe she'd forget about being
hungry for books."

"No, she wouldn't, not even if they fell in love. She'd want
him to read aloud to her while she knitted, after they finished
supper."

Larry did not answer immediately. He was thinking how
Clyde had told him about reading aloud to Lucy, evenings
after supper; how after she died, Clyde's book and her work-
basket had been found in this very room, just as they had been
left the last time. Probably Louise was right—she usually
was. . . . And now all this talk about reading aloud likewise
brought back the times his grandfather had read aloud to
him, out of Grimm's *Fairy Tales*, also in this very room—not
because he especially enjoyed doing it, but because he believed
that was the right thing to do, after supper, when you had a
wife or a child to consider. Hang it all, Larry said to himself,

307

wasn't the time ever going to come when he stopped thinking of this house in terms of his grandfather, and started thinking about it in terms of Louise and himself?

"You can't dry-nurse every discontented New Englander who comes to Louisiana, you know, honey," he said at last. "After all, they don't have to come."

"No, but their work brought them here—work that was important to them and that's important to us. I don't know about this young engineer, but the girl is doing a fine job as Dr. Taylor's office nurse. It would be a real loss if she left."

"You don't think she's going to leave a good job just because there's no public library in the settlement, do you?"

"No, not right away. I think she'd be very conscientious about staying as long as she'd agreed to. But I think she might leave after that. And meanwhile, I don't think she'll be altogether happy in her work. Which means she might not do it as well as if she were."

"Louise, we can't operate this big outfit just so one girl from New Hampshire will be happy. We're running it as well as we know how and there isn't a plant anywhere around that's doing as much as we are for our employees. Can't we let it go at that?"

"I don't think we should. I realize we're running it as well as we know how, but I think we ought to make an effort to find ways of running it better and better all the time."

"All right. When you think of some of those ways, tell me about them. But not tonight, if you don't mind. I've had a pretty rugged day; we've added another pipe line to the tank farm, and you know those aren't just clipped out of cardboard with scissors."

"Of course I don't mind, of course I know, and I'm sorry you're so tired. What would you like to talk about—or would you rather not talk about anything at all?"

"That's it exactly."

Of course it would have been ridiculous to suggest that the idea for the Clyde Batchelor Community Centre was conceived during the course of this conversation and Louise never did suggest it. But a few evenings later she broached another subject, of infinitely more interest to Larry than Myra Dale's book hunger; and since he failed to see the slightest connection between the two, Louise did not call his attention to that, either.

"This looks like a big house, doesn't it?" she remarked, apropos of nothing in particular. "I've never quite recovered from the surprise of discovering that actually there's so little space in it."

"What do you mean, so little space?"

"I should have said, so few family bedrooms. We do need one guest chamber, at least. That's why we've still got both little girls in one room. Sometimes I think they'd be better apart."

"You're not going to suggest next that you and I would be better apart, are you?" Larry asked, grinning.

"No. Not for a minute. But I am going to suggest that as long as we stay together, we'd better face the fact that sooner or later we're going to need more space for our family."

"Well, when we do, we'll have to manage it, I suppose."

He had never told her that he did not want to use Clyde's room, but though she had never proposed doing so, he had always thought that she understood how he felt about it and had deeply appreciated her forbearance. It was quite true that they needed at least one guest room—as a matter of fact, they often needed two. And he knew that the little girls frequently disturbed each other; they were just far enough apart, in age, so that their needs and their habits were not the same; and since Tudie still slept between them, they were crowded besides. Just the same, he hoped Louise was not going to say now that this arrangement simply would not work any longer. Instead, she said something quite different.

"Then maybe we'd better begin to plan about management. Because I think that in six or seven months——"

He leaped up and pulled her to her feet. "You're sure? You're not just kidding?" he exclaimed joyously.

"Of course I'm not just kidding. I suppose it's too soon to be *really* sure. But I'm as sure as I can be at this stage. And I've been wondering—just wondering, of course—what you'd think of moving over to Victoria. Because all kinds of rooms are going to waste there, and perhaps, until the children are older—and if we keep on having them—besides, it's such a *beautiful* house!"

Move to Victoria! The idea had never crossed his mind. And what a fool, what a consummate fool he was, that it hadn't! There *were* all kinds of rooms going to waste at Victoria. Enough for as many guests and as many children as they would ever have. And it *was* a beautiful house! Suddenly he realized that the classic simplicity of its chaste columns and wide wings must be far more appealing to Louise than the manifold embellishment of Cindy Lou, that it must always have been, though she had never said so, for fear of hurting his feelings. But he remembered now that once he had seen her looking at the cast-iron fountain of the little girl with the umbrella, and he realized she had done so in a rather strange way. If anyone had asked him, he would have been obliged to admit that he did not especially admire that statue himself—that or much of the other garniture about the place. He knew, he must have known for a long time, even if he had not admitted it to himself, that the architectural pattern of Cindy Lou was not ageless and enduring, like that of Victoria; it was the transient expression of a period which did not recognise the loveliness of the unadorned, but delighted in the intricate and the ornate. Now that its flamboyancy was faded, it lacked the resplendence which had once given it glory; and since the floating palaces had ceased to glide up and down the great river, the Steamboat Gothic style inspired by them had lost its meaning, except as a memorial to the men who belonged to their era and who had contributed to its greatness. *Except as a memorial to the men who belonged to their era and who had contributed to its greatness! Men like Clyde Batchelor!* And, as these thoughts flashed through his mind, another suddenly struck him: *there would be no memories to haunt him at Victoria!* And there would be no feeling that it really belonged to someone else. It was his own house, his and his wife's, and their children's, not Clyde Batchelor's. . . .

"Darling, I think your idea is the best ever!" he said, putting his arm around her. "And, if we moved to Victoria, Cindy Lou would become——"

"Why, it would become the Clyde Batchelor Community Centre, of course!" Louise answered promptly.

"Of course it would!" Larry echoed, in a tone of triumph.

And neither of them, at that moment, gave a passing thought to Myra Dale.

They did not think, either, of Michael Cobb and Daniel Keefe, two of the older engineers, who had been yearning for a quiet place where they could play interminable games of chess; or of Betty Ellsworth, one of the younger stenographers, who had formerly been a teacher in an Arthur Murray Dancing Studio, and who had been urged to start some classes of her own, with special attention to a certain group of little girls, primarily interested. Larry and Louise knew nothing of these hitherto unsatisfied yearnings, so naturally they could not consider them at the time of that significant conversation. But Cobb and Keefe and Betty all came to them, spontaneously, as soon as the plans for the Clyde Batchelor Community Centre were announced, to express their gratitude and pleasure—Cobb and Keefe rather diffidently, almost apologetically, and Betty with great exuberance. Mrs. Lapham, the wife of the oil field superintendent, also came, to say how much the ladies who did Red Cross work were looking forward to using the new centre for this purpose; and Mrs. Phippen, the harbour-master's wife, arrived to inquire about the feasibility of holding Eastern Star meetings there. She had been afraid that Mrs. Mattina, whose husband had charge of the machine shop, and who was herself an officer in the Catholic Daughters of America, might raise some objections; but she had consulted Mrs. Mattina, who had been lovely about it, who had even gone so far as to say that turn and turn about was fair play. So, if Mr. and Mrs. Vincent had no objection . . . .

Mr. and Mrs. Vincent had not the slightest objection. To be sure, they were somewhat preoccupied with their own affairs, in those days, and therefore did not give undivided attention to the plans other persons were making. Even so, they were taking such general satisfaction in the turn of events that it is doubtful whether they would have raised any objections in any case. The transfer to Victoria of their personal belongings and the other possessions which they wished to retain progressed in a gradual and surprisingly effortless fashion; and the installation of the family there was also a comparatively painless process, though Louise remarked once, in passing, she had always been told that next to having a baby the experience of moving was traditionally the most trying which a woman could be called upon to undergo! Victoria soon regained the inhabited atmosphere which had so long been lacking: the front door stood open, the sunlight poured in through the windows, busy footsteps and alert voices sounded through the hallways. The library and the gun-room, which led out of each other, both seemed to gain in virility of character because of this proximity; the formality of the drawing-room was tempered by the cosiness of the morning-room. Lucy was old enough to take great pride in the fact that she now had a room of her own, and Amy could talk well enough to echo her sister's expressions of pleasure. Larry did not voice his enjoyment of a dressing-room, almost as masculine in character as the gun-room; but Louise did not fail to note how readily he fell into the habit of using it; and he needed no prompting from her to admire the new nursery. Now that the household staffs in the two places were combined, there was not overmuch work for anyone, especially with the labour-saving devices unheard of only a short time before; and the servants, like their master and their mistress, were pleased over the change and excited over the prospect of the new baby.

After the baby came, Louise said laughingly she had always known there was not much truth in that old saying about trying experiences; she had really enjoyed the moving; and as to the feat of bringing Clyde Batchelor Vincent into the world, that had been done so quickly and easily that everything was all over before Dr. Mitchell and his starchy nurse had time to clutter up the scene—and meanwhile, Tudie had achieved new stature as a midwife. Larry accused Louise of having tampered with the calendar, so that there would be no question of rushing her off to Touro this time; and though she did not deny the accusation, neither was he able to speak with much severity, since it was true that both his wife and his son were pronounced, by the tardy doctor, to be in excellent condition. Besides, Larry suspected that if some tampering had been done, it was because Louise knew it would mean a great deal to him, from the viewpoint of sentiment, to have his heir born at Victoria; under those circumstances, how could he do otherwise than voice, to the exclusion of all other speech, his joy and pride?

The baby was nearly four months old before Cindy Lou was ready for dedication as a community centre—big enough, Louise said, to take there with them, if they could arrange in some way for his nap; and she thought he might like to be able to say, when he grew up, that he had been present on such an occasion, even though he would have to confess that he could not remember it! Having said this much, she waited, with no appearance of impatience or aggression, for Larry to make a certain suggestion. He did not disappoint her.

"Well . . . why not put him in my grandfather's room, on the big bed? There's no danger of his being able to move around enough to fall off, is there?"

"No, not yet, if you put him in the middle. But at the rate he's developing there might be, pretty soon."

"Well," Larry said again and then hesitated. "The youth bed used to have sides, when I first slept in it," he went on. "I haven't thought about them for years—I don't even remember when they were taken off. You didn't happen to see them, did you, when you went through the store closets?"

"Of course I did. I know exactly where they are, too. Would you like to have them put back on the youth bed?"

"It wouldn't be a bad idea. We might want to take Batch over again for the day sometime—after it wasn't best to put him down in the middle of the big bed any more."

Nothing further was said on the subject. But when the day of the dedication came, and Louise and Larry and their children arrived at Cindy Lou, Larry took the baby in his arms and went straight upstairs with him. Like most men, he was rather inept at carrying babies; no matter how carefully their clothes had been smoothed down before they were handed to him, he generally had everything hunched up and around their little bodies by the time he had been holding them two minutes. On this occasion, however, he kept the baby's fine lawn dress carefully in place; and when he laid

Batch in the middle of the big bed, even Louise could not have done so more expertly.

"There!" he said, looking down at the baby. "There you are, son! Just the right place for you, too, if you ask me."

Nobody asked him; but Batch looked up at him, gurgling and grinning and kicking. Larry snatched at one of the small pink fists and held it fast for a moment, before he went downstairs and took his appointed place as chairman. . . .

The yard was already full of people, and he was just in time to greet the dignitaries who had come from far and wide for the occasion and who were to be seated on the gallery, at the head of the grand staircase. The Chief Justice of the state, Charles O'Niell, a witty, pleasant-spoken man who was to make the principal address, came promptly at the appointed hour, with the congressman of the district, Paul Maloney. Shortly thereafter a vice-president of the Old Hickory Petroleum Company arrived, along with a member of the River Commission, the mayors of several neighbouring towns, Frank Waddill and his wife, the superintendent of the oil field, Captain Clovis Bourgeois, Valois Dupré, Father Le Grand, Blaise Bergeron—now chairman of the Levee Board— and Henri Laburre, who had realized his ambition of becoming a motor magnate.

The orchestra, organized at the time the pavilion was built and now stationed under the grand staircase, had played several lively airs by the time all these personages were assembled; from the rear of the yard, savoury smells were already wafting—gumbo and barbecue were to be served as soon as the exercises were over and preparations for these were well under way. The crowd now filled the grounds to overflowing; there was no reason to delay the proceedings any longer.

Larry rose and, after calling for order, asked Father Le Grand to pronounce the invocation. There was a flutter of hands as most of those in the gathering crossed themselves, then a general lifting of heads as the prayer came to a close.

"You all know why we are gathered here," Larry began rather diffidently. "And those of you who know me—and that's most of you—know well and good that I'm no speaker. I'm proud to be here and prouder still to be chairman. But you realize, and so do I, that I'm acting in that capacity, not because I'm good at this kind of a job, but because I'm Clyde Batchelor's grandson. He isn't here with us in the flesh. But what he stood for, what he meant in this community, is everywhere you'd care to look."

It was true that Larry was not an easy or natural speaker. He knew what it was in his heart to say, but he still felt doubtful as how best to say it. He glanced toward Louise, who was seated in the chair next to his, with Lucy standing on one side of her and Amy on the other, and she looked quickly back at him with a reassuring smile. In her face he read complete confidence that he would do justice to his grandfather's memory, and through long and joyful experience, he had learned that the candour of her countenance reflected the candour of her thoughts. Therefore no shadow of suspicion crossed his mind that he was not reading these correctly, too. Mercifully, he did not know that Louise was saying to herself at that moment: *He's never guessed, I must never let him guess that I lied to him. Just once. But it was a terrible lie. I told him I burnt that diary because I felt no one had a right to read it. That was true enough. But I didn't tell him I'd read part of it before I burnt it—enough so that I knew I mustn't read any more, that no one must ever have a chance to read any of it.*

"One of the first things I can remember having my grandfather tell me," Larry went on, greatly encouraged by the look in Louise's face, "was the story of the hidden treasure, and of how my mother used to dig for it. Lots of people besides her believed the treasure was there, but they believed it was gold, pirate gold, just as she did. Then when oil was brought in, those same people said that must be the treasure, for true—black gold instead of pirate gold, but treasure just the same, I said to myself. Now I know better. I know that the real treasure of Cindy Lou is the memory of what my grandfather said and did in the fifty years and more that he lived here."

In the fifty years and more that he lived here! Yes, it was before he lived at Cindy Lou that he had been a gambler, true enough, Louise was thinking; and the knowledge of his devious way of life had not come as too much of a shock to his bride. Lucy had known from the beginning that there was something he was hiding from her, something of which he was ashamed. He had told her, when he first asked her to marry him, that she had a right to know about his past life, and she had said there would be time enough for that, if and when she definitely accepted his proposal. Later she had sensed his fear that though their marriage would survive his confession, because marriage to her was an irrevocable sacrament, her love for him would not; and though she could have stilled that fear, this would have meant that she must, necessarily, be the first to speak of the possible causes for it. It was not until she and Clyde had been married more than twenty-five years that, in a moment of desperation, he had poured out his heart to her. A brief notation in her diary, dated April 10, 1896, had told Louise this: "Today my dear, dear husband, of his own accord, told me that he had been a gambler, and I am thankful that he will no longer bear the burden of silence which has lain so heavily upon him all these years." The notation was written in the form of a postscript to a much longer entry, penned years before on the *Richmond*: "I felt sure, from the moment of our meeting with Mr. Pettigrew, who called himself Major Fanchon, that the secret of my dear husband's past life had been disclosed. Now the gossip which I have overheard in the observatory, when I have gone there to drink afternoon chocolate—gossip hushed as soon as the scandalmongers noticed my presence—has confirmed my belief. But I shall never let Clyde know that I have learned the truth. Why should I sadden him when he is so happy? And why should I give even a passing thought to what he was in the past, when he is no longer the same man? Truly, he must have been born again, as the Bible tells us we may be; for I am sure that in all the world there is not another being so upright, so wise and so kind."

I should have burned the diary when I read that far, Louise said to herself, as Larry went on with greater and greater assurance and ease. *I'm not sorry I burned it, I'm not even sorry I lied to Larry and told him I burned it without reading it. It is a terrible thing for a woman to lie to her husband, even once. Just the same, I believe I did right in lying, that time. I didn't do right in reading the diary though, in reading any of it. . . .*

"As I've said, I'm no speaker," Larry was telling his attentive audience. "But we have someone with us today who

316

is one of the greatest orators in the state. He can do justice to the memory of my grandfather, even if I can't, so I'm going to let him carry on from here. He doesn't need any introduction. Lots of you know him as Uncle Charlie. All of you claim him as your neighbour Charles O'Niell, of St. Mary Parish. But since we want to show how proud we are to have him here with us today, I'm going to present him by his full title—Chief Justice of the Supreme Court of Louisiana."

Genial laughter mingled with the hand clapping which greeted the Chief Justice's approach to the railing between the two wings of the grand staircase. His figure was slight, but wiry, and he carried off the impediment in his gait without self-consciousness. The people who watched him were not conscious of it, either. Instead, they were noticing, with admiration and affection, that his snowy hair was as abundant as ever, that his keen blue eyes seemed to twinkle more and more blithely with advancing years and that there was something actually impish in his grin.

"Mr. Chairman, distinguished guests, ladies and gentlemen," he began formally. Then the grin became wider. "Ah, let's cut all that sort of thing short. Let me just say, 'Friends,' and then get right on to the rest. Because that's how I think of the people in a gathering like this, anywhere in the state of Louisiana, but especially in that part of the state where Clyde Batchelor left such a lasting mark. Yes, I'm from St. Mary Parish, and it was just a few miles from my home that Clyde Batchelor launched what proved to be the revival of the Mississippi River's golden age. It was in St. Mary that he raised an old towboat from the bottom of Lake Verret and negotiated his first barge line charter and built the first new towboat for his new company. Did I hear your chairman say something about being proud? Let me tell every one of you within sound of my voice that the proudest man here today isn't anyone who's listening to me. It's the man who's talking to you. As your Uncle Charlie, as your neighbour Charles O'Niell, as the Chief Justice of your state and mine, I'm proud and honoured that I've been chosen to dedicate this great memorial to a man like Clyde Batchelor."

A man like Clyde Batchelor! A man who had come to Louisiana to buy the house of his dreams for his betrothed bride, and who had fallen a willing victim there to the wiles of an adventuress! That shameful episode could not be excused on the ground that it was part of the life he had led before he was 'born again'; he not only knew and loved Lucy, when it had occurred; he had already sworn to himself and to her that from thenceforth her standards should be his, and that his love for her and his loyalty to her were so intermingled as to be inseparable. The very fact that he had fervently hoped and prayed she might never learn of his unfaithfulness was proof positive that he himself did not look on it in the same light as the errant ways of his youth; unquestionably, he had thanked God, over and over again, that this sad secret he had succeeded in keeping. But he had done so mistakenly. Another entry in the diary made this all too clear: Among the women who had taken chocolate every afternoon in the observatory of the *Richmond* had been a dressmaker, returning from New York with the latest models. Before hearing Lucy's name aright, this woman had complimented her on her beautiful clothes. They had come from Sophia Diedens, Lucy told her, with pardonable pride. Ah, yes, the dressmaker said, she should have known. She did not usually deal with so expensive an establishment; but she had once bought a complete outfit from it for an actress who was the toast of her day in New Orleans. The outfit had never been worn on the stage because the actress had died suddenly just as the play was about to open. But it had been bought in its entirety by a certain Mme Labouisse, who had just sold her plantation to some wealthy stranger, for an enormous sum. And the dressmaker would never forget how Mme Labouisse had insisted that the most striking dress of all—a crimson satin, made with the new tie-back skirt—should be an inch and a half smaller around the waist and an inch and a half lower at the neckline. . . .

"And I knew she was up to no good when she made that demand," the dressmaker had added, with a sly look. "Afterward, I heard—one does hear such things, you know, madame—that this scheming woman had worn it at the farewell dinner she gave at her plantation, in honour of the new proprietor. In fact, another customer of mine, a Mrs. Vincent, was present on that occasion."

There was more to the entry, enough to show Louise how fully Lucy had understood how and when and why the crimson satin dress had been worn, and where the money had come from with which to buy it. And this time there was no mitigating postscript added many years later. The entry stood in all its starkness, just as Lucy had written it on her honeymoon. . . .

With an effort, Louise wrested her thoughts from the disclosures of the diary and focused them on the eulogy of the day. The Chief Justice was tracing the eclipse of steamboat prosperity, the darkling days of Reconstruction, the rise of the New South. . . . Then she realized that he was talking about her, that he was referring to her first as a worthy successor of the great ladies from Old France who had come to New France during the early days of the colony; then as the mother of a second Clyde Batchelor, who was to carry on the great tradition of the first.

The Chief Justice held out his hand to her and she rose, acknowledging the spontaneous applause which included them both. Again she saw that Larry's eyes were resting on her with confidence and love, and this time there were no hidden reservations in the candour with which she returned his look. Suddenly she knew that everything which had been said about Clyde Batchelor was true, after all, that he had indeed been a great man, for the handicaps he had overcome would have defeated one who was not truly great. Even his disloyalty to Lucy was revealed in a new light: Clyde's bitter memory of his one transgression against her had been a constant incentive to atonement, and his reparation had been perfect and complete. Lucy herself had understood this, and compassion for her husband had, from the beginning, been mingled with her adoration of him. As Louise looked from Larry to the Chief Justice, and then out at the throng before her, she understood it, too; she was filled with pride that her son, who bore Clyde Batchelor's name, was to carry on his tradition.

The departure of the barge tow had been delayed in order that Captain Bourgeois and his crew might share in the dedicatory ceremonies. Now men swarmed like ants over the steel deck plates, tightening or releasing cables and hawsers and uncoupling huge flexible hoses. Finally the last cable was set free, the air whistle blared and the heavy diesel engines of the *Clyde Batchelor* took up the rhythmic drumming they would maintain without pause or interruption until the tow docked at Louisville.

Larry Vincent stood on the gallery of the Community Centre, with his son in his arms and his wife and daughters beside him, watching the vessels as they passed upstream. Just beyond the barges, purple in the gathering dusk, he could see the island where once a floating palace rode at anchor. Yes, it was gone for ever; but if it had not once proudly floated over the Mississippi, the barges would not be ploughing through the river now. The old order had changed, yielding place to new. But it had not died of desuetude. After a period of dormancy it had roused itself and revealed greater vitality than ever, just as a field which has lain fallow teems with fresh fecundity.

Holding the baby securely in one arm, Larry slid the other over his wife's shoulder and drew her closer to him. She still had both little girls by the hand. But once again she returned his loving look, and this time the glance had in it the quality of a caress, bringing her closer still. As he looked down at her, in the fading light, it seemed to him that he and she and their children were all welded together into a single unit, and that though this unit, too, might change with time, it would remain essentially indivisible and imperishable. A deep contentment filled his being, a sense of fulfilment and completeness such as he had never known before. But he was tired. Everything that needed doing had now been done. He wanted to rest.